DANGER FORETOLD

EERIE SIDE OF THE TRACKS BOOK 5

ELLIE FERGUSON

WELCOME TO THE EERIE SIDE OF THE TRACKS!

When I wrote *Slay Bells Ring*, I knew I had something special in Mossy Creek and its citizens. There was something about the characters and the town that wouldn't let me go. I love Mossy Creek and everyone residing there, no matter how eccentric or "different" they might be.

I hope you enjoy *Danger Foretold* as much as I enjoyed writing it.

———

To keep up-to-date about new entries in the series as well as other books coming out, sign up for my newsletter or follow my fan page.

To Mrs. Winslow who recognized an imagination needing to fly.

Welcome to beautiful Mossy Creek where even the ordinary is extraordinary.

JAX

1

"Doc, I'm going to let you out and then go find somewhere to park."

Rafe slowly drove up Main Street in the direction of the courthouse. Every parking space was filled with vehicles ranging from farm trucks to expensive sports cars. The two ground lots nearby looked full. Seeing it, I smiled. Not that it surprised me. Today was a special day in our town's life. History seemed to be coming full circle and I hoped it represented a good omen.

Heaven knows we could use one.

In less than half an hour, one of my best friends, my sister from another mister, would take the oath of office as Harkin County's newest District Attorney. More than fifty years ago, her grandfather stood on the steps of the courthouse and took the oath of office she would soon repeat. For one of Mossy Creek's problem children, she'd come a long way.

But then, we all had.

"Try the lot behind the law office. We might get lucky."

Rafe nodded and turned down Third Street, doubling back to the rear entrance of the law firm of Metzger, Grissom and Sheridan. The Metzger was Nathaniel Metzger, former DA and judge, dead close to eight years. The Grissom was his granddaughter Annie, Mossy Creek's newest DA. The Sheridan was Meg Sheridan Grissom, Annie's sister-in-law and another of my closest friends. Now to see if they'd managed to save a parking space for us.

Rafe chuckled as the pickup slowed. Following his nod, I grinned. Someone had put barricades up across the entrances to the rear parking lot. Tommy and Beau Lucchese stood in front of the nearest barricade. Dressed in blue jeans, concert t-shirts and battered baseball caps, they waved the two cars in front of us to drive on when they tried to enter the lot. Then, recognizing Rafe's truck, they grinned and moved the barricade so we could drive in.

"Hey, Dr. Jax, Mr. Sabatini." Tommy looked in my open window and then glanced back to watch his older brother move the barricade back into place. "Mrs. Grissom said to tell you they've already headed to the courthouse."

"Yeah." Beau moved to where his brother stood and watched as Rafe parked the truck. "She said they'd try to save spots for you."

"Then we'd best be on our way." I glanced around the lot, counting only two empty spaces. "Who's not here yet?"

Tommy rolled his eyes. "Miss Catherine."

I didn't blame him for rolling his eyes. Annie's mother always means well, but she was the dictionary definition of why Southerners say "bless your heart".

"Do you want me to call and see where she is?" Knowing Catherine, she probably planned a grand entrance, not understanding that running late threw the entire swearing in ceremony behind schedule.

"Thanks, but no. Miss Olivia said she'd take care of it." Beau grinned almost wickedly.

I chuckled softly in response. Olivia Soukis had been the judge's admin for years. She had come out of retirement to help—meaning make sure they didn't screw things up—Annie and Beth, Miss Olivia's daughter, when Annie returned to town and opened her own law practice. To say she knew how to handle Annie's mother was an understatement. Hell, Miss Olivia knew how to handle everyone in town and didn't hesitate to do so where necessary.

And handling Catherine today definitely fell under something that was necessary.

"We'll see you two later," Rafe said as he joined us.

I reached for Rafe's hand and we left the teens to guard the lot. As we did, I grinned. Knowing the boys, I didn't doubt for a minute Annie would not only pay them well but she would also make sure they had all they wanted to eat from the café. That was Annie, always taking care of people she cared for.

People filled the sidewalk and overflowed into the street in front of the courthouse. They were there to support Annie. She epitomized the hometown girl made good. Many of those gathered remembered her as the little red-haired girl who came to work with her grandfather. Others remembered her as the young woman the old man had been so proud of or as the new attorney he hoped would come home to join his law practice. Instead, she chose another path, one that took her to Austin, where she quickly earned a reputation as one of Travis County's best prosecutors in years. She hadn't come home until her mother, bless her heart, was caught standing over her lover's body, bloody knife in hand.

Annie had been the first of Mossy Creek's "problem children" to return to the fold. I was the last. In between, Mossy Creek had been, well, Mossy Creek. There's a reason another of our good friends says the town's motto shouldn't be "Welcome to beautiful Mossy Creek" but "Welcome to Mossy Creek, where the strange is common place and normal is nowhere to be found."

I only hoped normal was closer to the truth today. Annie deserved it.

After two days of rain, the sun shone and not a single cloud dotted the sky. Rafe and I moved through the crowd, stopping to greet some, nodding to others. Waiting for us at the base of the courthouse steps was our "family". We might not be related by blood, but experience proved family went far beyond genetics. I'd learned that lesson a long time ago.

"Auntie Jax!"

I grinned as my goddaughter all but launched herself into my arms. Rafe ruffled her hair before greeting everyone. With Ali on my hip, I made my way to her mother's side, knowing Quinn was as happy for Annie as was I.

As if our arrival was the cue, the courthouse doors opened. Ali wiggled out of my arms and dropped to the ground at my side. Then, as she jumped up and down to see who it was, Rafe smiled at her in affection. Smoothly, he lifted her onto his shoulders. As he did, Quinn glanced back and shook her head. Before she could say anything, I stopped her.

"She's fine."

Quinn nodded. Then we watched as Annie's family exited the courthouse. Judge Robert Caldwell and his wife Camille, Annie's father- and mother-in-law, led them to the chairs set to one side. Annie's husband, Sam, and their eight-year-old son, Robbie, were next. It didn't surprise me to see Sam and Camille gently cradling a twin in their arms. Next came Annie's grandmother, Mary Kate Metzger, and her mother. Following were Annie's twin brother, Drew, and his wife, Meg. He escorted her to a chair and watched closely as she sat down and tried to get comfortable. A smile touched my lips. Drew might have been a pain when we were growing up, but he was going to be such a good father—assuming Meg didn't kill him before the baby came.

As we waited for the ceremony to begin, I glanced around once again. So many faces, representing all walks of life and all ages. It looked like most of the town turned out. They might not understand the importance of one of their "problem children" returning home, but they were more than glad Annie was back. They knew she, like her grandfather before her and like her father-in-law now, would take good care of the town and of the county.

What did surprise me, however, was the media presence. A reporter for the local paper was front and center. That I'd expected. Annie was big news around town. What I hadn't expected were TV cameras from different stations around the Dallas-Fort Worth area, as well as a few others from around the state. Their presence went beyond the fact Annie would be Harkin County's first female District

Attorney. That was important, but it paled in comparison to the drama that she'd survived since coming back to town. I had no doubt some of the out-of-town media would focus on how Annie returned when her mother—bless her heart—was accused of killing her lover. Then there'd been the more recent dust up with former Joe Bob Sawyer, a former assistant district attorney and classmate of ours who now waited to stand trial on a number of charges. Looking around as some of the out-of-town reporters moved through the crowd, trying to find someone to interview, I grinned proudly. Mossy Creek might be many things, but we protected our own, something those reporters had been unprepared for. After all, we might gossip and laugh at and about one another, but no one else was allowed to.

When the courthouse doors opened once again, the crowd fell silent. Annie stepped outside, Jason Alvarez, the outgoing DA, and members of the county commissioners followed. As Annie took her place in front of the mics that had been set up, Sam and Robbie joined her, each carrying a twin. Then, breaking from what had been planned, Annie looked around and motioned for her mother, mother-in-law, brother and sister-in-law to join them. Alvarez grinned and nodded in approval. So did I. This was how it should be.

Judge Caldwell stepped forward. Mary Kate Metzger, Annie's grandmother, joined him. A moment later, Annie placed her right hand on the Bible her grandmother held, the same one her grandfather used when he took his own oath of office as DA. Her voice never wavered as she recited the oath. But, when the crowd erupted into applause and her son ran to her afterwards, she smiled and blushed and knelt to give Robbie a hug before stepping up to the microphone.

"Thank you." She looked out over the crowd and waited a moment before continuing. "I promise not to be too long-winded."

Laughter rose and Quinn nudged me with her elbow. I grinned, understanding. We both knew Annie hated public speaking. She hid it well, but if you knew what to look for, it was there. But she had this and I was proud of her. This is what she was meant for. She'd missed being a prosecutor after moving back home. Now she got to do a job she loved and protect the town that loved her. It was perfect for her.

"In many ways, today completes my process of coming home," she said. "I remember spending time with my grandfather in his office when I was a little girl. He was a judge then. That's when he taught me to respect the law. He and my grandmother—you, too, Mom—" She grinned at Catherine.— "taught me to love this town. Each of you helped get me elected, and I will not betray your trust.

"I would be remiss if I didn't thank a few very special people." She turned and held a hand out to Sam, smiling as he joined her. "I'll start with my family. I wouldn't have been able to do this without their love and support. I also want to thank Jason Alvarez, who encouraged me to run. Filling his shoes as DA will not be easy, but I'm going to do everything I can to be as strong and dedicated a DA as he was.

"I also have to thank my girls." She turned and smiled at Meg before finding Quinn and me in the crowd. "You've had my back when I've needed you. You've pushed me to be all I can be and you have never been afraid to tell me when I'm about to do something incredibly stupid. You're my sisters, my best friends and I'm trusting you to be there with me going forward."

Quinn gave her a cheeky grin as I simply inclined my head. We'd been there for one another and always would be. We had to if we were going to keep Mossy Creek safe.

Annie once again thanked everyone and stepped away from the microphone. As she did, I glanced around. Nothing but familiar faces, all as proud of Annie as I was, surrounded me. So why did I feel like the other shoe was about to drop? Ever since Annie took the mic, something had been eating at me. I wasn't exactly on edge, at least not the sort of on edge I was when trouble's about to happen. This felt more like something was wrong and I needed to figure out what.

Damn it, I hate when this happens.

Doing my best not to be obvious about it, I scanned the crowd. Whenever I caught someone's eye, I smiled and nodded or lifted a hand in greeting. Nothing and no one looked out of place. This was the same crowd I'd expect to see at high school graduation or Christmas Eve services.

So what the hell was bothering me?

My gaze slid over the small gathering of Miss Serena and several others. Serena Duchamp was not only the most powerful Other I'd ever met, she was a direct descendant of one of Mossy Creek's founding families. She was friend, mentor, teacher, and surrogate grandmother for me and so many others. She was also the leader of the Guardians, a group of four Others sworn to protect Mossy Creek and its residents.

Standing with her were her granddaughter, Amy, and Amy's fiancé, Brian. Next to them were Dr. Pat Reyes and her husband, Marcus. Dr. Pat was another of the Guardians, along with Quinn's mother, Judith, and me. Marcus taught at the local college.

Shit!

One person was missing from their group. I continued looking for a face almost as familiar as my own. Maddy Reyes, Dr. Pat's and Marcus' daughter, was nowhere to be seen. Damn it! Despite everything that had happened the last few months, I expected her to be here. She was one of us. Growing up, she, Quinn, Annie, and I had been best friends.

So where was she?

The sounds of clapping broke through my concern. I'd have to worry about Maddy later. I wouldn't ruin Annie's day—or do anything to worry her. That didn't mean I couldn't send Maddy a text, one she sure as hell better answer. Doing my best not to frown, I pulled out my phone.

Where are you? You're missing the fun.

I hit *send* and slid the phone back into my pocket. As I did, I caught Rafe looking at me in concern. I shook my head and once again reached for his hand, giving it a squeeze. I'd explain once we were alone. He nodded, accepting if not understanding.

"Let's go give Annie our congratulations." He swung Ali down off his shoulders.

She gave him a quick hug before hurrying to her mother.

"Sounds good."

As we climbed the steps to the courthouse, I looked up. Six crows perched on the roofline of the courthouse. A chill ran down my spine. From long ago, I heard my grandfather's voice as he read me a story, one where a gathering of six crows was an omen and not a good one.

Jackie, six crows are a sign of death.

Could this mean the trouble we'd been expecting had finally arrived?

2

_____

"Care to tell me what's bothering you?" Quinn asked as she slipped her arm through mine.

I didn't other trying to deny it. I simply hoped she was the only one besides Rafe to realize I was worried about something. Still, maybe I was making too much of it. After all, there were any number of reasons why Maddy missed Annie's swearing in and why she wasn't here now.

"Here" was Mary Kate's backyard. Annie's grandmother had opened her home to family and friends to help Annie celebrate this new phase of her career. The men, including Rafe, manned barbeque grills they'd hauled over last night. The kids ran around the yard, our dogs chasing after them. Annie's twins somehow managed to sleep in the travel crib set up under a large umbrella on the patio. Taking it all in, I should be relaxed and I wasn't.

Damn it.

Around me, friends and family mingled. Small groups and large. In the kitchen, Miss Peggy, Janny, and several others from the café worked. I smiled slightly at the memory of Peggy Russell running Mary Kate out of her own kitchen. As Miss Peggy said, this was an important day for Mary Kate as well as for Annie, so Mary Kate needed to enjoy it.

"Jax?" Quinn prompted.

"Tell me what you see."

It didn't answer her question and I didn't need to look at her to know she frowned at me. But she didn't argue. Instead, she looked around the yard, her gaze messing nothing. When she hissed softly, I nodded, more to myself than to her.

"Maddy." She spoke softly, but I heard the anger and concern. "Was she at the ceremony?"

I shook my head. Then, recognizing the look in her eyes, I frowned. "Don' t."

She looked at me, not sure she understood. "Quinn, don't start asking yourself why you didn't realize she wasn't here, and don't start imagining all the things that could be wrong. You had one job this morning besides being there to support Annie. That was to make sure no one tried to disrupt the swearing in."

She didn't look convinced. At least she didn't argue. How could she when we both knew the potential had been there? Jim Bob Sawyer might be under house arrest, but neither of us trusted him any further than we could throw him. To say he wanted nothing more than to cause Annie heartache was putting it mildly. I had no doubt he would have caused trouble today if he could figure how without violating the terms of his release on bail.

"Did you call her?"

"Texted and called."

Quinn's mouth tightened and her eyes flashed. "I take it she hasn't responded."

I nodded. When Quinn glanced around, looking for Dr. Pat, I stopped her. The fact Dr Pat hadn't said anything about Maddy not being here worried me. But, before I said something that might upset Dr. Pat, I wanted more information.

"What do you want to do?" Quinn asked.

That's the good thing about knowing someone as well as Quinn and I know one another. We didn't need to spend time figuring out what the other wanted to do, nor did we have to waste time explaining our plans. This time, however, I hoped Quinn understood why I needed to do this alone.

"I want you to stay here and cover for me. I'm going to have an 'emergency' I need to go check on."

I made air quotes to make sure she understood what I meant by "emergency".

"Jax." She drawled out my name, her displeasure clear.

I led her further away from the others, keeping an eye on Annie as I did. The last thing I wanted was for her to suspect something might be wrong.. She deserved to enjoy today. I'd tell her later if there was anything to worry about.

This was definitely one of those "better to ask forgiveness" moments.

"Quinn, listen to me and don't argue." I glanced at Annie as she laughed at something Meg said. "I'll check on Maddy and let you know what's going on. But let's not take away from her day." I nodded toward Annie.

"Are you sure you don't want me to go with you?"

I nodded. Both of us disappearing would cause too many questions.

"Stay here and cover for me. I'll let you know what I find out."

Not that it was that easy slipping away. When I tried telling Rafe I had been called out, he simply arched one brow and walked inside with me. It didn't surprise me when he said to be careful and let him know if I needed help finding Maddy. Then he handed me the keys to the pickup.

He wasn't the only one. As I stepped outside, I found Miss Serena waiting for me. Her expression troubled, she walked with me to the truck. She asked if I was going to look for Maddy. When I nodded, she said to be careful. Something was going on, something she didn't understand. I assured her I didn't plan to take any chances. She squeezed my hand and watched as I climbed in behind the steering wheel. I waited until she returned inside. Then I drove off, unsettled by her warning.

My first stop was the caretaker's house at Miss Serena's. She initially built it for Jimmy Reardon when he became her farm manager more than twenty years ago. Since then, he'd gotten married and moved to his own home nearby. Over the last few years, it had been a temporary home for several of us. Meg moved in when she first came to Mossy Creek. I lived there for several months as well when I returned. Even though Aunt Bitsy and others said I could stay with them, I'd refused. The caretaker's house, situated near the center of Miss Serena's property, was the one place I knew my parents would never dare bother me. So it had been home until Rafe and I moved into our place.

I followed the tree-lined drive, bearing to the left when it split. Several of the farmworkers waved as I drove past, and I waved in return. Force of habit had me preparing to pull up at the stables, but I stopped myself. Jimmy would let me know if I needed to check any of the stock before morning. Besides, I knew what I was doing. I wanted to stop simply to postpone what I feared might be an unpleasant meeting with Maddy.

I rounded another curve and parked in front of the single-story brick ranch-style house. The driveway was empty. The house looked just as empty. Frowning, I climbed out of the truck and walked around it. Keeping a watch on the house, I dropped to one knee. The fingers of my right hand lightly caressed the grass before digging into the soil. Some people relied on technology to warn them of trouble. I relied on my talents as an Earth Elemental and as a Walker.

Energies rose up, filling me. The world turned from light and shadow to energy patterns that swirled around me. Horses and cattle, crops, men and women, and so much more. The patterns let me identify life around the farm. But not from the house. I didn't need to look to know no one was inside.

Damn it, Maddy. Where are you?

I stood and dusted off my hands. For a moment, I studied the house, wondering what to do next. Not liking my options, I returned to the truck.

"Drew, it's me," I said the moment he answered my call. "Don't let on you're talking to me and make sure your sister can't overhear us."

I waited, listening as he walked away from the sounds of the party. A door opened and shut and then another. He didn't say anything until he was in the privacy of his car.

"Jax, what's wrong?" Worry roughened his voice.

"I'm at Maddy's. I came to see why she wasn't at your grandmother's. She's not here, Drew."

"Did you talk to her folks?"

I rolled my eyes even though he couldn't see.

"No."

What was I supposed to say? *Hey, Dr. Pat, I was just wondering if Maddy's gone over to the dark side again.*

"Drew, I figured it was better to see what I could find out before worrying them."

That was putting it mildly. Two months had passed since Ciara, Quinn's older sister, Rafe and I brought Maddy home from Ireland. Now I wondered if trouble had followed her here. I hoped not. That was the last thing we needed right now.

"What can I do?"

"Can you make sure there's no report of her having an accident or anything?"

"Give me a few minutes. Hang on."

I waited, checking email and texting Quinn to let her know I didn't have anything to report—yet. By the time Drew came back on the line, I worried he might have found something. Much as I didn't want anything to have happened to Maddy, it would be better knowing she'd been delayed by a car crash than to know she chose not to be there for one of her best friends.

"No reports, Jax."

"Thanks."

So now what?

"Do you want me to come help look for her?"

"No, but thanks." I thought for a moment. "Do me a favor though. If you do hear anything, let me know."

"Will do. I'd better get back before Annie gets suspicious. You watch your six, Jax."

"I will." I slid the key into the ignition. "Keep any eye on things there. This might be nothing or it might mean we've got trouble coming."

"I've got things here. Keep in touch."

I ended the call and dropped the phone onto the passenger seat. I sat there, the engine idling, my fingers drumming a beat against the steering wheel. Mossy Creek wasn't that big. Hell, it was barely a dot on the map. But that didn't mean you couldn't go to ground if you wanted to. Maddy knew the town as well as any of us. If she didn't want to be found, it would be damned hard to do so. At least I had one advantage most folks here didn't.

And it was an advantage I wouldn't hesitate to utilize if necessary.

But, before I decided to go hunting her in animal form, I'd drive around town. Who knows? I might get lucky.

My phone rang as I idled at one of the two red lights downtown. I tapped the earbud in my right ear.

"Hello?"

"Dr. Jax?" a woman's voice asked.

"Yes." I knew the voice, but couldn't quite place it.

"Doc, it's Darcy. You'd better get over here. I think we might have a problem."

I frowned. Then I cursed silently. There was only one reason I could think of for Darcy to be calling. As one of the two full-time bartenders at The Roundhouse, a bar on the outskirts of town, she not only knew everyone in town, but she also knew who to call if someone needed a ride home.

And there was only one person I knew who might need such help today.

"I'm on my way." I tapped my earbud again and ended the call. I thought for a moment before the light turned green. As I drove off, I reached up, tapped the earbud, and used voice controls to call Quinn.

"Jax?" She sounded worried, not that I could blame her. "Have you found her?"

"Maybe." I told her about Darcy's call. "I'm heading there now. Do me a favor and tell your mother what's going on. See if she can find out anything from Dr. Pat or, better yet, from Mr. Reyes. Even if it's just where they think Maddy is."

"I'll let you know what she finds out. Do you want me to meet you there?"

"No. Not yet. Let me see what I find. I'll let you know."

Ten minutes later, I sat in the truck, staring at Maddy's car parked across the lot. From its position, I didn't doubt she'd been the first one through the door when the bar opened. That wasn't good. She had turned to booze and pills to cope with what Anton Roben did to her before we managed to find her. The bastard beat her, raped her, pimped her out to help seal his business deals. The only reason he'd been able to do so was through the magical binding he put on her. Then, to insure her "cooperation", he had her mother kidnapped.

Had something happened to send her back into the hell she'd known while under Roben's thumb? I hoped not. In return for her testimony against Roben and others, she'd been offered a very lenient plea bargain, one that would leave her with no criminal record if she fulfilled its requirements. One of those was that she undergo regular and surprise drug testing. Another was that she not drink. Just being at the bar could be viewed as a violation.

Damn it, was Maddy trying to get into trouble?

At the front door, Frankie Hearne, the bar's part-time bouncer, nodded in greeting. Then he jerked his head in the direction of the bar. As he did, Darcy looked over. Seeing me, she shook her head before nodding at the far end of the bar. I scanned the interior, noting the regulars already there. But it was the sight of Maddy sitting at the bar, a beer mug and shot glass in front of her that had me frowning. It was worse than I thought.

"I've got this, Frankie."

He nodded and watched as I stepped inside. Before joining Maddy, I pulled out my phone. I had a feeling this was going to take more than just me.

Found her at The Roadhouse. There's a problem. Can you come? I texted.

Quinn's response was almost immediate. **On my way.**

I gave myself a moment to gather my thoughts. That was easier said than done. Part of me wanted to grab Maddy by the scruff of her neck and drag her out of there. Another part knew that was probably the worst thing I could do. Something had set her off and it had to be bad to make her risk violating her probation, not to mention missing Annie's swearing in. Finally, unable to put it off any longer, I crossed the room in her direction.

And, as I neared, Maddy slowly turned her head in my direction. It was an almost unnatural movement that set off every alarm in my head. Maddy's eyes narrowed and she levered herself up and off of the barstool.

"Go away."

A ripple of energy danced across my skin as she spoke. I felt the compulsion that came with it—greasy, unsettling and so very wrong. Fortunately, I'm a suspicious soul and had reinforced my shields before entering the bar. But now, knowing my childhood friend, someone I thought of as a sister, had tried to use her abilities to roll me, fury built. I didn't care why she tried it. She knew better. Not only was it an insult, but it was also dangerous for both of us.

"Maddy," I growled. As I did, I felt my tattoos come to life as my Walker aspect pushed for release.

"I said, go away," she repeated, pushing her will against my shields.

"No."

I wouldn't lose my temper. I couldn't. I'd seen her in a mood like this before, years ago. She was spoiling for a fight and that wasn't the Maddy we knew. Something had changed since I saw her a couple of days ago. But what?

"Don't push me, Jacqueline." She drawled out my given name, knowing how much I hated it.

"Magdalena, two can play that game." I stood there, keeping my gaze on hers. "Now pay Darcy whatever you owe her and let's get out of here before someone reports you to Probation."

And that someone might just be me if things turned out to be as bad as I feared.

"Go to hell."

Maddy shoved past me, leaving me staring at her in shock. Fortunately, there were only a couple of others there. They knew both of us and, judging from their expressions, they realized how lucky Maddy was that I cared for her. Otherwise, she'd be nothing but a puddle of goo on the floor. Instead, I dug into my pocket and pulled out a couple of twenties. After tossing them on the bar, I hurried outside. Hopefully, I'd get to Maddy before she managed to drive off.

Damn it, where the hell was Quinn? I could really use her help right now.

3

The door slammed open as I ran outside. It wouldn't take much to shift. Tempting as it was, I knew better. I needed to stop Maddy and convince her to come back to Miss Serena's with me. Whatever happened to cause her to act this way, we could deal with it, but only if I managed to keep her from driving off.

"Maddy, stop!"

I slapped my hand against the driver's door, stopping her before she could climb inside. Snarling at me, she grabbed my wrist with her right hand. As she did, she smiled as if she knew something I didn't. At the same time, the skin beneath her hand went cold, ice cold. The sensation crept up my arm. I started to pull away and she merely shook her head. Instantly, I stopped fighting against her grip.

No!

"Stop fighting it, Jax. You don't want to fight me. You want to do exactly what I say."

She spoke softly, almost conversationally. As she did, she shifted her grip from my wrist to my upper arm. With her other hand, she lightly caressed my cheek. If it weren't for the cold that followed the touch of her fingers, it could have been a lover's caress. Oh, God, what was happening?

"M-Maddy."

"Shh." She placed a finger against my lips and stole my ability to speak.

Fear beat a thundering rhythm deep inside me. Sweat rolled down my spine. I fought, screaming mentally, as she forced me to my knees. Never before had I felt so helpless. I was awake, aware of everything going on around me, but I had no control over my own body. I couldn't reach for my Earth abilities and I couldn't shift. All I could do was stare at Maddy and wait for her next command.

The sounds of tires screeching as brakes were slammed on sounded behind me. Maddy glanced over my shoulder and a slight smile lifted the corners of her mouth. But it was the look in her eyes that terrified me. This wasn't Maddy. At least not the Maddy I'd grown up with. Something had happened to her and it was as if this was her evil clone. I had to stop her before anyone else fell prey to her machinations.

But how?

"We have company, Jax." She ran a hand down my hair before lifting my face so I looked her fully in the eyes. "And you're going to take care of them for me. Down on all fours now."

I knew what she meant for me to do. Screaming that I needed to stop, I lowered to my hands and knees. This wasn't a show of submission. At least not the sort most would expect. She wanted me to shift and attack whoever arrived. Teeth clenched, muscles trembling as I fought against the compulsion, I waited for her order. I didn't know how long I'd be able to hold out if she gave me an explicit order to shift. It was hard enough to remain human just knowing what she had in mind.

"N-no."

It wasn't much more than a whisper, but it was enough. Even as panic rose as I felt my control slipping, Maddy once again focused on me and not on whoever was behind me. I had to hold out. I couldn't let her use me like this. But I couldn't. I knew it. The longer she looked into my eyes, the longer she maintained physical contact with me, the harder it became to think for myself. I forgot how to breathe.

All I could do was focus on fighting her commands because that's what they were. She was commanding me to act against my will.

Damn her!

"Now, now, Jax. You can't fight me. Be a good girl and make them leave us alone. Then we'll go somewhere and talk. You'd like that, wouldn't you?"

She sounded so reasonable, so much like the Maddy I knew. But the gleam in her eyes scared me as much as being unable to move. Even on hands and knees, I couldn't call to the Earth energies to help me. No, that couldn't be right. Being an Earth Elemental was part of me. Just because I couldn't move, that shouldn't prevent me from reaching for the nearest ley line. I just had to concentrate and pray she didn't do anything else to force me to do her will.

"Hey, Maddy, head's up!"

Quinn's challenge cut through the air a split-second before a fireball struck the pavement between us. Maddy looked up, fury suffusing her expression. But she didn't move her hand from where it rested on my head. Instead, her fingers twined in my hair, holding me in place.

"Leave or I won't be responsible for what happens." As she had with me, she didn't raise her voice. She sounded so reasonable, so *Maddy*.

"I don't think so," Ciara drawled from somewhere behind me and to my right.

A gust of wind buffeted us. Maddy cursed as she staggered back. Pain raked my scalp as she lost her balance and then her grip on my hair. In that moment, it felt like the world started turning on its axis again. I dragged in a ragged breath. My fingers dug down against the concrete of the parking lot. Earth energies raced into me.

"Shit, shit, shit, shit."

That became my mantra as I scrambled back, crab walking in the opposite direction from Maddy. I didn't stop until my back rested against the tire of someone's car. No, bigger than a car. An SUV? With my brain still reeling from what happened, I could only sit there, trying to catch my breath and still my thundering heart.

As I did, Quinn and Ciara stepped between Maddy and me. I didn't need to see their faces to know they were furious. Backs straight, energies dancing around them, they presented a united front. I needed to join them but I needed to figure out what happened and make sure Maddy didn't pull that little *trick* with either of them.

"You okay, Jax?" Quinn asked without turning to look at me.

"Not sure." I slowly, carefully climbed to my feet. For a moment, I stood unsurely, one hand on the SUV to steady me. Once the world quit pitching back and forth, I stepped forward, taking my place between the two sisters. "Maddy, I don't know what the hell you thought you were doing, but you went too far."

"Quinn?" Concern roughened Ciara's voice.

"I'll explain later." Now I had to figure out how to get Maddy out of here and keep the rest of us safe. Then we could figure out what the hell she'd done to me.

"Go to hell, each of you."

Maddy turned.

Or, to be more accurate, she tried to turn. Fury burst through me. I closed the distance between us in two quick steps. My left hand closed around her shoulder and I spun her to face me. Before she could react, my right fist came up in a savage upper cut. It caught the point of her chin. She cried out and staggered back. But she wasn't out and she made a futile grab for me. Well, two could play that way. She wanted to control me? I'd show her what control was.

I followed the upper cut with a left cross. Maddy's eyes rolled up and she started to crumple. Ciara moved quickly to catch her before she fell.

"Don't make contact with her hands." I panted like I'd run a couple of miles. Sweat soaked my shirt and my hands shook as reaction set in. "She tried to roll me. When that didn't work, she touched me. I couldn't move, couldn't do anything she didn't tell me to do."

For a moment, neither sister said anything. Then, while Ciara kept an eye on Maddy, Quinn hurried back to the SUV. When she returned, she carried a black duffle that she dropped onto the concrete next to Maddy. All I could do was watch as Quinn fitted what looked like modified mittens on Maddy's hands. Then she and Ciara used zip ties to secure her hands and feet. Between them, they carried her to the rear of the SUV and settled her in the back.

"Are you all right?" Quinn reached for my hand and I backed away, hiding both hands behind my back.

"Sorry." I licked my lips, striving for calm. "We can't risk whatever she did to me still being active."

"She's right." Ciara didn't sound happy about it.

Well, that made two of us.

"Now what?" Quinn asked?

"We take her to Miss Serena's. Maybe she can help us figure out what happened. Besides, I want her to have a look at Jax, make sure there's no long-lasting effects from whatever Maddy did." With that Ciara pulled out her phone and sent a quick text. Then she climbed in behind the SUV's steering wheel. "Jax, let her drive you. I'm serious."

Seeing Quinn pull on a pair of driving gloves, I nodded. A moment later, I tossed her the pickup's keys. She unlocked the doors and watched as I walked around to the passenger side. I waited, watching as Quinn leaned inside the SUV's driver's side window to say something to her sister. Ciara nodded and then pulled away.

"Easy, Jax. We've got this." Quinn slid the key into the ignition and started the engine.

I sat there, my forehead resting against the side window. Despite the warmth of the truck, I shivered violently. Reaction. That's all it was. Just reaction. Damn, that had been too close. If Quinn and Ciara waited just a few moments longer before distracting Maddy, it might have been too late. How had we not seen that Maddy was spiraling out of control like this?

"Thank you."

Quinn looked across the cab at me and smiled. Affection mixed with worry filled her expression. Then she reached over and lightly patted my leg. I stiffened and then relaxed. I needed the touch but didn't dare let her touch anywhere Maddy had. God, what if she'd managed to spell me and I turned on Quinn?

"Give me your cuffs." The words came out harsh, almost broken.

"No." She shook her head without taking her eyes off the road. "Listen to me, Jax. I don't know what the hell Maddy did, but she didn't break you. Whether you are ready to admit it or not, you were holding out against her. Ciara and I just gave you a chance to break her hold. Now trust yourself like we trust you and relax. We'll be at Miss Serena's soon and she'll know what to do."

God, I hoped so.

Despite Quinn's reassurances, I still worried. So I wrapped my hands around the armrest and held on as tightly as I could. I wouldn't release my grip until we were safe at Miss Serena's. Even then, I might continue to hold on until she figured out what Maddy had done to me.

It didn't take long to get there. As we approached the house, I didn't know whether to curse or collapse in relief to see the drive lined with cars. I recognized Miss Serena's Lincoln town car. Behind it were half a dozen other cars. As we parked behind Ciara's SUV, the front door opened. Lucas and Rafe were the first out. Miss Serena followed, Amy just behind her.

"C'mon, Jax." Quinn switched off the engine and opened her door. "I'll make sure the others know to give you room."

I nodded but didn't move. Instead, I sat there and watched as Ciara opened the SUV's hatch. She said something to Lucas as he joined her. He listened and then asked something. Once she answered, he nodded and reached inside. A moment later, he sat Maddy on her feet. Ciara bent and cut the zip tie around her ankles. Then, with his hand on her upper arm, Lucas escorted Maddy up the steps and inside the house.

I started nervously a moment later when my door opened. Miss Serena stood there, her expression concerned. She didn't say anything as she studied me. I started to move away from her when she reached out with one hand. Instead of telling me to sit still, she gave a small shake of her head. As she did, I felt a warmth emanating from the palm of her hand as she ran it from my head and down my arms.

"Jax, you need to come inside now." She spoke softly, her voice reassuring. "I know you're scared. I would be too. But we've got this. Lucas, Amy and Rafe are keeping an eye on Maddy and know not to let her touch them. Now I need you to tell me what happened."

She stepped back and waited. I drew a deep breath and released my seatbelt. Then I climbed out of the pickup. The moment my feet touched the ground, the wards reached out, welcoming me. I almost sobbed as I dropped to one knee and placed my right hand, palm down, on the ground. The Earth pulsed with energies that reached up and surrounded me, reassuring, refreshing, renewing.

"I'm sorry," I said softly as I climbed to my feet.

"You have nothing to apologize for, Jackie." She motioned me toward the house. "But now we need to figure out what happened and why."

I nodded. Slowly, we walked up the drive to the house. Quinn and Ciara waited for us by the door. As we stepped inside, I almost stumbled as a feeling of acceptance and a promise of protection filled me. The house was making its presence known just as the wards had. Maybe I hadn't fucked up too badly after all.

"Sit," Miss Serena said as we entered the kitchen. Without waiting to see if we complied, she busied herself putting on coffee and tea. When she finally joined us at the table, she had her emotions under control. "What happened?"

Sitting there, Quinn on my right and Ciara on my left, I described how I'd been worried because Maddy hadn't shown up for either Annie's swearing in or the party afterwards. Quinn confirmed I'd talked with her about my concerns. When it came to telling them about Darcy's call, Quinn hissed out a breath. Miss Serena rested a hand on her arm, stopping her from interrupting.

"Tell me what happened when she realized you were there, Jackie."

I thought for a moment, trying to recall everything. They listened closely. Miss Serena's expression hardened to hear how Maddy tried to roll me. But when she heard how I lost all ability to act when Maddy touched me, she paled.

"Drink your tea, dear heart." She did her best to smile in reassurance. Then she turned her attention to Quinn. "Call your mother and ask her to join us."

"Yes, ma'am." Quinn quickly did as Miss Serena said. "She said she'll be here shortly."

"Miss Serena, you have to have an idea about what Maddy did to me." I didn't try to hide my fear. "I've never felt anything like that. I'm not sure how much longer I could have held out. She wanted me to shift and attack Quinn and Ciara. I knew what she wanted me to do and I couldn't stop her."

"But you could and you did, child." She looked like she wanted to reach out to touch me but she stopped when I flinched. "I have an idea about what she did but I want to be sure. That's why I want Judith here."

"And Maddy?"

"She's not going anywhere until we know what's going on."

I nodded, knowing the house wouldn't let her out of whatever room Miss Serena told Lucas to put her in until Miss Serena said it was all right. There were definite advantages to having a semi-sentient house and that was one of them. But, sooner or later, we'd have to let her out and try to figure out what the hell happened and why.

Half an hour later, I watched as Miss Serena, Judith and Amy cast their circle. I sat there, shivering slightly in my underwear. Judith had taken one look at me when she arrived and told me to strip. I hadn't hesitated. I shed my clothes and watched as she carefully collected them and carried them outside. I didn't care if she burned them. I doubted I'd ever feel comfortable wearing them again.

"Lay back, Jax," Amy said softly as she knelt next to me.

I did as she said. As I closed my eyes, I focused on my breathing. All I could right now was try to remain calm and trust the others.

"Where did she touch you the first time, Jax?" Judith asked.

"My wrist. Then that upper arm."

"Which one?"

"The left."

"Did you feel anything strange?"

"Cold. So cold. Seemed to creep up my arm." I shivered again, this time at the memory.

"Did she touch you anywhere else?"

"Head, cheek."

"You're doing good, Jax, so very good."

I lay there, eyes closed, listening as they discussed the possibilities.

"Jax, you need to trust us," Miss Serena said from where she sat on the floor near my head.

"I do."

Even though trust was hard no matter who it was just then. I never suspected Maddy would turn against me. Now one very loud part of my brain wondered who else would turn against me.

No, I wouldn't listen to that voice. I wouldn't let what happened tear me from those who would do everything they could to help me.

"This won't be much different from what we did when all of you returned from Ireland. We're going to make sure she didn't bind you. Then we will neutralize whatever else she might have done."

"Just do it."

It wasn't like what you see in the movies. There was no dancing around the circle in the nude. No one drew a ceremonial blade down my body, offering my blood to some ancient god. Instead, they drew upon their elements and abilities. To the normal eye, they simply prayed over me, making some odd-looking hand motions as they did. But to anyone who could see the energies, they would have seen power building, seeking and probing. The air inside the circle was alive with those energies and I waited, forcing myself to remain relaxed and to remember to breathe.

It was over quicker than I expected.

"Well?" I sat up.

"No binding." Judith smiled in reassurance. "Go shower now. Make sure you take special care with anyplace she might have touched you. And quit worrying. I have a very good idea what happened and will explain when you're back. We'll leave clothes for you to change into."

"Miss Serena?" It all sounded too easy and that worried me.

"Go ahead, child. She's right." She smiled, understanding in her eyes. "Jackie, you're all right and you're in no danger of falling under Magdalena's control again. I promise."

"All right." I wanted to believe them. "Will you tell me what you *saw*?"

Judith nodded. "There's no evidence she bound you. Your shields are too strong for that to happen. The cold you felt when she touched you was a combination of her own abilities working with something she had on her hands. Think of it like a lotion or salve. The spells worked into it activated when she touched you skin-on-skin and took down your defenses. That allowed her to roll you, something she wouldn't have been able to do otherwise. The shower is simply to wash away anything that might remain on your skin or hair. It's also why we don't want you wearing anything you had on when this happened."

It made sense in a sick sort of way.

"And Maddy?"

"We'll deal with her together once you're back and feel up to it." Judith glanced at Miss Serena who nodded grimly. "And once Pat is here."

I closed my eyes and nodded just as grimly as Miss Serena. This was going to kill Dr. Pat. She'd worked so hard with Maddy since our return from Ireland, doing everything she to help her daughter regain her confidence and learn to control her abilities again. She'd gotten Maddy into therapy to help her get past the guilt she felt not only for how Roben used her abilities against his clients but also how he abused her. We all believed she was doing better and finally returning to normal. What had we missed?

"All right." I climbed to my feet.

"Go on, Jax. I've got a change of clothes in my go bag in the SUV. You can wear them." Quinn smiled at me in reassurance that did nothing to hide the anger and fear still reflected in her eyes.

"Thank you, both of you." I wanted to reach out to Quinn and Ciara but didn't dare, not until I was sure whatever Maddy had on her hands was no longer on me. "I don't want to think about what might have happened if you hadn't gotten there."

And I never wanted to feel that helpless again.

4

After showering, where I scrubbed until I worried I might scrub the skin from my bones, I dressed in the black cargo pants and black tee Quinn left for me. Good friend that she is, she even included a pair of panties and a support tank. Feeling more like myself, I padded barefoot upstairs. Quinn and Ciara followed. When Ciara glanced at my bare feet, I shrugged. I'd chosen to go sans shoes for the same reason Miss Serena and Judith wanted me in clean clothes. It was better to be safe than sorry, especially right now.

"What can you tell me?" I asked as I detoured into the kitchen. I wanted a drink, a very tall and strong one, but I'd settle for a cup of coffee.

"Dr. Pat got here while you were showering," Quinn said. "She and the others went to check on Maddy. Amy checked on you while you were still showering and asked that you join them when you're ready."

"Nothing else?" I didn't know whether to be relieved or not.

"Nothing else."

"All right." I glanced at the mug of coffee I held and decided I didn't want to take it with me. Why risk anything else happening?

There was one thing I needed to do before facing Maddy. I set the mug on the drainboard and turned to face Quinn and Ciara. One moment I stood there, searching for the words to explain how much I appreciated what they'd done. The next, we stood in a tight circle, arms around one another. Tremors wracked my body as they held me close, murmuring that it was all right. Their hands soothed as much as their voices. They loved me and were two of the very few I could let my defenses down with. Quinn knew firsthand what it meant to be abused and what Maddy did to me was abuse of a sort. They had my back as I did theirs. I needed to remember that.

"Thank you." I stepped back and scrubbed my hands over my face. I didn't say anything else. If I did, I'd lose it and I didn't dare, not until we dealt with Maddy.

"Jax." Quinn swallowed hard and reached for my hand. "You scared the hell out of me."

"Out of us," Ciara corrected. "And you need to reassure Rafe you're okay. He's about beside himself with worry right now."

I nodded. "Where is he?"

"In the den."

I was out of the kitchen in a shot. Hell, I might have teleported between kitchen and den. One moment I was talking to Quinn and Ciara and the next I was in Rafe's arms. He held me close, almost as if afraid to let me go. Then he stepped back, his eyes taking in every detail of my appearance. His expression tightened as he studied my face. I started to cup his cheek with my hand and hesitated, remembering what Maddy had done. Then I shook it off and reached up to kiss him instead.

"I'm fine," I murmured against his lips. "Just shaken."

"Oh, God, Doc." He rested his forehead against mine, his hands holding mine.

"I need to finish this and then I need you to take me home."

He nodded. "Darcy called to make sure you're okay. Said to tell you thanks for getting Maddy out of there. She'd been acting strange since she got there and it was starting to scare Darcy."

Which meant one of us needed to talk with the bartender and make sure I was the only one Maddy used her little "trick" on.

"We'll stop by later." I leaned into him one last time before stepping back. "I need to deal with Maddy now."

"Are you all right?"

I nodded.

"Then let's do this." He reached for my hand. "I'll wait outside, but you aren't going up there without me. Not this time, Doc."

I nodded and, with Rafe by my side and Quinn and Ciara following, made my way upstairs to the guest room where Maddy had been taken.

Lucas stood outside the door. Before I could react, he grabbed me in a bear hug. When he placed me on my feet again, he looked me over from head to toe. Then he nodded once. Whatever he'd seen, he approved of.

"Thank you."

I frowned. "For what?"

"For getting her out of that bar before she did anything to any of the patrons. For being strong enough to hold out against whatever she did to you. For having the sense to send for my wife." Now he gave me a look that had me considering hiding behind Rafe. "Although, next time, send for me as well."

I chuckled and lightly punched him in the shoulder. "I hope you don't mind if I say I hope there isn't a next time."

"Not at all." He gave me another quick hug, a big brother who had been worried about his little sister, and then nodded to Rafe. "She's inside. The others have been working with her."

I stood before the door and drew a deep, bracing breath. I needed to face Maddy, find out why she did what she did. That was my head talking. My heart was breaking. My childhood friend, a woman I considered as much of a sister as I did Quinn, Ciara, Annie and Meg, had tried to force me to hurt others I cared deeply for. She stripped me of my free will—or tried to. The Rogue wanted to make her pay for that.

And, just then, I wanted very badly to be the Rogue.

"Jax?" Quinn asked softly.

"I'm okay."

To prove it—to them and to me—I turned the knob and opened the door.

I could do this. I had to do this.

The door swung open and I stepped inside. Miss Serena, Amy and Dr. Pat stood on either side and at the foot of the bed. Maddy sat in the middle of the mattress, her back against the wooden headboard. Eyes swollen from crying, her cheeks stained by drying tears. In that moment, she looked like the Maddy I knew. But the memory of what she'd done to me remained and so did the suspicion this was all a ruse to lure us into complacency.

She looked up as I moved further into the room, Quinn and Ciara on my heels. Tears once again filled her eyes and rolled down her cheeks. Before the others could react, she launched herself from the bed. Arms open, her expression stricken, she all but flew in my direction. Whether she meant to hug me or attack, I'd never know. Instinct, more animal than human, took over. I sidestepped her, my hands held protectively in front of me.

"No, no, no, no," Maddy moaned as she all but collapsed onto the floor.

I stayed where I was. I hated the way I felt. I'd known Maddy most of my life. Until recently, I'd have trusted her with my life and the lives of my loved ones. Now I didn't dare turn my back on her. That hurt but I didn't know what else to do.

I wasn't sure we'd ever be able to get past what happened. The memory of what it felt like to be helpless as she tried to force me into a shift would take a long time to get past.

"Maddy, it's all right. Let's get you back to bed."

Amy's voice soothed as she bent and helped Maddy to her feet. As she did, she glanced at me. Instead of condemnation, her eyes reflected understanding and even approval. If that wasn't enough to reassure me that I hadn't overreacted, the way Quinn and Ciara reacted did. Somehow, without me realizing it, they'd placed themselves between Maddy and me, ready to stop her if she tried again.

I put one hand on a shoulder of each and assured them it was all right. Then, as Amy helped Maddy back to bed, I eased them back behind me. As much as they wanted to protect me, I knew I needed to protect them.

Damn it, how had we come to this?

"Miss Serena?"

"Maddy, you need to tell Jax what you told us."

Miss Serena might look like a much beloved grandmother but she had a spine of steel. That steel showed in her comment. Despite that, I saw the pain in her eyes, especially as she looked at Dr. Pat. Not that I blamed her. I felt pretty damned bad as well. Dr. Pat looked like we'd kicked her puppy, stolen her most favorite toy and then told her she couldn't go trick-or-treating. Worse, guilt radiated from her. She felt she'd failed her daughter and failed us.

Damn it all to Hell and back again.

Instead of saying something—there would be time for that later —I grasped her hand and gave it a quick squeeze. Then I turned my attention to Maddy, wondering what she had to say.

"Well?"

Okay, not the most encouraging thing I could say. But I didn't feel encouraging. Now that the initial panic had worn off, I was pissed. She'd better have a damned good story to tell. If not, it would be a long time before I had anything to do with her. It was bad enough she'd tried to roll me. But trying to force me to hurt Quinn and Ciara? That went too far.

I might never forgive her for that.

"Jax, I'm sorry. So sorry." She buried her face in her hands.

"That's not enough, Maddy. Not this time." I shook my head when Dr. Pat started to interrupt. "You tried to roll me, Maddy. Then you did—hell, I don't know what you did but I do know what you wanted. You wanted me to shift and attack Quinn and Ciara. Why?"

I stopped. If I said anything else, I'd go into a tirade. It might make me feel better but it would accomplish nothing. For the moment at least, I needed to keep my emotions under control. I'd be able to fall apart later, when she no longer presented a danger to anyone I cared for.

I waited, watching Maddy. She drew her knees up and wrapped

her arms around her legs. For a moment, she looked like a scared little girl. But I knew better. She'd taught me that lesson. She might be scared but she was far from helpless.

"I was stupid."

No argument there.

"I felt sorry for myself, something I've done a lot of the last few months." She dropped her head until her forehead rested on her knees. "You all have everything you ever wanted. Jobs you love, men who adore you. You even have one another. I'm the odd man out. My life's a mess. Today I couldn't take it any longer. I couldn't stand knowing Annie was getting yet another of her dreams. It hurt to know everyone would be there, telling her how wonderful she is and how happy they are for her. It was like my nightmares from school had come to life and it all became too much to handle.

"So I did what I've always done." She looked up and gave a bitter laugh. "I've become very good at hiding my feelings and my—let's call them my coping mechanisms. I didn't care if I violated the terms of my probation. All I wanted was to dull the pain and the best way to do that is with booze since Mom made sure I couldn't get my hands on any pills."

I sensed Dr. Pat stiffening where she stood. Anger slowly replaced her fear and guilt. Good. It was time for all of us to stop making excuses for Maddy. She was a grown woman and ought to act like one. That meant taking responsibility for her actions and facing the consequences.

"And you didn't think about what might happen, not just to you but to those of us who care for you, if your probation was revoked?" Ciara asked.

"As if you care about me," she all but snarled.

"Maddy!" Dr. Pat looked at her daughter as if she couldn't believe her ears.

"Let her talk, Dr. Pat." I lightly rested my hand on her arm, letting her know I didn't blame her for anything Maddy said or did. "As for you." I pinned Maddy with a firm look. "You know better than that. Quinn, not to mention Lucas and others, risked their lives to find your mother and arrest her captors after she'd been kidnapped. Ciara and Rafe went to Ireland with me when I went to find you and bring you home because we knew you were in trouble.

"Damn it, Maddy, I let Roben see some of what I'm capable of in an attempt to get you free from him. So don't give me any bullshit about us not caring for you."

I shook off Quinn's hand and moved closer to the bed.

"I don't know when you got it in your head that we didn't care for you. But it's wrong and it's stupid. So get the fuck over yourself. While you're at it, take a long look at what you almost did tonight. Consider what the consequences of it could have been."

"Jax is right." Dr. Pat spoke softly, her disappointment obvious. "Who else is going to have to be hurt before you realize you have to quit feeling sorry for yourself?"

Maddy laughed bitterly. Then she scrubbed at her eyes as tears once again rolled down her cheeks. Her laughter turned to sobs. Part of me wanted to go to her but the other part held back. If this was the breakthrough she needed, good. If not, I wasn't about to let her have the chance to control me again.

"Maddy, talk to us. Tell us what happened."

"Tell us how you managed to control me the way you did. I know you didn't roll me."

She sniffled and ran a hand under her nose. But she didn't say anything. We waited, giving her time. But that time was limited. If she didn't say something soon, I was out of there. I needed to make sure she hadn't done to anyone else what she tried to with me.

"Maddy, you have to talk to us," Amy said almost gently.

She nodded almost reluctantly.

"Everything seemed to crash in on me today. I wanted to be there for Annie but I couldn't. Everything about the day reminded me of all I've done wrong, all my failures. I couldn't take it. I didn't want to see her doing yet something else she could be proud of. I just wanted everything to go away. Since that wasn't going to happen, I wanted to forget the pain and the best way to do that was to have a few drinks."

Spoken like so many alcoholics and other addicts. I motioned for her to continue.

"I told Mom and Dad I'd meet them at the courthouse. I didn't want them to realize what I was thinking, much less what I planned on doing."

Dr. Pat frowned, frustration warring with guilt. Damn Maddy for doing this to her. Dr. Pat had gone above and beyond to help her, especially since her return from Ireland, and this was how Maddy repaid her.

"And?" Ciara prompted.

"Once they left, I showered and got dressed. I was on my way out when I stopped and went back to my bedroom. I knew I was on edge, so I used a lotion I brought back with me from Ireland. It has always managed to calm me down."

"Brought back with you?" I repeated.

The world came to a screeching stop. My lips peeled back, baring my teeth, and I growled. My animal aspects were so close to the surface, it would take little more than a thought to shift. Then I glanced at Ciara who winced slightly. She knew without asking what I wanted to know and she sure as hell better have a good answer.

Before leaving Ireland, Ciara helped Maddy get ready. Because we'd figured out Roben somehow managed to bind Maddy to him, I told Maddy she couldn't bring anything with her. I'd even made her change into clothes I'd brought with me. Ciara had one job that day: make sure Maddy left everything there.

And I had a pretty damned good idea how Maddy managed to bring the lotion back with her. If I was right. . . .

"What else did you bring back?"

"N-nothing."

"Don't lie to me, Maddy." My eyes flashed angrily.

"Tell her, Maddy. Tell her everything or, by God, I will bag up everything at the house and burn it," Dr. Pat said, her voice harsher than I'd ever heard.

"All right!" She slammed her right fist against the mattress. Then she named half a dozen other items, everything from jewelry to clothing to cosmetics. "I don't see why you're making such a big deal out of it."

I clamped my jaw shut before I said what I wanted to. Didn't see what the big deal is? Had she lost her damned mind?

"Tell me something, Maddy. Did you do anything to Ciara so she'd not realize you didn't do as we said?"

Looking defiant and miserable at the same time, she nodded.

"What did you do?" Quinn demanded. Flames danced around her hands and she cursed softly before extinguishing them.

"I still don't see what the big deal is. All I did was suggest she look the other way."

"You know exactly what the big deal is, Magdalena." Censure roughened Miss Serena's voice. "You knew the dangers of bringing anything back with you from Ireland. But you ignored those dangers and you took advantage of someone who was trying to help you. Worse, you tried to roll Jax tonight. When that didn't work, you used the properties of the lotion to do basically the same thing. You took advantage of someone who cares deeply for you. Worse, you tried to made her act in a way that would have injured, maybe killed, others and that would have broken Jax as a result. You knew that and yet you did it anyway."

"I didn't want to!" she wailed. "I didn't want to," she said more softly.

"Amy, she needs to shower and change. Quinn and Ciara will stay with you. Rafe and Lucas will be in the hallway."

The look Miss Serena gave her granddaughter spoke volumes.

"Yes, ma'am."

"The rest of us will be waiting downstairs."

Judith, Dr. Pat and I followed Miss Serena downstairs. No one said anything until we settled in the den. I'm not sure any of us knew what to say. I certainly didn't. But I couldn't stay silent, not when Dr. Pat blamed herself for what happened.

"Dr. Pat." I dropped down onto the edge of the coffee table in front of where she sat on the sofa. "Look at me." I took her hands in mine and waited until she did. "You love Maddy. We all do. I know how hard you've worked to try to help her since we returned from Ireland. What happened there and what happened today aren't on you. I mean it."

She nodded but I knew she didn't accept it. No mother who loved her child would, at least not easily.

"What can we do, Miss Serena?" I hoped she had an idea because I sure as hell didn't.

"That will be up to Judith and me. Amy will assist. It's clear to me that Roben still has some form of connection to her. We're going to have to dig it out and sever it once and for all." She sat next to Dr. Pat and reached for her free hand. "Pat, you don't want to be here for this. If we're right, we're going to see more of the same sort of behavior we just did, but worse. You don't need that and she's going to need you without those memories afterward."

"Serena." Tears glistened in her eyes.

"Pat, she's right. This isn't going to be easy. But if it can be done, you can trust us to do it."

"I do." She blinked back her tears and managed a tremulous smile. "We need to know who else she's influenced."

Influenced.

Such a benign word for what Maddy tried to do to me.

"We'll find out," I promised. We had to. "What do you want me to do?"

Miss Serena's expression warned me I wouldn't like what she had to say.

"Go talk to Darcy and make sure she didn't do anything there. Then find out how often she's been going to the bar. None of us." Now she pinned Dr. Pat with a firm yet understanding look. "None of us will stand in the way if a motion to revoke her probation is filed. We will do what we can to keep her from going to prison. But if the authorities feel she needs to be punished for her actions, we will honor that."

I didn't like it but she was right. For as long as I could remember, we'd protected Maddy. Maybe that was wrong and maybe it had something to do with how she viewed herself. It certainly hadn't helped her learn to stand up for herself and that was a cross I'd bear for a long time. Maybe it was time for all of us to grow up, at least where she was concerned.

"Pat, you and Marcus need to remove anything Maddy might have brought back from Ireland both at your house and at the caretaker's house. She won't be able to return to either location until that happens."

"Trust me, we'll make sure there is nothing from that time left." Determination replaced the despair in her voice and her body language.

"Then go on. Marcus should be here by now. Tell him what happened and let him know Judith and I are going to do everything we can to help Maddy break any binding that remains and remove any compulsions that might have been placed on her."

She nodded and climbed to her feet. As she did, she drew me up and wrapped me in a tight embrace. A tremor ran through her body as she held me close. Understanding, I rubbed her back, wishing I could do something to reassure her.

"You and Marcus return here when you're done. You'll stay with me until we're sure Maddy's all right," Miss Serena said as she, too, stood.

"Thank you."

My heart broke as Dr. Pat slowly left the room. She moved like a woman approaching the execution chamber. If nothing else, Maddy needed to make it up to her mother for everything she'd done.

"Miss Serena, Maddy would never willingly do anything to hurt her mother," I said softly once Dr. Pat was out of earshot.

"I know, Jackie, just as I know she would never do anything to hurt you, not willingly at least. That's one reason why I believe there is still another binding on her or a compulsion or both." She sighed softly and returned to her chair. "I also know you want to help. But this isn't the sort of thing your talents are good for."

I didn't like it but she was right. But there had to be something more I could do and I said so.

"Make sure the protections around your home, the clinic and

then each of our homes are still strong. As an Earth Elemental, you should be able to do that without any problem."

I nodded. I could do that. I could also make sure everyone was protected, whether they were in their homes or elsewhere. And I planned on starting here.

"All right."

The sounds of someone coming down the stairs reached us. Quinn and Ciara led the group. Maddy and Amy came next with Rafe and Lucas behind them. Maddy now wore a pair of grey sweatpants and white tank. Her hair hung damply around her shoulders. Gone was the rebellious, contemptuous expression I'd seen earlier. Now she looked almost beaten, as if resigned to her fate, whatever that might be.

"Jax." She swallowed hard, tears once again swimming in her eyes.

"Maddy, I'm not going to lie to you. I'm furious. More than that, I'm hurt. I don't know what's been going on with you beyond this: you haven't been honest with us." I stopped and stilled my swirling emotions when Judith placed a gentle hand on my arm.

"But you need to remember something. I love you. Each of us here loves you and we're going to fight for you, whether you want us to or not. All I ask is that you fight for yourself—for the Maddy we know and love and not the one Roben turned you into."

Her fingers twisted together and she nodded. "I will. I don't like the person he made me."

"Then quit hiding from us. Quit thinking you can do this on your own. Today proves you can't."

Harsh? Yes, but she needed to face the truth. And that meant answering a few more questions for me.

"Who else have your manipulated the way you did Ciara and me?"

She shook her head and started to tremble. My heart broke for her, but I couldn't turn soft now. Too much rode on finding out how deep the damage ran.

"Please." The word was little more than a whisper.

"I meant what I said, Maddy. We're past time for excuses or evasions." I waited until she met my gaze. "I don't know what else to do to prove we have your back, Mads."

"M-my parents."

God, this was going to kill Dr. Pat. Thank goodness, Miss Serena had her leave.

"We'll find out who else, child. You know what you need to do," Miss Serena said.

I nodded. "Do you need Rafe to stay?"

He looked like he wanted to protest but he didn't. Yet another reason I loved him.

"No." She shook her head. "I'm sure you can use him with what you have to do."

I nodded and held out my hand. A moment later, his closed around it. Together we walked outside. The moment the door closed behind us, he lifted me in his arms and carried me to the truck.

"Your shoes?"

That was it. Out of everything he could have asked, that was it. He knew I'd tell him the rest of it when I was ready. Fortunately, I was more than ready. But it needed to wait until we were home and I could finally fall to pieces.

"We need to stop by the office. I have a pair of boots there."

He nodded.

"I won't be long there. Promise." Just long enough to check the wards protecting the property. "Then we can go home. I'll explain everything while I change."

"Just tell me this. Are you all right?"

"I am." I turned in my seat so I could look at him. "Rafe, I am. I'll admit, she scared the shit out of me and I don't know what would have happened if Quinn and Ciara had been even a few minutes later. But I'm fine now."

"And this goes back to Roben?"

So much for waiting until we got home.

"At least partially," I answered as he parked in front of the stable where my temporary office and clinic were located. "I'll be right back."

"I'm going with you." He put the transmission into park and switched off the engine. Then he sat there, just sat there, and blew out a long, shaky breath. "Doc, Ciara told me a little about what happened. Don't you ever scare me like that again."

I walked into his waiting arms and held him close. "Not if I can help it." I rested my cheek against his chest. "I've never been that scared before, Rafe, but I can't talk about it right now. I need to make sure our wards are all in place. Then we can go home and I'll tell you everything. I promise."

Maybe by then, I could think about what happened and not want to dig a hole and hide.

5

"Are you sure about this?" Quinn asked softly as we walked from the stables to Miss Serena's house.

I looked at her and shook my head. "Honestly? No. But I don't see that we have any choice."

For the last two days, Miss Serena, Judith and Amy had worked with Maddy. While they managed to break more of the binding on her, they had been unable to completely sever it. All three had been at their wits' end when I spoke with them the night before. To say that conversation had been anything but uncomfortable was putting it mildly. They'd been dejected and worried. I'd been furious to see how badly they'd exhausted themselves. Finally, we agreed they couldn't keep working on their own. So, tonight, it would be the four of us, with Mary Kate, Quinn and Ciara casting an outer circle for protection and to support us if needed.

"Should we bring Annie and Meg in on this?" Quinn shoved her hands in her pockets and hunched her shoulders.

I smiled in understanding. Both of our friends would be seriously pissed when they discovered what we were doing. We'd deal with that later. For now, they needed to be protected. Annie was still learning to control her abilities. Hell, we didn't know yet everything she could do. The last thing I wanted was for her powers to go rogue while dealing with this mess Maddy had gotten herself in. As for Meg, no way did I want her near anything that might go South. Not until she had the baby.

"No. This is one time they need to be kept out of it."

She didn't look happy about it, probably because she knew how pissed they would be when they found out what we'd been up to.

"So what are we doing tonight?"

That happened to be the million dollar question.

"I don't know all the details." I wasn't sure I knew more than a few of them and they were enough to worry me. "But the main thing is we need to make sure your mother and Miss Serena don't overextend themselves."

And make sure Maddy didn't do anything stupid.

"And Dr. Pat?"

Now it was my turn to shake my head. I wasn't sure what to say mainly because I didn't know the answer. When I asked Miss Serena that very question at lunch, she said she and Judith were still considering their options. That worried me but I knew better than to tell Quinn. She'd already let me know more than once over the last two days how worried she was about her mother.

Half an hour later, I stood in Miss Serena's very large and very calming back yard. My boots rested on the back porch where I'd left them. Inside, the others waited, giving me the time I needed to connect with the wards and the ley lines running deep beneath the surface.

I knelt down and dug my fingers through the thick grass into the soil below. Carefully, I reached for the wards, making sure the connections between them, the ley lines and Miss Serena remained strong. Then, knowing Miss Serena would probably box my ears when she realized what I did, I tugged a strand of energy from the wards, tied it with the nearest ley line and then reached back toward the house and the glow of yellow-white energy. Smiling slightly, knowing Amy would approve even if her grandmother didn't, I tied her into the wards as well. I didn't know what was happening and did not want to risk Miss Serena by not having someone tied into the wards in case of trouble.

A few minutes later, I climbed to my feet and brushed my hands on my jeans. When I turned, I smiled slightly. Amy stood on the porch, her head cocked to one side, her blonde hair gleaming in the starlight. As I neared, she smiled and bent to hand me my boots.

"Thank you."

"For?"

She laughed and shook her head. "You know for what. I know we talked about it, but I wasn't sure you'd actually do it."

I sat down on the top step and motioned for her to join me. "Amy, I'm worried. Your grandmother has pushed herself as close to exhaustion as I've ever seen. Worse, I know she's worried about what might happen next. Then there's the very real fact that if someone wants to hurt Mossy Creek and weaken the Guardians, they will attack her. If tying you into the wards here helps protect her, then I'll do it without a second thought."

She nodded and waited as I pulled on my boots. Then she reached for my hand, holding it tightly between her own. "And that's why I thank you." She grinned and released my hand before turning serious again. "It is also why I know you tied into the wards yourself."

"I will neither admit nor deny it." That way I wouldn't be lying and wouldn't put her in the position of having to lie if her grandmother asked about it.

"Jax, you've always been there for Grandma and me." She leaned over and lightly shoulder bumped me. "I know I can trust you to do everything possible to keep her safe. That's important to me. I hope you know you can count on me to be there for you as well."

"I do."

"I know we haven't been as close as you, Quinn and Annie."

I noted she didn't mention Maddy and I didn't blame her. The closeness we had growing up might never return.

"But I always knew you were someone I could count on. I'm glad I can call you a friend now."

Emotion clogged my throat for a moment. I covered her hand where it rested on the decking and gave it a quick squeeze.

"Amy, you're family. You and your grandmother always have been." When she looked at me in question, I sighed a little sadly. "You know what my life was like growing up. The only thing that kept me from really going rogue was the fact I had people like Aunt Bitsy, Quinn's mom and you and your grandmother. You were always there, helping your grandmother help me. You were the big sister I'd always wanted. I'm sorry I didn't let you know it."

"I know it now." Suddenly, she grinned at me, mischief dancing in her eyes. "And think of all the years of picking on you I have to make up for."

I bared my teeth and mock-growled, reminding her I might not have gone rogue but I was still "The Rogue". Then I stood and held out a hand to help her to her feet.

"Let's get this done. Once we have, we'll both make sure your grandmother gets some rest and takes it easy for a while."

Hopefully, it would be that simple.

Ten minutes later, everyone gathered in the den. Without a word, Ciara, Quinn, Amy and I began moving furniture against the walls or out of the room. Once we had, everyone took their places. Quinn, Ciara, Mary Kate and Amy formed the outer circle. Miss Serena, Judith, Dr. Pat and I formed the inner circle. Maddy knelt in the center.

Before the circles were cast, I moved to crouch in front of Maddy. I had a simple question for her. Her answer would determine if we went forward or not.

"Maddy."

She looked at me, her eyes dark with an emotion I couldn't identify.

"You need to be honest now. I know you well enough to know if you aren't. Understand?"

She nodded.

"Do you want to do this? Do you want us to break the last of the bindings on you?"

She didn't hesitate. "Yes!"

That was all it took. Miss Serena nodded once and began issuing her last-minute instructions. The outer circle would be cast first. Then she and Judith would cast the inner circle. I would then tie both into the property's wards and the ley lines. Then the real work would begin.

It wouldn't be easy and it wouldn't be quick. It might not work. But we had to try.

"Are you ready?" Miss Serena asked.

I glanced at Dr. Pat where she sat opposite Maddy, her hands holding her daughter's. She wouldn't be taking part as one of the Guardians tonight. Her job was to act as Maddy's anchor in much the same way I'd anchor everyone else. We all knew our roles. Every possibility had been planned for.

So why was I so worried?

The next few hours were some of the strangest, most difficult I'd known as an Other. They made every test, every trial of vet school look like the proverbial walk in the park. I'd certainly never taken part in anything like it since returning to Mossy Creek.

I watched closely as the outer circle was cast. Amy wove the elements together with a deft hand. When she glanced at me, I reached out, physically and elementally, taking the thread of their combined energies and binding them to the wards, weaving them together to form a protective outer shell that arched above and below us.

Then it was Miss Serena's and Judith's turn. They worked with an ease that only years of practicing magic together could bring. Once their energies twined together, they looked to Dr. Pat. She added her own magic. This time, however, I felt it waver. Not that it surprised me. Dr. Pat was distracted, worried and it impacted her concentration. Before I could figure out what to do, Miss Serena softly encouraged her, somehow finding the right words to guide her through it. Finally, it was my turn and I added my Earth magic to theirs. All the while, Maddy sat in the center of our circle, silent, dejected.

Once our energies joined, it was my turn again. I knelt and placed my hands against the cool wood of the floor. Closing my eyes, I focused. Energy flowed down my arms and through my palms, into the floor. It went deeper, through the basement and then the foundation. Dark earth, filled with life most people never thought about. The call of the ley lines drawing me closer. It would be so easy to fall into them, to get lost in the power they held.

I inhaled, held it, and then exhaled. I opened my eyes and tilted my head back. Overhead, the energies of the inner circle danced, bright whites and blues, greens and browns. When I lifted my left hand, a tendril of energy snaked down toward me. Another and then another and yet another followed. My fingers moved, knitting them together. I then tied them to the energy thread Amy fed me earlier.

Once again, I closed my eyes. My awareness expanded and the energies built around me. They played over my skin, electric, enticing. I wove them around me and then through me, anchoring them to me before pulling once again on the nearest ley line. I drew it to me and joined it with the wards and the circles.

Someone gasped. My lips curled up, recognizing Quinn. For a moment, her magic wavered before she regained control. I opened my eyes and turned my head, searching for her. Seeing her surprised expression and guessing the cause, I winked. No doubt she'd pepper me with questions later, but this was necessary.

"It's time," I said.

I remained where I was, palms to the floor, monitoring the energies of the wards, our circles and the ley lines crossing the property. Miss Serena and Judith worked as one over a now reclining Maddy. They chanted softly and performed other arcane things I did not yet understand as they teased out a tendril of black energy from Maddy. My stomach churned to see it rising from Maddy's chest as sweat pricked out on her forehead. She jerked once and cried out when Miss Serena severed the tendril with the blade of her ancient athame.

"Pat, keep her calm," Judith said softly as they worked to draw out a second tendril.

I watched, focusing on the tendril. It fought to escape the circle, searching out its source. Part of me wanted to drop the protections so we could follow it but I knew better. Whoever was strong enough to bind Maddy in such a way was strong enough to cause any of us, even Miss Serena, a serious challenge. It was best to deal with one problem at a time.

Miss Serena and Judith teased another black tendril out. This time, Judith used her own athame to sever it. Instead of dissipating like the others did, it writhed above Maddy's chest. Twisting and turning, seeking, trying to reattach itself to Maddy as she lay there, eyes closed, trusting us to finally free her of the last of the bindings.

Worse, both women were tiring. I felt it as much as I saw it. I reached for the ley line again and began to carefully feed energy from it to the two women. Neither said anything but Miss Serena took a deep breath, almost like a swimmer emerging from too long under-water. As she continued, she looked steadier. So did Judith. Hope-fully, it would be enough.

"Almost done," Miss Serena said softly.

I narrowed my eyes to hear the worry in her voice. Had some-thing gone wrong? Before I could ask, she simply looked at Judith. Neither spoke, but they didn't need to. I felt them strengthening the protections of the inner circle. When I glanced at it, instead of dancing in the air like a concert light show, the energies seemed to solidify. Instinctively, I pulled on the ley line for more energy and fed it first into the circle and then into the wards around the house. If those two anticipated trouble, I wanted to be prepared.

Slowly, carefully, Miss Serena pulled what I hoped was the last tendril of evil—there was no other word for it—from Maddy. Sweat pricked out on Miss Serena's face. Maddy gasped and began strug-gling against her mother's hold on her. Judith reached forward, resting one hand on Dr. Pat's shoulder and the other on Miss Serena's right arm. I watched her feeding energy into the two of them. Knowing she couldn't do that for long, I reached across Maddy to lightly rested my right hand on Judith's thigh. She gave me a quick nod before accepting the energy I offered.

It couldn't have lasted long but it felt like an eternity. Miss Serena fought to pull the final tendril free from Maddy. She chanted, her words shifting from English to Irish to a language I didn't recognize. Energy built inside the circle, dark and light. The tendril pulsed angrily, solidifying until I felt sure it would split Maddy in two. From a distance, Quinn shouted something.

"Maintain your circle!" I yelled, pulling on more of my Earth magic to help fight the magic the dark tendril represented.

It rose high into the air. When it reached the top of our circle, it spread, creating a dome of black over us. Fear licked at me and I fought it down. Light dimmed and breathing became difficult. Knowing I risked singeing myself, literally and psychically, I sought for a second ley line, one I hadn't already tied into the wards and the circle. I plunged my metaphysical "hand" into it, drawing the power to me. Energy filled me. Every pore felt like it suddenly caught fire. Wrapping the power around me, I reached for my connection to the circle. I fed the new energy up through my left hand. Ignoring the tightness in my chest, I directed it out through my right which I removed from Judith's leg.

Go, go, go. Protect them. Have to protect them.

Blinding white energy, pulsating with browns and greens, flew from my fingertips. It wrapped around the dark tendril, starting just above Maddy's chest. Slowly, it wove in and out, encasing the dark force. As it climbed toward the top of the circle—dome, whatever the hell you wanted to call it—it began to pull the tendril down toward it. At the same time, I could swear it pulled the last grasping hooks from Maddy's body. She cried out, rising from her waist. Dr. Pat held her tightly against her. Miss Serena and Judith, seeing what I was doing, joined in. At least I thought they did. I sensed a shift in the energies but kept my focus on directing the flow from the ley line.

"Jax, release it! Do it now!"

My last conscious thought as the world around me exploded was to hope no one paid too high of a price for what I did.

6

I hurt.

Dear God, I hurt.

Moaning, I rolled onto my side. That's when I remembered to breathe. Not that it helped. It only confirmed that the pain was more than on the surface. Inside and out, everything hurt.

I gasped in another breath and tried to focus on my other senses. Unless my imagination was working overtime, smell was there. Sweat and fear and something I couldn't identify assaulted my nostrils and sent my stomach churning. Touch was there and I wasn't sure that was a good thing. The usually smooth wood floor felt jagged, painfully rough beneath me. Hysterical laughter bubbled up. Miss Serena was going to kill me—assuming I wasn't already dead—if I'd ruined her floors.

Since smell was there, I assumed taste was as well, especially since there was no mistaking the metallic taste of blood in my mouth. That left sight and sound.

Best to leave sight until I could actually move.

A dull roar filled my ears. Slowly, it cleared. At least I thought it was slowly. From somewhere in the distance, shouts sounded. I couldn't understand what they said. Didn't care what they said. There were other things to worry about first.

Open your eyes, Jax. You need to open your eyes.

My cheek against the floor, body curled almost into a fetal position, I forced my eyes open. The world swam dizzyingly before me. Gasping, swallowing against the bile rising in my throat, I slammed my eyes shut. One deep breath and then a second. My stomach settled.

This time the world didn't pitch and turn, it only pitched. I lay there a moment longer. Then I carefully leaned up on one elbow. Sweat drenched hair fell across my brow and I shoved it back. Hissing as pain shot through me, I sat up and climbed to hands and knees. I knew better than to try to stand.

Time to find out what happened.

No!

Fear slashed through me, threatening to send me back to my belly as my animal aspects cringed before fighting for release. Miss Serena and Judith half-lay, half-sat across the circle from me. They leaned against one another, as if they would collapse without the support. Dr. Pat lay on the floor, Maddy cradled against her. Eyes closed, pale as death, Maddy didn't move. My breath caught and my heart stopped as I stared at her, waiting, praying for her to breathe. Relief washed through me a moment later when she drew an all too shallow breath. It wasn't much, but it was enough for now.

Putting one hand in front of the other, I crawled to Miss Serena and Judith. They looked as battered and exhausted as I felt. But they were conscious. However, they weren't able to dismiss the circle. Hell, I wasn't sure I could do it just then.

"Damn it, Jax, take down the circle!"

I looked over my shoulder to see Quinn standing at the edge of the boundary between the inner and outer circle. Fear and something akin to anger filled her. Flames danced not just around her hands but up her arms. If she didn't get control and soon, she'd become a real-life version of a human torch. I giggled, a sure sign I wasn't all right, at the thought. Then I nodded, knowing she was right. I needed to dismiss the circle.

"Give me a minute."

I closed my eyes. Pain lanced through my head as I opened my connection with the Earth energies. Panting as the pain worsened, I checked the wards. Then I opened my eyes and looked at Maddy. Relief filled me to see the aura I knew when we were growing up. At least something good came out of this.

I released my connection and dropped to my knees next to Miss Serena. She looked up at me and smiled when I reached for her hand. For the first time, she looked older than I knew she was. Not that it surprised me. I had a feeling I looked like hell. I certainly felt like it.

"Is it safe to dismiss the circle?" My voice sounded hoarse even to my ears.

She nodded. Then she gathered herself to stand. I shook my head. I could do it.

I hoped.

Staggering to my feet, I walked the circle, dismissing it as Miss Serena and Judith had taught me so long ago. The moment it was down, the others rushed forward. Amy and Mary Kate dropped to their knees to check on Miss Serena and Judith before turning their attention to Dr. Pat and Maddy. Ciara slid an arm around my waist, taking on much of my weight while Quinn looked at me in concern.

"You need to sit down, Jax." Quinn spoke softly, worry in her eyes.

"Not yet." I stood straighter, locking my knees before they could buckle. "Ciara, you need to dismiss the outer circle."

She nodded and then motioned for Quinn to take her place.

"What about me?" Quinn asked as she wrapped my arm around her shoulder before sliding an arm around my waist.

"I'm going to help you check the wards again when the circle comes down. We need to make sure they weren't damaged."

And heaven help us if they were because neither Miss Serena nor I were up to dealing with them right now.

"Quinn, come help your mother. I can deal with the wards." Amy stood and hurried to us. Once she took Quinn's place, she eased me into a sitting position on the floor.

The moment the outer circle came down, Amy used her new connection with the wards to check them. I watched, ready to help. It wasn't long before she nodded and smiled. Then she knelt at my side, her hands gentle as she tipped my head this way and that.

"The wards held," she said. Then, hearing the sounds of cars racing up the drive, she smiled. "Probably too well."

The front doors flew open and people rushed in. Meg and Annie, looking like avenging angels—pissed off avenging angels—were the first through. Rafe and Lucas followed. Behind them came Sam, Drew, even Aunt Bitsy and Miss Peggy. All looked worried and angry and ready to take on whatever army we pointed them at.

"Someone better tell me what happened and quick." Annie stood where the two circles had joined a short time later. Hands on hips, blue eyes flashing, she was more than pissed.

"You'll have to wait for a minute." I batted at Amy's hands as she tried to wipe blood away from a nose I hadn't realized was bleeding. Then I stood, praying I didn't fall flat on my face. "We'll explain but after we take care of a couple of things first."

With Amy shadowing me, probably to make sure I didn't fall flat, I returned to where Judith and Miss Serena sat. Both looked a little better than they had. But Maddy still lay almost motionless. The only thing keeping me from panicking was seeing how Dr. Pat continued to cradle her daughter against her, murmuring softly, telling her she was fine. Everything was fine.

"Dr. Pat?"

"I think she's going to be all right." She bent and brushed her lips against Maddy's forehead.

"Is it safe to move her to a bedroom?" I looked to Miss Serena for an answer. If she hesitated any, I'd have the guys take Maddy down to the basement and set up a new protective circle around her.

"Yes." Miss Serena patted my hand before looking for Amy. "Go up with them. I'll be along shortly."

"No, Grandma. You are going to get some rest. You and Judith both."

I tried not to laugh. In that moment, she looked more like Miss Serena, at least her expression and body language did, than ever before.

"She's right. We'll take care of everything." I hoped. "Rafe."

He nodded and helped Miss Serena to her feet. At the same time, Lucas moved to his mother-in-law's side. Judith swatted at him, telling him she was perfectly capable of standing on her own. Instead of saying anything, he simply swung her up in his arms and asked Amy where she wanted Judith. Drew and Sam moved to help Dr. Pat and Maddy. Amy led them upstairs, talking to her grandmother and Judith over her shoulder, telling them that this was one time they would do as she said.

And that left me with the others. Too weary and hurting too much for a confrontation, I simply folded my legs under me and sank to the floor. If I didn't worry they'd call the EMTs, I would have curled up and gone to sleep. Instead, I inched back until I could lean against the wall.

"Peggy." Mary Kate looked at the woman who nodded once before disappearing in the direction of the kitchen. "You two." She pinned Annie and Meg with a look that warned them not to argue. "Go help. They need food and drink. Water first, then one of Serena's restorative teas." When they remained where they stood, she frowned. "Go!"

She waited until they followed Miss Peggy.

"Let's put the room back to order." She gave me a look that needed no words. I was to stay where I was. "Now," she continued a few minutes later as she returned to where I sat. "Let's get you to the sofa."

Before I could try to stand, Quinn and Ciara were there. They worked together to lift me to my feet and then all but carry me to the sofa. Under Mary Kate's watchful eye, they helped me to lie back. Quinn covered me with the afghan draped over the back of the sofa while Ciara slipped another pillow under my head.

"Ciara, go check on Maddy. You know what to look for."

She nodded and hurried upstairs.

"Quinn, Serena should have something in her refrigerator or pantry that will replenish her electrolytes."

Quinn squeezed my shoulder and then hurried off.

Once alone, Mary Kate sat on the edge of the sofa. Her hands were gentle as she checked me. I didn't need to ask to know she didn't like what she saw. Her expression darkened for a moment and then went blank. Worried, I sat up some, ignoring the pain in my head. Then I reached for her hand.

"Mary Kate?" Aunt Bitsy asked, worry thickening her voice.

I turned my head and tried to smile in reassurance. The last thing I wanted was to worry Bitsy. She'd been aunt and friend, more of a parent than either my father and mother. She was here now because she had always been there for me, whether I wanted her to be or not.

"I'm okay."

"She will be okay," Mary Kate corrected. "She needs rest."

"And?"

"You came close to frying your system as Annie would say. I could feel you channeling more and more energy to Serena and Judith. Amy said something about you feeding more into the wards as well. What did you do?"

"Tapped into the ley lines."

Mary Kate's eyes widened and she gasped in surprise. "Lines as in plural?"

I nodded.

Mary Kate paled and quickly stood. "Stay with her, Bitsy, and do *NOT* let her get up. I'll be right back."

"I've seen you look better, kiddo," Bitsy said as she took Mary Kate's place at my side.

"I've felt better." I tried to smile. I didn't like seeing the worry in her eyes. "Feel like a truck hit me, backed up and hit me again."

It wasn't long before the sounds of footsteps thundering down-stairs filled the air. I didn't know whether to smile or hide to see Rafe moving in my direction. Mary Kate followed him. Before I knew what he meant to do, he had me up in his arms and turned to face Quinn's grandmother.

"Take her into the downstairs bath. I'll be there as soon as I finish gathering what we'll need."

"What?" I didn't understand and wasn't sure I wanted to.

"You stink of power right now, Jax, not to mention sweat and a few other things I'd prefer not mentioning." Bitsy grinned to take the sting out of her words. "If my guess is right, Mary Kate's going to have you bathe and is going to ground your powers. If she doesn't, you'll burn out. You're still tied into the ley lines."

Mary Kate nodded.

"Take her on, Rafe. I'll be there shortly."

Half an hour later, I stood in front of the sink, staring at my reflection. My hair hung damply, released from the tail I'd worn it in earlier. My eyes looked like sunken hollows in my face. My lower lip was swollen where I bit it at some point. My hands shook and I felt weak as a kitten. But my skin no longer tingled and the flow of energy from the ley lines had been severed. Thankfully.

But it was the band of white in my hair that kept me staring at my reflection. An inch wide, it flowed back from my left temple. What the hell caused that?

A soft knock sounded at the door. A moment later, it swung open. Bitsy slipped inside. Without warning, she threw her arms around me from behind, holding me close. Emotion shuddered through her. Holding my robe closed with one hand, I turned. Then, confident I wasn't going to flash her, I slid my arms around her and held on.

"There are easier ways to change your hair style, child." Her voice quivered as she reached up to touch the band of white.

"I'll keep that in mind next time."

God, don't let there be a next time.

"I brought you come clothes. Amy sent word down that her grandmother and Judith are insisting on getting out of bed."

I thanked her and waited until she stepped out. Time to face the music.

The moment I stepped into the den, all hell broke loose. Annie and Meg wanted an explanation. Rafe moved me and held me at arm's length, studying me as if making sure I'd taken no further damage since he left me to bathe. Quinn and Ciara retreated to the far side of the room. They expressions said it all. They'd suffered through the demands and now it was my turn.

"Enough!"

I instantly regretted raising my voice. My head pounded and, for a moment, I worried I might throw up. Then Rafe was leading me to the closest chair. As he seated me, Mary Kate appeared, a mug of something in one hand. I took it and sipped, almost sighing when I did. The restorative herbs and who knows what else began easing the pounding in my head. I might actually want to live after a few more mugs of this.

"Someone had better tell me what happened." Annie sounded almost petulant and when I looked at her, I halfway expected her to stomp her foot. "I was in my office getting ready for court tomorrow when something literally knocked me from my feet. All I knew for certain was it came from here."

Meg nodded, her expression as stormy as her sister-in-law's. "And I damned near ran off the road trying to get here. Thank God I was in my car and not on one of my motorcycles when I was knocked on my ass."

Rafe shot them a look that warned them to back off. God, I loved that man. Then he knelt next to my chair and reached for my hands.

"We couldn't get in, Doc. We got as far as the property line and it was like an iron curtain came down. We could see the property beyond but we couldn't get through. And trust me, we tried. Lucas and I even tried climbing various trees to jump over and couldn't. It was like we hit a wall and just slid down."

Bitsy stood behind Rafe, her hand on his shoulder, remembered fear reflected in her eyes. "That was bad enough, but then it looked like the world's largest fireworks display had launched from the house. Except it wasn't fireworks. It was energy, from you and the others and from someone or something else, something evil. I could feel it and I never want to feel anything like that again."

"I'm sorry we worried you, but it had to be done."

And I hoped we accomplished what we set out to do.

"What had to be done?" This time Annie did stomp her foot.

"Annie."

"Damn it, Jax." She shoved a hand through her red hair, frustration seeping out of every pore. "You don't understand what it was like trapped out there and not knowing what was going on."

"I don't know?"

Rafe grabbed my mug as I pushed to my feet.

"I suggest you back off until everyone's here and then we'll tell you what you need to know."

Her eyes narrowed. "What I *need* to know?" Frustration turned to fury. "Let me tell you what you *need* to know. You keep telling us we have to work together and yet you kept us out." She rounded on Quinn who had the good sense to take a step back. "And if you want to keep your job, Moira Quinn, you'll start telling me what I want to know."

"Julianna, that is enough!"

Oops.

Like Quinn, I took a step back. We learned as kids to pay close attention when Mary Kate got that particular note in her voice. When she called Annie by her given first name, we didn't want to be anywhere nearby. Annie remembered as well and swallowed once before facing her grandmother. Not that she was ready to back down just yet.

"Grandma," she drawled.

"Don't you grandma me, young woman." She stared daggers at Annie and now everyone took another step back from the two of them. "I know you have a better head on your shoulders than you've been showing. I suggest you take a look around. Start with Jax. Take a look at her, a really good look. Then decide if you want to keep making a fool out of yourself."

Annie looked mulish before she hung her head. When she turned to look at me, she gasped softly. Then she hurried to me. Her left hand reached for one of mine while her right hand reached out to lightly touch the band of white in my hair. She released a shaky breath and then looked at the others. From her expression, I guessed she finally realized things had been no cakewalk in here.

"Are you all right?"

"She damned near burned herself out protecting everyone." Mary Kate glared at her granddaughter before turning that glare on me. "And that includes all of you. That so-called iron curtain you ran into was her, doing her best to keep the dark magic we were dealing with contained."

"She's right," Miss Serena said softly as she and Judith entered, Amy following close behind.

Sam and Lucas hurried to help the older women to chairs before returning to their wives' sides.

"I don't understand," Annie admitted.

"That can wait. It can wait." I repeated when Annie started to protest. "Are you all right?" I knelt in front of Miss Serena and reached for one of her hands before reaching for one of Judith's as well.

"Thanks to you." Miss Serena lightly cupped my cheek before touching the band of white. "But you are never to take that kind of risk again. Promise me."

I shook my head. "I can't. I will do whatever it takes to protect you, all of you, and this town."

"What exactly did you do?" Amy asked as she handed her grandmother and then Judith mugs of what I assumed was the same tea Mary Kate gave me earlier.

"I tied into the closest ley line at the beginning of the workings, just as we planned. But when I felt the bindings trying to fight against being broken, I knew I needed to channel more energy to your grandmother and Judith. I didn't dare take away from the energy I was channeling into the circles or into the wards. So I reached for a second ley line, this one a little further out on the property."

Amy inhaled sharply and I tasted her fear. But the others looked at us, not understanding what I had done or why Amy reacted as she did.

"Remember the movie *Ghostbusters*?" Amy asked.

The others nodded.

"She crossed the streams."

I couldn't help it. The image she brought in mind sent me into fits of laughter. They might have been more than a bit hysterical, but it beat running to the hills.

"Easy, Doc." Rafe rested his hands on my shoulders, anchoring me. "And remember to never cross the streams again."

I smothered another laugh and nodded. As quickly as it came, the humor of the situation fled.

"Did it work?"

"It did, thanks to you." Miss Serena smiled gently and then motioned for Rafe to help me back to the sofa. "And we're going to need to discuss how you knew we needed the extra boost you gave us. But that can wait until we've all had some rest."

"Maddy?"

At our friend's name, the others stopped grousing and demanding answers and turned the attention to Miss Serena.

"It worked but only because of you."

"I don't understand."

"Neither Judith nor I anticipated just how deeply the binding had connected with Maddy," Miss Serena said and then sipped her tea. She closed her eyes and sipped again. Color began returning to her cheeks and I relaxed a bit. "We probably should have after realizing we hadn't managed to break it earlier." She gave a slight shrug.

"I don't understand." Meg looked between Miss Serena, Judith and me as she waited for one of us to explain.

"We broke the binding we anticipated once Maddy returned home. That one had been put in place by Anton Roben."

Everyone nodded.

"We should have anticipated then there might have been a deeper binding, especially since Jax had already broken one level of it in Ireland."

"Serena's right," Judith took up. "We didn't because that level of binding takes a great deal of energy and requires it being recharged, for lack of a better word, from time to time. We simply didn't antici-pate Maddy being subject to a binding over such a long period of time."

Now it was my turn to frown.

"I don't understand."

"We found another level of binding by Roben. That was the first one we broke today. I recognized the feel at the time. There's no doubt in my mind Roben set it in place. Two of the threads we broke belonged to him." Now Judith smiled mercilessly. "I have no doubt he felt the bindings sever. It would have been more than a mental echo and it wouldn't upset me at all if he fell down a flight of stairs or something else and broke his neck when it happened."

Since I agreed, I didn't say anything.

"There's more, isn't there?" Bitsy asked as she settled at the end of the sofa by my feet.

Miss Serena nodded. "There were half a dozen other hooks into her, hooks set by two different people. Roben wasn't one of them.

"Several of the lines were set by a woman. I could tell that much, but I didn't recognize the feel—the flavor if you will—of her. All I know for sure is she's no longer alive. That's a concern because I've never heard of a binding existing after the death of the person who cast it. I need to do some research to see if there's an explanation for that happening.

"The remaining threads, in particular, the last one were set by a man. There was something familiar about the feel of it. If I'm right, I've come up against it before."

"Who?" I tried to stand but Rafe held me where I was.

"I may be wrong, Jax. So I'm going to do some research before I say anything more. If I'm right." She stopped and the color drained out of her face. Then she shook herself before continuing. "If I'm wrong, our town's facing more danger than we thought."

"One more question, Miss Serena." I carefully chose my words. "Are we in immediate danger?"

She shook her head. "If my suspicions are right, you tilted the odds in our favor, Jax, at least for the immediate future. He'll have withdrawn to figure out not only what happened but how. That gives us some time to plan our next move."

"Then you and Judith can take time to rest and recover from the last few days." This time Rafe did let me up.

"She's right, Grandma." Amy helped Miss Serena up and slid an arm around her waist.

"All right. I am tired."

The fact she admitted it worried me. She never admitted being tired.

"I would appreciate it if everyone stayed here tonight. Please."

"Of course, Miss Serena." I moved to her side and gently kissed her cheek. "I'll come up later to check on you."

"You too, Mom," Ciara said as she pulled Judith to her feet.

"The kids?" Annie asked as they headed upstairs.

"Where are they?"

"At my place. Lexie is looking after them for us."

Well, that explained why she hadn't shown up. But it also made what I was about to suggest easier.

"Let them stay there. Quinn or Ciara can fill Lexie in. You know that between her and the house, they'll be safe."

And that didn't take into account Ali's own abilities. My goddaughter might be only eight, but I had a feeling we didn't have a clue about everything she could already do.

"I'll call her," Quinn said and left the room, Annie on her heels.

"And I have a question you can answer, Jax," Ciara said as the rest of them gathered around me. "I promise we'll let you get some rest then, but put this down to me still being more cop than anything else."

I nodded, knowing the decision to leave the Rangers hadn't been an easy one.

"When Miss Serena and Mom were trying to sever the last hook the binding had in Maddie, you were channeling more energy than you should have. I gathered that from what you, Mom and Miss Serena said. What none of you mentioned was the explosion."

"Explosion?" Bitsy sputtered, eyes wide.

"That's certainly what it looked like from where we were." She licked her lips and I tasted the remnants of her fear. "What was it?"

"I'm not really sure." I wasn't lying. I didn't know for sure. "My best guess until I can talk about it with Miss Serena and your mother is that our combined magic, supplemented by the two ley lines, caused the binding to explode. All I can tell you for sure is it knocked me back and my ears are still ringing."

I scrubbed a hand over my face as exhaustion dragged at me.

"Until we figure out what happened and who is behind it, each of us needs to be careful. We go armed, mundane and arcane for those of us who are Others. Mundane for the rest of us." And I'd be talking with those with certain abilities to craft personal wards for our mundanes.

"We'll figure out security after you've rested," Ciara promised. Then she turned to Rafe. "Take her upstairs. Mary Kate and I will get everyone else settled."

That was all Rafe needed to hear. Before I could protest, he swung me up in his arms. As we started upstairs, he warned the others not to disturb me until I'd slept myself out. Instead of arguing, I rested my cheek against his chest and closed my eyes. Sleep was on me before we reached the bedroom.

7

—————

"You know, that band of white's kind of sexy." Rafe grinned at my reflection in the mirror before bending to kiss the side of my neck.

"Glad you like it because I'm not sure I do." I studied my reflection for a moment before turning. His arms went around my waist and he held me close for a moment before stepping back.

"Are you all right?" He looked down at me in concern.

"Getting there."

That much was true. I didn't hurt like I did yesterday and a marching band no longer resided in my head. Instead, I felt like I'd been on a three-day bender. Food and lots of water would help. But what would help most of all was getting answers to at least some of the questions that might turn the rest of my hair white.

"Doc, talk to me." One hand lightly caressed my cheek while the fingers of the other toyed with the dog tag hanging on a chain around my neck. His dog tag. My personal talisman.

"Rafe, yesterday scared me." I hadn't admitted that even to myself. Now that I had, the tense muscles of my neck relaxed some. "I could see Judith and Serena tiring. They'd been working so hard the last few days trying to break the bindings on Maddy. I don't think either of them knew how tired they were going into yesterday's ritual. I knew I needed to do something. I reached for that second ley line without thinking."

"You said it yesterday, Jax. You did what you needed to in order to protect them." He bent and lightly kissed me. "You did something else too and I don't think you've realized it."

I looked at him in question.

"You might not like it and I know you aren't going to agree, but you proved to everyone that you very well may be as strong as Miss Serena."

I looked at him, wondering if he'd taken a blow to his head. Nothing else could explain such insanity.

"Doc, think about it. Let's start with the obvious, you're a hybrid. At least that's what you've called yourself because of your Elemental magic and your Walker abilities."

Okay, I had to give him that one.

"I'll even agree that your Earth magic let you know there was more than one ley line under this property."

Again, he was right.

"Now think about what happened yesterday. You managed to maintain control of the circles and, yes, both Quinn and Ciara confirmed you anchored both circles as well as reinforcing the wards around the property. Then, when you realized how much trouble Serena and Judith were having breaking the bindings on Maddy, you began feeding them energy, first from yourself and then, when things started getting dicey, from the second ley line. At the same time, you continued to feed energy to the circle protections and to the wards. That much magical energy could have killed you. It would have killed most anyone else. But you managed it, controlled it and kept a number of people we both care for alive."

I shook my head. It hadn't been that simple.

"Yes." He gently gripped my chin and lifted my face so he could look me in the eye. "But you listen to me, Doc. Never, ever do anything like that again without proper backup. I don't want to lose you."

"You're not going to." I stepped into his embrace, drawing strength from him. "I need you to do something for me, Rafe, and I hope you won't argue."

"What?"

"Well, it's a couple of things, actually. Don't go anywhere without your gun, preferably without your guns."

I'd rest easier knowing he was armed whenever I wasn't with him.

"As long as you do the same." He waited until I nodded. Then he lifted his shirt to show his Glock .19 snugged in a holster at his waist. A moment later, he lifted the right leg of his jeans, revealing another gun in an ankle holster. "Yours?"

"In my bag right now. I haven't finished getting dressed." I arched a brow at him and then glanced down at the short robe I wore.

"So I see." His hand slipped inside the robe, his fingers finding my breast. He dipped his head and nuzzled my neck. "You really should go back to bed and rest some more."

I chuckled softly. "If I went back to bed, I doubt either of us would rest. "Besides, do you really want the house tattling on us to Miss Serena?" I kept my expression innocent—well, as innocent as I could —until he withdrew his hand. Then I reached up and nipped his lower lip. "But remember where you were. I think it's very important for you pick up where you left off when we get home."

He grinned, patted me on the ass and stepped back. "Get dressed before I change my mind."

"There's something else, Rafe." I crossed to the closet and looked inside. Since my return home, I'd spent more than a few nights here. It didn't surprise to discover Miss Serena now had jeans, shirts and even a couple of sweaters in my size hanging there. I selected a pair of black jeans and a black tee. "I want you to keep Fenris with you. He's bonded with you and you take him to work and around town often enough no one will think twice about it."

"Doc, he's your dog and we need to make sure you're safe more than me."

I shook my head. "Rafe, I love you. If whoever is behind all this does his or her research, they'll figure that out. They will also know the way to get to me is through you." I tossed the clothes onto the foot of the bed and moved to where he stood. Sliding my hands into her back pockets, I stepped close. "Rafe, please. I couldn't bear it if anything happened to you."

He lowered his forehead to mine and then nodded. I knew he'd find a way to make me take Fenris back—or at least try to. But for now he wasn't going to argue. I could live with that.

"All right. But you will go armed and you aren't riding your Ducati until this is over." He thought for a moment. When he smiled, I knew he was up to something and I probably wouldn't like it. "I'm also going to arrange for a new car for you, something with a bit more armor and protection than your truck."

"Rafe."

"It's that or I'm talking to Aunt Bitsy."

Oh, he was good. He knew I wouldn't want him to do that. Bitsy not only would agree that I needed to be careful but she would buy me the most heavily armored vehicle she could find. Hell, I didn't doubt for a moment, she'd try to arrange for a tank or something similar. Well, two could play that game. I just played it better than Rafe. He wouldn't know what I planned until I sprung it on him.

Ten minutes later, we split off to go our separate ways, him to the kitchen and me downstairs to Miss Serena's workroom after a quick detour for coffee. By the time I stepped inside the workroom, the others were there. Judith and Miss Serena sat in two of the four chairs. Dr. Pat paced the room, her expression thunderous. Worried, I looked to Miss Serena, hoping for some indication about what was wrong.

"Pat, you need to calm down," Judith said and, from the look on her face, I had a feeling this wasn't the first time she'd said it.

"Calm down?" She spun to face the others before turning and glaring at me.

What the hell had I done?

"Would someone care to tell me what's going on?" I kept my voice even, hoping I didn't exacerbate the situation.

"What's going on is these two." Dr. Pat pointed to Miss Serena and Judith. "Refuse to see reason."

"And that would be?"

Why couldn't I keep my mouth shut?

She looked at me and threw her hands up in the air. I fully expected her to scream in frustration and I still didn't know what was going on.

"I've clearly walked into the middle of something and I'd really like it if someone would tell me what so we can deal with it."

Dr. Pat whirled to face me. I braced myself, unsure of what she might do. Then her eyes widened and she gasped softly. In the blink of an eye, she crossed the workroom to stand in front of me. Her hand shook as she reached out to touch the band of white in my hair. Her mouth worked and she looked over my shoulder to the others. A moment later, she sobbed once and dropped to the floor as if her legs simply refused to hold her any longer.

I caught her before she finished her fall and eased her into a sitting position. She turned to me, her arms going around me. I held her, looking helplessly at Miss Serena, as Dr. Pat sobbed against my shoulder.

"I'm sorry. I'm so sorry."

She kept saying it over and over again. I held her, rocking back and forth, trying to figure out what she was apologizing for. When Judith and Miss Serena joined us on the floor, I looked at them for guidance. Instead of explaining, they looked as much at a loss as I felt.

"Dr. Pat, it's okay. Truly. But you need to talk to us. Please." I rubbed her back, much like I did with Ali when she was upset. "Tell us what's wrong."

She sniffled and tried to pull away. Before I let her, I hugged her, reminding her we all loved her. She was our sister and friend. She needed to trust us and let us help her.

And, I added mentally, stand out of my way if Maddy was what caused this meltdown.

"I failed you, each of you, and I failed Mossy Creek."

Okay, now I was confused. What the hell did she mean by that?

"M-Maddy."

I gritted my teeth. I knew it! What the hell had she done now?

"Dr. Pat, how does any of that mean you failed any of us?"

"How can you say that?" She looked at me, doubt in her eyes. "My own daughter. I didn't see what was happening."

"Pat, none of us did."

She shook her head, not willing to accept the truth.

"She used her abilities and the magicked items on me and on her father. Who knows how many others she also did it to. How much harm has she caused others because she wouldn't ask for help?"

Miss Serena started to answer, but I stopped her. To give me time to think, I carefully stood and helped Dr. Pat to her feet. Once I had, I led her to one of the chairs and seated her. Then I crossed to the antique table in the far corner of the room and poured tea from the pot I knew waited for us.

"Drink this and listen to me." I pressed the china cup into her hands and guided it to her lips. "We all missed what was happening. If you're to blame, then so are we. But we aren't. We didn't realize how deep the bindings were that held her. We thought we were dealing with the Maddy we love, the one who never really believed she was as good or as strong as the rest of us." And that was something she needed to get over.

"If you want to assign blame, then put it where it belongs—with Anton Roben and the others who hurt Maddy, who bound her against her will." God, I hoped it had been against her will. "This doesn't fall on you or on Marcus. You two did everything you could to help her, to protect her. Don't you dare let this shake you or make you doubt yourself."

"I should have seen it, Jax. I'm her mother and I'm a doctor. The signs were there." She set the cup on the table to her right. "I missed something that was right under my nose." Tears ran down her cheeks.

Miss Serena hurried to her and pulled her close. "We all did. Jax is right about that. But we stopped it and we will get through this together."

Dr. Pat shook her head. "You don't understand. Maddy's going to need help now. Jax was right when she said Maddy has always doubted herself, especially when she looked at Jax and the others. She knows they love her and she loves them, but she never felt like she measured up. But now she's tried to hurt them. She did hurt Jax. It's going to be a long time before she can forgive herself for that and move beyond it and I need to be there for her."

"What are you saying, Pat?" Judith asked.

"I think it will be best if Marcus and I take her away from Mossy Creek. I don't know if she can face her friends, knowing what she's done."

I ground my teeth in frustration. That was the last thing Maddy needed and it sure as hell was the last thing Mossy Creek needed.

"No."

Everyone looked at me in surprise. Although, to tell the truth, Miss Serena and Judith looked at me with more relief than surprise.

"If you do that, you are playing into the hands of whoever is behind everything that's happened. Do you really think it's just a coincidence that Maddy was bound and that we found out about it now?"

"But—"

"No." I stalked across the room, searching for the right words. "We're past being anything but brutally honest. Am I pissed at Maddy? You bet your ass I am. But I am also more relieved than you can imagine. Her trying to control me like she did revealed what was going on. We all knew there was something wrong. You can't deny that, Pat, because you and I discussed it on more than one occasion. But none of us expected the level of binding we discovered yesterday. You want to blame yourself for what she might have done before yesterday. Well what about what she would have done if she hadn't tried to roll me and then bind me?"

"Jax—"

"No." I didn't care if I stepped over the line. She needed to listen to me. What I wanted to know was why Miss Serena or Judith didn't say something.

"Now ask yourself something else. You said you failed this town. What would happen if you did leave town with Maddy and the trouble we've been expecting comes and we only have three Guardians to meet it?"

"There are others—"

"Who?" I made a sweeping gesture even though it was just the four of us in the room. "Who else is ready to step up if you leave? For that matter, I think I proved yesterday that I might be stronger than I thought but I'm also nowhere near trained enough. I'm lucky I didn't blow us all to pieces when I drew upon the second ley line.

"She's right, Pat." Judith spoke much more gently than I had. "Much as I love my daughters, neither of them is ready to step up yet." Now she chuckled. "Can you imagine how Quinn would react if we told her she was the next Guardian?"

I knew what she meant just as I knew she was wrong. Quinn might not be fully comfortable with her role as an Other after spending most of her life believing she was a normal, but she also did what she felt was her duty. If necessary, she would accept the role as Guardian. Of course, she'd bitch long and hard to me about it afterwards.

"And Amy isn't ready yet," Miss Serena said.

"No way is Annie and Meg would leave town," I put in and returned to crouch in front of her. "Dr. Pat, we love you, we need you and, most of all, we each trust you with our lives and with the lives of those we love."

"Jax is right about everything except knowing what she needs to." Miss Serena smiled at me in affection. "We learned a valuable lesson this time. We now know we need to be more watchful and pay closer attention when something doesn't feel right. I might not approve of Jax going off to confront Maddy without one of us being nearby to assist her if she needed it, but she did us a huge favor by doing so. Who knows how much more time would have passed before any of us realized what was going on?"

Dr. Pat didn't say anything for several long moments. Then she reached for my hands. Holding them firmly in her own, she thanked me. I smiled slightly, relieved to see some of the guilt easing. Hopefully, we were getting through to her.

"You may each need to remind me of this from time to time." She rubbed her face, as if by doing so, she could rub away her doubts.

"We will," Judith assured her.

Dr. Pat blew out a long breath. Then she nodded, as if making a decision. "I swore an oath to protect Mossy Creek just as a swore an oath to be their doctor and to do no harm. I won't forget that again."

"We love you, Dr. Pat." I smiled and gave her hands a squeeze.

"You called me Pat earlier." She grinned when I blushed. "I liked it."

"Our Jax is still conflicted." Miss Serena's eyes danced with humor. "She isn't quite ready to accept she's our equal."

"Except for me." Judith laughed as my blush deepened.

"It's not that," I protested. "You all but beat it into me once I graduated from high school," I reminded her. "Dr. Pat, you've been my doctor for years. It's hard to break the habit of addressing you as such." Now I looked at Miss Serena and my expression softened. "As for you, you are the closet thing I've had to a grandmother since I was a little girl." I blinked by sudden tears. "Each of you are family and you'd better accept the fact that I will fight for you as such, even if it means knocking your heads against the wall if you're doing something stupid."

"And we love you," Miss Serena said with a gentle smile.

"Before you have me crying again." Dr. Pat smiled slightly. "We need to discuss one more thing about Maddy."

"Pat, we don't have to, not right now," Judith told her, clearly anticipating what she had to say.

"No, I need to say it. We all admit Maddy has always had issues with self-confidence. Whether that helped make her easer for Roben and the others to bind her or not we may never know. But that tendency means she's going to be a long time getting over what happened. It also means we'll have to be vigilant to make sure she doesn't become a victim again. We're all going to have to work with her on strengthening and maintaining her shields."

She looked at each of us, her expression both serious and somehow relieved.

"We've talked many times over the years about who would replace each of us when the time came. Maddy's name has been mentioned more than once. There was a time I thought she would make a good Guardian. It's clear to me now that can never happen. We can't risk our friends and family or our town by putting her in that position."

My heart broke for her as she spoke but she was right. Maddy didn't have the strength, the self-confidence needed to be a Guardian. Hell, I still wasn't convinced I did.

"That's not a decision we need to make right now," Miss Serena said. "But if you are right, that doesn't mean she can't and won't be a valued part of our team. It does, however, mean she can't be part of our inner circle. At least not for a while."

"I agree." She reached for her cup and sipped her now cold tea. When I started to retrieve the pot to pour her some more, she waved me off. "Jax, I know you don't want to hear it, but thank you. You've given me my daughter back. But never risk yourself again like you did yesterday. Please."

"I'm always going to do what I think is best for each of you and for this town, Pat." I grinned when she smiled at my use of her given name. "Maddy is my sister by choice, just as Quinn, Ciara, Amy, Annie and Meg are. I am always going to do whatever it takes to protect them and the three of you."

I stopped and my eyes narrowed at Miss Serena's expression. She was up to something.

"Since you said that," she began, amusement dancing in her eyes.

"Miss Serena?"

"It is obvious the trouble has come for us. What happened with Maddy is just the latest in the attacks. We need to go on the offensive and part of that is making sure we have people we trust at our backs."

Dr. Pat and Judith nodded.

"I don't understand."

I didn't. I thought we already had that with the others. Was she saying we needed to expand that number?

Miss Serena smiled almost gently, as if she knew I wasn't going to like what she said.

"We've been pretty insular since before you returned home, Jax." She looked at the others who nodded in agreement. "But we did make sure we had those like Mary Kate, Amy, even Peggy and Bitsy to watch our backs. Since Annie, not to mention the rest of you, returned to town, we added them as well. You made the Guardians complete again. But what we haven't done is take an apprentice of sorts to train to step in for us if something happens."

"You're wrong." It was out before I knew what I meant to say. "You've trained Amy and I doubt any of us would say she couldn't step in for any of us."

"If she becomes a Guardian one day, I'll be proud, but it won't be because I trained her to take my place when I can no longer perform my duties as such."

That didn't make sense but I knew better than to argue.

"And it is clear after yesterday that you and I need to start working more closely together, Jackie. It still terrifies me to think what could have happened if you hadn't been able to control the energies of the two ley lines. What you did was beyond foolish and even more brave."

"Miss Serena." I stopped. *No, no and hell no.* She couldn't mean what I thought she did. No way was I going to ever be ready to step into her shoes. But she was right about one thing. I had been damned lucky.

"Shh." She cupped my cheek with her hand before continuing. "I'll take Quinn on as my apprentice. Judith, I'd like you to work with Meg. Pat, you and Amy will work well together. And that leaves you, Jackie."

I shook my head. I seemed to be doing a lot of that recently. But it was that or run to the hills.

"I'd like you to work with Ciara. You have similar temperaments and you can teach her that there are times when you have to ignore the rules. It's learning to know which rules and under what circumstances that will work."

I swallowed hard and then nodded.

"Now." Miss Serena checked her watch. "The others should be upstairs and ready to hear what we have in mind."

"Maddy?"

Dr. Pat looked at the ceiling. "She's still sleeping."

"Before we go upstairs, are each of you all right? You scared the hell out of me last night." Which was putting it mildly.

They each assured me they were fine. Still, I couldn't help looking at Miss Serena in concern. She still looked tired. There was a shadow to her expression that worried me. When she didn't answer right away, I glanced at Dr. Pat who wouldn't meet my eyes.

"Miss Serena, talk to me. Please."

"I'm tired," she admitted. "I'm not as young as I used to be and all the workings of the last few days have taken it out of me."

"What can we do?"

"Exactly what you have been." Then she chuckled. "Maybe without almost blowing my house up next time though."

"Spoilsport." I grinned back at her before turning serious. "Let us tell the others what we have in mind while you get some rest. Please."

"I can't. But I promise to rest once we've talked with the others."

"You've remembered something," Judith said.

Miss Serena nodded. "I'm still not sure. But, if I'm right, we're facing more trouble than I thought."

"What do you mean?" Dr. Pat asked.

"If I'm right, everything started here years ago and has been fomenting under the surface for a very long time without any of us realizing it."

SERENA

8

1964

"Serena, it's time."

I closed my eyes, fighting the tears that never seemed far away. Yesterday, I sat stoically as the military honor guard carried my husband's coffin into the church. I allowed only a single tear to escape when the flag draping his coffin was presented to me at the cemetery. Last night, I held our daughter and cried, much as I had every night since learning of Preston's death.

It wasn't supposed to be this way. We were supposed to raise our daughter and grow old together. Instead, he died on a hill in Vietnam, far from home, and there was nothing I could do to change it. At least he hadn't died alone. I had that comfort, small though it might be.

His captain wrote me a letter and assured me Pres died a hero, protecting his squad. Others who were there that day told me they wouldn't be alive if it weren't for Pres. He sacrificed himself so they could live.

That was Pres. It was one of the things I loved about him. It was also what I hated right now.

"Serena?"

Mary Kate crossed to stand behind me. Her hand was gentle as she rested it on my arm, a reminder shew as there for me. There as friend and there to give support. All I had to do was accept it. But I didn't want to accept it because that meant accepting Pres was never coming home. I wasn't supposed to be a widow before my thirtieth birthday.

"I can't."

Mary Kate didn't say anything. Instead, she stepped forward and slid an arm around my waist. Together, we looked out the window. The yearlings grazed in the field to the left of the drive, enjoying the morning sun. The only indication today was different from most other days was the line of cars parked in the drive.

"What am I supposed to do now, Mary Kate?"

"Exactly what you have been."

Mary Kate turned me so I looked at her. She'd been there for me since learning of Preston's death. I still didn't know who told her. But she arrived at the house less than twenty minutes after the Army captain and our priest left. She'd been with me almost constantly since then. She and Nathaniel, her husband, stood when me when Preston's flag-draped coffin was removed from the belly of the plane at Love Field. They rode with me as we followed the hearse back to Mossy Creek. Along with my parents, they made sure I ate and slept. Now she was there to help me through this next step in dealing with Preston's death.

"You mean sleepwalking through life?" I gave a humorless laugh.

"No, I mean doing what you have to do and remembering to let yourself grieve." She took my hands and gave them a squeeze. "You've always demanded too much of yourself, Serena. No one expects you to act as if nothing happened. We know how much you loved Pres. It's going to take time to accept he's not coming home. I won't say get over his death because you never will, not completely. But I want you to remember something."

"What?"

"That he is still alive in your memories and in that little girl of yours. You lean on Nathaniel and me, on your parents and all the rest who love you. Let us help you as you've helped us all your life."

"Even when I want to climb into bed and pull the covers over my head?" I managed a slight smile.

"If that's what you want to do, do it. Nate will deal with everyone for you."

It was tempting, too tempting. But I couldn't. I'd get through the morning. Maybe then I'd return to bed and pull the covers over my head.

But there was something I needed to do first.

"Thank you." I hugged Mary Kate. "I wouldn't have made it through the last few weeks without you."

"Serena." She shook her head and reached up to dash away the tears that hadn't yet fallen. "You were there for me when the Army told me Nate had been hurt. You made sure I was there when they brought him back to the States for treatment. When he was strong enough, you and your parents arranged for him to be brought home to finish his recovery. I know you won't admit it, but he kept his leg because your father pulled strings to get him the best possible treatment before he was back to the States. Then you and your mother *supplemented* his treatment with healing sessions." She swallowed hard against the emotion closing her throat.

"But I'd have been here anyway. You're my best friend. When you hurt, I hurt." Now she smiled and I saw the girl I met the first day of grade school. "Besides, we made a pact a long time ago to always be there for each other."

I sniffled and smiled through the tears once again threatening to fall. She gave me another hug and then produced a tissue from somewhere and wiped my face. When she finished, she looked at me for a moment before moving to my closet.

I sat on the foot of my bed and watched as she looked through the clothes hanging there. She ignored the black dress hanging on the back of the closet door, the one I'd chosen the night before. When she turned back to me, she held a navy, short-sleeved dress in one hand and a matching pair of pumps in the other.

"No arguments," she said before I could comment. "It's suitable for today but it also shows you are going to celebrate Preston's life, not dishonor his memory by shutting yourself off from the rest of the world forever."

I couldn't help it. She sounded so much like her mother—or mine —that I smiled. It might have been my first real smile since learning of Preston's death. It felt strange but she was right. Pres would probably come back to haunt me if I spent the rest of my life mourning. We both knew the potential for him being injured or killed when he received his orders to go to 'Nam. I'll never know if he had a premonition, but he made sure everything was in order in case he didn't come back. It was yet another way he showed how much he loved our daughter, Ashley, and me.

Ten minutes later, we made our way downstairs. My parents waited at the foot of the stairs, worry reflected in their eyes. I took the last few steps at close to a run. As I did, my father opened his arms. He pulled Mama and me into a hug and held on tight. Their emotions were as strong as mine just then. They'd loved Pres like a son. His death had shaken them almost as much as it had me.

"I'll let Nate know you'll be in shortly." Mary Kate slipped past us and disappeared inside Papa's library.

"You look like you feel better, Serena." Mama pressed her cheek to mine before stepping back.

"I do, at least a little."

"Are you sure you're up to this?" Papa asked.

"This" was the reading of Preston's will, something that included not just us but his family as well. That also meant his brother, Carson, would be here. Assuming, of course, he could stand after last night.

I frowned at the memory. Preston and his brother had been close when they were younger. That changed before Pres and I met in college. All Pres said was his brother wasn't the man he once knew. The few times we did get together, always at some family gathering,

Carson proved he was not the man his younger brother was. He drank too much, often to the point of blacking out. He was, as Mama said more than once, about as useful as a steering wheel on a mule. Papa believed he wasn't worth the air he breathed. After Carson's behavior last night when our families got together to remember Pres on what would have been his thirty-second birthday, I knew they were both right and prayed this was the last time I had to see Carson Alexander.

"I am, Papa." I had to be.

"Then let's get this done."

With Papa on one side and Mama on the other, we entered the library. Preston's parents stood and hurried to us, making sure I was all right. Mary Kate stood next to Papa's desk, watching as Nate made sure he had everything he needed. Remembering our earlier conversation, I took a moment to study him. His wounds had been life-threatening. He'd been in hospitals from South Vietnam to San Francisco to Dallas for months. It had taken Papa time and a number of favors being called in to get the Army to agree to let specialists in Dallas treat him. But it had been worth it to see him healthy and whole.

Since his medical discharge, he had opened his law office. Papa was his first client. In fact, Papa was waiting outside the office when Nate arrived that first day. Since then, Nate proved to be a gifted attorney and, more importantly, a loving husband and father. Now he was here not only as Preston's attorney but as my friend—our friend.

Thank goodness.

"Serena." He moved to my side and led me to a chair in front of the desk.

The moment I took my seat, Carson approached. I don't think I reacted, but I must have. Nate, his expression as cold as I'd ever seen it, turned to face my brother-in-law. I'm not sure what Carson saw, but he quickly backed off without so much as another word. Then Mama took her place on one side and Papa on the other. Preston's parents sat behind us, leaving Carson to stand behind them. I might not like having him at my back but it was far better, at least in this moment, for him to be there instead of next to me.

Nathaniel knelt on his right knee and studied me. Then he nodded once, a slight smile on his lips.

"This won't take too long. I promise." He spoke softly. "Preston was as thorough and careful with his will as he was with everything else, especially where his girls were concerned."

I nodded, tears once again burning my eyes as I that last day before Preston shipped out. He'd held our daughter in his arms and looked at me, love written all over his face. He smiled and called us his girls and promised he'd be home soon.

It was the only promise he'd ever broken.

"If you need a break, let me know," Nate said.

"I will."

I reached for Mama's hand as Nate climbed to his feet. A moment later, he sat behind Papa's desk. On the desktop in front of him was a file folder. He opened it and withdrew a sheaf of papers. The blue backing indicted they were legal documents. He placed them on top of the folder and then looked at each of us.

"Before we get started, I want to once again offer my condolences to each of you. Preston was one of my best friends. He loved Serena and little Ashley more than life itself. He's going to be missed by all of us.

"Preston was also a practical man. When he and Serena were married, he wrote his will. He updated it when Ashley was born. When he learned he was going to ship out to Vietnam, he came to me and updated the will again. I assure you, it is legal and that he took everything into consideration."

"Just get on with it," Carson muttered.

I reached out and stopped Papa before he could respond. I couldn't stop Nate, not that I wanted to. He stood and leaned forward, hands on the desktop. His posture spoke volumes. Not only did it warn Carson to keep his mouth shut but it warned him that Nate would gladly wipe the floor with him if he said another word.

"We will, once you understand that you will be removed if you interrupt or cause Serena any heartache."

I didn't turn, but I heard Preston's father stand. Whatever Alan said to Carson, it seemed to work. Carson muttered an apology and fell silent. Nate nodded once to Alan and then returned to his seat.

"One last thing. It isn't legally necessary to handle Preston's will like this. State law allows for it to be filed with the probate court and go through the legal process simply by notifying anyone named in the will and any creditors of the probate hearing date. However, Preston was as smart as he was loyal. He asked that Serena and I do it this way so everyone knows what he did and why."

At that last, Mary Kate looked past me, looked past the rest of us to where Carson stood. Her expression spoke volumes and I frowned. Never before had I seen that particular expression on her face. It was close to hatred. Had Carson said or done something last night I wasn't aware of? Then, as suddenly as the expression formed, it disappeared. I filed it away for later. It was most definitely something we would be discussing.

It took time. Nate warned me it would. Preston wanted to make sure the will would stand up to any challenges his brother might raise. Despite all that, it came down to some very simple terms. There was a bequest for his parents, one that would allow his father to retire if he wanted. Pres, with help from my father, had made some very successful investments since we met and, while he wasn't rich, he had more than enough to help his parents. When they protested, I reminded them he loved them and he wanted to take care of them just as they had taken care of him when he was younger.

He also set up a trust for our daughter. With careful investments, it would pay for her college when the time came and leave her with enough afterwards to start her life as an adult. Except for several items bequeathed to his parents and to Nate and Mary Kate, the rest of the estate came to me. To avoid problems with his brother, he named Nate as the trustee. What Nate didn't say and I knew only because Pres showed me the trust documents before he signed them, was I would become trustee if Nate stepped down for whatever reason.

"Preston included a letter to all of you. You'll be given copies of it along with a description of the bequests listed in the will before you leave." Nathaniel shuffled the will to the bottom of the stack of papers in front of him. "I will let you read the letter for yourselves. But I do want to point out one thing from it. He asked that each of you respect his wishes as laid out in the will. He hoped you would continue to love and support one another, especially Serena and Ashley. Lastly, he said he loved all of you."

I didn't realize I was crying until Papa handed me his handkerchief. Behind me, Preston's mother, Alice, sniffled and reached into her purse for a tissue. Mama sat stoically next to me, doing her best to be strong for me.

"That's it?" Carson demanded as he stalked toward the desk.

"It is." Nathaniel slid the paperwork back into the file folder and handed it to Mary Kate. Then he climbed to his feet. "Your brother took into account the number of times you came to him for loans and he gave them to you. Loans you never paid back. Loans that came to more than he would have left you otherwise."

"He can't do that!"

"He can and he did." Nathaniel moved around the desk, putting himself between Carson and me. "You're lucky he didn't add a provision for the estate to go after the monies you owe. But that doesn't mean that, as the executor, I can't do just that.

"Pres wouldn't want this." He spun to look at me. "Serena, you know he wouldn't."

I patted Mama's hand and stood. Stepping around Nathaniel, I faced my brother-in-law. It hurt—God, how it hurt—to see his resemblance to Pres. But he wasn't Preston and he never would be.

"What I know is that you broke Preston's heart." I didn't want to do this. Not today. But I wouldn't let him make this day any harder than it already was. "Please, leave it be, Carson. This is what your brother wanted. I assure you, I will do everything I can to make sure his wishes are followed."

"As will your mother and I," Alan said as he and Alice moved to join my parents standing with me.

"Dad!"

"I suggest you leave, Carson." He pointed to the door and then followed, making sure Carson left the house.

"I'm so sorry, Serena." Tears swam in Alice's eyes.

"Don't." I hugged her. How dare Carson hurt her like this on today, of all days? "He'll come around."

Probably for more money, but I'd let Nathaniel deal with him. That's what attorneys were for, right?

"Come on. I know a little girl who would love to see her grandma and grandpa."

"Really?" Alice looked at me with such hope, it broke my heart.

I took her hands and held them, willing her to believe what I said next. "Alice, you and Alan are my family as much as my parents are. I want you to be part of Ashley's life. I'm counting on you to help her learn exactly what kind of a man her father was. I want her to know him through your eyes." I swallowed against the lump in my throat. "I hope the two of you will be a large part of her life. I want you to be."

She sobbed once and drew me close. We clung to one another for a long time before she stepped back. When she did, Alan's arm went around her waist.

"We'd like that more than anything, Serena," he said, his voice thick with emotion.

"Then let's go upstairs." Mama smiled and slipped her arm through Alice's. "Serena will join us once she and Nathaniel finish all this boring legal business."

Thank you, I mouthed.

She nodded and led my in-laws and Papa out of the library, leaving me with Nate and Mary Kate.

"Well, that was unpleasant." Mary Kate looked toward the front of the house and shook her head.

"But not unexpected." Her husband slid the paperwork into his attaché case. "I want to know if he gives you any grief, Serena."

"You will." Not that I expected Carson to try anything soon. He was smarter than that. "Will the two of you stay for lunch?"

"No. You need to spend some time with your family, both of them. Then you need to get some rest. I'll check on you later," Mary Kate said.

I walked with them to the door and watched as they drove off. Then I climbed the stairs to join the others. The worst was behind me, at least for today. Mary Kate had been right about one thing. Preston lived on through my memories of him and through our daughter. I needed to hold that close.

9

1967

"What do you mean Carson showed up without warning?"

Mary Kate's voice held equal parts surprise, concern and anger. Not that I blamed her. I'd felt pretty much the same way when Mama appeared to tell me he was there. Her own disapproval was plain on her face and in the way she held herself. Then she informed me she was dumping him in the sunroom where he could wait until I was ready to see him.

Her message had been clear. I had work to see to and I wasn't to cut it short just because Carson suddenly decided to pay us a visit.

Not that I could. Since Papa's death last year, I'd been running the farm. I had also taken over the management of the farm management firm he established a decade ago. We worked with local farmers and ranchers, helping find workers and negotiate contracts with various markets. Papa had been good at it. I took over and would keep the company going until I found someone who shared his views about locally owned farms to sell it to. Running our own farm and raising Ashley were more than enough to keep me busy.

"Just that, Mary Kate. He showed up about half an hour ago and announced to my mother he was here to take me out."

"Oh my." She actually chuckled. "I bet that went over well with your mom."

I laughed softly. "About as well as finding out her prized filly had been sold to the glue factory would."

And she'd probably take that better than seeing Carson on our doorstep.

"What are you going to do?"

"Finish reading this last report and then go see what he wants."

She fell silent for a bit and I had a feeling she was pacing her kitchen, a worried look on her face. "Are you going to let him take you to dinner?"

"I don't know."

Part of me wanted to send him on his way, preferably without seeing him. I'd been right the day Preston's will was read. After his outburst, Carson laid low for a while. I didn't hear from him for several months. Then he sent a short note apologizing for his behavior and hoping I understood it was due to his heartache over the loss of his beloved brother.

Less than a year later, Carson showed up wanting another "loan". I didn't know about it until after the fact. Papa had been home when he arrived. To be more precise, the wards Mama and Papa had in place around the property let him know Carson was approaching and he made it to the front gate before Carson did. He met Carson, shotgun in hand, car parked across the drive. With the shotgun nestled under one arm, he stood in front of the car and asked what Carson wanted. Then he turned him away, telling him he wasn't welcome and not to return unless invited.

Now he was back and he'd caught Mama and me off-guard. That told me two things: he knew Papa was dead and I needed to strengthen the wards on the property. They should have warned me he was nearing.

"Get rid of him." Mary Kate paused and said something to her daughter, a very demanding two-year-old. "Or, better yet, bring him to the café. Nate and I are having dinner there. I know Nate would just love to see him again."

The emphasis she put on love said it all. Nate would quickly let Carson know just how unwelcome he was and then make sure he never bothered any of us again.

"We'll see." I scrawled my signature at the end of the report I'd been reading and put it to the side. I'd send it off in the morning. "I'd best see what he wants before Mama decides to turn him into a toad or something."

She chuckled almost evilly. Mama's patience for fools or for those who threatened her family had lessened over the years. Since Papa's death, she made no secret of the fact she would do whatever it took to protect Ashley and me. She might not actually be able to turn Carson into a toad—at least I didn't think she could—but she most could make him believe she had. While it might be amusing to see him hopping around the parlor, trying to catch flies with his tongue, it wouldn't be for the best.

"Let me know what you decide."

"I will. Give my love to Nate."

"I will." Left unsaid as she hung up was she would also let him know of Carson's sudden appearance.

I stopped by the kitchen long enough to let Mama know I was going to see what Carson wanted. She nodded, her expression neutral. I arched one brow and shook my head. I recognized the signs. She was considering the best spell to throw at him.

"Spoilsport," she muttered.

I grinned and left the kitchen. As I made my way to the sunroom at the back of the house, I was glad Ashley wasn't there. Five days ago, Preston's mother flew in. She spent two days with us before she and Ashley flew out to California. She wanted to take Ashley to Disneyland and then to SeaWorld in San Diego. They'd be gone for another week. Thinking about it, I knew without a doubt Carson timed his visit so his mother wouldn't be here. His father was back in

Tennessee where they'd moved a year after Preston's death. As far as Preston was concerned, he could do whatever he wanted.

He really was a fool.

I opened the door to the sunroom and stepped inside. As I did, Carson turned from the window he'd been looking out of. He wore dark trousers and a white shirt, open at the collar. He didn't look like he had aged any since I last saw him. Tanned, his light colored hair neatly trimmed, he looked as if he could have walked out of a fashion ad. From the expression he wore, he knew it.

He always had been too cocky for his own good.

"Serena!" He crossed the room in three steps and took my hands in his. "You look wonderful." He bent and lightly kissed my cheek.

Every instinct screamed for me to break the contact and get away. I pushed it down. I was overreacting. This was Carson, over-confident but harmless, at least to everyone but himself.

"Hello, Carson. This is a pleasant surprise."

Except it wasn't. I didn't know why I said that. It certainly wasn't what I planned on saying. I shook it off, putting it down to Mama raising me to have good manners.

"What brings you to town?" I motioned for him to have a seat and then sat in my favorite chair near the windows.

"I had some business in Dallas and thought I'd drop by to check on my favorite sister-in-law and niece."

Charm oozed from him but not so much that it fooled me. Alice told me before she and Ashley left for California that the last time she heard from Carson he was unemployed—again. She and Alan had cut him off not long after the funeral. He called or showed up once or twice a year, always promising that he had new prospects and needed just a little bit of cash to tide him over. No doubt that's why he was here.

"I wish you'd called ahead to let me know you were coming. I have plans tonight already."

"Surely you can change them. I'm only in town for the evening."

"I am sorry, Carson." I stood, ready to get him out of my house.

He climbed to his feet. Before I could avoid it, he once again reached for my hand. He gently caressed it, his gaze holding mine. A warmth spread from where his hand held mine followed by a bone chilling cold.

"Change your plans, Serena," he all but purred. "We'll go into town and try the new café I saw as I drove through. We can catch up over dinner."

The world blurred and turned hazy. Even as I tried to tell him I couldn't go, I heard my voice telling him I'd be happy to go with him. My brain yelled for me to stop, to think. Something was very, very wrong.

But I couldn't stop myself. He kept talking, his voice soft, soothing. I wanted to be with him, to go wherever he told me. With my hand tucked into the crook of his elbow, I let him lead me out of the house. Not even the sense of warning it blasted at me stopped me. I walked down the steps and let him help me into the front seat of his car.

We talked. Or he talked. I'm not sure which. Then he parked down the block from the café. He'd been wrong about it being new. Peggy opened it almost three years ago and it had quickly become a favorite. My heart skipped a beat as he took my hand and helped me out of the car. Mary Kate said she and Nate would be there. They'd help me.

They had to.

If they realized anything was wrong.

Hope flared again when we entered the café. Mary Kate and Nate sat two tables from the door. Even as all conversation stopped and heads turned in our direction, Mary Kate was on her feet. Before she could say anything, Nathaniel stepped around her. The smile on his face didn't reach his eyes. Adroitly, he managed to place himself between Carson and me.

"You have to join us, you two." He smiled again and escorted me to the seat next to Mary Kate's. "It's been a long time, Carson." He didn't shake hands. Instead, he motioned for Carson to take the chair across from Mary Kate, at a diagonal from me at the table.

"We don't want to intrude, Metzger."

"It's no intrusion at all." Nate rested a hand on his shoulder and only a close look showed the way his fingers dug in. Once Carson dropped onto his chair, Nate took his place at the table and signaled to Peggy for two more menus.

"Are you all right?" Mary Kate whispered urgently while Nate kept Carson's attention.

I nodded, smiling. Beneath the table, my hands clinched. What was wrong with me? It was like someone had taken control of my body. I did and said what they wanted even as my mind screamed in fear. Cold fury lit Mary Kate's eyes and her mouth firmed. Maybe she realized something was wrong.

Please, God, let her know I was in trouble.

Dinner was the most surreal meal of my life. I ate. I answered questions. But I felt powerless to initiate anything. Once, Mary Kate reached for my hand under the table and jerked back the moment her fingers touched mine. It was as if she'd been burned. Nathaniel grilled Carson, not that Carson realized it. As long as he was talking about himself, Carson was happy. Throughout it all, Peggy kept an eye on the table from behind the counter, her expression unreadable.

"I don't know about the rest of you, but I think I want to freshen up a bit before Peggy brings dessert." Mary Kate smiled and lightly dabbed at her mouth with her napkin. As she stood, she looked down at me. "Why don't you come with me, Serena? You probably want to touch up your makeup, right?"

Yes!

My brain screamed it but I continued to sit where I was. Fear spiked, my heart raced.

And I couldn't move from my seat.

"Go ahead, Serena." Carson didn't like it but he apparently thought he needed to agree, especially since most everyone else in the café was looking at him.

I stood and would have followed Mary Kate had she not slipped her arm through mine and drawn me next to her. The moment we turned the corner and stepped into the short corridor at the far end of the café that led to the restrooms, I breathed easier. Part of me wanted to turn and run back to Carson but the "me" part wanted to run in the opposite direction. Instead of doing either, I let Mary Kate guide me inside the small restroom and lock the door behind us.

"Serena, what the hell is going on?" She shook me, all but frantic as she looked me over as if searching for injuries or some other explanation for what was going on.

"C-can't."

I wanted to say more but couldn't. I was little more than an observer in my own body and I did *not* like it.

"You can't what?" She started to reach for my hands again and stopped, as if remembering how she'd jerked back earlier.

Before she could say anything else, a key turned in the lock and the door opened. All five foot nothing of Peggy Russell stepped inside. Her auburn hair was tied back with a white scarf. A white apron covered her blouse and dark slacks. But nothing disguised the way the air swirled around her or the fury blazing in her eyes as she locked the door, making it very crowded in there.

"Mary Kate, wash your hands. Now!" she snapped.

"What?"

"I saw how you jerked back when you reached for her hand. There's only one thing I can think of to cause you to do that. So wash your hands. Do it!"

Putting actions to her words, Peggy shoved Mary Kate toward the sink. While Mary Kate complied, Peggy looked at me. If possible, her expression darkened. She shoved my sleeves up my arms and studied my hands. Then she stepped back against the door and looked at me. I saw her pupils go wide as her gaze unfocused. Swallowing hard, hoping she could *see* something I didn't, I waited, fighting the urge to return to the table and Carson.

"Damn it," she muttered. If she could have paced, she would have. Instead, she drummed a beat on her leg with the fingers of her right hand. Then, careful of where she touched, she grabbed my arm, unlocked the door, and dragged me out and up the back stairs in the direction of the apartment she kept over the café.

"Peggy?" Mary Kate asked as she followed us.

"He used something on her. I can see the echoes of it." Now she paced. When I took a step toward the door, she jabbed a finger at me, eyes flashing. "Don't even think about it, Serena."

She stopped pacing and faced us. "Look at her aura. It's muted, like something slick and oily is coating it. My guess is he had something on his hands and that opened her to suggestion." Her expression softened and she stepped closer. "Serena, did you want to come with him?"

It seemed forever before I could form one simple word. "N-no."

"Mary Kate, get her in the shower. Make sure she washes all over. Hair, body, everything. Don't let her put her clothes back on. Melissa Avery is downstairs. I'll have a word with her and have her grab what Serena needs from her store. Wait up here until I get back."

"What about Carson?"

"I'll put a bug in Nate's ear. Once Serena's ready, we'll deal with Carson." She gave me a reassuring smile then. "We're going to make sure he never tries to do anything like this to you again, Serena. I promise."

With that, she left the apartment and Mary Kate managed to get me undressed and in the shower.

"Stop!"

Pain tore through me at the first touch of water. For a moment I considered fighting my way out of the apartment. It didn't matter I was naked. Nothing mattered but getting back to Carson. He'd protect me.

Another splash of water as Mary Kate moved me back under the spray. I hissed as pain flared again, not as badly this time. Breathing through the pain, I realized she was using soap and wash cloth to get rid of whatever Peggy had seen. Embarrassment flared, not because I was naked but because I'd been such a fool. I'd not kept my guard up when I knew better.

That was a mistake I'd never again make—assuming I got out of this relatively unscathed.

"Give me."

I grabbed soap and cloth and began scrubbing. Pain flared time and again, but each time it was less than the time before. I washed my hair, rinsing it and then washing again. I don't know how long I stood in the shower, scrubbing not only whatever Carson had used on me but the memory of his touch from me. When I finished, I stepped out of the shower and found Mary Kate still there, a white towel in hand that she wrapped around me before handing me a second towel for my hair.

"Peggy left clothes in the bedroom. I'll be in the living room once you're dressed."

"Mary Kate, wait." Hesitantly, I reached for her hand. I wouldn't blame her if she pulled away. Instead, she pulled me into a tight hug, ignoring the fact I was getting her wet or that I was crying all over her.

"Shh, Serena. It's all right. You're safe now." She patted my back and gently pushed the hair back from my face. "Let's get you dressed and then Nate and I will take you home."

"Thank you."

The outer door opened and Peggy slipped inside. This time, she grinned wide enough to split her face. If possible, her grin grew even wider as she studied me.

"How do you feel?"

"Furious and ready to let him know I do not appreciate being manipulated like that."

"Good." She nodded and her eyes sparkled. "But you'd better hurry. He knows something happened. About the time you got into the shower, he all but fell out of his chair. If I didn't know better, I'd say he felt his spell snapping back on him."

Good. It served the son of a gun right.

Mary Kate and I made our way back downstairs a few minutes later. Thanks to Melissa Avery, I now wore a pair of black slacks, red silk blouse and even had underwear and a pair of sandals to wear. My damp hair was pulled back into a tail. The fact both Mary Kate and I wore new clothes was lost on no one as we entered the café except, perhaps, Carson.

Silence fell over the diners as they watched us march toward our table. One corner of Nate's mouth twitched up as he rose and moved to my side. With him on my left and Mary Kate on my right, I felt safe. Carson wouldn't be able to bespell or manipulate me again.

"Serena." Carson's brow furrowed as he realized something was different.

"Nathaniel, I have a question." I didn't take my eyes from Carson nor did I attempt to hide my anger or distaste.

"Oh?"

"Tell me what the penalty is for an Other who uses his or her abilities to bespell or manipulate someone against their will or without their consent."

"If the Other is found guilty, they are sentenced to a time in prison ranging from one year to life, depending on the seriousness of their crime. During that time, they are held in specially built cells and are not allowed access to anything they can use to enhance their abilities or to make any potions or the like."

"And how do the authorities enforce the prohibition against using their abilities?"

"There are a number of different ways that can be used, ranging from allowing them no items in their cells save for a change of clothes, bed and bedding and a toilet to placing a binding on them to keeping them under sedation light enough to allow them to function but heavy enough they are unable to use their abilities."

"I see."

Carson swallowed hard and pushed his chair back. I waved my hand and his chair shot forward as if someone shoved it from behind, trapping him against the edge of the table.

"And what sort of steps do you see being taken against a man who tried to bind and compel a woman against her will?"

Nathaniel's expression turned hard and Carson paled. "That man would find life very challenging in prison. Cons look poorly on any man who tries to take advantage of a woman or child. One who used his abilities as an Other against a woman will find himself facing a very short lifespan."

"I see."

More importantly, so did Carson.

"You have one choice to make," I said, speaking to him for the first time. "You leave town and you never come back. You never try to contact me or mine again. If I learn of you abusing your abilities, I will make it my life's work to see you in prison for the rest of your miserable life."

"You can't prove I did anything."

"But we can," Nate said coldly. "You're so damned full of yourself and convinced no one would ever look beyond the surface that you forgot that magic leaves traces. Every spell carries the signature of the Other who cast it."

Now he glanced at me. "Let him up, Serena."

I nodded and waved my hand again. Carson's chair screeched back from the table, almost tipping over backwards.

"The only reason I'm not pressing charges against you myself is because I will respect Serena's wishes. But know this, every person in this town will know to be on the lookout for you within the hour. Show your face here again and you will be arrested. Try to manipulate or bespell anyone and I will make your life a living hell. I'll do it because Serena is special to my wife and me and because your brother was one of the finest men I've ever known."

"You don't scare me." He pulled himself up to his full height, all bluster and hot air. "This isn't the end of this. I'll be back and I'll be the end of each of you."

Nathaniel extended his right hand, palm up, and smiled as three flames danced above it, stretching toward the ceiling. "You're a fool. Serena doesn't need any of us to deal with you. Unluckily for you, she has each of us standing with her and we will do whatever it takes to protect her and her daughter. Now get the hell out of our town."

"Now!" I looked at the door and it swung open and stayed that way, the message clear.

"Let me help, Serena dear," Mrs. Kyber said.

She made a shooing motion with her hands in Carson's direction and an expertly controlled gust of wind sent him head over heels and out of the café. The door slammed shut behind him. As it did, several of the men stood. After kissing their wives and assuring them they would be back soon, they stepped outside. The last I saw of Carson was of them hauling him to his feet and dragging him down the street to where his rent car waited.

"Now, will someone explain what happened?" Nate asked as he seated first Mary Kate and then me at our table.

Peggy was there almost instantly with three Irish coffees and the warning to everyone else that the café was closed—the only way she could get away with serving alcoholic anything.

I quickly told them how Carson showed up and my plan to send him on his way. Several of those gathered hissed angrily to hear how I found myself unable to resist his "suggestions". From the look on Nate's face, Carson was lucky not to be there. All I could do was thank each of them for standing up for me.

"I'll make sure everyone knows to keep an eye out for him," Peggy said softly before disappearing into the back of the café, no doubt to activate the grapevine.

"You need to tell your mother, Serena," Mary Kate said softly. "She and the others can make sure there's no remaining connection to him."

I nodded. As embarrassed as I was to know I fell for such a cheap trick, I knew better than to risk letting any binding he might have started get a hold on me. The Guardians would be able to tell if I had anything else to worry about and they could deal with the binding if it was there. As for me, as soon as they were finished, I'd be strengthening the wards around the house and our lands. He would not get near me and mine again without me knowing he was coming.

JAX

10

Present Day

I couldn't believe it. Miss Serena could have said almost anything, even that the Earth was flat, and I'd have accepted it easier than what I just heard. The very thought someone could manipulate her in such a way was beyond imagination. Worse, the similarities between what happened to her and what Maddy tried to do to me made my blood run cold.

"What happened to him?" Quinn asked.

I looked around the living room. Everyone save Maddy was there. She still slept upstairs. I didn't doubt the house made sure she couldn't hear anything that was said. As for the rest of us, disbelief and worry filled the room. Mary Kate had moved to sit next to Miss Serena. She held Miss Serena's hand and now softly reassured her everything was going to be all right. But I saw the worry in her eyes and an anger that still lingered after so many years.

"He left town." Miss Serena glanced at her fingers linked with Mary Kate's before looking at the rest of us. "Perhaps I should say he was escorted out of town. He never came back and I never heard from him again."

"Do you know what happened to him?" Judith asked.

Miss Serena shook her head.

"You said Peggy told you to tell your mother what happened," Dr. Pat said.

Miss Serena nodded. "She was one of the Guardians then. I wouldn't become one for another several years. They made sure Carson didn't leave any hooks in me."

"That is how you knew what to do with me." At least that answered one question.

She smiled slightly and nodded. "You were even luckier than I was, Jackie. You were able to fight the compulsion and that gave Quinn and Ciara time to get to you."

"That wasn't luck, Miss Serena. I doubt Maddy is as strong as that bastard was. Remember, she was acting under several bindings at the time. Besides, you were blindsided and I wasn't, not completely anyway. We knew there was something going on with Maddy, just not what."

And that brought up questions we needed to discuss but later, after we dealt with what we just learned.

"I agree," Judith said. "But it does raise a question or two. There are too many similarities between what happened to you, Serena, and what happened yesterday. Is it possible this Carson could be responsible for one of the bindings we found attached to Maddy?"

Miss Serena didn't answer right away. Then she shook her head. "I don't think so. He was several years older than I am. It's possible he's no longer alive." She paused and we waited, giving her time to process the memories and the emotions they evoked.

"I haven't thought about that day in years. Now that I have, I am confident he wasn't responsible for any of the bindings we found on Maddy. I remember what I felt like that night; the feel of his talent leaching into me, stealing my ability to act. I was locked inside my head, aware but unable to fight back." She shuddered and wrapped her arms around herself.

Pat gently draped an afghan from the back of the sofa around her shoulders. Then she knelt in front of her, concerned friend and worried doctor. While she and Mary Kate took a few moments to make sure she was all right, Amy standing behind them, I moved across the room. The only sounds were Dr. Pat softly asking questions and Miss Serena answering. The sound of liquid being poured into a glass joined it as I poured myself a shot of whiskey. It didn't matter that it was early morning. I needed a drink after what happened last night and after hearing what happened to Miss Serena.

"Jackie."

I turned and saw Miss Serena holding a hand out to me. I set my glass down and rushed to her. Her hand was so cold when her fingers wrapped around mine. Worried, I looked at Dr. Pat who shook her head. Whether it was to stop me from asking questions or something else, I didn't know.

"You need to rest, Miss Serena." I lowered to sit on the arm of her chair, refusing to let go of her hand. It didn't surprise me when Amy mirrored my actions. Her eyes were dark with a concern I shared. "We have enough to get started."

"Not yet." She released my hand and accepted a cup of hot tea from Mary Kate. "As I was saying, I don't think Carson was responsible for any of the bindings we found on Maddy. But one of them did feel similar to what I felt that night. It was stronger, however, and much more pervasive and evil."

I swallowed hard at that last word. Then my anger began to build. One of the first lessons any Other was taught was never to abuse our talents. Those talents made us different, yes, but not special. What made us special was how we used our abilities. They were meant to help others, to make our homes, our towns and, yes, even the world a better place. Abusing our talents by using them for personal gain or against another person in anything but a defensive manner was tantamount to committing a sin for most of us.

"That's more than enough to get us started, Miss Serena." Quinn knelt in front of her chair. "We can start looking into what happened after he left town. You let Amy and Dr. Pat take you upstairs to rest."

"She's right, Grandma."

"In a moment." She smiled and lightly patted Amy's hand. "Preston's family wasn't one of the early settlers here in town. They moved here when Preston was in high school. He was three, almost four years older than me. That's why we didn't meet until college. After he died, his parents returned to Tennessee. For a while, they kept their house here. It made it easier for them when they came to visit. But after what happened and then when his father died, his mother sold the place here. Part of the money we put into a trust for Amy's mother." Now she gripped Amy's hand as if it were a lifeline.

"Alice never said anything, but I've always suspected something happened between Carson and his parents after that terrible night. Never again did they mention him. When Alice died and Ashley and I flew out for her funeral, Carson wasn't there. From what I heard afterwards, he hadn't been to see his parents for years. The fact they left everything to Ashley seems to confirm some kind of falling out."

"All that will be public record, Miss Serena. We'll start looking into it right away. If there's a connection between him and what happened with Maddy, we'll find it. If not, at least we'll be able to put that possibility to bed." Ciara stood behind her sister, a hand on Quinn's shoulder.

"The girls are right, Serena," Judith said. "You need to rest some more. I know what the last few days have taken out of me and it was worse on you. Come on. Let us take you upstairs."

Miss Serena nodded before letting Amy and me help her to her feet. As they slowly made their way upstairs, I watched, my worry spiking. Then I dropped onto the chair Miss Serena had been sitting in. The others waited and I felt their eyes on me. I needed to say something, but what?

"Doc?" Rafe crouched in front of me, his expression worried.

I smiled slightly, not trying to hide how I felt. As I reached for his hand, I looked at everyone else. God, what I wouldn't give to wake up and find this had all been a nightmare.

"Mary Kate, can you tell us anything else?"

She quickly glanced upstairs, as if worried she might be overheard. Then she nodded. "Serena needed to put what happened out of her mind. She was still dealing with having to take over management of the farm here as well as her daddy's business when it all happened. She was also doing her best to spend as much time as possible with her daughter and help her mama. That was also about the time she started training to become a Guardian. But that didn't stop my Nathaniel from checking on Carter. I don't know if he found anything but, if he did, it will be in his files." She glanced at Annie who sat on the hearth, Sam at her side.

"I'll look into it." Then she frowned and shook her head, remembering she had her plate full getting settled in as the new DA. "Meg?"

"I'll check the files. You might come over at lunch or after work and give me a hand."

"What can we do?" Sam asked.

That was my cue. "I want the security setup here checked. If possible, camera feeds of the entire property line. I know the cars have GPS, but let's get a backup in place."

"We'll take care of it, Doc," Rafe said and Sam nodded in agreement.

"Ciara and I will look into that bastard who hurt her."

We didn't need to ask who Quinn meant.

"Quinn," Lucas drawled.

"She's right, Lucas." I continued before he could interrupt. "You might want to check around town to see if there have been any strangers around. Let's make sure no one's keeping an eye on Maddy for Roben or anyone else."

"All right. I'm also going to see if there's any connection between the bastard who hurt Miss Serena and Roben."

"And Maddy?" Meg asked.

I blew out a breath. To say I was torn was putting it mildly. However, before I could answer, Judith came downstairs. She waved off our questions about Miss Serena and crossed the room to pour herself a cup of tea.

"Mom?" Ciara asked in concern.

"Sorry. It's been a long couple of days." She smiled slightly, exhaustion turning her complexion ashen.

"You need to rest as much as Miss Serena," I told her.

"And I plan on it." She sipped the tea and then smiled slightly. "To answer your question about Maddy, when she wakes, her mother is taking her back to their house. Marcus has cleared out everything she might have brought back from Ireland." Now she did smile, humor dancing in her tired eyes. "She said he told her he'd thrown out everything that didn't have a local tag on it."

I winced slightly. I didn't doubt he had done just that. Maddy would be pissed, but it was a small enough price to pay to keep her—and us—safe.

"And Miss Serena?"

"She's beyond exhausted. Pat's giving her something so she'll sleep and Amy's going to stay with her." Now she looked at me. "Amy told us you boosted the wards here and tied her into them, Jax. Thank you."

I nodded, understanding. "Then understand, I'll be checking the wards at each of our places. We can't let our guards down now."

I pushed to my feet and stood there, studying each of them. "I don't know about the rest of you, but what Miss Serena told us shook me. It was too close to what Maddy did to me. But Miss Serena was right. There was something else to what Maddy did. It was more than just bending me to her will. She wanted me to hurt Quinn and Ciara and who knows what else she would have forced me to do.

"But we all have to accept it wasn't really Maddy. We knew Roben had bound her. We knew it was possible he still had a hook into her but she wouldn't let us do what was necessary to make sure and to break the binding if it still existed. We need to learn from what happened and make sure we aren't that vulnerable again."

And I was going to have to find a way to remember—and accept —it wasn't really Maddy who did what she did.

"You need to get some rest too, Jax." Mary Kate looked at me in concern.

"Soon." I looked at all of them, not liking how they seemed to be waiting for me to tell them what to do. Then, as I glanced at my watch, I almost winced. It was later than I thought. "Annie, you and Meg both need to get to work. You too, Lucas."

Annie cursed softly as she looked at the time. Then she nodded. I waited as the three of them hurried out of the house. As they did, I knew they'd be checking in and seeing not only how our own research was doing but what they could do to help.

"Sam, Rafe, after you finish here—and let me know how long you think it will take—we need to talk about what can be done to help protect everyone else." Seeing Aunt Bitsy standing in the doorway to the kitchen, I gave her an almost apologetic smile. "That includes your place."

She nodded, her expression grim. "As long as you make sure your place is secure as well and you promise not to run the land on your own."

I didn't like it, but she was right. Until we knew what was going on, I had to follow my own advice.

"Amy, will you let me know how your grandmother is after she wakes?"

"I will." She blinked back what looked suspiciously like tears and then smiled slightly. "The last few days have been difficult on all of you, but she's not as young as she used to and she tires more easily."

"I promise I'll do everything I can to make sure she doesn't overdo again."

"We all will," Judith said. "We should all get on our way. I need to rest some and the rest of you have things to start working on."

"Jax, we need to talk for a moment," Mary Kate said softly as everyone started moving toward the front door.

"Feel like walking a little? I need to check in with Jimmy and make sure nothing needs my attention right away."

"That sounds good."

The two of us retraced the steps Quinn and I had taken the day before. At the "clinic", I put on a pot of coffee and told Mary Kate to make herself comfortable while I checked for messages and popped into the main stable to check in with Jimmy. By the time I returned, Mary Kate had poured coffee for the two of us and then, with a grin, told me she'd been playing receptionist before handing me two messages.

"Mary Kate, I can tell you're worried about something. What?"

For a moment, she studied her coffee mug. When she looked up, my heart clinched. She looked as old as Miss Serena had. Neither were young women but they'd never looked their ages, but fear and worry would do that to anyone.

"I wanted to discuss a couple of things with you." She sipped her coffee and I leaned back, crossing my ankles. "There's not much more I can add to what Serena told you until we see if Nate learned anything else. If he did, I know he will have notes about it some-where. I haven't found any at the house, but I will make sure to look again when I get home."

"After you get some rest." I pinned her with a firm look.

She smiled slightly and nodded.

"Even so, I can't help feeling that we need to be very careful right now. That means I agree with Serena and the others about Maddy. She can't be part of the inner circle. She probably shouldn't even know what is being planned until after it has been put in motion."

"I agree, but why?"

"I have nothing to support this except a feeling. You need to understand that."

I dipped my chin.

"We can guess the approximate date when Roben first bound Maddy. We're talking months ago, but not quite a year."

Another nod.

"What we don't know is how long the other bindings had been in place. It is possible they are years old. The long-term effects of such things are tricky to anticipate at best. She's going to have to work on her shields and she will always be susceptible if she get careless."

"I was afraid of that and I agree with you." And it broke my heart. I might still be furious with Maddy but I still loved her.

She sighed softly in relief. "We're going to need to keep an eye on

Serena as well. This has shaken her, especially having to remember what that SOB did to her. It took her a long time to start trusting herself again after that. I don't want to see her return to anything like she was back then."

"I will do whatever I can, Mary Kate. You have my word."

She reached over and lightly grasped my hand. "There's one more thing—Annie."

No we got to her real worry. Not that it surprised me.

"Mary Kate, I'll admit I've been trying to think of a way to talk to you about her. You know I love Annie. Hell, I love your entire family, even Catherine."

Mary Kate laughed softly, her eyes sparkling. "I love my daughter dearly, but she is a challenge, especially for poor Annie and Drew."

"That she is." No sense in denying the truth, especially when she tended to jog around town with Aunt Bitsy and the rest of the Terrible Trio, all of whom wore pink jogging suits. "As for Annie, she's got a lot on her plate right now, more than usual. So she's going to be distracted. I was hoping you'd figure out a way to suggest you stay with them at her house. It's more than big enough for all of you, as you know, and there's room for Ranger as well." I knew she wouldn't agree to go anywhere if she had to leave her beloved German shepherd behind.

"Besides, that way you can help protect her and the rest of the family and, to be honest, give her extra training on how to use and control her talents."

Something very important right now. In the months since Annie finally realized she was an Other like the rest of us, she'd worked hard to accept she wasn't a normal and to learn exactly what she could and couldn't do.

"Well now." Mary Kate looked as if she was considering what I said. Then she grinned and the resemblance between her and Annie had never been so evident. "I will admit, it might be enough to save me from Catherine's 'babies'."

I groaned at the mention of the 'babies'. Catherine's 'babies' were two of the most evil geriatric poodles to ever exist. By all rights, they should have died years ago. I'd wondered more than once if they were like some of Lexie's family and simply returned to their 'mama' after dying. One of the only good things to come out of the troubles to come to Mossy Creek the last few years was the influx of "real" dogs like Mary Kate's Ranger. The poodles were terrified of the dogs and life was much better as a result.

At least for everyone except Catherine who mourned the fact she could no longer inflict her babies on everyone in town.

"I will talk to Annie and Sam about it as soon as I get home." She shook her head when I started to object. "I'd need to go home to pack and pick up Ranger anyway. This way, I kill two birds with one stone."

"All right." I drained my mug and stood, stretching until my back popped. "Come on, I'll drive you back to the house. Then I'm going home to grab a nap before figuring out what my next step should be."

11

The moment we crossed the property line, I felt the wards reaching out. It was like an embrace almost, welcoming Rafe and me, assuring me we were safe. For the first time since entering The Roadhouse, I relaxed. I trusted the wards, not to mention the security measure Rafe and Sam put in place, to keep out those who shouldn't be here. Even so, I planned on adding another layer of warding as soon as I'd rested some.

"You okay, Doc?"

I turned my head and smiled at Rafe. He'd been waiting for me when Mary Kate and I returned to the main house. Then he'd followed me back to the clinic. I left my work truck there so he could drive me home.

"Honestly?"

He nodded.

"I don't know."

I leaned my head back and closed my eyes. When I sat up a few moments later, he was parking in front of our house. He switched off the engine and then reached for my hand. He didn't have to say anything. He always seemed to know what I needed, usually before I did. Thank goodness I found him. Or maybe he found me. It didn't matter which. He was part of my life. He helped ground me and I loved him more than I ever thought possible.

"You need to get some sleep."

I nodded as we walked up the steps to the front door. His keys jangled. Then he looked at me, his head cocked to one side.

"Doc." He pulled me close, gently pressing my head against his shoulder. His hands were warm as they ran from my shoulders to my waist. Sighing, I wrapped my arms around him, smelling in his scent. "I know you're worried about what's happened and what might happen next. But I want you to remember something, you aren't alone. I'm here with you and always will be. So don't try to take all this on by yourself." He lifted my hand and rubbed the pad of his thumb over my engagement ring.

"And I know you. I know you want to shift and run but you made a promise to Miss Serena and the others."

I stepped back and looked up at him, trying to figure out how to convince him to change his mind.

"Sweetheart, you're dead on your feet. Even shifted, you're going to be exhausted. So get some sleep. Then you can shift. As long as you let Fenris run with you, I won't argue if you run the fields for a few minutes—after you rest."

I looked at him, surprised. "You're not going to say I should wait until you or someone can be with me?"

He looked down at me, his expression serious. "Jax, if you can't protect yourself when shifted—or at least get away from trouble—then we are all truly fucked. But I do want you to take Fenris with you."

"I will."

"Then let's get you upstairs so you can rest. The house might not eat intruders like Quinn's, but it will make sure no one gets in you don't want to."

I smiled and held him close for a moment. Leaning up on my tiptoes, I brushed my lips over his. Then, grinning a little apologetically, I slipped off first my engagement ring and then the chain with his dog tag that I wore around my neck.

"You're right about the protections, but I need to be sure." I whistled for Fenris. "I promise I won't be long but I need to do this. I *need* this."

For a moment, he looked like he might argue. Then he nodded. He didn't like it, but he understood. Thanking him, I stripped and dropped to my hands and knees. I focused on my Walker side. The fingers of my right hand lightly traced the coyote tattooed on my left arm. The coyote that now sat on its haunches, head raised as it howled at the moon. The world disappeared into a swirl of energies and everything. . . shifted.

"I never get used to how quickly you shift." Rafe grinned and scratched between my ears as I butted him with my head. "Don't be too long, love, and don't get into trouble."

In a very non-canine movement, I nodded. Then I padded down the steps on four paws, Fenris at my side. The German shepherd looked at me as part of his pack in this form—thankfully. Even more thankfully, he recognized me as the alpha. Now, however, he shoulder checked me and ran toward the trees, barking playfully. The human part of me laughed as the coyote part raced after him.

Fenris and I ran the property line. Remembering Rafe's concern, I made sure we kept to the shadows. Once reassured no one had tried to gain entry, Fenris and I played tag, making our way slowly back to the house. There was a freedom in this form—or any of my other animal forms—I didn't feel in my human skin. That was why I needed these few hours after the events of the last few days.

"Feeling better?" Rafe asked.

I looked up from where I knelt on the back porch, once again human and very naked. Fenris lay at my side, his head resting on his paws. Rafe, dressed only in a pair of jeans, helped me to my feet and draped a robe across my shoulders. He watched as I slid my arms into the sleeves. Then he reached out and belted it about my waist.

"Yeah." I reached for his hand and lifted it to my lips, brushing my lips against his knuckles. "Thanks for understanding."

He drew me against him. For a long moment, we stood there, looking out across the lawn. From the angle of the sun, I guessed it was around noon. Exhaustion dragged at me, but I wasn't ready for bed. Not yet.

"Sweetheart." He chuckled and his arm tightened around me. "You need to remember I've known about your Walker side pretty much from the start."

I nodded, remembering my surprise to find him waiting after I shifted back to human that first time. I'd only been back to Mossy Creek for a few days. He'd been helping keep an eye on Annie after she'd been attacked. That evening, I'd gone back to his house ostensibly so I wouldn't drive after having several drinks. My real motive was because his house was closer to Annie's and Sam's than Aunt Bitsy's, where I'd been staying. Once I thought he was asleep, I crept out, shifted, and made my way to Annie's. Finding him waiting after I shifted back had been a surprise. That's when I admitted to my Walker side and he assured me he had no problem with. He'd served with shifters in the Army and, as long as it helped keep Annie and the kids safe, he was all for it.

"Did you find anything we need to be concerned about?"

"No." Thankfully. I lifted my face and looked at the sky. To the naked eye, it was a beautiful day with barely a cloud in the sky. But to anyone who could see the energies and recognize the wards, it was something very different. The wards wove a complicated pattern—by design—over the property. Those patterns would alert me if anyone tried to trespass or if something as small as a drone broke the plane. It was the best passive protection I could give us. But was it enough? I hoped so because I couldn't shake the feeling the worst was yet to come.

"Come inside. You need to eat and get some rest." Rafe took my hand and led me across the porch in the direction of the back door. As he did, Fenris lifted his head and then lowered it back to his paws. His eyes closed and Rafe chuckled softly. "You wore him out."

"More like he wore me out." I smiled at the shepherd in affection. "Did you get any rest?" I asked as we stepped inside the kitchen.

He shook his head. "I took care of a few things while I waited for you." He studied the contents of the refrigerator. A moment later, he turned and tossed me a bottle of water. "What do you want for lunch?"

"Nothing right now." I cracked open the bottle and took a long drink. "I'm too tired to eat."

"Then let's get you to bed."

"Not yet." I shook my head and took my place at the kitchen table. Seeing his look of exasperation, I shrugged slightly and tried to smile. I might be exhausted, but my brain was still working overtime. If I didn't talk it out, I'd never get any rest. "Please." I lightly patted the chair next to mine.

He sighed and then joined me. When he did, I reached for his hand. As our fingers touched, I felt grounded again. Drawing a deep breath, I tried to order my thoughts, not the easiest thing tired as I was.

"Doc?"

I might as well start with the elephant in the room.

"Maddy."

He nodded, his expression grim. Worse, anger flashed in his eyes.

"Don't." I used my other hand to cover his. "I'm all right. She didn't hurt me."

"She damn sure wanted to," he growled.

"That wasn't her, Rafe." I shook my head when he started to interrupt. "Sweetheart, it wasn't."

He simply arched a brow and I sighed.

"All right. Part of it was. But it is something she never would have tried had it not been for the bindings." I released his hand and reached for my water. "Maddy always struggled with self-confidence." I thought for a moment. "No, that's not quite right. She struggled with self-esteem, at least where the rest of us were concerned."

"How so?"

"Annie was the academic of us. Always made good grades, voted class president, that sort of thing. Quinn was a good student and an even better athlete. She was on the swimming team, the tennis team. Hell, love, she could have played football on the varsity team if that was allowed back then. Me, well, I was the Rogue even then. My grades were good enough." They had to be or I never would have gotten into college, much less vet school later. "But I had my fair share of trouble."

He grinned. "Sam used to tell me about the Rogue and how she stood up to anyone and everyone when you were all in school. You never picked a fight, but you always did your best to end them, especially if one of your friends was being picked on."

"Yeah." And it seemed I hadn't changed much over the years. "Maddy was different. She was a good student but she didn't see it. It wasn't that we didn't try to encourage her. It sure as hell wasn't because of her parents. They did everything they could to support her. Even so, she felt like she could never live up to the rest of us. I always thought it was because of her gift. She had to be so careful not to use it to influence anyone and that was hard, especially when we were all going through puberty. That uncertainty may be why she was susceptible to being bound."

He thought for a moment. "It makes sense."

I climbed to my feet and crossed to the refrigerator where I claimed another bottle of water. "It means we need to keep an eye on her now." I turned to face him. "Not only to protect her but to protect her parents and Miss Serena."

Rafe's expression told me he agreed. "That was one of the things I was working on while you were outside."

Now it was my turn to look at him in question.

"Nothing much beyond what we discussed with the others."

He led me out of the kitchen and upstairs. As he did, he outlined what he'd discussed with Lucas and Sam while I'd been running the property. Knowing they'd keep an eye on her eased at least some of my worry.

"You're worried about something else, Doc. What?"

"Miss Serena." I shrugged out of my robe as slid between the sheets. "Whoever is behind all this has done their homework."

For all we knew, the bindings had forced Maddy to tell whoever it was everything she knew about Mossy Creek and those of us living there. If so, the danger was greater than we knew. Worse, it meant they knew the best way to hurt the town was to target Miss Serena.

"Sam and I will be updating security at the farm, Doc. We've already discussed some changes we want to make with Lucas and Drew. I know you and the others will do everything you can to increase the arcane defenses."

I nodded. "How long will it take for you to do the updates?"

Now he frowned. "At least a week. Some of the equipment we need has to be ordered."

"Is there any way to get it here quicker?" Every instinct told me time was running out.

He shook his head. "No. That timeline is with us paying for expedited shipping, etc.."

I didn't like it but didn't see any way around it. Rafe would have done everything possible to get the equipment here sooner. We'd just have to find a way to keep Miss Serena safe until then.

And wouldn't that be fun—not. One of the reasons the farm didn't have the level of mundane security as the rest of our homes was because Miss Serena put it off until she was sure the rest of us were well-protected. Part was because all of us tended to think of her as invincible. Not that I would any longer. The strain of removing the bindings from Maddy had been plain for all of us to see. It was time the rest of us understood we needed to take up the slack, starting with me.

"Rafe, I'm going to be the Rogue right now. I want the updates done as quickly as possible to the farm. But we aren't going to stop there. I want the same thing done at the café, at Miss Peggy's house, Bitsy's and the Caldwells. Hell, even Catherine's." Although I wasn't sure I wanted to know what went on in her house. I had a feeling it would warp me even more than my aunt's love life.

"Consider it done, Doc." He slid into bed at my side and drew me close, nestling me against him. "We discussed those locations and several others. Sam and I are getting started in the morning. We need to inspect the current security systems at each site and figure out whether to start from new or if we can just tie into them."

"Thanks." I brushed my lips against the line of his jaw.

"Sleep now, Doc. You're exhausted. We'll figure the rest of it out later."

He was right. I was exhausted. But I wanted to talk to him about one more thing first.

I leaned up on one elbow and smiled down at Rafe. That smile deepened as the fingers of one of his hands played with my breast, fanning a lust I thought I was too tired for.

"Rafe, thank you."

"For what?"

"For understanding, for being there for me. For loving me." Most of all for loving me.

He smiled and leaned up to kiss me. "I do love you, Doc, more than you know."

"I do know." I settled back, resting my head on his shoulder. "You've been there for me. You've never asked for anything. Why?"

He slipped his arms around me, his hands warm on the bare skin of my back. "Because you are all I've wanted." He moved one hand so he could touch the dog tag I wore before touching the mate on its chain around his neck. "You make me whole, Doc."

"I love you." More than he would ever know. "Another question?"

He chuckled softly. "You need to shut that brain of yours down and get some sleep."

"After you answer my question." I smiled even as I hoped he didn't hear my heart pounding.

"All right."

"Why haven't you ever asked me why I won't set a wedding date?"

He carefully sat up, still somehow managing to cradle me against his chest. His hands gentle, he held me close, letting me feel the beat of his heart. It remained steady, just as he'd been a steady anchor for me in our time together.

"Doc, I know you love me. You prove it to me in so many ways every day. I can wait. You have a responsibility right now to help keep the people we love and this town we love safe. I'll wait, just as I will stand with you as we make sure nothing else happens to those we love."

I didn't deserve him. I knew it, just as I knew he'd argue if I said so. Just as I knew he expected me to. Instead, I decided to surprise him, not something I managed to do very often.

"And how do you plan on doing that?" I grinned up at him as my left hand moved slowly down his chest.

"Well." He inhaled sharply as my fingers closed around him. "By letting you finish what you're starting." He dipped his head and kissed me. "And by making sure you don't push yourself too hard. We can't risk you overextending. Not knowing what we do now."

"And if I do try to push too hard?"

"Then I'll just have to take you in hand." He grinned as his hands gripped my waist.

"I think I'm the one taking you in hand." I nipped at his lower lip and put actions to words. We could talk about the rest of it later.

Three hours later, I padded downstairs. Overhead, I heard the shower and knew Rafe would soon join me. For a moment, I considered my options. Then I made my way to the kitchen. It might be mid-afternoon, but in many ways it was the start of our day. At least it felt that way after sleeping so long in the middle of the day. But Rafe had been right. I needed the rest and so did he, not that he'd admit to the latter. Besides, I knew what the next day would be like. We'd be lucky to get home before eight or nine at night. He had work and then everything he and Sam planned to do to help increase security around our loved ones. As for me, well, I had work. I needed to check on the status of the construction of my clinic. I needed to meet with Bitsy about the upcoming board meeting for Powell Properties. I also needed to talk to Meg about that as well as a few other things, including the latest attempts by my parents to work around Grandpa's will. Then there were my duties as Guardian.

There simply weren't enough hours in the day.

As I waited for Rafe to join me, I fixed lunch for us. One of the traditions we quickly settled into was eating together whenever possible. We managed it at least once a day and usually twice. I didn't plan on letting today be any different.

"Looks good." He slid his arms around me from behind and looked over my shoulder. Lunch rested on a table at the far end of the deck. "But you didn't have to."

"I wanted to." I turned in his arms and smiled up at him. "Besides, you still have a question to answer for me." I gave him a wicked grin and led him to the table.

"What question?" Suspicion filled his eyes as he sat across from me.

"There's no need to look like that," I laughed as I poured iced tea for both of us. "It's just that I've been doing some thinking."

Eyes twinkling, he cocked his head to one side and looked at me. "That could be dangerous."

I barked out a quick laugh. "You do know the same could be said for you, right?" I reached for his hand. "Rafe, everything that's happened these last few days did make me start thinking about some things."

"Doc." He sounded worried and I mentally kicked myself.

"No, Rafe." I squeezed his hand. "This isn't an inept way of saying I want to break up. Just the opposite in fact." Mouth suddenly dry, I took a sip of tea and prayed I didn't screw this up.

"Rafe, I love you more than I thought possible. I want nothing more than to spend the rest of my life with you. I want to have your children." And I couldn't believe that. Until I met Rafe, I never thought of myself as mother material. My own mother certainly hadn't set a good example for me. "I want with you what Annie has with Sam, Quinn with Lucas and Meg with Drew."

I stopped, scared I'd said too much.

Or maybe not enough.

Then, without warning, Rafe pulled me onto his lap. He nuzzled my throat. Then he leaned back, smiling.

"I want the same thing."

"Then let's do it. Let's get married. Now."

He looked at me, just looked at me. Then he grinned broadly

enough I was surprised his face didn't split. Hopeful, I waited. Why hadn't he said anything.

"Are you sure?"

I nodded. "Rafe, if we keep waiting until things are settled, who knows how long it will be. Besides, I finally figured something out." Well, to be honest, my subconscious did. "We'll be stronger with that additional bond between us. I want that. So, will you marry me?"

"Of course I will." Still holding me, he carefully climbed to his feet. It was probably a good thing he didn't put me down because his kiss turned my bones to water. "When and what are we going to tell the others?"

I kept my arms looped around his neck as my feet finally touched the floor. "Now. We can tell them afterwards."

Even if they killed us for not telling them beforehand.

"Are you sure?"

I smiled and nodded. I didn't want to wait while we found the perfect date, planned the parties, that sort of things. We already had the license. We'd gotten one not long after Rafe asked me to marry him. We renewed it several times since then.

"We can call Judge Caldwell and ask him to officiate. The only thing I want is for Bitsy to be there."

"Of course." He framed my face with his hands and kissed me. "She's been the closest thing you've ever known to a mother. I'd like Sam to be there as well."

I nodded, understanding. Sam talked to Rafe about Mossy Creek when they were in the Army together. When he realized Rafe was having a hard time adjusting to civilian life, he brought him here, gave him a place to stay and a job. Without Sam, we wouldn't have met.

"See if his dad will marry us. If he will, ask Sam to meet you there. Don't tell him why."

Annie would kill all of us, but I didn't want this to get out of hand.

He nodded and pulled out his phone. Less than ten minutes later, we were on our way to pick up Bitsy before heading to the judge's house.

"It's a damned good think you kidnapped me, Jax." Bitsy grinned as she pulled me into a tight hug. "You might have interrupted my *supervision* of the pool boy—and you know how much I enjoy making sure he does a really *good* job—but this was worth it."

Laughing, I shook my head. "You're incorrigible, Aunt Bitsy."

"I'll have you know I am very encouragable." She winked and linked her arm with mine. "But seriously, thank you. It means a great deal that you wanted me here."

"Bitsy." I took her hands in mine and gave them a squeeze. "Rafe said it earlier when we decided we didn't want to wait. You've been the closest thing to a mother I've had. There's no way I would do this without you."

She freed and hand and lightly patted my cheek. "You're a wonderful young woman, Jax. If I've had anything to do with helping you become you, it's been my pleasure."

"You can get away with being glad to be here, Bitsy," Sam said with a chagrined smile as he joined us. "But my wife is going to kill me."

Rafe slapped him on the back. "She won't kill the father of her children. She might torture you, but she won't kill you."

"Easy enough for you to say," Sam muttered. Then he brightened and pointed a finger at the two of us. "She won't kill me!" He suddenly looked like a man who'd been given a last-minute reprieve. "Not when I tell her Rafe kidnapped me at gunpoint and Jax threatened to have the Earth swallow me whole if I didn't come along peaceably."

"Samuel, don't be foolish," his mother chided. She might have sounded serious but her amused expression betrayed her true feelings.

"Don't worry, son. Jax and Rafe will do the right thing and tell everyone really soon, won't you?" Judge Caldwell pinned both of us with a firm look. "Because I know for a fact if they don't let Miss Serena and your mother throw them a party, I'd be forced to ask Catherine to do it."

Rafe swallowed hard and the blood drained from my face. We

knew Catherine well enough we were willing to just about anything to keep Annie's mother well away from any party planning that involved us. So we did the only thing two grown, sane adults would do—we promised to tell our friends soon. Judge Caldwell shook his head, a smile tugging at the corners of his mouth. Seeing him like that, I knew now why Annie kept telling me how much he'd enjoyed pulling little "surprises" out of his metaphorical bag when she first returned home.

"Forty-eight hours. If you don't tell them by then, I'll file your marriage license certificate and you know what the grapevine will do with that."

"Forty-eight hours." Rafe extended his hand and shook they shook, on it.

"Now, everyone sit down and let's toast the newlyweds," Camille said as she entered from the kitchen, a tray with six glasses of champagne in her hands.

The judge handed out the glasses and then led the toast. With Rafe's arm around my waist, I sipped and smiled at this part of our extended family. Each of them meant a great deal to both Rafe and me.

"Thank you, all of you. It means more than you know that you were part of this today." I looked at Sam and grinned. "And, yes, we'll tell the others and probably redo our vows and have a party that will hopefully help them get over their pique."

"Pique?" Sam shook his head as he looked at me as if I was some poor fool without a clue how badly I'd stepped into it. "Annie is going to kill all of us and that's nothing compared to what Quinn's going to do to both of you. Hell, to all of us."

"Oh ye of little faith." I winked, hoping they understood. "But there is something we need to discuss right now."

"Jax, I think I can guess what's on your mind and Sam's already talked to Camille and me," the judge said. "And don't worry about us. We told Sam to do whatever he thinks is best to make sure our security system is top of the line."

"Thank you."

"As I told Sam, Camille and I both realize there's something going on. We've suspected it since Catherine took up with Spud. She might be flighty and she might not have the common sense God gave a flea, but that was out of character even for her. With everything that's happened since then, it's been clear something's going on, something aimed at our town."

"Bob's right," Camille said as she sat on the arm of his chair. "All anyone has to do is look at Serena, or any of the rest of you, and know you're worried. So tell us what we can do to help. You don't have to shoulder everything by yourselves."

I glanced at Bitsy who nodded, her expression serious. She knew much of what we suspected, thankfully. Now I hoped she hadn't changed her mind about doing as I asked when it came to her safety.

"Sam's probably told you this, but I want to repeat it. We love each of you. If whoever is targeting Mossy Creek has done their research, they're going to know that. It means you could be targets."

"Shh, Jax. We know. It's all right. We're going to be careful," Bitsy said.

"Thank you." I smiled and reached for her hand. "We're doing everything we can to protect you and the town. But I'm asking you to not take any chances."

"We're asking you to take extra precautions," Rafe put in and Sam nodded in agreement.

"What do you mean?" Camille looked slightly concerned.

"The guys are going to make sure your security system is top of the line. Rafe's already talked to Bitsy about hers. I'd appreciate it if each of you would be sure to carry concealed. You don't have to worry about being licensed under the new law and Sam and Rafe will be glad to take you to the range or bring you out to my place to get in some target practice."

"Jax, I think it's safe to say we all do that already," Camille said.

I nodded even as I glanced at Bitsy. "I have a feeling some of you do it more consistently than others do." Which reminded me to have a talk with Annie about it as well.

"Jax, you're talking about a lot of people if you're worried about the extended family." She made air quotes around family. "We need to make sure everyone's covered."

I nodded and internally blanched at the thought of how expensive it might run.

"Jax, look at me."

I closed my eyes for a moment and held Bitsy's hand even more tightly. I knew what she was going to say before she did.

"Sam, Rafe, do whatever you feel is necessary. Let me know if anyone needs help paying for it. Or, better yet, don't tell them it will cost anything. The newly formed Foundation for Public Safety will take care of."

I looked at her, not sure I followed. "What foundation?"

"The one I'm talking to Meg about as soon as I leave here." She smiled almost innocently and patted my shoulder. "We're going to do whatever it takes to protect our town and loved ones, Jax. You may be on the front line but that doesn't mean the rest of us can't do what we can to help."

"Thank you." I hugged her, tears stinging my eyes. "Thank all of you."

"Remember that when we tell Annie and the others about your wedding," Judge Caldwell teased.

"You promised forty-eight hours," Rafe reminded him, grinning. "I'd hate to think you were a man who didn't keep his word."

"Well," he drawled, his eyes twinkling. "I can't be held responsible if the news happens to slip out."

Bitsy laughed, Camille shook her head and I glared for a moment before chuckling softly.

"Judge, Annie warned me about your little surprises." I looked him in the eye, letting him see that I might just have something up my sleeve as well. "I suggest you not let anything *slip* for those forty-eight hours. Otherwise, I might just have to tell Annie about that other little surprise you've been holding onto until it's 'just the right time'."

Sam looked between me and his father, his brow furrowed. The judge's eyes narrowed as he studied me. Then he grinned and slapped his thigh. Laughing, he pointed a finger at me.

"Deal. I won't let it slip and neither will you."

"Deal."

"Will someone tell me what's going on?" Sam asked.

"Nope." I grinned at him.

"Sorry, son, you'll just have to wait and see," the Judge said easily.

"Jax?" Sam almost ground it out.

I shrugged and winked at the judge. "I gave my word."

"Then I am definitely telling my wife you kidnapped and threatened me with dire consequences if I told her about all this." He waved a hand at the gathering. "And I'm telling her you know about Dad's next little *surprise*."

Rafe moved to his best friend's side and rested a hand on his shoulder, his expression a mix of humor, understanding and something else I couldn't quite understand.

"Sam, think hard before you do that because you will be admitting to Annie—very possibly after the fact—that you knew your father had something up his sleeve and didn't warn her. I guarantee our getting married today will take a backseat to that. I don't think this is a battle you should take on."

"Not you too!" Sam looked at his best friend and then chuckled. "I have a feeling you're right. But you two." He pointed fingers at his father and me. "You are both the immovable object and I know better than to keep beating my head against you."

Laughing, I toasted him with the last of my champagne. This had to be the most unconventional wedding ever and that was saying a lot when it came to Mossy Creek.

12

Rafe and I managed to shut out the rest of the world until morning. Then responsibilities intruded. While he headed out to meet with Sam to go over what they needed to do to update the security systems for our various loved ones, I left to start what promised to be a very long day for me. Throughout it all, I never forgot the wedding band that hung from the same chain as Rafe's dog tag. I slipped the band on the chain before leaving the house to prevent the questions I knew it would raise. But now, dragging home as the sun went down, all I wanted was to slip it back on, a shower, a large drink, and a quiet evening with my husband.

Husband.

That really had a nice ring to it.

Smiling—and I seemed to be doing a great deal of that today—I pulled onto the wide, tree-lined drive. At the end of the drive, in almost the exact center of the property, waited home and husband.

And far too many cars.

I slowed and then stopped my F150. Hands on the steering wheel, I studied the half dozen cars lining the drive. Annie's Mustang. Quinn's SUV. Ciara's SUV. Meg's Discovery. Lucas' official SUV, with the Sheriff's Department logo on the driver's side door. Behind it was Drew's pickup. The gang was all here.

Damn.

Groaning, I considered climbing out of the car, shedding my clothes and shifting into my coyote form. That way I could hide in the trees until everyone went home. Surely, they wouldn't stay too late. Then Rafe and I could enjoy what was left of the evening.

Sitting there, studying the cars, I frowned as a niggle of worry forced its way in. They wouldn't be there if it wasn't important. The only question was if something happened I didn't know about yet. I wasn't going to find out sitting here. I slid the transmission into drive and continued toward the house, praying the proverbial other shoe hadn't decided to drop.

By the time I parked and started up the steps to the front porch, Rafe waited for me. I stopped, watching as he closed the front door behind him and hurried toward me. He took my hands and pulled me close. Then, realizing I was worried, he kissed me and stepped back.

"Rafe?"

"I'm sorry, Doc. I would have warned you if I'd had the chance. They were waiting here when I got home."

My stomach flipped and then flopped. "What happened?"

God, had they found out about yesterday?

"No." He grinned as his fingers found the chain around my neck and pulled it out. "They don't know."

"Then what?"

"It seems like everyone's been busy. Quinn said they found some things out based on what Miss Serena said that they want to discuss with us before bringing everyone in on it."

"All right." Even it if meant we wouldn't have the private evening I'd planned on. "Sorry."

He looked down at him, his brow furrowed. "For what?"

I glanced down the drive at the collection of vehicles. "For that."

"Doc, don't." He cupped my cheek and then pressed his forehead to mine. When he straightened, he smiled. "You need to accept that our friends look to you as the leader of our merry little band" Now he grinned, mischief dancing in his eyes. "At least they brought dinner."

As if that was the cue, my stomach rumbled, reminding me it had been much too long since lunch—assuming you could call a protein bar and a cup of coffee lunch.

"One more thing. Annie and Quinn brought the kids. She and Sam have the twins right now. Robbie and Ali are in your office doing their homework."

I smiled, affection filling me. I loved Ali, Robbie and the twins. Anytime I could see them was a good time. But, tired as I was, their presence meant something else. It meant this wouldn't be a late night, not with school the next day.

Still. . . .

I rested my head against his chest and sighed. I loved my friends. Really, I did. I also loved the fact they were as dedicated to protecting the town and everyone who lived here as was I. Every one of those waiting inside for us would risk his or her life to keep danger from coming to Mossy Creek.

But, damn it, couldn't they have waited one more day and let me have the evening alone with my husband?

Since standing out here only delayed the inevitable, I laced my fingers with Rafe's and together we made our way inside.

"Go clean up," Annie said as she entered from the kitchen. As she did, she smiled in affection. "Dinner will be ready by the time you're back."

"Thanks."

I took long enough on my way upstairs to greet everyone. When it came to Quinn, I looked at her, arching one eyebrow in question. She shrugged, gave a small smile, and tilted her head toward the stairs, her message clear. I wasn't going to learn anything until I came back down.

I had to admit Quinn and Annie had been right. The shower helped. Not only did it wash away the stress of the day, it also washed away the exhaustion that started dragging me down about an hour earlier. Now if they would just get to the point and let me know the reason for this impromptu get together, I'd be much happier.

I hoped.

"Where are the kids?" I nodded to Quinn in appreciation as she handed me a bottle of beer.

"We fed them earlier," Annie said. "So they're finishing their homework and playing while we talk."

I nodded, catching the looks passed between her, Quinn and Meg. Then there was the way the men looked at one another. They knew something and they weren't sure how to tell me. That did not make me feel any better. Maybe my news would make them feel better.

I hoped.

"How about I kick this off?" I finished fixing my burger. "I ran by the caretaker's cottage today to check on Maddy."

All conversation ended and everyone looked at me in various stages of surprise. Rafe was the exception. His disapproval radiated off of him and I knew we'd be discussing this once we were alone. Maybe by then, I would know what to say to reassure him that I hadn't lost my mind.

"You went alone?"

Oops, Quinn wasn't any happier than Rafe.

"I did, but only after making sure your mother knew what I was doing." I took a bite of the burger, giving them time to consider what I said. "And Dr. Pat was there. She's taken the rest of the week off so she can be with Maddy."

Rafe relaxed a little but Quinn still eyed me in a way I knew meant she wasn't happy.

"And?" Annie prompted.

"She's better. Her aura was more like what it used to be." It was going to be a long time before I forgave myself for not recognizing the change in her aura. "She and her mom have done a lot of talking. Maddy's still beating herself up about being an idiot, but she's trying to remember who besides Roben might have placed a binding on her. The key is figuring out when it happened."

Until then, we were shooting in the dark.

"Did she say anything else about what happened at The Road-house?" Meg asked.

I shook my head. "She tried apologizing again. I told her words were easy. Now she needs to show us that she's going to do everything she can to make sure something like that doesn't ever happen again."

"And?" Annie looked at me from where she sat on the sofa, Sam next to her. Concern darkened her blue eyes.

"She surprised me." I took a sip of beer. "She called Liam today. According to Dr. Pat, they talked for more than an hour."

Ciara sat up, her dinner forgotten. She might not realize how much her reaction betrayed. Whatever happened between her and Liam once we got Maddy home from Ireland, it hadn't changed what she felt for the man. She'd been hurting since he returned home but, like Quinn, was too stubborn to admit her feelings had been hurt. Now, however, anyone with eyes in their head and a working brain cell could see her interest.

"I got this from both Dr. Pat and Maddy. Seems like Maddy had been blowing off Liam and his questions as much as she did us. She apologized, told him about what happened the other day and promised to be fully cooperative going forward. To prove it, she answered all his questions and even offered to turn herself in to Lucas here if that made Liam feel better about leaving her here instead of returning her to Ireland to face charges."

"What did he say?" Ciara asked.

"They are to talk every day until he's confident she isn't just bull-shitting him. He admitted to Dr. Pat he was about to ask Lucas to pick her up and file a motion to terminate her probation. He's pretty pissed at our Maddy and isn't sure he believes her right now."

"Maddy's lucky." Annie spoke so seriously, I looked at her in concern. "Jason talked with me about her before I took office. He reminded me I was too close to her and would need to recuse myself if further legal action needed to be taken. Then he told me he was hearing rumors of her going to places like The Roadhouse, violating the terms of her probation."

"How the hell didn't we know about it?" Quinn asked. The look she gave Annie promised they would be discussing how Annie hadn't said something sooner.

"My guess?" Annie asked and we all nodded. "She didn't go far enough to have the cops called and no one wanted to worry us."

Or Maddy used her talents to influence anyone who might have said something so they didn't.

And that was something else we needed to find out.

"I'll have a chat with the bartenders." Lucas looked at me and nodded once. He'd obviously had the same thought as had I.

"So what brings you guys over tonight?" I smiled, hoping they realized I wasn't upset. "And why didn't you bring the others?"

The women looked at one another and the guys looked everywhere but at me. This was not good, not good at all.

"Well?" I leaned back, looking from one to another.

"Meg and Beth spent part of yesterday and today looking into Carson Alexander and what happened to him after he left town. Ciara and I started a deep dive into everyone from Stephanie Dinsmore to Meg's maternal bloodline to Sawyer and Mia," Quinn began. "We're trying to find anything that ties them all together besides Mossy Creek."

"Why don't you start with Alexander?" I suggested, linking my hand with Rafe's as he handed me another beer before sitting on the arm of my chair.

"We'll start with what happened after Preston's funeral." Meg pulled out her phone and swiped a finger across the screen. I didn't need to look to know she had notes on it she referred to.

"After Annie's granddad read Preston's will and Carson showed his true colors, he left town. It wasn't easy to find, but he made his way to the West Coast. For six months or so, he traveled between San Francisco and Northern California. He had minimal contact with his parents during that time. After Mr. and Mrs. Alexander moved to Tennessee, he showed up there once that we were able to confirm. There is an old police report from that time. Apparently, Carson got drunk and became so out-of-control that his sister called the police.

Charges weren't filed but the cops made sure Carson left. He basically dropped out of sight until he showed up here in Mossy Creek three years after Preston's death."

"What did he do during that time to make a living?" Rafe asked.

"I'm working on getting that information," Meg said. "But, for the moment, I don't know."

"We need to know that and we need to know where he's been," I said.

And if he's still alive.

"What else?" Rafe asked.

"Miss Olivia is going to talk with Miss Peggy and some of the others who might be able to help tell us more about the last time he was in town. As soon as I know anything, you will." Another swipe of her finger across the cell phone's screen and Meg glanced at me. "I did manage to confirm Miss Serena's suspicions about there being a falling out between Carson and the rest of his family after she last saw him. The attorney who handled Mrs. Alexander's estate made copious notes about his meetings with her as she drew up her final will. She was very open about why she was leaving him out of the will. The attorney's retired since then, but his partner is still practicing. I had a discussion with him this afternoon. He promised to get me copies of all pertinent documents tomorrow. Apparently, Mrs. Alexander left instructions to do whatever they could to assist Miss Serena if Carson ever tried to cause her trouble. He said he considers the fact we are making inquiries cause enough."

"We know what Miss Serena suspected about the falling out. Did this attorney give you any details?" Rafe asked.

"Nothing much. He said he needed to review his partner's notes." Meg held up a hand before anyone could interrupt. "I believe him. He wasn't with the firm when all this happened, so he doesn't have any firsthand knowledge. My gut tells me he saw enough on a quick review to know he had a duty to share the information. That means we need to know whatever he can tell us."

"All right." I thought for a moment, considering the possible implications. "Did he say if he knows if Carson is still alive?"

Meg shook her head. "So far, we haven't found any indication he's died, but we have no data on him that is newer than ten years old."

"Get me the pertinents. I'll run it through law enforcement databases," Lucas said.

"Lucas, you can't," Annie reminded him. "Not yet at any rate."

"She's right." Quinn reached for her husband's hand, understanding and approval reflected on her face. Then she looked at me. "He has to have probable cause that a crime has been or will be committed. He doesn't have that yet. If he were to run this bastard just because of what he did so long ago, he risks not only losing his certification as a peace officer but charges as well."

I thought about what she said.

"This goes for each of you." I pinned them with a firm look. "I don't want any of you doing anything that puts your professional lives in jeopardy. That could play into the hands of whoever has been targeting us as much as misusing our talents. We do this right and we do it solid. But we don't put the town or our loved ones in danger because we cut corners."

"I agree," Rafe said. "Whoever is behind everything that's been happening, we know a couple of things. They are patient but that patience is starting to wear thin."

"What do you mean?" Quinn asked.

"If this goes back to Miss Serena and Carson, this plan has been in play for decades. So why start taking direct action all of a sudden and why so close together?"

I considered what he said for a moment and then nodded. He put to voice something that bothered me from the moment I heard of Judith's kidnapping and everything Quinn went through with her ex. Looking back, in a period of two years, less really, Mossy Creek had seen more attacks on its very fiber than it had in the last quarter century or more.

"Could it be whoever it is recognized that with us coming home, things would change here, helping strengthen the town?" Ciara asked.

"No." I frowned slightly as I tried to figure it out. "Each time, circumstances brought us home that we had no control over. It is more like we were lured here instead of coming home and forcing the bad guy's hand."

Quinn nodded grimly. "Jax is right. We left of our own accord after high school. Meg grew up away from here. But family circumstances brought us back. None of us have asked why our loved ones were targeted. We just came home to deal with it and make sure they were all right."

"So what's our next step?" Sam asked.

"We keep doing what we've been doing. We keep our eyes and ears open. We continue looking into Carson as well as into everyone from Stephanie to Mia and Sawyer. Annie, you and Lucas keep your ears to the ground when it comes to trouble in the county. You two are uniquely situated to know if something out of the ordinary happens."

"What else do we know about Carson?" Drew asked from where he stood behind Meg's chair.

I glanced at Meg, hoping she found something we could sink our teeth into.

"Preston had a sister as well. I asked Miss Serena about her. She didn't meet the sister until after Preston's death. She went through a period of time when she thought she wanted to be a nun. Her parents didn't discourage her but did suggest she take time to do service without taking her vows first. So the sister did just that. She went to Africa and worked with the Peace Corps and other groups there. She didn't come home until a year after Preston's death. By then, she'd decided the life of a nun wasn't for her.

"She initially moved in with her parents but quickly got her own place, went to college and graduated. She went to work as a teacher in the local school district. She married and had two children. Those children have married and had their own kids.

"Financially, the daughter and her family are comfortable. Not rich but they had enough that, along with the scholarships and grants their kids received, they didn't go into debt putting them through college. There are no legal bumps except for the occasional traffic ticket and a couple of minor drug busts/drinking busts for some of the grandkids. On paper at least, they look like the All-American family. A little judicious digging beyond the official databases shows the family is about evenly split between Others and normals. Family talents are much like what you'd expect. Kitchen witches, a couple of hedge witches, nothing else popped there. Certainly nothing like what Miss Serena and the others saw with Carson."

"Do we know anything about him after he last left here?" Lucas asked.

"Some but, as I said earlier, we don't have anything for the last decade." Meg once again consulted her notes. "He surfaced back in California a few months after he tried to bind Miss Serena. He stayed in that part of the country, dropping out of sight every few years for anywhere from a month to half a year, until we lost track of him for good.

"Before then, he married and divorced three times. Two of the three wives alleged mental abuse. There are records for two children from the second marriage. I'm still looking into them and looking into whether Carson fathered any kids out of wedlock."

"What about criminal history?" Annie asked.

Meg shook her head and looked at Ciara.

"I called in a favor. Don't worry, it won't come back on any of us," she said before I could object. "My source could find nothing for the last ten or eleven years. Before then, Carson filed for bankruptcy several times. Each of those times, he skipped out just ahead of the authorities when it was discovered monies had mysteriously disappeared. Somehow, he managed to avoid prosecution. My best guess is he used his talents to influence anyone who could have filed charges against him."

"The attorney did say Carson made noises about breaking his mother's will. The sister stopped him cold. She authorized the attorney to file for repayment of all the loans their parents had given him over the years. Carson finally had to sign an acknowledgment that he had no rights to his mother's estate. In return, the sister released him from the debt to the estate. The attorney told me he doubted Miss Serena ever knew because the sister was trying to protect her and Ashley."

It made sense in a way. But it also made our jobs now more difficult.

"Has the sister had any contact with him since then?"

"Not that I know of but I'm going to try to talk to her tomorrow," Meg said.

I thought for a moment. "Hold off on that. Let's not tip our hand just yet. If he's not involved, we'd only be bringing up bad memories for the sister. If he is involved, I don't want to put her in the middle if we don't have to. At least not until we have a better idea about what's going on."

"So what do we do now?" Drew asked.

"Exactly what all of you have been. I'll talk more with Maddy and Dr. Pat. It's obvious the initial binding had to have happened when she was still living here or after she moved to Dallas to go to college." There was more. There had to be. But what?

"Ciara, can you look into whether or not there is any kind of connection between Roben and Carson or anyone in his family?"

"I'll start on it as soon as I get home."

I looked at her, almost reading her thoughts. Not that I needed to be a mind reader to do so. Not when they were written so plainly on her face.

"Ciara, if you need to talk to Liam about it, do it. Just let the rest of us know."

Before anything else could be said, Ali appeared from my office. She stood at on the landing, looking down at us. Her mouth opened to say something only to snap shut as an excited gleam shone in her eyes. Seeing it, and seeing where she was looking, I cursed silently. We—I—so did not need her spilling the proverbial beans tonight. Hoping she understood, I grinned, slowly closed one eye in a wink and lifted a finger to my lips. Then I was on my feet and moving up the stairs to see what Ali wanted.

"Auntie Jax!" Ali threw her arms around me the moment we were in my study.

"Hey, kiddo." I hugged her and then sat back on my heels. "Don't get me wrong, but why the over-the-top greeting?"

Your aura looks different again. Like it's really happy and dancing and stuff. Did something happen?"

Leave it to her to see what the adults hadn't.

I so needed to remember to keep a lid on my emotions.

I held a hand out to Robbie who stood several steps back watching us. He grinned and hurried to stand next to Ali. I hugged them both and then looked at them, my head cocked to one side.

"I need you two to help me keep a secret for a little bit. Can you do that?"

They nodded, eyes wide.

"You have to promise not to tell anyone, not even your parents, until I say you can. It won't be long." Especially since I knew the judge would stick to his threat to tell Annie at the end of forty-eight hours.

"We promise, Auntie Jax," Robbie said and I grinned. Over the last few weeks, he'd taken to calling me that as often as he did "Dr. Jax".

"Then what would the two of you say if I told you Rafe and I got married yesterday?" I laughed as they launched themselves at me, hugging me even as we fell to the floor in a tangle of arms and legs.

"That's great, Auntie Jax. Mr. Rafe's cool." Robbie grinned as he hugged me once more before standing up.

"Does that mean we can call him Uncle Rafe now?" Ali wanted to know.

"Once we tell everyone. But not before. Remember, it's a secret for a little while longer."

"How come, Auntie Jax?" Robbie asked.

"We want to tell everyone at one time, kiddo." Which meant I needed to figure out how before these two or the Judge let the cat out of the bag.

"Are you going to have a party?" Ali's excitement at the prospect made me smile.

"We are." Somehow.

"Cool." Ali climbed to her feet and the two of them pulled me up.

"Okay, what did you need?" I asked as I stood.

"Oh, we have math homework and there's a problem we can't figure out," Ali said and Robbie nodded grimly.

"Okay, let me see if I can help. Then we'll go down for dessert."

Spurred on by the prospect of chocolate cake baked by Mary Kate, they hurried to where their books and notebooks waited. I followed and my thoughts went back to Carson Alexander. These two, and everyone else in Mossy Creek, were why I'd do whatever it took to protect the town. If that meant having to deal with someone from Miss Serena's past, so be it.

So why did I keep thinking the danger came from a different quadrant?

And what if it came from somewhere closer to home?

A few minutes later, the kids thundered downstairs, racing ahead of me. I stepped into the guest bathroom and closed the door behind me. After locking the door, I pulled out my phone. It didn't take long for Miss Serena to answer.

"It's me, ma'am."

"Jackie." She sounded better than when I spoke with her earlier, thankfully. "What can I do for you?"

"This may sound strange, but I was wondering if there's a list or database or something of all the Others in town, their families, their talents, that sort of thing. I know we have the historical records, but I am interested in something more up-to-date."

"Maybe?" She sounded close to uncertain. "I have no doubt that between Peggy, Olivia, Mary Kate, myself and Judith, we know most of what you're asking. But I know of nothing that's been formally put together. Why?"

"It may be nothing, but it may also be important." I wish I knew which. "But it will help us figure out our weapons if trouble does finally come."

"Let me talk to Olivia. If anyone's compiled such a list, she will know about it."

If I knew Miss Olivia, she would compile the list if she didn't already have access to it.

"Thanks." I shook my head as Ali yelled up the stairs for me to hurry up so they could have cake. As I did, I remembered something else. "Miss Serena, one more question. I've always assumed the judge is a normal. But he's not, is he?"

She chuckled and I had my answer. Still, it would be nice if she confirmed it one way or another.

"No, he's not. He's an Other. He simply doesn't advertise the fact." She chuckled softly.

"And his talent?"

"Talking to the dead."

Well, that explained how he knew what Annie's grandfather wanted and why he kept the law office until Annie returned home.

"Why?"

"It's just something I'd been wondering about." I'd explain later. "What about the rest of the family?"

"Camille is a Sensitive. Sam hasn't shown any tendencies. Again, why?"

"Have you or anyone else checked Robbie to see if he's an Other?" I considered how I'd seen Ali's aura expand to include the boy on several occasions. I'd assumed it was because she was trying to protect him, especially after the trouble with Mia. But now. . . now, I wondered if she wasn't shielding him for some other reason.

"Jackie, what's going on?"

"I'm not sure." That much was true. "How about we discuss it tomorrow morning?" Maybe I'd have some answers by then.

Or at least some idea to explain why I asked.

"All right."

We chatted a few moments more and then ended the call. By the time I joined the others downstairs, I knew there was one thing I needed to do before anything else could be discussed.

"Ali," I said as I stepped into the great room. "Come here, sweetheart."

The eight-year-old ran to me. As she did, her mother looked at me in question. Man, I hoped Quinn—not to mention Annie—was ready for this.

"Ali, I have a question for you and I need you to be completely honest with me. You aren't in any trouble. I promise."

"Jax," Quinn started.

I shook my head.

"Okay," Ali said, her dark brows drawing together as she tried to figure out what I was going to ask.

"Ali, I know Robbie's your best friend."

She nodded.

"I know you want to do everything you can to protect him, especially after what happened before. Right?"

Another nod.

"Sweetheart, have you been shielding him?"

She cocked her head to one side, as if trying to figure out what I meant.

"Ali, are you extending your aura over his?" I wasn't sure how else to put it.

Quinn and Ciara gasped. Then their eyes narrowed as they looked between the kids. I didn't spare them much more than a glance as I turned my attention back to Ali.

"It's okay, kiddo. In fact, I'm really proud of you for trying to take care of him. Just answer my question." I needed to know if she was doing it consciously or unconsciously.

"I'm not in any trouble?" She cast a quick look behind me in her mother's direction.

"Not one little bit. You have my word on it."

She smiled a little before looking at the floor. "I've been doing it."

"That's okay, Ali. Why have you been doing it?"

"Because I don't want anything else to happen to him."

I nodded and pulled her close. I could think of several explanations for what she meant. Now to figure out which was right.

"Okay, Ali." I sat on the floor and pulled her into my lap. Then I held a hand out to Robbie and waited for him to join us. "Ali, I want you to pull back your shielding. When she does, Robbie, you're probably going to feel a little different. Don't be afraid. Just let me see what happens."

"Okay, Auntie Jax," they replied in unison.

"Jax?" Annie stood next to Quinn, holding her hand.

"Let's see what happens."

I waited, watching as Ali closed her eyes. As she did, I focused on the energies surrounding her and Robbie. Slowly, almost reluctantly, the energies withdrew from around Robbie and snapped back into place around Ali. Quinn's quick intake of breath told me she'd been watching as well. I tightened my arms around Ali, hugging her close. then I turned my attention to Robbie.

Oh my.

Robbie stood there, holding my outstretched hand. The soft colors of Ali's projected shields were gone. But that didn't mean energies didn't swirl around him. I glanced first at Annie and then at Sam. Laughter bubbled up inside of me and I fought to keep it from emerging. Now was not the time.

"Robbie, do me a favor. I'm going to let go of your hand. When I do, hold it right there. Turn you palm up to the sky. Okay?"

He looked uncertain but he nodded. I let his hand go. Then I held mine, palm up, next to his. A moment later, an eagle's feather appeared on my palm. Someone, maybe Ciara, chuckled softly. Everyone else remained where they were. The room was silent, so silent I wondered if anyone remembered to breathe.

"Robbie, watch."

I concentrated and focused on manipulating the energies around my hand. Soon, the feather lifted. Robbie's mouth formed an "O" of surprise as the feather floated above my palm. Then it slowly turned until it stood on its hollow shaft. Still focusing, I smiled slightly as it began to spin slowly on its shaft before floating over to his upraised hand.

"That's pretty neat, isn't it?" I asked and he nodded, a grin on his face. "Would you like to be able to do something like that?"

"Yes, ma'am."

"Then let's see what you can do."

Carefully, I slid my hand under his, so close I could feel the warmth of his skin even though our hands didn't touch. For a moment or two, I studied his aura, trying to figure out what part was his and what part was a remnant of weeks, maybe months of Ali shielding him.

"Okay, Robbie. I want you to focus on the feather. Let your eyes go wide. Relax. Tell me what you see."

He didn't say anything for a moment or two. "Everything looks funny, Auntie Jax, like it's out of focus. Except it isn't. But there are different colors and they are moving in and out and all around the feather and everything."

"Very good, kiddo. What you're seeing is the energy that makes up everything in our world. Not everyone figures out how to see it."

"Can Ali see it?"

I glanced at Ali and nodded, letting her know that she could answer.

"I do. Isn't it cool?" She sounded so excited that I winked at her in approval.

"What do all the different colors mean?" Robbie wanted to know.

"We'll talk about those later," I promised. "But let's see if you can do anything with the feather."

"How do I make it dance?" He sounded so excited I smiled.

"Focus on the energies around the feather." I spoke softly, gently, directing him on what to do. As I did, I watched as he reached out and clumsily began to manipulate the energies. The feather wobbled and he inhaled sharply. As he did, the feather bent, almost as if he grabbed top and bottom and pulled them toward one another. "Easy, Robbie. That's it."

The energies relaxed as he did. The feather once again stood tall above his palm.

"Watch what I do."

I focused, gently teasing the energies until they moved clockwise around the feather. It rose slightly higher above his palm. Then it began turning. He looked quickly at me and then back.

"Can I try?"

I nodded and eased my control of the energies, letting him take over. The feather tilted this way and that. But he soon had it spinning very slowly above his palm. He grinned gaily and looked at me, losing his control over what was happening. The feather floated toward the floor. I caught it and handed it to him.

"I think you're going to be joining Ali in her lessons with Miss Serena. But your mom can help you too." I hugged him tightly. As I did, I pulled Ali into the hug. Then I looked at their very stunned parents.

"What just happened?" Sam asked.

"Your son just proved what I've suspected for a while now." I climbed to my feet and moved to where Rafe stood. "I'll talk with Miss Serena about it in the morning. But, unless I miss my guess, Robbie takes after your mother, Sam."

"Mom?"

I rolled my eyes. "Yes, your mother. Camille is a sensitive and the judge talks to the dead."

"I knew it!" Annie practically shouted it as she pointed a finger at her husband. "I told you he was too dam-darned smug when I first came back to town."

"How did you figure it out?" Ciara asked.

"I caught a glimpse a couple of times that made me wonder if Ali wasn't somehow protecting him." I looked down at my goddaughter as it started to make sense. "You were protecting him, weren't you?"

She nodded. "He said everything felt like the world was crushing down on him."

"Robbie, do you feel that way now?"

He looked a little scared but he nodded once.

"Okay. Come here." I waited until he stood in front of me. "I'm not going to make your talents go away. But I am going to make it easier for you until Miss Serena teaches you how to do it on your own. Okay?"

Another nod.

"Annie, come here." Once she joined us, I continued. "Robbie, what I'm going to do is help you build your own shields. Think of it as a form of protection that will keep you from feeling all the emotions people around you are feeling."

It didn't take long. When I finished, I stepped back. Annie rushed to him, Sam just behind her. They held him close, assuring him they were proud of him. Then I realized Ali stood halfway behind me, watching her parents as they tried to process what just happened.

"Jax?" Quinn asked softly as Lucas lifted Ali and, as she wrapped her legs around his waist, settled her at his hip.

"Your daughter saw what we missed. She's been shielding him since Mia," I said softly. "You're going to need to talk to Miss Serena about that because she shouldn't have been able to. Hell, I'm not sure I could, not for as long as she has.

For a moment, Quinn looked like she might run for the hills. Then she nodded., her gaze going from Ali to Robbie as his parents reassured him they were proud of him. When he asked Annie if this meant they'd be taking lessons together, I pursed my lips to keep from laughing. Quinn's eyes twinkled and she reached over to ruffle Ali's hair.

"I think you guys need to take the kids home," I said softly. "We can talk about this and the rest of it tomorrow."

"I'll go get their things," Ciara volunteered.

With that, the evening wound down. Rafe told Annie not to worry about cleaning the kitchen. We'd take care of it and get their dishes back to them the next day. She nodded, her expression still a little dazed as she took Robbie's backpack from Ciara. One thing you can say about Mossy Creek: life is never dull.

13

"This is the final straw."

I paced the length of Meg's office. Fury coursed through me. My parents—and I hated admitting any kind of relationship to them, especially after today—had gone too far. It was bad enough they did all they could to harass Aunt Bitsy and me but this? This was too much. Now they were striking out at innocents and I wouldn't stand for it.

"Jax, sit down." Meg looked up from the pleadings she'd been studying.

"I don't want to sit down."

What I wanted was to find my parents and teach them a lesson they wouldn't soon forget.

"Jax, we won't get anything accomplished as long as you're pacing like a caged animal."

I looked at Bitsy and nodded once. She was right. Not that it eased my anger any. A moment later, I took the free chair in front of Meg's desk. When I did, Bitsy leaned over and grasped my hand. As she did, she assured me we would deal with this together, just as we always did.

"Who else got hit with these?"

I waved a hand at the stack of filings on the desk. Three of them had been served on me that morning as I arrived at the clinic. The process server looked apologetic as he climbed out of his car and approached before I could go inside. Since I knew him—we'd gone to school together once upon a time—I understood. Frankly, it hadn't surprised me when I saw him waiting there. The last I heard, he worked as an investigator for a law firm in Denton. That explained how he got the task of serving the various filings. I felt for him because I knew how his family would react.

To say my parents were vindictive was putting it mildly. I'd never been the daughter they wanted. I was too independent, too head-strong and had the temerity of being an Other. Worse, when my grandfather died, he'd left dear old dad a relatively small trust fund to be administered by Bitsy and some stock in the family business. The rest was split between Bitsy and me. Bitsy turned out to be an excellent trustee and she did everything she could to protect and grow the business. That included kicking my father off the board when she learned he tried to sell his shares against the express condi-tions of Granddad's will. She bought them through a proxy and split them between the two of us.

Since then, they'd tried to convince us to return the stocks—and pay a penalty for enforcing Granddad's will. When that didn't work, they filed a lawsuit. Which was promptly thrown out by the trial judge. Now they were trying to throw out the will, use intestacy laws to get what they saw as my father's "fair share", cutting me out in the process.

And as if that wasn't enough, there were even slander allegations and more. I'd been too angry after reading the first filing to keep reading. When I contacted Bitsy, she sounded a cross between resigned and amused. Resigned because she'd played this game with my father all their lives. Amused because she knew we would prevail this time just as we did every other time. So she let me rant for a bit and then told me to meet her at Meg's office where we would draft a formal response to this latest attack.

By the time I arrived, I knew it was worse than I thought. My parents had really outdone themselves. Not only had they filed multiple lawsuits against Bitsy and me but they targeted others around town as well. The only questions was how many and what it would cost in the long run to deal with the problem once and for all.

"Meg?"

"I'm not sure I have the final count, but they are suing Miss Peggy and Janny for denial of service, slander, and several other spurious allegations. Wanda's Salon has also been named as have the bank, the B&B, and half a dozen other businesses. Caldwell Construction and Powell Properties have also been served.

"But they aren't the only ones serving paper today. Attorneys for both Sawyer and Mia have filed change of venue motions. Even though Annie and Judge Caldwell are not taking part in their trials, they have filed motions for recusal for both of them as well. My last count is at least a dozen people and businesses have been served this morning."

"What are they trying to do?" Bitsy asked.

"That is a very good question. The fact their motions come at the same time the attorneys for both Mia and Sawyer filed their motions has all my internal alarms going off," Meg admitted.

"Any connection between the attorneys?" I asked.

"Not that I know of but I'll be checking."

"Meg, even if the attorney took Daniel and Emma on as clients on a contingency basis, wouldn't they have to pay filing fees and that sort of thing?" Bitsy asked and I grinned at her refusal to call my father by his "chosen" name of Dante. Never one to be pretentious, Bitsy hated the way parents personified the word.

"That would be how it usually works in contingency cases." Meg chewed her lower lip for a moment, clearly thinking about what to say next. "Here's something else we need to consider, except for some of the cases filed against the two of you, none of the filings are what most attorneys would touch as contingency cases. They are more nuisance filings and not worth the time or effort—or the possibility of being sanctioned by the Bar."

No big surprise there.

"Then there's the simple fact those cases don't have the potential for a large payout associated with most contingency cases."

"Then we need to find out where the money to file and pay the retainers for those cases is coming from because I guarantee my parents don't have it." Not unless they had a secret bank account somewhere we hadn't been able to find yet. Now it was my turn to think for a bit. "Do you know anything about the attorney representing them?"

Meg shook her head. "Not a thing. Beth checked the Bar listings and his online presence after Bitsy called to say she'd been served. He passed the Bar two years ago and moved to Dallas three months ago. He'd been in West Texas before then and moved here when his wife, who is a teacher, accepted a job with one of the local school districts."

"The timing of all this bothers me." And that was putting it mildly. "Put someone on doing a deep dive into both my parents. Find the money and find out if there is anything tying them to Roben, Maddy, even Carson Alexander. Hell, run them against all the players in everything that's happened since Spud's murder. There's something there, some connection. We just haven't found it yet."

Meg nodded and made a note. "Now, how do you want to respond to these?" She waved a hand at the stack of filings directly related to Bitsy and me as well as to the company.

Before I could answer, Bitsy placed a hand on mine, stopping me. Her eyes burned with a depth of anger I'd never seen before. Worse —or maybe better. Who can tell in situations like this—it was an anger I shared. I knew without asking that she felt we were finally at the point where we could no longer try to play nice with my parents and that was fine by me.

"I don't care what it takes, Meg, or how much it costs. I want the two of them stopped once and for all. It was bad enough when they were only going after me and the company. I held back when they started including Jax in their misguided attempts to extort the estate and the company because I didn't want to make life harder for her. So I'd toss them a few thousand here and there, knowing it was little more than emotional blackmail, but it was worth it to keep her out of their line of fire."

I looked at Bitsy in surprise. "What?" And why was I just now hearing about this?

"Hush." Bitsy once again reached for my hand. "They threatened to move away, taking you with them, after Dad died. I knew what your life would be like and, yes, I paid them off to keep them here where I could keep an eye on you."

"Bitsy." My throat tightened with emotion. It didn't surprise me that she'd paid my parents off to keep them from taking me away. I'd always known she loved me like a daughter. Hell, she'd been my mother in all but the biological sense. Still, it infuriated me to know her feelings for me had been used to bilk her out of anything and especially by the two people who should have my back and never did.

"Don't." Her eyes flashed.

I clamped my mouth shut and then nodded. "Thank you." It wasn't enough but it had to do, for the moment at least.

"My apologies, Meg." Bitsy smiled slightly. "You wanted to know what you should do now."

Meg nodded much as I had a moment before.

"Daniel—who will never be a Dante no matter how hard he tries —and Emma have gone too far this time. If Jax agrees, I want you to do whatever it takes to shut them down once and for all. I will get you a full accounting of everything I've given them over the years."

"I assume you have documentation about how and why the payouts were made."

Now Bitsy's smile turned every bit as predatory as mine could be. "Of course."

"Good." Meg sat back and thought for a moment. As she did, I could almost see her mental gears turning. "I'm going to see what criminal charges we might be able to bring against them. If the statute of limitations hasn't run on even one of them, we've got them for extortion and blackmail at the very least."

"I'll have it to you by end of day," Bitsy promised.

"What else?" Meg looked between Bitsy and me, knowing neither of us would be satisfied unless every person hurt by my parents had been made whole at least financially.

"For everything we're parties to, file motions to dismiss with prejudice or whatever the proper legal terminology is. Include a demand for attorneys fees and expenses. Then file countersuits for anything and everything you think we can prove against them. If you think we can get a judge to grant it, file for restraining orders against them as well. Look into the attorney and file for sanctions if it looks like he either didn't do his homework or is abusing the system. I'm tired of playing this game and I will not let them pull the rest of the town into it."

"What can we do to help the others they targeted this time?" Aunt Bitsy asked.

"Annie and I already represent most of them on other matters. Annie won't be able to take part in this but I'll pull Ciara in to help if the others agree."

I nodded even though I still had a hard time thinking of the kick ass Texas Ranger—or should I say former Texas Ranger—as an attorney.

"Beth is contacting those we know are included in this round of filings and asking them to come in for a meeting among everyone. If they agree, we'll file the necessary paperwork listing us as their counsel of record and then we'll file the appropriate responses and counter suits."

"Is there any way Jax and I, and possibly even Powell Properties, can join and go after them?"

Meg thought for a moment and a slight smile touched her lips. She had something in mind and I had a feeling I was going to like it.

"I think so, but it could be expensive."

Bitsy waved her hand again, dismissing Meg's concern. "Anyone who needs help covering the expenses will have it."

I had a feeling she would set up another "foundation". Bitsy loved this town and the people in it. She wouldn't hesitate to use any means she could to protect them. If that meant opening her pocketbook, she would without a second thought. Since I agreed with her, I'd be writing a check myself and I knew others who would as well.

"Let me do some research and see what the others have to say. Then I'll file the appropriate responses as well as our countersuits. Before I do, I'll go over everything with both of you and I'll be coordinating with the company's corporate counsel."

"Thanks, Meg." I glanced at my watch and blew out a breath. "Sorry, but if you don't need me for anything else, I have to run."

"Go on, Jax. I have a couple of other things to discuss with Meg."

I narrowed my eyes at my aunt. "Don't do anything I wouldn't do."

Bitsy grinned wickedly. "I always do things you wouldn't do, Jax. You really are much too conservative."

Laughing, I climbed to my feet. "No, you do things I wouldn't do because you love to try to scandalize me."

"True, and I usually manage to succeed."

Since she had a point, I nodded. Then, after saying my goodbyes, I left. When I stepped outside, I paused and looked around. Mossy Creek has never been what one would consider "normal". But, unlike so many towns, we look out for our own. Sure, there have always been a few malcontents or those like Meg's maternal grandparents who would love to see the Others in town long gone. But they were the minority. Now my parents were trying to tear the town apart and I planned on stopping them. Meeting with Meg and Bitsy was step one. The next step was stopping by the café to talk to Miss Peggy and Janny.

The bell over the door jingled as I entered the café. I hadn't taken two steps when Miss Peggy appeared from the kitchen. All five-foot nothing of her marched around the counter in my direction. The look on her face had me swallowing hard and seriously considering backing out the door.

"Not one word, Jacqueline Elizabeth Powell." She stopped in front of me and waved her finger under my nose. I nodded even as I shuffled my feet and fidgeted like a kid called to the principal's office.

"Miss Peggy."

"I said not one word." Her eyes flashed and it took every ounce of courage not to step back. "I don't want to hear a single word of apology from you, Jax. What your parents are doing is on them and them alone and they've finally overplayed their hand. This is the chance we've all been looking forward to—and I do mean all. It's our chance to put them in their place once and for all."

All around us, heads nodded in agreement. From the far end of the café, I heard Les Robach say, "Preach it, Peggy."

"I will close the doors here permanently before I give them a single penny. But I won't have to. I *know* it."

Hearing the slight emphasis she put on "know", I relaxed a little. One of Miss Peggy's talents as an Other is a touch of foresight (which is the only reasonable explanation for how she always knows what's going on, usually before those involved know). But, if she was wrong, she wouldn't have to close. I'd make sure of it, even if it emptied out my own bank account. I would not let my parents—God, I hated calling them that—hurt anyone else. Their reign of terror was over.

"You listen to her, Jax." Mala Okoro's voice held a hint of the Islands. She and her husband moved to Mossy Creek a little more than ten years ago. Once here, they bought the old Zahn place, a three-story Tudor-style house. It took them two years to bring the place up to code and transform it from what had been the local "haunted house" on Halloween to a B&B that now ranked as one of the best in this part of the country.

"I appreciate it, all of you." I did my best to make eye contact with everyone there. As I did, it dawned on me that most of them were the most recent targets of Dante and Emma. Others had been taken advantage of by them in the past. "Since you're all here, Meg's going to be touching base with you." If she hadn't already. "Aunt Bitsy and I would appreciate it if you'd agree to meet with her. We have a plan forming and Meg will run it down for you."

"Does it include running them out of town on a rail?" Janny asked as she appeared from the kitchen.

"Something like that."

Murmurs of approval filled the air.

"Don't worry, Jax. We'll meet with Meg. Consider this our pre-meeting." Miss Peggy's grin was even more predatory than Meg's had been earlier.

"Thank you." I slid an arm around her shoulders and gave her a quick hug. "Thank all of you. Since I returned home, you've each been there for me. Now I want to do something to show my appreciation." I waved off their objections. "Miss Peggy, I'm picking up the tab for everyone here. If you'll just let me know what I owe later today, I'll take care of it."

"Jax," she started.

"Please. I want to do this."

I walked down the sidewalk, a go-cup of coffee in hand, considering what I'd seen and heard the last few minutes at the café. My parents might have thought they were striking a blow against the town with this latest stunt of theirs but it had been far from that. Everyone was pulling together. I wasn't going to argue with that, no matter what the reason.

My cellphone buzzed and I reached up to tap the Bluetooth earbud. "Dr. Powell."

"Jax, your parents just proved they are complete idiots. Not that there's ever been any doubt about it."

"Lexi?"

Lexi Smithson was not only Amy's best friend but she was also another of Miss Serena's proteges. Her family was odd even by Mossy Creek standards. Her father, Jacob, was a wizard with all things mechanical. Her mother was a stereotypical uptight Bible Belt Bible thumper. It made Lexi's home life growing up interesting to say the least. Especially once the family's dead started returning to the homestead after they were buried. It started with her granny and progressed from there. They weren't zombies or vampires, none of what you'd see in modern fiction. They were dead and needed regular "treatments" from the local mortician but they were most definitely sentient and as "alive" as they had been before death—much to her mother's chagrin.

"What did my parents do?"

And did I really want to know?

"They are suing my dad, claiming he sabotaged their Mercedes when they brought it to him for a tune-up six months ago."

I stopped, forgetting I was in the middle of the sidewalk. "You've got to be kidding me." The very idea Jacob would do anything to harm a vehicle was beyond belief.

"Nope, and it gets better. They also filed—probably with encouragement from my mother—complaints with the city about our dearly returned."

For a moment, I didn't say anything. I couldn't. I opened my mouth and nothing came out.

"Lexie, tell your dad and the others not to worry about it. I'll deal with those two. If you haven't done so already, get copies of anything they had served on your father to Meg."

"Jax, that's not why I called."

"I know. But they are trying to bluff the entire town and Bitsy and I aren't going to let them get away with it. Not this time." When she didn't say anything, I cursed loudly enough Miss Treacher looked at me in surprise as she walked by. I silently apologized before realizing Lexie hadn't explained.

"What else did they do?"

"They sent letters to the school board and my principal questioning my suitability to be teaching 'our impressionable youth'."

I started to answer and then snapped my mouth shut. Speaking of the devil—or, to be more accurate, devils. My parents rounded the corner and headed in my direction. From the smirk on Dante's face to the way Emma look so smug, I didn't doubt for a moment they'd been waiting for me, especially since my truck was parked nearby.

"I'm about to have a close encounter of the unwanted kind. Talk to Meg. I'll check on you later."

I tapped the earbud again, ending the call. Then I pulled my phone. I didn't try to hide the fact I was doing something. I doubted either of them would realize I was activating the video camera. Now to see if I could get them to incriminate themselves, preferably before I decided to pound them into greasy stains on the sidewalk.

"Jacqueline." Dante drawled my name, making sure his distaste and disappointment in me were clear.

"Hello, Daddy." Two could play that name.

"Always so disrespectful." Disgust dripped from Emma's voice.

"You have to earn my respect and neither of you have done anything to do so." Still holding my phone, I crossed my arms, being careful to make sure the phone was aimed at the two of them. "That's certainly true after today."

One corner of my father's lips twitched upward before he controlled the reaction. "We are well within our rights to protect ourselves against those in this town who are out to get us."

"True." I nodded, as if in agreement. From the looks on their faces, they didn't know where I was going with this. Good. "Just as it is within our rights to protect ourselves against you and your machinations."

"Perhaps we can come to an agreement that benefits all of us."

Oh, he was smooth, but not as smooth as he thought.

"Gee, Daddy, what would your attorney say if he knew you and Moms there waylaid me in the middle of downtown and offered to enter into a settlement negotiation?" I cocked my head and made a show of studying them. "I have a feeling he wouldn't approve. Besides, I have no intention of giving you a single penny."

"Don't be a fool, Jacqueline," Emma hissed as she reached out and grabbed my arm before I could walk off. "We'll ruin everyone in this town if you force our hand."

I looked at her hand where it rested on my arm and then I looked back at my parents. No, not my parents. They hadn't been that for a very long time. Any love I once felt for them died a little each time they attacked me or Bitsy or the others I loved. I don't think any remained. Now, instead of being willing to give them a second chance, I fought the urge to teach them both a lesson they would never forget. It would be so easy and it was so damned tempting.

Tempting as it was, I refused to fall into their trap. Not this time.

"I suggest you remove your hand now." I might not get to deal with either of them the way I wanted, but that didn't mean I couldn't remind them exactly who and what I was. I eased my control slightly. My eyes bled to amber as my cougar aspect looked out from them. "I did not give you permission to touch me, much less hold me in place." My voice roughened slightly, its pitch lower than usual.

"You're just like that bitch of an aunt of yours," Emma hissed.

She dropped her hand but not before I saw what she planned. I blocked her slap, knocking her hand to one side.

"Dr. Powell!"

I didn't know whether to curse or not. A quick look behind Emma and Dante showed one of Lucas' deputies striding in our direction. His hand rested on the butt of his gun and his expression darkened. Then he reached behind his back, pulling his handcuffs free from his belt. They dangled from the fingers of his left hand as he stepped to us.

"Is everything all right, Doc?" Deputy Chip Inuye eyed my parents closely. "We had several complaints about a disturbance and possible assault."

I clamped my lips tightly together to hold back the laugh building inside me. Anyone along Main Street could have made the call, but my money was on the café. They had a clear view of what was happening and no love lost for my parents. Of course, that latter described a whole bunch of people around town.

"Let's just say that there was a technical violation of the law, Deputy, but it's one I'm willing to let slide—this time."

"Is there anything I can do?"

"You might want to explain to Dante and Emma here the dangers of grabbing someone who doesn't want to be grabbed or threatening them or those they care about."

"Bitch," Dante rasped.

Inuye tsked-tsked and pulled out his citation book. "Run along, Dr. Powell. I'll make sure these two understand we don't take kindly to anyone disturbing the peace."

"Thanks." I grinned and started toward my truck.

"Doc?"

I turned back. "Yes?"

"The sheriff would appreciate it if you stopped by the office before heading out."

"Will do. Thanks."

I changed directions and hurried off. As I did, I slid my phone back into my pocket and tapped my earbud, using vocal commands to call Meg.

"Are you all right?" she asked the moment she answered.

"I take it the grapevine is working up to its usual speed."

"Did you expect anything else today?"

I shook my head, chuckling softly. "Add what happened to your filings. I'm emailing you a copy of the video I took of our little encounter. It should show that they not only threatened everyone but a few other things I'm sure you can use somehow."

"What else?"

"Deputy Inuye is having a discussion with them. He had his citation book out when I walked off."

Meg chuckled and I imagined her rubbing her hands together in anticipation. "I'll touch base with him later this afternoon. Where are you now?"

"On my way to see Lucas. Inuye said he wanted me to stop by the office." I paused outside the front entrance to the Sheriff's Office. "Any idea what he wants?"

"Not a one. Touch base when you're done and let's compare notes."

"Will do."

And, somewhere along the way, I needed to stop in and check on Maddy. Hopefully, she'll have some answers for me—if I figure out the right questions to ask.

14

"I hope iced tea's okay."

Maddy crossed the porch and set the tray she carried down on the table between two deck chairs. I watched as she poured tea into two tall glasses filled with ice. As she turned to hand one to me, I smiled in appreciation. I'd much preferred a beer, especially after everything that happened today, but tea worked. Especially since it meant she didn't have any liquor in the house. Not that I wouldn't do check before leaving.

"It's fine. Thanks." I took a sip and smiled again. "Sorry I was late."

She waved it off. As she did, I caught the shadows of doubt lingering in her eyes. Worried, I leaned one hip against the porch rail and looked at her in concern.

"Maddy, what's going on?"

She gave a wavering smile and half a shrug. I waited, knowing better than to push. Instead, I settled on one of the deck chairs. Leaning back, I watched as she looked out across the field in front of the house.

"Mads, are you okay?"

"Sorry." She gave a shaky smile and took the other deck chair next to mine. "I was worried you weren't going to come."

I frowned, not understanding.

"When you called and said you were running late, I thought it was your way of trying to get out of coming here," she admitted without looking at me.

I sighed and rolled my eyes. Sitting up, I swung my legs off the side of the deck chair and turned to face her. Frustration warred with understanding as I did. Frustration because she should know better and understanding because, for whatever reason, she still felt unsure about me and the rest of us.

"Maddy, believe me, I want to be here. The only reason I was late was because it has been a lousy day and I had some things I needed to take care of." To put it mildly.

She looked at me, worry clouding her expression. "Are you okay?"

I nodded, hopeful. This was the Maddy I knew. The one I grew up with. The one who worried about her friends and did whatever she could to help. It had been a long time since I'd seen her.

"Yeah. Just tired."

I sat back and reached for my tea. For several minutes, we sat in comfortable silence. Glancing at Maddy out of the corner of my eye, I frowned slightly. She looked tired, drawn. I expected that, especially after everything she'd been through the last few months. But she did look better. There was a spark in her eyes that hadn't been there since our return from Ireland. It looked like she had put on a few pounds. She was still too thin, but she no longer looked gaunt. Best of all, the dark shadows under her eyes had lessened. No longer did she look like she'd lost the fight. She still wasn't sleeping well, but at least she was sleeping.

"Can you tell me what happened?" she asked.

I heard a touch of resentment and did my best not to react. She knew there were things we wouldn't be talking about with her. That bothered her. Hell, it bothered me. But there were more than just the two of us involved. This—whatever "this" might be—involved everyone we cared for. If that meant keeping her in the dark until we knew for certain she no longer presented a danger to herself or to us, we'd do it.

"My parents."

She groaned and shook her head. "What did they do this time?"

"The question is what didn't they do?"

"Worse than usual?"

I nodded. "They've found themselves a new attorney and filed new suits against Bitsy, me, pretty much anyone they ever had a grievance against."

Maddy's brow furrowed and looked as if she couldn't believe it. "Don't tell me someone from around here took them on as clients."

"No. Someone from Dallas who moved to this part of the state a short time ago." Which didn't excuse him not doing his homework before filing the cases against us.

"What are you going to do?"

"Bitsy and I met with Meg and she's going to see what our legal options are." I didn't mind telling her about the lawsuits, but I wasn't ready to tell her all of it. Not yet, at any rate.

"There's more, isn't there?" That familiar doubt crept into her voice.

"Does being ambushed by Dante and Emma count?"

Her eyes went wide and her jaw dropped just a little. Over the next few minutes, I gave a heavily edited and much more humorous than it really was accounting of the encounter. By the time I ended, Maddy looked like she didn't know whether to laugh, shake her head in disbelief or what.

"What are you going to do about them?"

"I'm waiting to see what Meg says our options are. Then I'll talk with Bitsy and figure it out." That was as much as I was willing to tell her. "After that, I needed to check on the progress at the clinic which was another headache because one of the suppliers sent the wrong equipment. It's going to slow things down until they get the new shipment out. If that's not enough, one of Miss Serena's geldings came down with colic and I needed to check him and make sure Jimmy knew what I wanted done."

"Sounds like a hell of a day, Jax."

I nodded.

"And I didn't help with my attitude when you got here, did I?" She looked at me, her expression serious. "Be honest with me, Jax. I'm so tired of everyone walking around on eggshells whenever I'm in the same room with them."

I didn't answer right away. Instead, I opened my senses and looked at her. She might look better physically, but the toll of what she'd been through was still visible if you looked arcanely. The only thing that reassured me was I no longer saw the black threads leaching out of her. Intellectually, I knew the bindings had been broken, but it as going to take a long time to convince my animal side of it. The memory of her trying to force me to submit was still too fresh.

"Mads, I'll be honest. I don't get the insecurity. We've always been there for you. You know that. We're sisters in everything but blood."

She blew out a breath and ran her hands over her face and then up, through her hair. I watched, worried, as she climbed to her feet. She crossed the porch to the railing and stood there, her back to me. Somehow, we needed to get through to her. But how?

"Maddy." I stood and moved to her side. I didn't touch her. I still remember what happened at the bar. It was going to take time to put that behind me. "Talk to me. Tell me what's wrong."

"Mom tells me I need to be honest about how I'm feeling."

I nodded.

"When you called and said you were going to be late, I heard enough to know you were downtown. To me, that meant you were going to the café, or stopping in to see Annie or one of the others instead of coming to see me. I was hurt and angry and even jealous."

"Maddy." Despite my misgivings, I slid an arm around her shoulders and hugged her. "All you had to do was ask. I would have explained." I paused and kicked myself mentally. "I'm sorry. I should have explained."

And she should have trusted me.

"Jax, what happened to us? We used to be so close, all of us."

Now I frowned, not understanding. "Maddy, we still are."

"Not like we were in school." Tears pooled in her eyes.

I wanted to roll my eyes but didn't. This was it. We were back to the old insecurities that plagued her when we were younger. But she needed to be specific. Otherwise, none of us would be able to address the issue and, hopefully, solve it.

"I don't understand."

"It used to be the four of us: you, me, Quinn and Annie. You remember how it was. We were inseparable. I always knew I could count on the three of you, especially you."

I leaned against the railing and waited, hoping she kept talking.

"Then we went to college and we drifted apart. But whenever we were all home at the same time, it was like nothing changed. Then she came along."

"She?"

I had a cold lump in the pit of my stomach. I had no doubt who "she" was.

"Meg." Maddy all but spat out her name.

My hands tightened around the railing. Anger flared before I pushed it down. I needed to be careful here. The last thing either of us needed was for me to do or say anything to confirm her paranoia.

"Maddy, look at me." I waited until she turned in my direction. "I understand. I really do."

The look she gave me spoke volumes. She didn't believe a word I said.

"I do understand. I felt like the third wheel the first time I came home after Meg moved here. Both Annie and Quinn told me about her." Boy had they told me about her. By the time I came home that first time after her arrival, I figured she had to be ten feet tall and walk on water. "It was so clear they had a relationship with her like what the four of us shared. I didn't know where I'd fit in—if I'd fit in.

"I told myself it didn't matter. After all, I wasn't going to move back here. No way did I want to return to Mossy Creek as long as my parents lived here and I knew the chances of them ever leaving were slim to none. Then Ali called me, telling me something happened to

Annie and asking me to come home. I forgot about my reservations where Meg was concerned. All that mattered was making sure Annie was all right."

I paused, swallowing against the remembered fear of that morning.

"What I found when I got here was that Quinn and I fell instantly back into the relationship we've had since we were kids. Yes, there was uncertainty about Meg. I didn't know her, didn't know what she could do and, to be honest, didn't know if she'd fight for Annie the way Quinn and I would. What I found when I gave her a chance was someone who would have been one of our group if she'd grown up with us. She's someone I trust as much as I do any of the rest of you."

Maddy shook her head, her lips trembling slightly. "Not me. Not now."

I wanted to pull my hair in frustration. What the hell would it take to finally get through to her?

"Maddy, stop!" I snapped.

She blinked and looked at me in surprise.

"We all love you. Accept it. We're going to fight for you. So you'd better accept that as well. As for trusting you, yeah, it's hard right now. Intellectually, I know what happened at The Roundhouse wasn't so much you as it was the bindings and their effect on you. Emotion-ally, I'm working on it. But that doesn't mean I'm going to turn my back on you. If I were, I wouldn't be here right now." I pinned her with a firm look. "So accept that as well."

She shook her head.

"Damn it, Maddy. I get it. I do and I don't know how to convince you I'm telling the truth." I wanted to pace but knew she'd take it the wrong way. We were at a critical moment and I didn't want to blow it. "If me simply being here isn't enough, I don't know what else to do."

Tears filled her eyes and spilled down her cheeks. When she reached up to wipe them away, her hands shook. Her aura had muted as we talked, worrying me. We were still a long way from making her whole.

"You don't understand," she said softly.

"You're wrong, but why don't you explain it to me then?"

"I-I can't." She sniffled and rubbed her arm under her nose like a kid.

I knew better. She could but she wasn't ready to talk about it. I understood. She'd always been the more fragile of our group both emotionally and when it came to knowing how much we loved her. She'd never really believed she had anything to offer like the rest of us did. That lack of self-confidence may have made it easier for whoever placed the first binding on her to do so. It most definitely was something Maddy needed to work on. Unfortunately, I had a feeling I'd pushed her about as far as I could along those lines for the moment.

Time for a change of targets, so to speak.

"How are you feeling? I know the last several days were difficult."

"You think?" She laughed humorlessly. Then she gave a half-shrug and ducked her head. "Sorry. I feel like everything's off right now."

"It's going to take time, Maddy. But you're going to be all right. *We're* going to be all right."

"I hope so." She stared at something far away, probably something she didn't see, some image in her mind. "I've been talking to Liam every day, answering his questions, telling him what I can about Anton and the others."

"I'm glad." I smiled, hoping she saw the truth in my expression.

"And Mom has me set to see a counselor tomorrow."

"If there's anything I can do." I left the rest off. She either understood what I meant or she didn't. "Will you do me a favor?"

She didn't respond for a moment. Then she nodded once.

"Talk to your counselor or to your mom, even to Amy if you're comfortable talking to her, about Anton. See if you remember more about that conversation you overhead when he was on the phone and he mentioned Mossy Creek."

She didn't look happy about it, but she agreed. I smiled and gave her another one armed hug.

"Is there anything I can do to help you?"

She gave me a teary smile and nodded. "Come back?" The mix of helplessness and hopefulness in her voice about did me in.

"Of course." I pulled my phone and checked my schedule for tomorrow. "How about I stop by the café and bring lunch tomorrow?"

She smiled happily and then shook her head. "I can't. I have a doctor's appointment tomorrow. Mom said we'd be gone until mid-afternoon probably."

"Then we'll do it the next day." After I talked with Dr. Pat about the appointment. "Call me tomorrow and we'll set it up."

We chatted for a few more minutes. Then, as her father pulled up in the drive, I said my goodbyes. The visit raised more questions than it answered and that bothered me. But now it was time to head to Miss Serena's. Maybe she'd have some answers for me.

Man, I hoped so.

15

"I think that's about it, Jimmy."

I leaned back and stretched my arms over my head. The day might still be young, but we'd been at it since just after midnight. But it was worth it. Miss Serena was now the proud owner of a beautiful newborn colt who, unless I was sorely mistaken, would be as successful on the track as his sire. Now all I wanted was to find my bed for a couple of hours before facing the rest of the day.

"You did good, Doc."

Jimmy Reardon, the farm manager, smiled in approval and I grinned back. I couldn't help it. I'd been a kid, probably no more than five or six, when Jimmy put me on the back of my first horse. As I grew up, he encouraged my love of animals and introduced me to the local vet. Between the two of them, they set me on the path to becoming a large animal vet.

"Thanks." I grinned.

"While you were checking the colt, another delivery for the clinic came in. I signed for it and had them put it with the rest of the equipment."

I blew out a breath. Assuming construction continued on schedule, my vet clinic would be completed in another month. Over the last week or so, some of the final equipment and supplies had been arriving. My "investors" wanted to make sure everything was ready to move in as soon as the clinic was ready to move into. As a result, one of the overflow stables here had been turned into a storage area for me. Miss Serena insisted and I learned long ago not to argue with her when her mind was made up.

"Was it at least on the equipment list I put together?"

I couldn't—quite—keep the exasperation out of my voice. Mindful of the cost of setting up a large animal vet clinic, I'd been careful about what equipment I ordered. Yes, I had investors. Mainly because they pushed their way in. Oh, they did it out of love and with full knowledge I wouldn't order everything they thought I needed. To make sure the clinic had everything they thought it needed, Miss Serena recruited Jimmy to tell her what items I talked about but put off buying. Meg pestered Quinn who talked with the trainers who furnished her dogs—as well as dogs for most of the rest of us—about what they thought I should have. And Aunt Bitsy. . . .

Well, let's just say it wouldn't surprise me if my aunt didn't find the most successful large animal vet in the state before wining and dining him to get not only his list of equipment but his phone number for "personal consultations". I love her. She's been more of a parent to me than my mother and father ever have been. While most of the world looks at her and sees a woman with more money than brains, I know better. Just as I know she loves the male of the species. I'm only half joking when I say her love life scarred me from an early age.

At my question, Jimmy grinned. "It was." He leaned forward, elbows on knees, his expression suddenly serious. "Doc, I know all this makes you uncomfortable. We all do. But you need to understand something. Miss Serena and the others know you'd never buy all the equipment you should have. At least not right off the bat. Miss Bitsy explained how you've not touched your trust fund except when she's all but forced you to. Even then, you've done your best to pay every penny back. So look at this as an expression of how much those women love you and how much they love the animals you're going to be taking care of."

He was right. But that didn't make it any easier to accept. But I was working on it. After all, what other choice did I have?

"Okay." I gave him a nod and looked at the empty mug on my desk, wishing for a fresh cup of coffee. "I'm going to take a look at what came in and then I'm getting a couple of hours sleep. Someone needs to check on our newest addition every hour. Let's make sure he and mama are doing okay."

"I'll see to it. We've already got the video feed set up, so I can monitor them from my office or while I'm out on the farm."

That had been one of the updates I suggested for the stables when I agreed to work with Miss Serena's stock. Not only did it make it easier for me to keep an eye on my charges, but I knew she'd enjoy watching the horses she loved so much. Besides, Jimmy wasn't getting any younger and this way he didn't have to spend nights with the stock. That alone had been enough to convince Miss Serena to make the investment.

"I'll keep an eye on things as well."

He gave me a look I knew all too well. He thought I'd just said something exceedingly foolish.

"Doc—Jax, you're exhausted. Anyone with a pair of working eyes and an ounce of sense can see it. You need to go home and get some sleep. You know me and the rest of the crew will keep an eye on the colt and his mama."

I nodded. I couldn't deny being exhausted. In the week since my parents—No. They weren't my parents. Not now and not for most of my life.—sued what seemed like most of the town, sleep had been a very rare commodity. I had patients to see and the clinic's construction was at the point where I spent at least some time there every day checking on things. Or I was dealing with equipment deliveries. Every evening was spent with either Miss Serena and the other Guardians or with all of our inner circle, training and planning. We might not know what the trouble was we all felt coming, but we were doing everything we could to be prepared for whatever it might be.

Then there was Maddy. Quinn, Ciara and I took turns visiting her every day. Annie went as often as she could but, with the twins and trying to settle into her position as DA, she didn't have much free time. As for Meg, we decided it was best to leave her out of that part of the plan. Maddy needed time to accept the fact Meg had not taken her place as our friend. Besides, we were doing what we could to make sure Meg didn't overdo. Drew would have our heads if anything happened to her or the baby she carried.

"I'll make you a deal, Jimmy. I'll go home and get some sleep if you promise to do the same. You said it. We have the video system. The crew can keep an eye on the colt and his mama. They know to call both of us if they think there's anything wrong. What do you say?"

"I'd say you have a deal." He stuck his hand out and I shook it. "You going to let Miss Serena know about the new colt on your way home?"

I stood and nodded. Then I checked my watch. It was still early, but I knew she'd be up. I'd texted her and left word that the mare had gone into labor. I didn't doubt for a moment that she was waiting for news. Then I'm heading home."

"You do that, Doc. I want to look in on mama and son and then I need to make sure the crew knows their assignments."

"Thanks for helping, Jimmy."

He lifted a finger to the battered brim of his equally battered ball cap. As he left the office, I watched, hoping he'd find his own bed before long. He wasn't as young as he used to be but he refused to admit it. That usually manifested in him pushing himself too hard. I understood, just as I knew I wasn't one to tell anyone they were doing too much right now. Not after Rafe made me take a long, hard look at my reflection only a few minutes before Jimmy called to tell me the mare was in labor. All I could do now was hope he did as he promised.

Fifteen minutes later, after checking on the equipment delivered earlier, I climbed into my Dodge Ram. With the engine idling, I sent a couple of quick texts. The first was to Rafe to let him know I was heading home. Almost instantly, he responded and promised to be there within half an hour. I started to tell him he didn't need to and then changed my mind. I needed a few minutes alone with him just as much as I needed to find my bed.

The next text was to Amy. If anyone could get around Jimmy's stubborn streak, it was her. She assured me she'd check on him in an hour or so and if he hadn't gone home by then, she'd make sure he did. Then she told me in no uncertain terms to get some rest.

Texts sent, I tossed my phone onto the passenger seat, slid the transmission into gear, and headed toward the house. It was a short drive. I could have walked it and gotten there almost as quickly as I would driving. But I wasn't Jimmy. I had no problem admitting I was tired. I'd let Miss Serena know about the newest addition to her stock, show her the pictures we took during the delivery and hopefully cadge a mug of coffee off of her before heading home to shower and then get some much needed sleep.

I turned, smiling to see the three-story plantation style house at the end of the drive. Then the Ram sputtered once before rolling to a stop. Frowning, I turned the key in the ignition. Nothing. No click. No flicker of lights. No nothing.

"What the hell?"

I climbed out and stared at the pickup. I'm no mechanic, but even I knew the Ram shouldn't have just died. For one, it was new, less than six months old. For another, Jacob Smithson took care of it for me. To say he was a talented mechanic was putting it mildly. An Other, his talents ran to all things mechanical. He had given the truck a full check up just the day before. No way anything could be wrong with it now.

Not that it helped me right then. I pulled my cellphone and cursed again. Not only no bars but no power. It didn't make any sense. The phone had a full charge just a few minutes ago and I'd never had any reception problems here. Had we fallen through the rabbit hole while Jimmy and I delivered the colt?

Or was it something else?

I'm going to learn not to ask that sort of thing, even if I do it silently. It almost always rises up to bite me on the ass. As soon as the thought formed, the ground felt like it pitched beneath my feet even though I knew better. A wave of vertigo hit. My stomach rolled and I dropped to one knee, as much to keep from falling as to shelter behind the truck. Every instinct screamed for me to run. Something was wrong. Very wrong. But what?

Gasping for breath, fighting the urge to vomit as another wave of vertigo hit, I pressed my palms against the ground. My fingers dug through the dirt, searching, seeking. Almost blindly, I sought the ley lines running beneath the property. Energy flooded through me, around me. Colors, brilliant and vibrant, pulled me in, soothing and invigorating. I gasped, drawing in what felt like my first breath in a year.

Danger. Danger. Danger.

The defenses woven into the energies that were a very real part of the farm rose up. For a moment, they threatened to overwhelm me. I closed my eyes and focused, grounding myself. As I did, a spike of fear raced through me. I pushed it down and drew the energies close, reaching out to the defensive wards I had helped reinforce not that long ago.

Where?

More importantly, what?

My consciousness rode the energy, splitting and splitting again. So much information. Too much. Not enough. Where was the danger?

A wave of fear and pain washed over me so strong, so *real*, I looked and felt for injuries. Then anger washed away the fear and pain. The sky overhead turned dark. Clouds formed. Wind swirled, bending trees dangerously in its path. For a moment, I expected to hear warning sirens in the distance. But this was no natural storm. I doubted it extended beyond the edge of Miss Serena's property. Weather radar certainly wouldn't pick it up.

I turned my head, focusing, watching as the energies centered over the house. I felt the wards strengthening. In that split second I knew at least some of the answers. The danger was here and, whatever it was, Miss Serena felt it as well and was mounting a defense.

Lightning crackled across the sky and thunder rolled. I pushed to my feet. One step. Two. Each step faster, more urgent than the one before. The sound of my boots slapping against the drive was lost in the sounds of thunder and rain pounding down. Hail the size of dimes and quarters pelted me. The very air around me felt charged, dangerous.

Lightning struck the ground mere feet in front of me. I stumbled, veering to the side. Through rain so heavy it obscured my vision, I glanced around. The property was under attack. I knew it just as surely as I knew my own name. But from whom and where?

I slid to a stop ten yards from the front porch. I turned, facing away from the house. I needed to find the attacker. If we managed to deal with him—her?—now, maybe we could finally quit looking waiting for the proverbial shoe to drop.

Almost without thought, I moved off the drive onto the grass. It squelched under my boots and then under my knees as I knelt down. The fingers of my right hand sank through the grass into the dirt below. One distant part of me recognized the vibrations of my phone in my hip pocket as someone called. I ignored it, focusing on the Earth energies and reaching again for the ley line. As I did, wave after wave of energy beat against the property's defenses, searching for a weakness.

Foolish. So very foolish.

And that told me whoever it was didn't know Miss Serena, or at least not well. Anyone who did would also know the defenses here had no weaknesses. At least none that could be exploited quickly or easily.

Overhead, the dome created by the defenses Miss Serena set up so long ago, defenses reinforced by the Guardians little more than a month ago and then once again by me last week, flared as another attack landed. Sparks and flashes of color reminded me of fireworks or, more accurately, images I'd seen of rocket attacks hitting the Iron

Dome. But I didn't have time to think about that. I needed to follow the energies back to their source.

God, let me be able to follow them back to their source.

Find them, find them, find them.

The words echoed, reinforced as thunder once again sounded overhead, so loud this time I felt it vibrating through the ground. Or maybe that was my phone as it once again came to life in my hip pocket. In the distance, a siren sounded. Then another. Not the warning sirens, set up to let folks in town know if a tornado neared.

Car sirens.

Cop sirens.

Coming closer.

God, I needed to end this before they became pawns in this fight.

I slammed my left hand down on the ground, those fingers digging in much as the fingers of my right hand had earlier. I pulled on the Earth's energies, twinging them with my own Elemental abilities. Picturing the nearest ley line, a river of energy running deep below the surface but almost directly beneath me, I tied into it. Energy filled me once again. I no longer saw the world through normal eyes. I saw the energies of the trees and grass, the power of the defenses overhead. It was like looking through a filter some insane scientist invented. Every color of the spectrum danced before me.

Where? Where? Where?

Suddenly, the world exploded around me. One moment, I knelt in the grass, mud leaching up through the grass, rain soaking me. The next, I lay on my back, arms splayed as if I'd been tossed aside by the gods of old. My ears rang. I tasted blood and my tongue hurt. My ears felt stuffed with cotton, all sound muted. Spots danced drunkenly before my eyes. Somewhere along the line I needed to learn how to breathe again.

God, what happened?

Groaning, I rolled to my side. That sent the world pitching for a moment. Once it subsided, I slowly levered onto an elbow. Then to hands and knees. Lifting my face, I slowly opened my eyes, afraid of what I'd see—or not see.

A sob tore from my throat and I blew out a breath I really couldn't afford to release yet. The defenses held. But they no longer looked as strong as they had been. Someone—someones?—had thrown everything they had at the wards. Miss Serena and I had turned it back but at what cost?

God, at what cost?

I stumbled to my feet like a staggering drunk. For a moment, I wavered, my legs rubber bands of muscles without bones. Chest heaving, stomach pitching, I took three unsteady steps to the nearest tree and leaned against it. I needed to get to the house, but I had to do so without falling flat on my face. All I had to do was put one foot in front of the next. So simple. Right?

I pushed away from the tree. I could do this. I had to.

"No!"

All doubts, all thought about what happened over the last few minutes disappeared at the sound of Ali's scream. Instinct took over. I raced across the lawn. As I did, I spotted her on the front porch. She looked so small, so scared. Heart pounding, I pushed forward, knowing only that I needed to get to her. My boots slid across the wet grass but I didn't care. Nothing mattered more than getting to Ali.

"No, no, no, no."

I repeated it like a mantra as I leapt onto the porch and dropped to my knees. In that moment, the world skidded to a stop and I wasn't sure I wanted it to start again.

"Aunt Jax, is she okay?"

Miss Serena lay motionless between us on the porch. It looked as if she simply collapsed. Pale to the point of being ashen, she looked drained of blood. She looked old and frail and I swear I felt Death hovering nearby. Not that I'd let her go without a fight. Not here and not now and certainly not in front of Ali.

Oh God, Ali.

Somehow, I kicked my brain into gear. I wasn't helping anyone and certainly not Miss Serena sitting there, babbling incoherently albeit silently.

"Ali, I need you to go inside. Now."

She stood there, eyes wide with fright. Tears rolled down her cheeks. For a moment, she stared at me, as if not quite comprehending what I said. Then she shook her head, her lower lip quivering. I knew what that meant. Unless I found just the right words to convince her otherwise, she wasn't about to move from where she stood.

Not that I blamed her. Unfortunately, that didn't make what I needed to do any easier.

"Ali, I'm not going to lie. I don't know if Miss Serena's going to be all right." God, it hurt on so many different levels to say so. "I need you to be brave and I need you to help me help Miss Serena right now."

She rubbed her fist under her nose. "H-how?"

"I need you to go inside and call your grandma. Tell her I need her to get here as quickly as she can. Call your mama too."

Her lower lip quivered some more and she shook her head. I reached out and pulled her to me. For a moment, I held her close. Then I retrieved the cellphone I felt in her back pocket and pressed it into her hands.

"Please, sweetheart."

"D-don't make me leave her, Auntie Jax."

"D-do as Jax says."

I gasped and looked down. Miss Serena's eyes were open. She still looked so pale, too pale. But her words broke through to Ali. The little girl sniffled once and then scurried inside. As the door slammed shut behind her, I bent, placing my forehead against Miss Serena's. Tears burned my eyes and I blinked them back.

"J-Jax."

"Shh, you're going to be all right." She had to be all right.

"Y-you're in charge. T-take the book. A-answer's there."

"All right." I pulled my phone and sent texts to Rafe, Amy and Dr. Pat. I knew Quinn would contact the others as soon as Ali called her.

Hell, for all I knew, everyone was already on their way. "You just lie still. What can I do to help you?"

"You already did." She smiled and lightly grasped my hand. "You were here and you helped reinforce the wards. You kept him out."

Him?

Him who?

I had so many questions I wanted to ask but didn't dare. Not yet.

"Help's coming, Miss Serena." I lightly brushed the hair back from her brow. As I did, I wished I possessed even some of Amy's healing talents. "You just lie still and hang on."

"So tired."

"I know, Miss Serena. You'll be able to rest soon. I promise."

She nodded and closed her eyes. As she did, I held my breath, waiting for her to take her next breath. Her chest rose slightly and I relaxed a little. Then, knowing I couldn't just sit there and wait for what happened next, I closed my eyes. There was one thing I could do, if only I found the strength to do so.

I pressed my fingers to Miss Serena's wrist. Her pulse was slow, thready. Her breathing worse. I didn't need to see her aura to know she was dying. Fear spiked and I fought the urge to shift and run somewhere I could hide from the world. I didn't want to face losing her. But I couldn't run. I wouldn't. I needed to do whatever it took to keep her alive until help came.

Carefully, every muscle and nerve ending screaming in protest, I once again reached for the ley line. Focusing on its energies and hers, I wove them, one strand at a time, with the other. As I did, I prayed I didn't fuck up. Normally, I didn't mind flying by the seat of my pants but not when Miss Serena's life hung in the balance.

God, where was everyone? Surely, they knew something was wrong. Why weren't they here?

I glanced over my shoulder as the sounds of tires skidding to a halt nearby broke through my concentration. Even before the pickup came to a complete stop, men jumped out of the bed and ran toward the porch. A moment later, Jimmy Reardon emerged from the cab, his expression as worried as I knew mine was.

"Doc?"

"Check the property. Pull in the stock. I want armed guards here at the house and on the gates. Now!"

He took one look at the scene before him and then nodded. Instantly, the crew with him split up. Several took positions on the drive, rifles or pistols in hand. Others piled back into the pickup and drove off. As they did, Jimmy moved in my direction, suddenly looking every one of his almost sixty years.

"Jimmy, I need you to go inside and stay with Ali." God, why hadn't I known she was going to be here this morning? "She's supposed to be calling for help. Make sure she has."

He nodded as my phone came to life in my hand. I slid my thumb across the sensor and then tossed the phone to Jimmy. He could deal with it. I had to focus on Miss Serena.

"Miss Judith is almost here. Amy's with her. Quinn's following." He placed the phone on the porch next to me. "I'll sit with the girl. You do what you can for her." He nodded at Miss Serena.

Expression grim, I nodded in response. As I did, the sound of another car coming up the drive filled the air. Moments later, it parked where Jimmy's truck had been just a few moments before. Help was here. I hoped.

"Grandma!"

I sagged in relief to hear Amy's yell. The blonde piled out of Judith's car and raced up the steps to the porch. She dropped to her knees opposite me, her hands already searching out her grandmother's pulse, checking her respirations. Then she looked at me, fear in her eyes but her expression determined.

"What happened?"

I shook my head.

"Jax, damn it, pull it together and tell me what happened!"

She was right. I could fall apart later, after we knew what happened and why.

"It felt like someone tried to batter down the wards. I was at the stables with Jimmy. By the time I got here, it was all I could do to feed energy into the wards. Next thing I knew, I was thrown head over heels and was flat out on the ground. Then I heard Ali scream and found Miss Serena like this."

As I spoke, Judith disappeared inside the house. She returned a moment later with two quilts. She draped one over Miss Serena and the other around my shoulders. Then she softly said Jimmy was calling the others.

"Jax, look at me." Amy waited until I did. "Grandma's alive and that's because of you. Right now, I need you to keep doing what you're doing. When Dr. Pat gets here, we're probably going to take her to the hospital. That means I'm going to have to ask you to do something else."

"Anything."

I'd do anything for Miss Serena and Amy knew it.

"Make sure the wards here are secure. Then get to the hospital. She's going to need you when she wakes up."

I nodded. What else could I do?

As I did, more cars sped up the drive, parking wherever they could. Dr. Pat ran up the steps to join us. Behind her came Quinn, Meg and Annie. Not far behind them were Lexie and her father. Others came as well. Rafe, Sam, Lucas and Drew. Miss Peggy. Aunt Bitsy. Others as well. Too many others.

"Jax."

That's all Amy said as she and Dr. Pat checked her grandmother. I didn't respond, at least not vocally. Instead, I nodded and climbed to my feet. Only to stagger back as Bitsy all but threw herself at me. I held onto her, fighting to maintain control. Then I looked at the others. They looked as scared and worried as I felt.

Worse, they all looked to me as if I had the answers they wanted.

"Jax?" Bitsy looked from me to the porch and back.

"I can't explain it all just yet." I shook my head when I saw Quinn open her mouth to protest. "I don't have the answers. But someone tried to hurt Miss Serena. I don't know how. Amy and Dr. Pat are working on her right now. She's alive but she's unconscious."

"What can we do?" Annie asked.

"Keep your eyes and ears open. Anyone new to town, I don't give a damn if they're just passing through, I know about it. Be sure to tell Lucas too."

Heads nodded.

"If you hear of anyone talking about what happened today or saying anything that rings wrong with you, same thing."

More nods.

"And watch your backs. Watch out for one another. Something is going on, something we don't yet understand. If we're to keep our town and our loved ones safe, we need to be careful and we need to be watchful. Don't try to be heroes, but don't just shrug off something if it doesn't feel right."

"Are you all right?" Bitsy held my hand tightly, worry reflected in her eyes.

I nodded. Then I led her a few feet away. "I need a favor."

She glanced past me to the porch. "Anything."

"Go to the hospital with them. Keep me informed. If they need anything, get it—specialists, anything. You keep telling me to use my trust fund. I will empty it out if it helps her." I glanced back to where Dr. Pat worked on Miss Serena.

"Don't worry. She and Amy will have whatever they need."

"Thanks. Something else you can do for me. Get with Miss Peggy. If anyone can rally the town, it's the two of you. Call a meeting of those you feel need to be there at the café for tonight. Keep word on the down low. Let's not advertise it." If the person responsible for the attack remained nearby, I didn't want them knowing we were rallying the troops.

Bitsy thought for a moment before giving a decisive nod. "My house, not the café."

"Thanks." I turned back to the others. "I know you want to be here and I know Amy and Miss Serena appreciate it. But right now, you need to let Amy and Dr. Pat do what they can for her. I need you to get back to town. Don't take chances and let me know if anything seems out of the ordinary."

"She's right," Miss Peggy said before she started ushering everyone back to their cars.

Before long, the only ones remaining were our inner circle and our men. We stood several feet from the porch, watching and waiting.

"Jax, what the hell happened?" Quinn looked as worried as I felt.

"It's like I said, Quinn. Someone tried attacking the wards here. I don't know if they were actually trying for Miss Serena or what. But it was enough to weaken the wards even though I tied into the ley line and was feeding energy back to the wards."

"And Miss Serena?"

"She was unconscious by the time I got to her." I reached for Quinn's hand. "I'm sorry. I didn't know Ali was here. She found Miss Serena before I could get to her. She's inside with Jimmy right now."

Quinn paled even more. Then she took off running. I watched her leap onto the porch, completely ignoring the steps. A moment later, she disappeared inside. As she did, I blew out a breath.

"Whether they take Miss Serena to the hospital or not, we need to talk. She was conscious for a few moments before everyone got here."

"What did she say?" Meg asked.

"Not much. She knew I'd tapped into the ley lines to help reinforce the wards. She said that kept him out."

"Who?" Annie demanded.

I shook my head. "I don't know. She said to take the book." At least I didn't need to explain what book. All of us were familiar with the old, leather-bound book that detailed so much of our town's history. "Said the answer's in it."

I paused as Amy joined us. Worried, we waited for her to say something. Instead, she reached out and pulled me into a tight hug. I held on, feeling the tremor of emotion run through her. Scared as I was, she must be terrified. Miss Serena basically raised her. Now she lay unconscious, fighting for her life.

"Jax, we need to talk." Amy's expression turned so serious all I could do was nod and follow her away from our friends, away from where Dr. Pat worked with Miss Serena and away from the ambulance roaring up the drive.

"Your grandmother?"

"I think she'll be all right, but Dr. Pat wants to get her to the hospital so she can run some tests." Tears glistened in her eyes and she reached up to dash them away before they could escape. "You saved her." She shook her head when I started to deny it. Then she gave my arm a shake. "You saved her. You helped reinforce the wards and you fed her energy from the ley lines after. That helped her own abilities begin healing her. So yes, you saved her."

"I love her, Amy." It was as simple as that.

"I know." She smiled and squeezed my hand. "And she loves you. We both do."

Now tears burned my eyes.

"Jax, I need to go with her."

I nodded.

"Jimmy will make sure the house is locked up. He and the crew will keep watch here, but I need you to do something. Make sure the wards are reset and do as Grandma asked. Take the book. Her workroom will seal behind you once you do. But keep that book safe."

"Do you know why she wants me to have it?"

Amy shook her head. "No. All she told me was the answer will be in there. Find it."

I glanced at the porch and watched as the paramedics gently lifted Miss Serena onto a gurney. "All right. Go. We'll be along as quickly as we can. I'll get with Jimmy to make sure everything's taken care of here and then I'll do what I can with the wards."

Amy hugged me again and then hurried to the ambulance. I watched as she climbed in the back. A few moments later, the ambulance roared down the drive toward town. Dr. Pat followed in her car. As they sped off, I closed my eyes and drew a deep breath. Somehow, I needed to make sense of what happened and prevent a repeat.

"Doc?" Rafe slipped his arms around me and held me close.

I turned and rested my cheek against his chest. For a long moment, we stood there. He didn't say anything. He didn't try to make me explain. He gave me the time I needed to gather my thoughts. Miss Serena was depending on me, on all of us, to protect the home she loved. With that accomplished, we needed to protect her town, our town. I wouldn't and couldn't turn my back on that.

"I need to talk to you and the others." I reached for his hands, linking my fingers through his. I glanced around and didn't know whether to smile or not to see Quinn carrying Ali in our direction, Jimmy on their heels.

"Jax?"

Ciara looked at me in concern as Quinn and Ali joined us. The little girl wrapped her legs around her mother's waist. Her arms wound around Quinn's neck in what looked like a death grip. Not that Quinn's grip on her daughter was any looser. Mother and daughter needed one another right then. I only wished I could give them the time they needed to reassure themselves they were all right and Miss Serena would make a full recovery.

"I don't know nearly enough right now and you've already heard the basics. Someone attacked the wards Miss Serena has on the property." I went on to describe how my truck died moments before I felt the wards being attacked. "We need to make sure the wards are complete and recharged. That means we need the four Elements. Judith and I represent two of the Elements. We need the other two as well."

"Quinn and Mary Kate," Judith said.

I shook my head. After seeing what happened to Miss Serena, I didn't want to risk Annie's grandmother. But who did we have who could represent Water?

"Meg instead of Mary Kate." I hated to ask it of her. She was pregnant and shouldn't be in the proverbial line of fire. Because of that, I'd do everything possible to protect her. "I'll take Earth, Quinn Fire, Judith Air and Meg Water." Before Meg and Quinn could run to the hills, I reached for their hands. "It's not permanent. Just for this. I promise."

I hoped.

"And us?" Rafe asked as he moved to my side.

I thought for a moment, not as easy as it sounded. Exhaustion dragged at me. Sooner or later, I'd fall face first to the ground. Hopefully, not until after we reinforced the defenses here.

"Lucas, you or Drew need to go to the hospital. Make sure security is solid there. We can't risk anything happening to either Miss Serena or Amy." I looked down the drive, as if by doing so I could see where the ambulance was in that moment. "The other stays here to find out what you can by searching the perimeter. Whoever attacked the wards had to be close. They weren't on the property, the wards would have kept them out. That means they needed to be nearby. It's the only explanation for not only the strength of the attack but the precision of it. It felt like they were hitting specific points in the wards trying to weaken them."

"You're sure?" Lucas asked.

"No." I was so far over my head just then. I hoped I wasn't leading us all down the wrong path. "But it's the only thing that makes sense." I turned to Rafe and Sam. "One of you also needs to go to the hospital. The other stays here to help with the security system. We put in all the cameras for a reason. Let's see what they can tell us."

"Consider it done." Rafe brushed his lips against the top of my head and then led Sam off. As they disappeared inside the house, Drew climbed into his SUV and sped after the ambulance.

"Jax, this is your show right now," Judith said.

I swallowed hard. I didn't want it to be my show. Hell, I wanted it to be a nightmare I'd wake up from. But that wasn't going to happen and, for whatever reason, the others looked to me for guidance.

"Mary Kate, Lexie, get to the hospital. I don't want Amy to be alone. Let me know the moment Dr. Pat says anything about Miss Serena." I considered what to do next. Then, seeing Ali watching me closely, I had my answer. "Hey, kiddo." I smiled and moved to stand in front of her and her mother. "You okay?"

Ali shook her head and buried her face against her mother's neck. Quinn closed her eyes as she fought to stay calm. A moment later, she brushed her lips against the top of Ali's head.

"Ali, will you look at me?" I kept my voice soft, gentle, and waited until she did. "Sweetheart, I am so proud of you. You did exactly what Miss Serena needed you to. You made sure I knew she needed help and then you called for more help. You stayed calm and you did everything I asked and everything Jimmy asked. Now I need you to be a big girl and do one more thing for me. Can you do that?"

She shrugged her little shoulders. "Don't know what you want."

I laughed softly. "It's nothing hard, but it's really important." I gave a quick shake of my head when I saw Quinn about to object. "I need you to go to the hospital with Lexie and Miss Mary Kate. You can help them look after Amy and Miss Serena until your mom and the rest of us get there."

"Mama?" She looked up at Quinn, her expression hopeful.

"I think that's a good idea, sweetheart." Quinn gently placed her on her feet. "You have your phone. You can call me or Daddy or Auntie Jax if you need to before we get there."

Ali threw her arms around her mother's waist and hugged her. Then she ran to me. I held Ali close for a moment and then knelt on one knee in front of her. "We won't be long, Ali. I promise."

She nodded, her expression serious. "You find the bad guy, Auntie Jax, and make sure he doesn't hurt anyone else."

With that, she hurried to where Mary Kate and Lexie waited. Lexie took her hand and led her across the drive to where she'd parked her Toyota. A few moments later, they headed off. That was my cue and I didn't like what had to come next.

"This sucks."

I didn't mean to say it out loud. But when the others nodded in agreement, I knew I had. What they didn't realize—yet—was I meant more than they knew.

"After we reinforce the wards here, each of us needs to do the same with our own homes and anywhere else you might have set protective wards. I mean it." I pinned them each with a firm look. "It must be done before we go to the hospital. Whoever attacked here might get the idea to attack one of us and we need to be prepared."

"She's right." Judith moved to stand next to me. "What else?"

"There's one other thing we need to do." I scrubbed my hands over my face. God, I hated this. "Ciara, it's something I think you need to do."

She frowned and narrowed her eyes at me. Then she cursed as

imaginatively as I'd ever heard. Quinn, Meg and Annie looked at her, expressions concerned.

"Maddy," she said simply.

I nodded.

Now it was Quinn who cursed as she looked around. Our childhood friend hadn't made an appearance despite the fact half the town had been here. Why? Was she a part of this or had she fallen victim again?

"I'll go with you," Annie said.

I smiled in appreciation. Between the two of them, they'd find out what was going on with Maddy. Annie could keep the situation from escalating and Ciara would do whatever it took to keep her safe. I could trust them to find out why Maddy was MIA.

"All right. Let's get to work. Let's see what we can do to make sure the property's safe until Miss Serena can come home."

Dear God, let her be able to come home.

16

The next few hours crawled by. We reinforced the wards at Miss Serena's. Judith and I sent the others on before making our way inside. Jimmy waited for us. He listened closely as we told him what we could. Then, before I could ask, he assured me he would make sure the property was safe. This wasn't the first time they had to take precautions and it wouldn't be the last. All we were to worry about was Miss Serena. Leave the rest to him. With that, he tapped a finger to the bill of his cap and left the house. As he did, he pulled his phone and began issuing orders to the crew like a seasoned soldier preparing for a long siege he had no intentions of losing. Which meant I needed to have a discussion with him before long to find out what he meant by this not being the first time they'd had to take precautions.

Damn it, there was too much about all this I still didn't know or understand.

Before heading downstairs to Miss Serena's workshop, Judith firmly put herself in my way. Arms folded, expression stern, she looked pointedly at my soaked clothing and then pointed to the nearest bathroom. Her message was clear and her expression all concerned mother, something I didn't ever remember seeing on my own mother's face. Before I could open my mouth to protest, she assured me she'd be able to find something for me to wear, even if she had to send Quinn to my place to pick something up. For now, I was to get out of my wet clothes before I caught cold.

Fortunately for both of us, I had a change in my pickup. Ten minutes later, we left the house, the door closing and locking behind us. Judith carried a small suitcase with things she thought Miss Serena might want or need while at the hospital. I clutched "the book" to my chest, holding onto it for dear life. Quinn followed, her phone pressed to her ear as she spoke with Ali, assuring her daughter we were on our way.

We stopped at my place long enough for me to secure the book in my own workroom in the basement. I didn't know whether to laugh or scream hysterically when I closed the door and prepared to head back upstairs. In one moment the door was there, just as it had been since I bought the place. The next moment, only solid wall remained. I swallowed hard and blinked, as if by doing so the house would return to normal. When it didn't, I glanced at the ceiling and pictured Quinn and her mother waiting for me in the main room. Never again would I laugh when Quinn groused about how her house had a mind of its own. Clearly, mine did as well. I only hoped it let me into the room so I could retrieve the book.

But that was for later, after we'd checked on Miss Serena.

At the hospital, people came and went. All offered their thoughts and prayers for Miss Serena. Janny arrived an hour or so after Judith, Quinn and I did. She handed around coffee and tea, promising to send lunch within the hour. If we needed anything else, all we had to do was call. Then, as she started to leave, she gave me a jerk of her head. I nodded and followed her into the hallway outside the waiting room.

"My mother said to tell you no one's reported seeing anyone who doesn't belong here. But we're keeping eyes and ears open."

"Thanks."

"Are you all right?" Concern roughened her voice.

"Just tired and worried."

She lightly patted my arm. "You hang in there, Jax."

I nodded and watched as she moved down the hall toward the elevator.

"Come sit down," Judith said softly as she joined me. "It shouldn't be too much longer."

I nodded and turned to follow her. As I did, the doors to the ICU swung open. I stopped and waited, forgetting how to breathe. Then Amy appeared. Seeing me, she hurried in my direction. I didn't say anything. I held out a hand and waited. She took it before leading me into the waiting room.

"Your grandmother?" Mary Kate asked softly.

Drew moved to his grandmother's side and slid an arm around the woman's shoulders. As he did, all eyes turned to Amy.

"Dr. Pat and others are still working with her." She paused and swallowed hard. Understanding, I eased her down onto the nearest chair. Then I sat next to her, letting her know she wasn't alone. "Grandma's alive. It looks like she had a heart attack. We'll know more soon."

"What can we do?" Drew's mother, Catherine, asked.

For a moment, Amy didn't answer. Then, as if realizing how many people were there, she closed her eyes. A moment later, she opened them and smiled slightly.

"Right now, you're doing it. You're saying prayers that Grandma is all right. You're helping by keeping your eyes and ears open for anything that might help Jax and Lucas identify who attacked her." She nodded at the coffee go-cups several of them held. "You're doing it by making sure everyone staying with me is taken care of."

"What else, Amy? There has to be something else we can do," Sam's mother, Camille, said.

"There is." She nodded her thanks when Mary Kate handed her a cup of coffee. "Check in with the café. Miss Peggy is setting up a visitation schedule. That way we have someone here all the time while Grandma's here. Knowing Miss Peggy, she also has a schedule of who is going to bring food, that sort of thing. And don't worry. We'll let you know if there's any change in Grandma's condition."

"She's right, everyone." Catherine looked around the waiting room. "You call me if you need anything, Amy, you or your grandma." She gave Amy a quick hug and then looked at her son. "I expect you to if she doesn't, Drew."

His eyes wide with surprise at the sudden maturity his mother showed, Drew nodded. I watched, unsure whether I should laugh or run for the hills. Miss Serena was hurt. Catherine was acting like a mature adult. What next? Would pigs finally fly?

I looked on, still not sure this wasn't all a dream, as Catherine herded most of those gathered out. She paused at Amy's side and gave her a hug, reminding her to call if she needed anything. Even more of a surprise than seeing her acting like a mature adult, she placed a gentle hand on my shoulder and simply nodded, a slight smile full of understanding on her lips, when I looked up. Then she stepped into the hallway, closing the door behind her.

"What just happened?" Drew asked as he dropped onto one of the chairs across from where I sat.

"I don't know." And that was putting it mildly.

"Neither do I, but I'll take it." Amy sipped her coffee and we waited. "Dr. Pat and the others haven't said much yet, but they did confirm Grandma had a heart attack. My take is she expended too much energy trying to hold off the attack before you got there, Jax."

I nodded. It made sense. But it also meant Miss Serena and I would be having a very long talk when she was better. She made a mistake, one that might still be fatal. She should have tied into the ley lines running beneath her property. If she had, she wouldn't have had to expend so much personal energy trying to shore up the wards.

Damn it, none of this made any sense.

"Has she regained conscious?" Judith asked.

"She came around a few minutes ago."

Well, that was good news. I hoped.

No, I knew it was.

"Did she say anything?"

"Only that she wants to see you and Judith. The doctors want her to rest but she informed them in no uncertain terms she wouldn't be able to until she'd seen you two."

I smiled. I couldn't help it. That sounded exactly like something Miss Serena would say.

"What else did the doctors say?" Quinn asked.

"Not much more than I've already told you. They're convinced it was a heart attack even though she has no history of cardiac problems. They've managed to stabilize her and have already said she will be here several days at least. They aren't going to take any chances where she's concerned, so they'll be putting her through a whole battery of tests."

"Good."

"Can I see her?" Ali asked softly from where she sat next to Meg.

"Not yet, sweetie. Hopefully, you'll be able to in the morning. Right now, my grandma needs to see your grandmother and Auntie Jax. Then she's going to have to rest. I promise as soon as she's strong enough, I'll come get you myself so you can see her."

Ali's lower lip trembled but she nodded in understanding.

"You two go on. I need to call my mother and let her know what's happened." Amy's tone spoke volumes. She did not look forward to making the call and I didn't blame her. "Tell Grandma I'll be back in a few minutes."

I nodded and then gave her a hug.

"After you make your call, you need to eat something, Amy," Mary Kate said.

Before Amy could object, Mary Kate took matters into her own hands. She pulled her phone and called the café, telling whoever answered that we needed food sent to the hospital now rather than later.

With Judith at my side, I entered the intensive care unit. A nurse at the station in the center of the unit looked up as we did. Her expression was unmistakable. Any moment now she'd be telling us we couldn't be there. Then, recognizing us, she smiled almost gently and motioned to the room directly across from the nursing station. Judith softly thanked her.

I paused at the door and braced myself. As I did, I wanted to be anywhere but there. I didn't want to see Miss Serena ill. Still, it could be worse. I needed to remember that. I needed to remember she lived and she would get better. Nothing else was allowed.

Inside the small room lay the woman who was grandmother, mentor, friend, teacher and so much more. Standing there, I swallowed hard. Miss Serena looked so frail as she lay in bed, covered by a sheet and light blanket. At least the machines monitoring her vitals remained silent. If they'd been beeping like they do in the movies, I might have run to the hills.

I was still trying to decide whether to step inside or run and hide when she lifted her head. Her eyes, not as alert as usual, focused on me. A relieved smile touched her lips and she held a hand out to me. With Judith moving to one side of the bed, I moved to the other. I grasped Miss Serena's hand between mine and bent to press my lips to her cheek. As I did, tears burned in my eyes and I blinked them back. I wouldn't let her see how scared I was.

"You need to do what the doctors tell you," I said softly.

"Jax is right, Serena. You scared us."

"Scared me too." She freed her hand and lightly patted the mattress, waiting until I carefully sat next to her. "Did you get the book?"

"Yes, ma'am. It's safe. I'll keep it that way until you're home. I promise."

"You're a good girl, Jax. Too good for your parents." Her eyelids drooped and she forced them open. "You keep the book. It's yours now."

I shook my head, panic racing through me. Nope. No way.

"Miss Serena."

"Hush." She waited until I nodded. "Jax, you did more than save my life today. You proved what I've suspected since you returned home."

"Miss Serena, please. We can talk about all this after you're better." I didn't try to stop my tears now. Instead, I reached up and wiped them away as they rolled down my cheeks.

"Don't be scared, child. I'm not going anywhere." She lifted a hand and wiped away a stray tear I'd missed. "But things are changing. Today proved that."

"I-I don't understand."

"You knew there was trouble before any of the other Guardians did. You tapped into the ley lines and use their power to help maintain the wards over the land. Then you used them to help stabilize me until Amy arrived. You acted on instinct honed by training and a determination to do whatever it took to protect not just me but Ali and everyone else." She paused. Her eyes closed. I waited, fear building until I saw her chest rise and then fall with a breath.

"Miss Serena, I only did what I needed to." I swallowed against the lump in my throat. "I love you."

"Love you too." She forced her eyes open. "Tired, but I need to say this. Judith, you witness."

Judith nodded, her expression doing nothing to reassure me.

"Jax, you've never turned away when someone's needed your help." Miss Serena winced slightly as she changed positions in bed.

Worried, I glanced at the monitors over her bed. I might not be an MD, but as a vet, I knew how to read the monitors and translate what they meant. She was far from healthy right now, but she wasn't in immediate danger either.

"Lie still. Let me get the nurse. She'll help you get comfortable."

"In a minute." She held my hand more firmly than I expected, forcing me to stay where I was unless I wanted to jerk free. "I need your help now. The Guardians, Mossy Creek needs your help."

"You have it, Miss Serena. I accepted my role as a Guardian. I'm not changing my mind."

"I'm not doing this well." She struggled to sit up. Judith hissed in displeasure but moved to help her. "Jax, bend down."

I did as she said. I'm not sure what I expected. Maybe she wanted to kiss my cheek. Hell, maybe she wanted to smack me up side the head. So why did I feel like she was about to upturn my world again?

She rested her palm against my cheek. When she did, I leaned into it. Slowly, so slowly I almost missed it, my cheek warmed under her touch. The world narrowed to the two of us. Then the world exploded around me. It was like the way the land greeted me whenever I returned to town but on steroids that were on steroids. For a moment—or an eternity—I felt the town, every acre, every person, every living thing. Then, with a *snap!*, I was back in Miss Serena's room, Judith's arms holding me on my feet.

"What the hell was that?" I rasped it out as I struggled to remember how to breathe.

"I hadn't wanted it to be like this, Jax. I'm sorry." Miss Serena looked and sounded exhausted. "But it's necessary. I'll be here to help, but it's your time now."

"I-I don't understand."

"Judith?" Miss Serena looked at her, her eyes imploring Quinn's mother to explain.

"Jax, let's let her rest. I'll explain."

I nodded, knowing I wasn't going to like what she had to say. But instead of protesting, I bent and once again lightly kissed Miss Serena's cheek. Then I promised to be back as soon as the doctors let me. Judith, her arm still around my waist, led me into the hallway outside Miss Serena's room. As she did, Amy moved in our direction. One part of my brain realized she'd been waiting for us. My inner alarms went off again. If someone didn't explain what just happened and soon, I was going to lose it.

"Jax, let's step in here." Judith indicated the next room, this one unoccupied.

I nodded and let her lead me inside.

"Sweetheart, you have every right to resent what just happened, every right to be angry. But I want you to think about one thing before you say anything. None of us planned this. The last thing Serena wanted was for you to feel trapped. But she's been worried for more than a year that she wouldn't be strong enough if anyone or anything tried to attack the town. When you came home, she knew her prayers —our prayers—had been answered. Even then, she refused to try to force your hand into accepting your place as a Guardian."

"I really don't understand."

"She just stepped down as a Guardian, Jax, and passed the leadership to you."

My eyes went wide and I stumbled back a step. Now I knew this was a dream. No, a nightmare.

"I can't." I looked at Amy, convinced she wouldn't go along with this. Instead of outrage or hurt, I saw understanding and approval.

"You can, Jax, but only if you want to," she said.

My knees gave out and I slowly sank to the floor. As I did, Amy softly told Judith to give her a few minutes alone with me. Judith didn't say anything. Instead, she knelt next to me and lightly kissed my cheek, much as I had Miss Serena's not so long ago. Then she left, closing the door behind her.

"Amy."

"Shh." She sat next to me and slid an arm around my shoulder, pulling me close. "Grandma planned for this, Jax. She didn't think it would happen so soon though."

"She can't step down, Amy. We need her. *I* need her."

"And she will be there for you. But she's old now, Jax. Her strength isn't what it once was. Today showed all of us that. Isn't it better to learn now, when we all have time to adjust to what we need to do to protect our town than later, in the heat of battle?"

I knew she was right but that didn't make it any easier. Hell, who was I kidding? I'm surprised I didn't piss my pants and run from the room screaming. I wasn't ready for this. In so many ways I wasn't ready for it. I'd barely started accepting the fact I was a Guardian. Now I was supposed to step into Miss Serena's shoes and make sure nothing else happened?

No fucking way.

"Jax, look at me."

I did.

"Grandma's going to recover. You have to believe that first and foremost."

"I do."

Of course, I might kill her when I quit fighting the urge to run and hide.

"Then accept this. Grandma would never pass on the leadership of the Guardians, the protection of the town she has devoted her life to, if she didn't believe you not only could do the job but that you would do it with the same determination she has."

"Amy."

"Jax, think about it. Be honest with yourself as you do. Think about everything that's happened since you came home. You fell back into the role of the Rogue. You finally stood up to your parents and accepted—at least to a degree—everything Bitsy's been telling you for years. All of us from this generation have looked to you for our cues on what we should do. All you're doing now, if you agree, is taking the next logical step."

"Amy, I never wanted this."

"Neither did my grandmother. Will you at least think about it?"

No matter how much I wanted this to be a dream, it wasn't. Damn it.

"Be honest with me right now. Is your grandmother going to be all right?"

"I wouldn't lie to you about this, Jax. If nothing else happens, if she doesn't have to extend herself like she did today, she will be. But she is going to have to slow down and take the time to recover. She will be able to be there for us as an advisor and teacher. But the fighting for Mossy Creek falls to the rest of us now. It is a fight we have a much better chance of winning with you leading us."

"It means we're one Guardian short again."

And we all know where that led us before.

"All right. I want everyone to meet back at your grandmother's house. You too. You and Judith can help explain what happened."

Maybe by then, I would figure it out as well.

17

It took time, but two hours later we all gathered at Miss Serena's. Rafe, realizing something bothered me, didn't ask questions. He knew me well enough by now to understand I needed time to think, to process what happened. Except there wasn't enough time to process it all. There never would be. Once again Mossy Creek hit me with that cosmic two-by-four. It caught me right between the eyes and kept swinging.

God, what had I gotten myself into?

As we climbed out of Rafe's SUV, the front door opened. A moment later, two figures came flying down the steps in our direction. I braced myself and opened my arms. At almost the same time, Ali and Robbie dove for me. I held them close, knowing they needed reassurance as much as I did.

"Auntie Jax?" Ali lifted her face and fear lit her eyes. She didn't need to ask her question.

I dropped to my knees and hugged the kids to me. Then, feeling Rafe's hand on my shoulder, I smiled up at him. He gave me a reassuring smile in return before stepping back to give us some privacy.

"Miss Serena is doing better. I promise."

"Is she going to be all right, Dr. Jax?" Robbie asked.

"The doctors think she has a really good chance of being all right. But she's going to have to stay in the hospital for a while and then she's going to have to take it easy." I carefully considered what else to say. "And that's where the two of you can help. Once she's home, do you think you can come over and read to her and keep her entertained so she doesn't try to do too much?"

They nodded emphatically.

"Will she be able to keep teaching me stuff, Auntie Jax?"

"Once she's better. In the meantime, think you can put up with your grandma and Miss Mary Kate and me, maybe even Aunt Ciara working with you?"

Another nod.

"I promise I will always tell you the truth where Miss Serena's concerned, kids. I know she's as important to you as she is to me."

"What happened to her, Auntie Jax? She was fine. Then she told me to stay inside. She looked like something bad was happening. The house wouldn't let me out. I tried and tried and it kept me inside. Then the door suddenly opened and she was laying on the front porch."

"We're still figuring it all out, sweetie, but the doctors think she had a heart attack. That's serious but treatable if she does what they tell her and if nothing else happens." I stood and held a hand out to each of them. "Let's go inside and let your mamas know you're okay. I bet they're worrying about you."

Rafe waited for us on the front porch. I sent the kids ahead and stopped, reaching for his hand. He deserved a head's up about what happened.

"Doc?" Concern roughened his voice as I led him around the house.

"We need to talk before we go inside."

He stopped and pulled me close. "What's wrong? Do you know something about Miss Serena the rest of us don't?"

I nodded and then shook my head.

"I guess the answer is yes and no."

"Doc, you're not making any sense."

Why should I when the situation didn't make any sense?

"The doctors really do think she's going to be all right. But something has changed."

"Doc, you're worrying me."

I chuckled softly but with little humor. "I'm worrying me too, love." I looked down at our hands, fingers twined. "Rafe, Miss Serena wanted to talk to Judith and me because she feels she can no longer be a Guardian."

For a moment, he said nothing. I'm not sure he could. He might not have lived in Mossy Creek for long, but he knew how important she was to the town and to me. Hell, I knew she meant a great deal to him too.

"Damn. No wonder you've looked so unsettled. Is Judith taking over for her?"

"I wish." I stepped away. I wouldn't blame him if he wanted to run for the hills. Hell, I was still considering doing exactly that.

"You?"

"Yes."

As if things weren't strange enough already, he grinned and nodded in approval. "You probably don't want to hear this, Doc, but it makes sense. Anyone with eyes in their head could see she's been preparing you for this."

I swallowed hard and then licked my lips. If that was true, why hadn't I seen it?

Because I didn't want to.

"Are you really okay with this?"

"It's what you're meant for, Doc." He reached for my hands again and lifted them to his lips. "You're a protector, a warrior. But you are also someone who cares deeply and who will do everything she can for those she loves. So, yes, I'm okay with it as long as you remember you aren't in this alone. I'm right here with you and always will be."

"Thank God."

We stood there another few moments before heading inside. It was time to face the music, whether I wanted to or not.

"Are you all right?" Bitsy asked the moment we stepped inside.

I nodded, thanking Judith as she handed me a beer. "Honestly? I'm still shaken by everything." I glanced around the room, wondering where the kids had gotten to.

"They're in the kitchen with Camille and Peggy," Mary Kate said. "We thought it best all of us talk before we eat."

I nodded again. At least someone was thinking. I was still babbling silently and considering the quickest way out of town.

"Security?"

"Jimmy has guards posted and Rafe and Sam added more cameras and sensors to the security system," Amy said from where she sat next to Lexie on the sofa. "Jimmy also pulled the stock in and they're safely in the barns or fields nearest the house."

"Good." That, at least, was one worry off my mind.

"He and Sherry are going to see Grandma and will stay at the hospital until Brian and I get there."

"Where is Brian?" I frowned because I'd expected her fiancé to be here.

"He needed to take care of a situation at work. He'll be here shortly."

"Anything else from the hospital?" God, don't let there be any more news, especially bad news.

"Grandma's resting comfortably and her condition has stabilized. They're going to keep her in the unit another day or two and, if she continues improving, will move her into a step-down room next."

"Then I guess we should get down to business." I took a long draw on my beer and sank onto the raised hearth.

"Before Jax says what she needs to, there's something you all need to know. Grandma sent for Brian and me last night. It's no secret that she's been worried about everything that's happened the last few years. Last night, she told me she felt like the danger was getting closer and she wanted me to know some things in case something happened to her."

"Amy?" Lexie looked at her in concern.

"I don't think she had a premonition. If she had, she would have warned us. I think this was just Grandma being pragmatic like she always is. Basically, she wanted to make sure I knew what to do if anything happened to her and I think we all agree having her in ICU qualifies as something happening to her."

We all nodded.

"Most of it came as no surprise. She wanted Brian and me to move in here. She told me at the hospital she still wants that and asked us to move in now. She doesn't want the house left empty, even for a short time. So we started moving in this evening."

"I'll get with Brian and arrange for a crew to help move your things here," Sam said.

"Thanks. That will help."

"What else?" Quinn asked, looking from her mother to Amy and then to me. She knew there was more to it. I saw it in her eyes.

"All the town records, the histories, everything related to the Guardians will go home with Jax. Grandma has charged her with holding and protecting them just as she has all these years."

"Amy, I don't understand. If Miss Serena's going to be all right, why send all that with Jax?" Ciara asked.

Amy looked at me and I recognized her unasked question. I dipped my chin. She could tell them. Hell, it would probably be best if she broke the news. Then we could explain what little we knew.

"Grandma is stepping down as a Guardian. Today's events proved to her that she isn't strong enough to continue in that role. She passed her position with the Guardians to Jax who accepted—after considering running for the hills."

"Still considering it," I muttered.

"I don't understand." Quinn looked as lost as I felt.

"Join the club." I climbed to my feet. "As much as today scared each of us, I think it made Miss Serena face her mortality. We all know she would never put Mossy Creek or any of us in danger. Right now, she feels like she is no longer able to protect us as she has. I'll be honest, I hope she changes her mind. But, in the meantime, I will do everything I can to live up to the faith she's put in me and in all of us."

"Before any of you start jumping to conclusions, this is something Serena talked with me, not to mention Pat and Mary Kate, about on a number of occasions. We knew she was training Jax to take over for her even if Jax didn't realize it." She smiled at me and I grinned in return. "We also agreed. The head of the Guardians needs to be strong, stronger than Pat and me. Jax more than meets that qualification. She also loves this town as much as any of us. Then there's the little fact that the town recognizes her, responds to her. That is very important."

"But that leaves us a Guardian short again," Annie commented. "Are you taking the empty slot?" She looked at Amy who, in turn, looked at me.

"We'll talk about that in a bit." I held up a hand to prevent any of them from interrupting. "I promise, it will be discussed tonight. But right now we need to talk about what happened today.

"Someone tried to attack this house and Miss Serena. I don't know why and I don't know who. But I plan to find out. I hope each of you will help me do so."

"Just tell me what you want me to do, Doc," Rafe said.

"Rafe speaks for all of us," Lucas added.

"Thanks." I relaxed a little. At least they seemed to be taking this more in stride than I was.

"From what I understand, the attack itself didn't hurt Miss Serena. The wards held. They may have held even if she hadn't thrown everything she could into strengthening them. But you know her. She wasn't going to let anything happen to the people who were on the property." People who included Ali, Jimmy Reardon and his crew, and me. I'd be dealing with that guilt for a long time.

"So she threw everything she had into strengthening the wards. Best I can tell from what Amy's had to say, it was that strain that was too much for Miss Serena."

"Jax is right." Amy stood and moved to sit next to me on the hearth. "And I will say what Jax hasn't. It was also unnecessary and it was foolish. I don't know why, but Grandma didn't pull on the ley line running beneath the house. If she had, she wouldn't have needed to pull on personal energy to feed the wards."

"That doesn't sound like Miss Serena," Quinn said.

"Actually, Quinn, it does."

I looked at Judith in surprise, especially when Mary Kate nodded in agreement.

"Why?" Amy and I asked at the same time.

"I love Serena like a sister, but I'm the first to admit she's stubborn to a fault. That's especially true when it comes to believing she can handle anything that gets thrown at her. I doubt she even thought about the ley line until you were here, Jax. By then, she'd already overextended herself." Judith moved to stand in front of me. I let her pull me to my feet. A moment later, she turned so the two of us faced everyone.

"That attitude is also something Serena is well aware of. She knew it was her weakness, if you want to call it that. Realizing she put herself and, through extension, the town in danger because she reacted instead of thinking and utilizing the tools at hand played into her decision to step down as a Guardian. But, and each of you need to remember this, she was already planning on stepping down and she had already talked with Amy, Pat, Mary Kate and myself about Jax taking over for her. So yes, we can be upset with Serena for acting foolishly enough she put herself in danger. But this decision of hers is not something she did on the spur of the moment and it is something she feels is best for our town."

"Judith's right." Mary Kate moved to stand to my left while Judith remained on my right. "Remember too that Serena will still be here. She is still going to be a very important part of our lives."

She'd better be because I sure as hell needed her help and guidance, now more than ever.

But she'd made her decision just as I'd made mine. Now we needed to figure out where to go from here.

I hugged first Mary Kate and then Judith. They studied me for a moment and then returned to their chairs. Once they had, I held a hand out to Rafe. If I was going to do this, I wanted him with me.

"What happened today leaves us needing another Guardian. I am not willing to go even a day without there being four of us, not after today and not after everything that's happened these last few days." I blew out a breath. I could do this. I had to do this. "Miss Serena always represented Air but we all know she could have represented any of the Elements."

Heads nodded.

"Judith represents Fire, although it isn't her strongest Element and Dr. Pat represents Water."

More nods.

"That leaves us needing an Air Elemental."

Meg's eyes went wide and I laughed softly when she started shaking her head, her hands up as if to ward off a blow.

"No, Meg, not you. Not right now at least."

She narrowed her eyes at me and didn't relax. But at least she hadn't made a run for it—yet.

"I've had a chance to talk with Judith, Mary Kate, Amy, Dr. Pat and even Miss Serena about this. Judith is going to become our Air Elemental. Air has always been her strongest Element."

I looked at Quinn who didn't gasp and didn't try to run away. Instead, she closed her eyes for a moment. It didn't take a mind reader to know she was remembering an earlier conversation. That day, she promised to do whatever she could to protect Mossy Creek. Now the day had come for her to fulfill that promise. It was sooner than either of us expected.

When she opened her eyes, she nodded once. The hint of uncertainty in her eyes did nothing to take away from the determination on her face.

"Thank you." I reached for her hand, drawing her to my side. "Quinn will be our fourth, our Fire Elemental."

"Are you sure about this?" Ciara asked her sister.

"Maybe?" She gave a shaky smile. "I already promised Jax I'd do whatever was necessary to help protect the town. I had a suspicion this was going to happen, but I'd been hoping it was a long time off."

"We all did, child." Judith smiled proudly at her youngest.

"And I'm holding Jax and Miss Serena to their promises to help me. God knows I still need training." As if to prove her point, she looked down at her hands and then cursed to see small flames dancing around them. She closed her eyes and the flames died out. "See?"

"Quinn brings up a good point," Meg said from where she sat next to Drew. "Isn't it dangerous having two untrained or relatively untrained Guardians right now? No offense, Quinn, but you're still learning the extent of your abilities."

"None taken and I'd like an answer to that question as well."

"It's a risk, but it can also work to our advantage."

"Jax is right. Whoever has been targeting the town and some of us sitting in this room, they know Serena, Pat and me. They don't know Jax and Quinn. They won't know how they will respond to any given situation nor how they will work together. Adding Jax to our number changed our dynamic. Serena stepping down and Jax taking over for her does so again. Add my Quinn to the mix." Judith grinned and then shrugged expressively, clearly looking forward to the battle to come.

"Quinn's the protector, the enforcer. I'm the Rogue. We've all seen Judith become a warrior to protect each of us from the time we were kids. Dr. Pat's our healer. Whoever attacked Miss Serena, whoever has been trying to disrupt the town, will soon learn they made the worst mistake of their lives when they decided to come after us." I took a step forward.

"Will you help us? Will you join this battle of ours and have our backs as we have yours?"

I knew the question didn't need to be asked but there's power in voicing vows and that's what we each were doing. We were pledging to protect our town, to support one another, to stand against the darkness coming our way.

"Thank you." I smiled at each of them once they agreed. "So let's get started before dinner's ready and the kids want to know what we've been talking about. Ciara, Annie, what did you find out about Maddy?"

I returned to my place on the hearth and waited. From the way they looked at one another, I had a feeling I wasn't going to like what I heard. Since I hadn't liked a lot of what I'd seen and heard today, why should this be any different?

"Jax?"

I turned from where I'd been brewing tea and smiled slightly. Three hours ago, we ranged around the den at Miss Serena's. Now Quinn and Judith sat at my kitchen table. Lucas and Rafe were holed up in Rafe's study, going over the various video feeds from the security cameras around Miss Serena's property. For the arcane attack to be as strong as it had been, the person responsible needed to be nearby. Maybe we'd get lucky and one of the security cameras caught a glimpse of him—or her. Even if they didn't, it was possible the cameras caught something to help us figure out who was responsible for the attack.

While they did that, Judith and I needed to have a heart-to-heart with Quinn. She needed to know what she was getting into. I'd sprung becoming the fourth Guardian on her. Part of me felt guilty for it. Another part was surprised she hadn't beaten me to a pulp for ambushing her with the possibility.

"Jax, quit fussing," Judith said.

"Sorry." I smiled slightly and gave a little shrug. "I'll admit I want to shift and run."

And probably not stop until I was very far from here.

"Tell me about it."

To my surprise, Quinn chuckled and patted the chair next to hers. Bringing the teapot with me, I moved to the table. As I did, Judith handed around the three mugs I'd put out earlier. The next several minutes saw us pouring tea and fixing it to our own tastes. Then I couldn't put it off any longer. It was time to talk to Quinn and make sure she knew what I was asking of her.

"Jax, quit tying yourself in knots trying to figure out what to say."

Quinn turned slightly in her chair so she faced me. "I'm not dumb. I knew when you asked if I was ready to step up that this was probably going to happen. Like I said earlier, I didn't expect it to happen so soon."

Judith smiled and reached for her daughter's hand. "None of us did, Quinn, not even Serena."

"I want you to be sure, Quinn. I don't want you to feel like I trapped you into agreeing."

"Well." She drawled it out and then grinned mischievously. "Like I said, Jax, I'm not dumb. I've been keeping an eye on what you've been up to since you came back to town. You slid back into your role as the Rogue as if you'd never left. But it's been more than that. You, me, Annie, even Meg and Ciara, slipped back into our roles from when we were younger."

I nodded. She was right. We had slid back into our childhood roles with one exception. Meg filled the role Maddy played back in school. Even now, she was more a part of our inner circle than Maddy. That was something I needed to think long and hard about, especially in light of what Ciara and Annie said earlier about their visit with our friend. But that was something to worry about later, after talking with Quinn.

"I'll always need you standing with me, Quinn. You're my sister in all the ways that matter."

"As you are mine." She reached for my hand and gave it a quick squeeze. "Mom, I guess we could blame you for all this." She grinned wickedly at Judith who simply shook her head, her eyes sparkling with affection.

"That is something I will happily take responsibility for." She lay a hand on top of Quinn's where it still rested on mine. "You both have always done whatever's been needed and that's what we need right now."

"I'll do it, Mom. You know that. But I still have a hell of a lot to learn about my abilities. That's what I'm trusting the two of you for. I need you to know this all goes beyond my discomfort with the woo-woo stuff."

I couldn't help it. I grinned. I had a feeling Quinn would never be completely comfortable with her abilities, not after spending most of her life thinking she was a normal.

"We will all do whatever we can, Quinn, but you know more than you give yourself credit for," Judith said.

"Your mother's right."

"Maybe." That was the closest she'd come to agreeing with us. "Just understand this. I'm doing this to protect this town and the people I love. I will do whatever it takes to do so. That means I'll use arcane and mundane means, Fire and guns, the dogs, whatever is necessary."

"Understood. That's pretty much where I stand and both of you need to accept it. I will use my arcane abilities but I also won't hesitate to shift and use those abilities if I think they are best for the situation."

"So we're on the same page." Quinn sipped her tea and I waited. She had more on her mind. "For me at least, I'm going to look at what's happening like I would a criminal investigation. When that SOB attacked the farm, they injured Miss Serena just as surely as if they'd fired a bullet at her. I'm not going to let them get away with it."

"We aren't going to," her mother corrected.

Quinn had the good grace to agree.

"Since that's settled, I might as well prove you probably made a mistake tapping me for this, Jax."

I looked at her in concern.

"Look, I know I'm probably out of place saying this and you can tell me to mind my own business, but this all feels like we're about to go to war. Someone, maybe more than one someone, has been systematically trying to attack the people we care for as well as our town. We can't just sit back and wait to see what happens next."

She drew circles on the table top with her mug. "Jax, I know you're more than willing to fight for those you love and those you know need your protection. That's what the Rogue has done for as long as I can remember.

"Mom, same for you. I've watched you fight for those you care for all my life. Hell, where do you think learned to do it? You taught both Ciara and me, even Ciaran, to stand up for those we love and for those who aren't able to stand up for themselves."

I nodded, knowing where this was going.

"But what about Dr. Pat? Does she have it in her to fight like I fear we're going to have to? More than that, does she have the time and the mind space for it? She's still dealing with Maddy. Now she's taking care of Miss Serena. Is she going to be able to step up or will she be a weak link?"

For a moment, no one said anything. I frowned slightly. Quinn put into words one of my concerns. It was also a concern I didn't feel qualified to address. That had to be Judith, at least initially. She knew Dr. Pat better than Quinn and I did. She'd have a better idea what Dr. Pat was prepared to do to protect Mossy Creek.

"If you had asked me that six months ago, I would have told you there was nothing to worry about."

My stomach did a slow roll. That was not what I wanted to hear.

"Now, all I can say is she will do her best. But you're right, Quinn. She is distracted right now. Maddy is a constant source of worry for her. With Serena ill, her focus will be even more split. But she will be there when we need her. She may be a healer, but she will fight to protect those in her care."

I hoped it was enough. It had to be enough.

"All right." I thought for a moment. "Until this is over, we don't go anywhere unarmed. That means both mundane and arcane methods of protection."

"Jax," Judith began.

"Mom, she's right." Quinn waited until her mother looked at her. "We can't take any unnecessary risks. This fight doesn't have any rules. So we make sure the playing field is as level as possible."

"Quinn, at least one dog for each of the Guardians as well as for Amy." Annie, Meg and Mary Kate already owned dogs Quinn selected for them.

"I'll take care of it come morning." She pulled out her phone and made a note. "I'm also making sure there are a couple of extra dogs at Miss Serena's to not only protect her but the stock as well."

I nodded in appreciation.

"What about Dr. Pat? She won't be able to have a dog in the hospital and will raise hell if we try to get her to keep one with her in the office."

"Sam will know who to talk to about getting her armed escorts to and from work. Lucas can talk with hospital security to make sure she has eyes on her whenever she's there."

It wasn't enough to satisfy me but it would have to do until we figured something else out.

"There's something else you can do, Quinn, if you would."

"What?"

"Get with Lucas, Drew, Sam, Rafe and your sister. Figure out what can be done to tighten security around town. I'm going to talk with Miss Peggy and Miss Olivia in the morning. They'll make sure word is spread to the right folks about what they need to be on the lookout for."

"Let me talk with them, Jax. You have enough on your plate already," Judith said.

"Thanks." I leaned back and considered how to broach this next bit. "That leaves me free to talk with Ciara. There's something I need to take care of and she can help smooth the way for me."

Mother and daughter narrowed their eyes at me as they waited for me to explain.

"Don't look at me like that."

Instead of saying anything, they arched almost identical brows.

"Look, it's simple. I need to have a conversation with Maddy's ex-boss. I need to do so without Liam or anyone else interfering. Ciara can help set it up for me."

"See what Ciara thinks. Then we'll talk." Quinn waited, her expression serious, until I nodded. Then she relaxed some.

"That's not all." Here's where it got a bit trickier. "We need someone to have a little *chat* with the Luíseachs, Sawyer, Mia and everyone else involved with the troubles we've seen since Catherine was charged with Spud's murder. There's a thread running through everything and we need to know what it is. You and Lucas can sense patterns, so I'd appreciate it if you both looked at the case files again. But we need someone not associated with the Sheriff's Department, the DA's Office or the law office to talk with them."

"I'll talk with Meg and Sam tomorrow. I'm sure they know someone we can use."

"Thanks, Judith." I blew out a breath, suddenly so tired I could put my head down on the tabletop and fall asleep. "I need you two to do one more thing for me."

"I'm not carrying you to your bed." Quinn grinned and shook her head.

"That might be easier." When they looked at me in concern, I waved it aside. "I've done my best since morning not to let on how scared I am. On the inside, I want to curl up in a corner and hide from the world."

"Jax, we understand." Judith scooted her chair closer and leaned in, sliding an arm around me for a quick hug. "But think about this. If you run, Quinn's going to beat you to the city limits." She grinned at her youngest daughter. Quinn did the mature thing and stuck her tongue out at her.

"Mom's right. Don't even think about leaving me to deal with all this." She waved a hand in front of her and I knew what she meant.

"Remember this as well, child. Serena's been planning for this for years, long before you returned home. She always knew you'd be the one to step into her shoes where the Guardians are concerned. You only have to accept it."

"Yes, ma'am." I scrubbed my hands over my face. "I'm not going to run away."

"I know." Judith tilted her head and studied me for a moment. "Something else, Jax. It means you can't go haring off on your own anymore. You are what will hold the Guardians together, just as Serena did. You need to trust us to have your back and do whatever we can to help you."

"I do trust you to do just that. I'm not making any promises about the rest of it. But I'll try." Unless I believed by doing something on my own, I could keep everyone else safe. Then it would be better to apologize after the fact than get their permission before.

"Let's all meet for breakfast in the morning. It will need to be early so Dr. Pat can join us."

"I'll set it up. We can meet at our place," Judith said and Quinn nodded. "And now you need to get some rest. I'll go see if Lucas is ready to leave."

"Are you all right?" Quinn asked once we were alone.

"I ought to be asking you that." I climbed to my feet and crossed to the counter. Quinn watched as I dug in one of the upper cabinets. A few moments later, I turned. In one hand I held a bottle of tequila and in the other two shot glasses. I poured each of us a shot and handed her one before returning to my chair. "I sort of ambushed you. Sorry."

"Don't be. Of the two of us, you were blindsided more than I was."

Wasn't that the truth?

"But we're good?"

"We're good, Jax." She tapped her shot glass against mine and then downed her tequila. I chuckled softly as she grimaced at the burn. Then I shot mine back and poured us each another shot. "Before your mother gets back. I share your concerns about Dr. Pat. We need to keep an eye on her and on Maddy." I tossed back the second shot and slammed the glass down on the tabletop. "I don't think she'll turn on us. Never that. But she has a lot on her plate right now."

Quinn nodded and finished her shot. Then, hearing the others moving in our direction, she stood. "You get some rest, Jax. We'll discuss it some more tomorrow."

"I'd tell you to get some rest as well but you're going to have to deal with your daughter first." I grinned when she looked at me in question. Then her eyes went wide and she cursed inventively. "I'm going to get you for this, Jax. You know she's going to want to know what's going on."

"No, she's going to want to know why you're glowing." I laughed and ducked under the arm she swung at me.

"Just remember that payback's a bitch, Jax."

Maybe, but that was so far down my list of things to worry about it was non-existent. For now, all I wanted was to get some sleep. Maybe when I woke, I'd have a better idea about what to do to keep Miss Serena and all the others safe until we figured out what the hell was going on.

QUINN

18

It finally happened. Jax had lost her mind. Either that or I had. That was the only thing that made any sense.

Me, a Guardian.

Jax—and, by extension, my mother—had lost her mind. I couldn't be a Guardian. I was still learning how to control my abilities. Now Jax and Mom expected me to help protect the town as an *Other*?

I dropped onto a chair at the kitchen table and slowly beat my head against it. I'm not sure what I hoped to accomplish. Mom always said my head is too hard to beat anything into it. So maybe I was hoping to beat myself into unconsciousness.

It didn't help that the house laughed in my head.

Yes, laughed. Damned house.

At least Ali didn't have too many questions about what happened. That would change. My little girl was nothing if not curious. But right now she was more worried about Miss Serena than she was about any change she might have seen in me. Petty as it was, I'd take it.

In the distance, a clock struck midnight. I sat up, listening. The house around me was silent. Ali was safely tucked into bed. Lucas had gone up half an hour ago. Mom retired shortly after, once she made sure I was all right.

The only problem was I wasn't. I was worried and pissed and stunned in equal parts.

I was worried about Miss Serena. I was pissed—and that's putting it mildly—that Lucas and I, not to mention everyone else, might have missed something that led to what happened today. Yesterday? Most of all, I couldn't get past the fear I'd finally lost my everlasting mind. But like it or not, I made the same decision Jax had not that long ago. We both did whatever was necessary to protect those we loved, even if doing so made us question our sanity.

But, if I was honest, I didn't question my sanity. Not about this. I might have done everything possible to avoid returning to town until I had to. Ali kind of took care of that for me when she called Fire and Wind that first time. Now we were both part of Mossy Creek. That meant I'd protect it and those who live here.

The only question was how.

First things first. Jax gave me that step at least. I needed to put in place security for my fellow Guardians.

I closed my eyes and fought the urge to beat my head against the tabletop again. Guardian. I was a freaking Guardian. How the hell had that happened? I usually know before someone hits me with a two-by-four, even a metaphorical one. Despite everything I said earlier, I had not seen this coming so soon.

I needed to shake it off. The only way to do that was to get busy. That meant coffee. Lots and lots of coffee.

Mug in hand, I returned to the table a few minutes later. As I did, I opened my laptop and reached for my cellphone. I quickly texted Annie and Meg, telling them to meet me for lunch. To say we needed to talk was an understatement. But I wanted time to talk with Sam and Drew first. There were things the three of us needed to set in motion before I informed their wives what I had in mind, especially since I knew Annie and Meg would not appreciate it one little bit.

Before long, a pad and pen joined the laptop and cellphone. Emails were sent. Notes were taken. More texts went out. Slowly, a plan began to form. With it came a determination I recognized and welcomed. I felt this way every time I got my teeth into an investigation. I had the scent, so to speak. All I had to do was follow the trail to the perp.

"Quinn?"

I saved my work and glanced over my shoulder. Lucas stood in the doorway. Dressed in jeans and a black golf shirt with the sheriff's logo at the left breast, he looked ready for work. The only thing missing was his gun. But it was his look of concern that had me climbing to my feet. My muscles protested and I groaned slightly.

Damn it, I was getting too old to pull these all-nighters.

"Sorry if I woke you." I moved to where he stood and reached up to kiss him.

"You didn't." He nuzzled my neck and then stepped back, studying me. "You didn't come to bed. Are you all right?"

I started to reassure him and then gave a half smile and a shrug.

"I feel like I've been hit over the head and tossed into the middle of a tornado. Except I didn't land in Oz."

He chuckled and moved to the counter to pour himself a mug of coffee.

"Jax?"

I nodded. "And everything else."

He topped off my mug and then moved to the table. Instead of sitting, he reached over and moved my notepad so he could read what I'd written. I waited, sipping coffee, and none-too-subtly stretching to ease my cramped muscles. When he looked up a few minutes later, he nodded once, his expression thoughtful.

"I think I see where you're going with this." He sat next to me and pushed my notes to the side. "Before we get to that, tell me one thing. Are you all right?"

I reached for his hand where it rested on the tabletop. As our fingers twined, I studied them. Lucas had been there for me from the moment I returned to town and learned Mom was missing. He'd bent to the point of breaking department rules to let me assist in the investigation. Oh, he'd been an ass as well and learned firsthand how dangerous it was to have the house decide he might present a danger. But through it all, I'd known he had my back and, even more important, that he would do everything possible to protect my little girl.

"Honestly?"

He nodded.

"I'm not sure."

He scooted closer to me and slid his arm across my shoulder. "Quinn, I'd worry if you didn't feel a little off-stride this morning. Between the attack, Miss Serena's heart attack and Jax asking you to be one of the Guardians, yesterday upended everything."

I nodded. Of course, he understood. He knew how learning I wasn't really a normal did more than surprise me. He helped me get past the doubts I still had as an *Other*. Fortunately, those came less frequently now, but I still found it hard from time to time to realize I wasn't what I thought myself to be for the majority of my life.

"You think?" I grinned up at him.

"I'll be honest, love. I expected you to fight Jax and your mom about everything."

I frowned and sat up.

"Quinn, don't get mad." He held up a hand before I could interrupt. "Admit it. You didn't expect to become a Guardian."

I grimaced slightly. Seeing it, he frowned. Then he arched a brow, a clear indication I needed to explain my reaction.

"I didn't expect it to happen so soon, but Mom and Miss Serena have hinted at the possibility more than once."

And, if I was being honest, I'd given the possibility some thought.

He nodded, his expression thoughtful. Then he looked at me and grinned.

"You've always done your duty, love. Whether it's your family, the job or this town, you've always stepped up. This isn't really all that different."

"I wouldn't say that." Not by a long shot.

"What can I do to help?"

This was just one reason I loved him. He took things like this in stride.

"Jax gave me several assignments last night while you were talking with Rafe."

He nodded for me to continue.

"She asked me to make sure we have solid security in place for not only the Guardians but our families as well as Annie, Meg, Mary Kate and Amy. I've already emailed the trainers and will be getting additional dogs. I don't see any problems about it with anyone except Annie."

Lucas knew what I meant. More than once, Annie put herself in danger by not taking precautions. She wasn't careless. She simply didn't think the way either of us did. But that was changing and part of me mourned. I didn't want Annie to lose that faith in humanity but I also didn't want her putting herself in danger because she wanted to believe in the best of people.

"Tell me what you have in mind."

"You can help, at least the SD can, when she's at the courthouse. I'll keep an eye on her when I'm in the office but even without the added responsibilities of being a Guardian, there will be times when I have to be out of the office investigating our cases. When I'm not there, I need to know she's covered."

"You're right. That is where I can help. I'll make sure we have a deputy doing regular patrol through the courthouse. I'll get with Miss Olivia as well. You know she'll have a few ideas on the matter."

I grinned. Talking with Miss Olivia was probably the best way to deal with the situation. Besides, Annie wouldn't dare argue with her.

"Thanks." I squeezed his hand. "I'm also going to have a chat with Stephanie Dinsmore. Everything seems to go back to her. I want to know why."

"Quinn." Censure roughened his voice.

"Don't." My eyes flashed in warning. "Lucas, you know I'm right. At the very least, the current round of trouble began with Spud's murder. That brought Annie home. Catherine could have ended up in prison if Annie hadn't played hard ball with Sawyer. Think about all that could have happened and then think about how nothing about the case makes sense."

"Explain."

Oh, he didn't like it. Not that I cared.

"First, the shoddy investigation into what happened, including how the lead detective didn't follow up on any other leads because Catherine was found at the scene." I ticked off one finger.

"Second, Sawyer's prosecution of the case. He ignored Annie's notice that she was representing her mother and tried to get Catherine arraigned before Annie could get here from Austin. He conspired with that bastard Rhodes to direct the investigation in such a way Catherine would be railroaded straight into prison." I ticked off another finger.

"Then there's the fact Jason Alvarez who, from everything I can tell, was an excellent DA allowed Sawyer to stay on the case until Annie presented him with enough evidence to have Sawyer brought up before the Bar. Even then, he didn't immediately act to remove Sawyer or to dismiss the charges against Catherine." A third finger ticked off.

"Then there's Stephanie herself. She didn't need to show up at Annie's office that day. Yes, Annie had managed to pull together enough evidence to clear her mother, not to mention enough to bring serious attention to how both Rhodes and Sawyer acted during the investigation of the case. But from everything Annie's said, she had no clue Stephanie was involved in either Spud's murder or Bruce's. So why expose herself when she did?"

Lucas didn't say anything for a moment. Then he pushed back his chair and climbed to his feet. I sat back, watching as he moved to the counter. He poured another mug of coffee and stood there, staring out the window over the sink. Then he turned, his expression serious.

"You know I've never liked what happened then."

I nodded.

"What I haven't told you is that when I took office, I had the files for the investigation pulled. Someone, and I don't know if it was Rhodes, my predecessor or someone else, had removed Rhodes' investigative notes as well as any correspondence he had with Sawyer. The only reason we had any of it when Stephanie went to trial was because Drew and Annie kept records, as did the others assigned to the case."

I bit back a curse. This just kept getting worse and worse.

"Do me a favor. Check the case files into the Luíseach family and everything else that has touched on any of us since Spud's murder. Then do whatever you can to secure them and back them up."

He nodded grimly.

"I'm going to meet with Alvarez today and get his approval to see if the Luíseachs will speak to me."

Lucas opened his mouth to interrupt and snapped it shut when I shook my head.

"Don't. I have an angle. If Alvarez agrees, I'll tell them that talking to me gives them a chance to earn some good will with the court by cooperating. I have no doubt they will refuse. Winston Reed might not. The last thing he wants is for the town to learn he raped Meg's mother. That would open up too many cans of worms, some of which very well could lead to similar charges where the statute of limitations hasn't run."

"You make sure you record everything they say. I don't want this blowing back on you, Quinn."

I rolled my eyes. My husband, bless his heart, sometimes forgot I'd been in law enforcement longer than he had.

"I know the drill, Lucas. Don't worry."

The look he gave me spoke volumes. But before he could say anything, the sounds of a herd of elephants running downstairs filled the air. A few moments later, the kitchen door swung open and Ali raced inside. Seeing us, she stopped. Then she all but launched herself into my arms.

"Mom, how's Miss Serena?"

I brushed my lips against her hair. "She's getting better, sweetheart. I checked with the hospital a little while ago and they said she'd slept well."

"Can we go see her this morning?"

"Not yet, sweetie."

Tears gathered in her eyes and I saw the doubt reflected there. Damn it.

"Ali, Miss Serena's in a special part of the hospital," Lucas said as he joined us at the table. "It's one where the nurses and doctors can keep an eye on her all the time. That way, if she needs anything, they can handle it without any delay. But it means they limit who can see her."

"Lucas is right. But that doesn't mean you can't call her later." I hoped that would be enough to satisfy her.

"Really?" She looked from Lucas to me.

"Really." I ruffled her hair. "Besides, you have school this morning."

"Mom," she drawled.

"C'mon, squirt. Your mom's been working most of the night for her new job with Aunt Annie. So why don't the two of us fix her something special for breakfast?"

"Okay."

She hurried to Lucas. He gave her a hug and then lifted her until she wrapped her legs around his waist. Together, they crossed to the refrigerator and looked inside. Smiling, knowing he loved my little girl as if she was his own, I slipped out of the room. And, with that, it was back to the normal morning routine.

So simple and so grounding, and so something I needed.

19

By the time lunch came around, I felt like I'd run a marathon. I'd arranged to go by Longhorn Breeders early Saturday morning to look at several dogs they were currently training. Until then, they had two others trained for personal security where the sale fell through. Live video of the two convinced me I wanted them. I transferred payment and they would be delivered that evening. That relieved at least some of my concerns.

At least until I told Jax they were for her.

I stepped onto the sidewalk outside the Sheriff's Department and glanced around. I love Mossy Creek. I always had. I left because I needed to grow up. Not that I knew it at the time. Now I was back and I would do whatever it took to protect the town and those who lived here.

In other words, I had grown up. I'm not sure I liked it, but I wouldn't change it and I sure as hell didn't want Ali growing up anywhere else.

As I strolled down the sidewalk toward the café, I thought about the last hour. I'd stopped by the Sheriff's Department expecting to meet with Lucas and Drew. Finding Sam and Rafe there as well surprised me. Then I realized it shouldn't. They were as invested as

Lucas and Drew were in making sure we did everything possible to keep the town safe. So, closed away in one of the conference rooms, we started laying out our plans on what we needed to do and how to accomplish it.

Details still needed to be worked out, especially from the financial end of things, but we had a starting place. Additional cameras, most of them small enough or well placed enough not to be noticed to a casual observer, would be situated around town. Lucas and Drew would meet with local business owners to check their security systems. Upgrades would be arranged where needed. It would be expensive but between those of us dedicated to protecting the town, the money was there. Besides, if Lucas couldn't massage the city and county into footing at least some of the bill, he wasn't nearly as good as of a politician as I knew him to be.

The bell over the door tinkled as I entered the café. Instantly, silence fell and all eyes turned to me. It didn't surprise me to find the café filled with locals, all of whom I not only knew but trusted with my life and with Ali's. Grim faced, determined to make sure nothing else happened, they wanted to know how Miss Serena was. Even though I wanted to wind my way to the back booth where both Meg and Annie waited, I knew I needed to deal with this first.

"I talked with Amy less than ten minutes ago. She said her grandmother is holding her own. Dr. Pat was in first thing this morning. Miss Serena's vitals are stronger and she had no complications overnight. If she remains stable the rest of the day, they will move her into a step-down room tomorrow."

"Can we see her?" Mrs. Haverstock asked.

I shook my head. "Not yet. As long as she's in the ICU, visitors are limited to immediate family and a very few others."

"What can you tell us about what happened?" Mr. Watson asked.

I didn't answer right away. Mom and I talked about this earlier. We knew as soon as one of us appeared at the café, questions would be asked. The problem was how much to tell them. Since those present were the backbone of town, I decided to be honest, at least up to a point.

"Someone—and we don't know who—tried to attack Miss Serena. She could have easily turned them aside but you know her. Instead of focusing on protecting herself, she worried more about protecting those who were working the farm, including Jax, as well as my daughter who was there for a lesson. She spread herself too thin and she's not as young as she used to be."

Several heads nodded.

"Sounds just like her," Mr. Watson said. "But she's going to be all right?"

"That's the way it looks."

"And the SOB who attacked her?" Anger filled Mrs. Petric's voice.

"Got away. But we're doing everything we can to find them."

"What can we do?"

I blinked against the sudden burning in my eyes. These men and women, young and old alike, stood ready to do whatever it took to not only avenge their friend's injury but to protect our town. That was something whoever was behind all this didn't understand. Hopefully, it would be enough to tip the advantage to our side.

"Keep your eyes and ears open. Let Miss Peggy know if you see or hear anything out of the ordinary."

"My mother will be here in an hour and she'll have assignments for everyone," Janny said from the kitchen door.

I didn't wince but it was a close thing. I had no doubt Miss Peggy had her head together with Miss Olivia right now, planning our next move. Hell, for all I knew, my mother was with them. If the bastard who tried to hurt Miss Serena knew what was good for him, he'd be long gone from Mossy Creek and would never return.

Much as I hoped that was the case, I knew better. Whoever attacked Miss Serena's the day before was waiting somewhere close by, biding his—or her—time as they waited for the right moment to strike again. All I had to do was help Jax and the others figure out who and where before that happened.

"Let her get some lunch now," Janny said and motioned me to the back booth where Meg and Annie waited.

"One more thing." Much as I wanted to join the others, I needed to say this. "If you do see or hear anything out of the ordinary, do more than let Miss Peggy know. Your first call needs to be to me. If I'm not available, call Jax or my mother. Then contact the Sheriff's Department." Now I grinned. "Well, you can call Miss Peggy before you call my husband."

Everyone laughed. Then they assured me they understood. With that much accomplished, I gratefully slid into the booth opposite Annie and Beth and thanked Janny as she placed a tall glass of iced tea on the table for me.

"You okay?" Annie asked.

I nodded. "Just tired."

And then some.

"And I owe you an apology."

I ducked my head. I should have been at the office with Annie that morning. We were both new enough to the jobs that I shouldn't have taken the morning off. But I didn't see any other choice, not after what happened yesterday. I only hoped she understood.

For a moment, she looked at me in question. Then, as under-standing dawned, she frowned. Before I could react, she reached across the table and slapped me none-too-gently up the side of my head. It was exactly what Mom would have done in the same situation. Not knowing whether to laugh or not, I gave a quick shrug. That seemed safe enough.

I hoped.

"Don't be stupid, Quinn. You are doing what you need to. As far as I'm concerned, you're investigating an active threat against the town. You have a good team at the office. They are handling the current cases. That is something you already set up. So check in once or twice a day until we get to the bottom of this."

"Sure thing, boss." I grinned as she frowned at the new nickname.

"Fair warning, Quinn. She doesn't think of herself as the boss. At least that's what she kept telling me." Meg grinned at her sister-in-law.

"She'd better get over it because that's exactly what she is." This time I ducked away from Annie before she could swat at me again.

"Both of you will pay for picking on me."

"Promises promises." I grinned and then sobered. "After everyone left Miss Serena's last night, Jax, Mom and I got together. There were some things they wanted to discuss with me."

"We figured." Now Meg looked at me in concern. "Are you really all right with everything that's happening?"

I nodded. "That's one of the things we talked about."

I went on to tell them what I told Jax. I was going to treat being a Guardian like an extension of being in law enforcement. Right now, I happened to be in full agreement with Jax and Mom. My main duty was to make sure the Guardians and the rest of our inner circle were protected. Then came the town and everyone else.

They listened closely, occasionally asking a question. By the time Janny delivered our lunches, they seemed satisfied. Then they assured me they were both armed, although it was easy to see Annie didn't like it. That didn't surprise me. She might be more than an adequate shot, but that didn't mean she liked guns.

"Quinn." Annie sounded so serious, I looked up from my burger. "Keeping everyone safe includes making sure you aren't taking any unnecessary risks. So where are your dogs?"

I placed the burger back on the plate. The answer was simple enough. The reason behind it? Not so much and something I knew both of them would not approve of, even if for different reasons.

"They are with Lucas at the station right now. I left them there because I have an appointment when I leave here where their presence could be a problem."

Annie frowned and I knew she was trying to remember if I had anything for the office on the schedule. A hint of suspicion touched her expression and she leaned in so she wouldn't be overheard.

"What meeting?" She held my gaze, all but daring me to look away.

I swallowed hard and cut my eyes in Meg's direction. Unfortunately for me, she saw and, if possible, suddenly looked more formidable than Annie in that moment.

"I had a talk with Jason Alvarez this morning. We discussed his trial strategy for the Luíseachs and for Reed. He agrees there is still something about the case we don't know. So I'm going to have a talk with Reed."

"Jason's not considering offering him a deal, is he?" Annie looked ready to hunt down the man who she replaced as DA if I answered wrong.

"No, he's not. That bastard is going to do hard time and a lot of it for what he did to Meg. Unfortunately, we can't prosecute him for what he did to her mother." I waited until Annie relaxed a little. Then I turned my attention to Meg who had yet to say anything.

"Meg, I promise you, he's not getting any deal."

"But?"

"But we are going to make him think he is."

"How?"

"Once Jason figured out I was going to take over as head investigator when Annie took office, he contacted me and gave me some leads he'd developed where that bastard's concerned. That led to two other women who confirmed he raped them much as he did your mother. There are others. The statute of limitations has run on those cases, but not the first two I mentioned. I'm going to lay all of it out for Reed, including the two we can still prosecute. What he doesn't know is Jason has no plans to put those women through a trial."

"Why?" Meg ducked her head and dashed at her eyes.

Worried, I reached across the table and rested my hand on hers. "Meg, I promise he is going to pay for everything he did. But if I can use the other cases to force him to tell us how they knew you would be here, not to mention the rest of it, I will. The two women I mentioned know what we are doing and have agreed. They've even agreed to testify if it helps put him in prison and keep him there."

"I don't like it." She ground it out.

"I don't blame you. I'm asking you to trust me to protect you and get justice for you and for your mother. But this goes beyond the two of you. If he knows anything about what's happening now, I want that information. That doesn't mean, however, that I'm willing to let him get away with what he did to you two."

For several long moments, she said nothing. Then she looked down at her hands where they were wrapped around her glass of water. When she glanced up a short time later, she nodded once.

"All right."

"It's not all right." Annie almost growled out the words.

"Annie, think as a prosecutor and not as a friend." Seeing how her eyes turned amber, I thanked my good luck that I was sitting across from her. "And get control of your Talents." I didn't—quite—snap it out.

"We will discuss this later."

"Fine, but only if you promise to think about the whys of what I'm doing and not just go with emotion. I mean it, Annie. Jason agreed with you that it was best he stand as special prosecutor for this case. He's signed off on what I want to do and you know he wants to see not only Reed but the Luíseachs rot in prison."

She nodded once, her expression grim and her jaw clinched so tightly I could almost hear her teeth grinding.

"If we can put that behind us, there's more to discuss."

Both took deep, cleansing breaths and then nodded. Relieved, I relaxed a little. Then I grinned to myself. I knew how to take their minds off of what we just discussed, at least for a few moments.

"What?" Meg asked.

"Actually a couple of things. First, I'll be in the office in an hour, two at the most. I doubt my conversation with Reed will take long. Besides, there are cases you and I need to discuss before I hand out assignments." I shook my head before she could say anything. "Annie, you hired me as the office's chief investigator. Yesterday doesn't change that."

"All right." She didn't try to hide her relief and I smiled in understanding.

"Besides, I need to figure out how to tell Jax that she's getting a couple of new dogs."

Annie grinned and Meg laughed. I'm glad they saw the humor in it.

"Of course, if you two really loved me, you'd tell her." I grinned as they both sobered and suddenly became very interested in their lunches.

"Nope." Annie took a big bite of her burger, making me wait for her to continue. "That's all on you."

"I'm not arguing, but why two dogs?" Meg asked.

"One, she somehow managed to convince Rafe that Fenris was better suited to be his dog." And I planned on having a serious discussion with him before the new dogs arrived. They were to be Jax's dogs, whether she liked it or not. "Two, they were trained together as a working pair."

"We'll back you on them, Quinn. I promise."

"Thanks, Annie." I ate the last bite of my burger and stuffed the last few fries in my mouth. "I need to run. Meg, I'll let you know what happens."

With that, I left them to finish their meals. Hopefully, by the time we spoke again, I'd have at least a few answers.

Ten minutes later, I stepped inside the building that had housed Reed Financial. After he was charged with everything from assault to attempted murder and more, most of Derek Reed's clients left like rats fleeing a sinking ship. To add insult to injury, state and federal regulators opened a series on investigations into his business practices. Four months later, he closed his office. But he still owned the building and had insisted we meet there instead of at his house or his attorney's office in Dallas.

The reception area had a musty smell, confirming what I already knew. No one had used the office in weeks. A thin coating of dust covered everything. I stood just inside the door and looked around, noting the light coming under the door set in the opposite wall and the security camera in the far corner. The same camera with the green light indicating not only that it was powered but active just then.

I waited, checking my watch. As I did, I made a bet with myself about how long Reed would keep me waiting. I didn't doubt for a moment that he sat in the back, watching me on the security monitor. He was playing a dominance game, one designed to throw me off-stride. Too bad I knew not only what he was doing but how to counter it.

At the three minute mark, I pulled out my phone and programed in Lucas' number. The call rolled over to voice mail, not that Reed would know. This was as much a power move as him making me wait.

"Sheriff, I thought I'd let you know that I arrived for a meeting with Derek Reed, one I arranged through his attorney. I was assured Mr. Reed would be at his office here in Mossy Creek. I've been waiting—" I checked my watch—"close to five minutes. The front door was open but it appears no one is here. Since it is possible this is a crime scene, I don't want to make entry into the rear of the office without someone from your office being present." I paused, as if listening to a response. "Yes, I understand. You're going to check with Probation to see where his ankle monitor shows him to be. In the meantime, I'm to make entry and assume that anyone here is not authorized."

I ended the "call" and slid my phone back into my hip pocket. Then I reached under my light jacket and pulled the Glock-19 from its holster. Before my jacket fell back into place, the inner door opened and there stood Derek Reed in all his fury.

"Mr. Reed." I made a show of replacing my gun. "Have you changed your mind about speaking with me?"

"No."

He stepped back and motioned me through the door. Then, when I indicated he should lead the way, he frowned in frustration. I'd bested him again. He expected to intimidate me by walking behind me where he could do anything he wanted before I'd be able to respond. Instead. I put him in the vulnerable position. Too fucking bad.

I followed him through what had obviously been a work area to his private office. Unlike the rest of the office suite, his office had been cleaned and showed signs he still used it on a regular basis. As he took his place behind a large glass and steel desk, I arched one brow. Interesting. His attorney had yet to make an appearance.

"Sit the hell down." He jabbed a finger in the direction of one of the two chairs sitting in front of his desk.

"Thank you." I once again pulled my phone. This time, I placed it on the edge of the desk within easy reach. "Is your attorney joining us?"

"Hell no. I'm not paying him a couple hundred an hour just to hear me say I'm not talking to you."

"Then it seems you could have saved all of us some time by telling me that before now." I shook my head, making a show of being disappointed. "However, I need to put that on the record." I leaned forward and activated the phone's recorder. Without asking permission, I identified both of us and our location. Then I read Reed his rights, ending by asking if he understood his rights as I'd read them to him.

"Yeah, I understand and I'm not saying a word."

I leaned back and crossed my ankles. "That is your privilege, Mr. Reed. However, before I leave, let me explain why I wanted to speak with you. The special prosecutor is willing to offer you a deal in return for your cooperation."

I waited, watching him process what I said. A moment later, he leaned forward, elbows on the desk, hands folded in front of him.

"What deal?"

"You answer my questions about why you targeted Meg Grissom when she first came to town and the special prosecutor will agree to not file any further assault charges against you for offenses that occurred prior to your arrest."

For a moment, he sat there. Then his eyes went wide and the blood drained from his face. I waited, my eyes never leaving his face. Anger replaced shock and his hands fisted on the desktop. But the thin sheen of sweat dotting his upper lip told the tale. He might not know who I referenced but he knew I had him by the short hairs.

As long as I didn't blow it.

"You're bluffing."

Too bad he didn't sound convinced.

"I don't bluff."

"If you really had proof, you'd have me in cuffs right now."

"No, it means the special prosecutor is willing to save your victims the pain of having to recount what you did to them if—and this is a limited time deal—you not only confess what you did but that you tell us everything about the charges currently leveled against you. The deal will be in writing and our interview will be recorded. If Mr. Alvarez or I discover you have lied or failed to be completely forthcoming, all deals are off and we will do everything we can to make sure you never see another day of freedom."

"Bitch."

"You aren't the first to say that." I leaned forward and tapped my phone, making sure he looked at it. "The recorder is on. I've told you what Mr. Alvarez wants from you. I've read you your rights and have given you the basics of the deal the special prosecutor is willing to offer you. I now have two questions for you. First, do you want to adjourn this meeting until your attorney can join us?"

"No, because there's not going to be any deal."

"Very well." I stood. Leaving my phone where it was, I reached behind my back and pulled a pair of handcuffs from where I'd secured them earlier. "Winston Reed, you are under arrest on charges including but not limited to sexual assault, sexual assault of a minor, and human trafficking."

I moved around the desk, handcuffs in hand. He stood motionless until I reached for his arm. As I spun him so he faced the wall, he flailed out. His elbow connected with my jaw. Pain flared. Stars danced before my eyes. Then I shoved him against the wall, smiling ferociously as his head hit with a satisfying *thud*. I had his wrists secured behind him before he recovered.

"Sit." I pointed at his chair and waited as he dropped onto it. Then I reached for my phone. "I tried to make this easy. Now we'll see how well you do when your fellow prisoners learn you're a rapist. I suggest you not turn your back on anyone."

I programmed in Drew's number. He deserved to be the one who booked the man who raped his wife's mother and who then took part in the plot to rob Meg of her inheritance and her life.

"Wait!" Reed struggled to his feet only to drop back down when I planted my hand in the center of his chest. "Let's talk about this."

"Nope. You made your decision. You can contact your attorney once you're booked. Who knows, maybe he'll catch Mr. Alvarez feeling charitable. I wouldn't count on it, but there's always the possibility."

"No, wait. Please."

Sweat covered his face now and he looked like he might pass out at any moment. Either that or piss himself. Maybe both.

"You had your chance. Believe me, I'm more than glad you refused the offer. I can't wait to tell the judge we offered you the chance to cooperate and you not only refused but you resisted arrest and assaulted an officer of the court."

"I'll sue you!

"Sue ahead." I laughed softly, letting him see I wasn't afraid. "Remember, I recorded everything that happened since I entered the office. Who do you think the jury will believe?"

"I want it all in writing before I say anything."

"No." Let him see I didn't mind playing hard ball one bit. "You need to give me something to prove not only that you are finally willing to cooperate but that you have something of value."

He didn't like it, not that there was much he could do about it.

"Before you make a decision I promise you'll regret, think about this. The charges against you are more than solid. You attacked Meg in front of half the town. You confessed to earlier attempts on her life and to raping her mother. Even if you are tried outside of Harken County, there's more than enough evidence to convict you and send you to prison for the rest of your life.

"Consider this as well. With the additional charges, Mr. Alvarez can argue a pattern of behavior that can and will be used to increase your sentencing. Not only will you not be eligible for release until after you're dead, you will be sent to a max security prison. If you think you're going to be able to survive in that setting, you have another thing coming. Cons hate sex offenders. When they find out you not only are a serial rapist but that you then tried to kill the daughter born from one of those rapes, your life expectancy becomes a matter of months, if not days."

"You can't tell them. You'd be killing me just as surely as if you pulled the trigger."

"I wouldn't have to. Your prison record will have a full listing of the crimes you're charged with and the ones you will be convicted of. Even if marked not to be released, word will get out. That's the way of prisons. Your only hope is to cooperate—and I mean fully—and hope Mr. Alvarez can convince the Feds to place you in one of their prison far from Texas and do so under an assumed name."

"I want it in writing," he repeated.

"After you prove you have something of value. Consider it a showing of good faith."

"Like I'm going to believe anything you can tell me." He sneered and I shook my head.

"Are you really going to let your prejudice against Others send you to what very well could be your death?"

"You have to give me something!"

There it was, the desperation I'd been looking for. Like so many bullies, he didn't know how to react when he didn't hold the power. He tried his games on me and they hadn't worked. Now, finally, he began to understand how those he'd taken advantage of over the years must have felt. That didn't bother me one little bit.

"I already have. Everything is on the record." I tapped my phone once again. "Now decide. Are you going to help me and, in doing so, help yourself or do I let Deputy Grissom take you to jail and book you on the additional charges?"

As if that was his cue, Drew entered the office. This wasn't the easy-going man I knew. Nor was it the country bumpkin cop he often played to put people off their guard. This was the solemn, all-business deputy I knew him to be, one who dearly wanted a piece of the man who raped his wife's mother. Then there was the little fact he'd tried to kill Meg.

"All right." He slumped in his chair. "What do you want to know?"

I tossed Drew the key to the cuffs. Once he freed Reed, he handed the cuffs and key back to me. Then, making sure Reed knew he was waiting in the outer office, he left us alone. But the look he cast in my direction before doing so spoke volumes. I was not to take any chances and if Reed tried anything, he wanted the chance to deal with him. I dipped my chin, letting him know I understood, not that I'd let him do anything to jeopardize the case against Reed or his job with the Sheriff's Department.

"We'll start with something simple." I returned to my chair. Before sitting, I pulled my gun and rested it on my thigh, letting him know I wasn't taking any chances where we was concerned. "When did you first hear of Meg Sheridan and how did you learn she was coming to town?"

I waited, watching as he considered his answers. Idiot. Didn't he realize I could see him thinking about the best way to answer without actually telling me what I wanted to know? How long before her proved he was yet another criminal too stupid to be anywhere but behind bars?

"I didn't know about her until she was already in town. Then old man Luíseach told Mathew who told me. It wasn't too difficult to figure out she'd come here for what she figured was her piece of the pie. I wasn't about to let her blackmail me for everything I had."

God, he sounded so smug. Worse, he expected me to believe his lies. I looked forward to what happened next.

"Wrong answer."

I stood and moved to the door. The moment I opened it, Drew stepped inside. This time, Lucas entered with him. I nodded and turned to face Reed.

He might not have said anything, but his expression spoke volumes. As the three of us approached, he stumbled to his feet. His eyes darted around the office, searching for an escape route. Unfortunately for him, his only option meant going through us. I almost hoped he tried.

"Winston Reed, you're under arrest." In a repeat of what I did earlier, I grabbed his arm and spun him to face the wall. This time he showed enough common sense not to try to escape. Instead, he stood silently as I cuffed him and once again read him his rights. Then I turned him and shoved him in Lucas' direction. A moment later, I emailed the recording of our conversation to Jason Alvarez and Lucas. "I'll be in later today to sign my statement but everything is in the recording I just sent you, Sheriff."

"Mr. Alvarez briefed me while we waited." He handed Reed off to Drew. "We'll get him booked and processed. He can call his attorney then."

"Wait!" Reed struggled against Drew's grasp on his arm. "I'll tell you what you want to know."

"Sorry, you had your chance." I slid my gun into its holster and then pocketed my phone. "Take him on."

"Benjamin Luíseach! It was Benjamin who told me about the bitch!"

I jerked my head at Drew. He nodded and dragged the still struggling Reed from the office. The moment I heard the front door close behind them, I turned to Lucas. He looked at me, his expression mirroring mine. Of all the names Reed could have named, that had to be one of the last I expected. Benjamin Luíseach was the youngest of the Luíseach sons. More than five years ago, he moved from Mossy Creek. As far as I knew, he hadn't been back. More importantly, nothing in the investigation into the attacks on Meg and the subsequent knowledge of her mother's rape and the attempts by the Luíseachs to gain control of her inheritance raised any flags where Benjamin was concerned.

"Well?" Lucas asked as we followed Drew and Reed more slowly.

"It doesn't make sense." But then when had anything over the last few years made any sense? "What do you know about him?"

"Nothing really. Let me do some poking around. For now, let's keep this to the three of us and Alvarez."

In other words, don't tell Annie and Meg. Since I completely agreed, I nodded.

"Let me know what you find out. I'm going to pull some strings of my own." I paused and watched as Drew once more gave Reed his

Miranda warnings before placing him in the back of his SUV. "I'll brief Alvarez."

"Tell him I'll send over the booking information as soon as it's done." Instead of walking to his SUV, Lucas reached out and gently grasped my chin, tilting my head this way and then that. "Did he do this?" He lightly touched my jaw where it throbbed painfully.

"Yeah. He didn't take kindly to being cuffed."

"Then I'll make sure that charge is added." He took a step and then turned back. Before I knew what he meant to do, he lightly kissed the bruise I knew had to be forming. "Next time, make sure he hits somewhere else. I happen to like your face."

I chuckled and brushed my lips against his. "You'd better get him transported. Make sure Drew's recording anything he says on his way to the SD. Let's not give him any reason to claim police misconduct."

"Done and done." He signaled to Drew to head on. "Are you going to be able to pick up Ali after school?"

I shook my head. "Mom's picking both Ali and Robbie up. After they have a treat at the café, she's dropping them off at Camille's."

"Sounds good. That way she should have her homework done by the time we pick her up. Let me know if you're going to be late."

"You do the same."

With that, I made sure the outside door locked behind us. I climbed into my SUV and settled behind the steering wheel. I sent a quick text to Mom, reminding her about Ali. A second text went to Jax, letting her know I'd be by the "clinic" in a couple of hours. But now I needed to get to the office and find some way to keep Annie from going ballistic when she saw my face.

Maybe I had time to see Amy and let her do a quick healing before heading to work. Woo-woo stuff or not, it was a hell of a lot better than facing Annie's wrath.

JAX

20

I pulled into the parking lot at the hospital and just sat there, my head resting against the steering wheel. Exhaustion dragged at me. It felt like I hadn't slept in days and that wasn't far off. In the four days since the attack on Miss Serena's farm, I'd managed only a handful of hours in bed. I spent the rest of the time doing whatever I could to make sure my town and my loved ones were protected.

How in the hell had Miss Serena done this for so long?

I sat up and blew out a breath. I was stalling. I knew it. Just as I knew there was no reason to. Less than an hour ago, Amy assured me her grandmother was doing better. Even so, I didn't want to **see** Miss Serena ill and in bed. Knowing how close we'd come to losing her, I felt like a kid scared she might suddenly be left all alone in the world. I didn't want to think about a world without Miss Serena in it. She'd been grandmother, friend, teacher and mentor. I didn't want to lose that—now or ever.

My phone buzzed as I climbed out. A quick glance had me nodding. Maybe things were finally starting to fall into place. God, I hoped so.

"Ciara?"

"Hang on a moment." She paused and I heard the unmistakable

sounds of an airport in the background. "Sorry. We were dealing with Security. I wanted to let you know we're on our way home."

"We?"

I leaned against the side of my truck and smiled to hear her softly curse. Obviously, she hadn't meant to say it that way. That meant only one thing, Liam was coming with her. Part of me wanted to tease her about it. That same part couldn't wait to let Quinn know. She'd been merciless with both her teasing and her demanding to know everything there was about Liam Murphy and his relationship with her sister.

Come to think of it, I wanted to know more about Murphy. Yes, I knew from the moment I saw them together that he'd won Ciara's heart. He claimed to love her as much as she did him. Yet, in the end, he returned to Ireland after Maddy told him what she could—or would—about Anton Roben and his criminal activities. I didn't doubt he and Ciara kept in touch but there'd been a sadness to her since that I knew he was responsible for. That alone put him on my shit list.

Okay, he had helped us locate and bring Maddy home from Ireland. He made sure Anton Roben, the bastard who not only raped Maddy and abused her physically and mentally but who also coerced her into using her Talents for his profit, spent the rest of his life locked away from the rest of the world. It was even possible that was why he was returning to Mossy Creek with Ciara.

But if he hurt here again, he would pay. No one played that sort of game with my friends.

"Jax," Ciara drawled.

I heard the note of warning in her voice. "Before you start reading me the riot act, perhaps you ought to tell me what's going on."

For a moment she didn't say anything. Then she sighed, as much in resignation as in frustration. Interesting.

"I'll fill you in when we get home. I don't want to go over it on the phone. But I think we've got a solid lead, at least for part of our problem."

"All right. Are you flying straight to Dallas?"

"We are, assuming everything goes as planned."

I didn't like the sound of that. "Ciara?"

"Don't pay any attention to me. You know I hate flying, especially over the ocean and in anything smaller than a 747."

I chuckled. Her answer explained more than she probably meant it to. Even though she'd flown commercial to Dublin, she was coming home on a charter flight. That meant either Liam had set it up or, more likely, Meg. That also meant they did have information they felt we needed to know ASAP. The fact she didn't want to discuss it over the phone worried me. But, since there was little I could do about it right now, I pushed aside my concerns.

"Do you need someone to meet you at the airport?"

"No. My car's there. I'll let you know when we land. We need to talk as soon as I get back to town."

"Understood." I thought for a moment. "Do I need to arrange a room for Liam?"

Okay, maybe it wasn't the most mature thing I could have asked. After all, she was a grown woman and her mother knew she had sex. As long as the house let Liam in, he'd be welcomed to stay with them. For that matter, he could stay with any of us. Frankly, with everything going on, I wanted him to stay with one of us. That way we could not only make sure he was safe but we could keep an eye on him. Ciara might trust him but I was still withholding judgment. There was just too much I didn't know about him and that bothered me.

"Just don't say anything to my sister. She'd probably tell the house to *play* with him some."

From the frustration in Ciara's voice, I guessed Quinn had done just that the last time he was here.

"Have a safe flight and let me know as soon as you land. I'll let you know then where we're meeting."

We said our goodbyes and I slid the phone back into my pocket. I took two steps and stopped. Retrieving my phone, I sent a quick text to Rafe. A moment later, my phone buzzed and I smiled slightly.

"What's going on?" He sounded worried.

"I need you and Sam to do something but not let anyone else know. Not yet at any rate."

"Doc, are you all right?" Worry turned to concern.

"I am." I quickly told him about Ciara's call.

"And she wouldn't give you any hint about what she found out."

"Not a clue. Said she didn't want to go into it over the phone."

"I don't like it."

"Neither do I," I admitted. "I need you two to do a run on Liam. I want to know more than the official story." I'd respected Ciara's request not to go rogue the last time. But not now. Not when so much rested in the balance. "And find out the current status for Roben."

"Will do." He paused and thought for a moment. "Doc, get with Meg. Tell her your concerns and ask her to contact her former CO. He might have information or access to information we won't be able to get to."

"Not yet." While Rafe's suggestion was a good one, it came with potential problems I didn't want to deal with unless absolutely necessary. "I'm about to head inside to check on Miss Serena. Then I need to meet with Judith. Quinn's working this morning, so she'll meet with us at lunch. I'm hoping to check on how the clinic's progressing this afternoon."

"Call me when you're on your way and I'll meet you there."

"I will."

"If you're at the hospital, where are your dogs?"

I rolled my eyes. I was still pissed at Quinn. I didn't need a dog, much less two. But she'd played dirty. Not only had she used my own instructions concerning the Guardians and our inner circle when I argued I was more than capable of protecting myself but she'd pulled Miss Serena into it. She reminded me how worried Miss Serena would be to learn I wasn't doing everything I could to protect myself. Much as she'd hate to do it, she wouldn't lie if Miss Serena asked. Nothing I said changed her mind. As a result, I found myself the owner of two matched Rottweilers.

"At Judith's. I left them in the dog run since I was heading to the hospital."

"All right. Let me know how Miss Serena is."

"I will. Talk to you later." I paused, looking around. It was silly, but I didn't want anyone listening in. "Love you."

"Love you too."

Smiling, I slid the phone into my hip pocket and quickly crossed the parking lot. By the time I stepped off the elevator, I managed to push aside my concern about Liam. I couldn't do anything about him or why he was coming until later and I certainly had more than enough to worry about otherwise.

Walking down the corridor in the direction of Miss Serena's room, I smiled slightly to hear Amy say something and Judith respond. Good. That meant they would have given Miss Serena another healing session. As much as I trusted Dr. Pat and the others looking after Miss Serena, I knew first-hand what Amy and Judith could do. I also had no problems making sure Miss Serena received all the mundane and arcane treatments she needed to make a full recovery.

"Serena, you need to rest now," Dr. Pat said as I entered the room. "If you do and if you continue to improve the way you have been, I'll sign off on moving you into a regular room tomorrow."

Relief washed through me. Dr. Pat wouldn't say something like that if she didn't mean it. Not wanting to interrupt, I stayed by the door, watching as Dr. Pat finished her exam. After telling the others to make sure Miss Serena didn't overdo, she left the small room, motioning for me to come with her.

"How is she?" I asked when we finally stopped next to the nursing station.

"Hang on a moment."

I waited as she entered her notes into Miss Serena's file and gave the nurse on duty a series of instructions. Then, when she turned and looked long and hard at me, I shifted uncomfortably.

"She's doing much better, Jax. She knows she was lucky you were there and able to help until the EMTs arrived." She slanted her eyes in the direction of the nurse and I understood. She didn't want to say too much in front of the woman. Since I didn't recognize her, I nodded slightly. No sense in advertising things best kept to ourselves.

"She has responded well to treatment. If she continues to do so, she should be out within the week."

Relief washed through me. "That's wonderful news." And it was.

Dr. Pat nodded. Then she cocked her head to one side and I shifted uncomfortably again as she studied me. She saw too much. She always had.

"Walk with me."

I glanced back at Miss Serena's room and then shrugged. Dr. Pat had something she wanted to say and she wasn't going to say it until we were alone. I had two choices: go with her and get it over as quickly as possible or delay it and accept the consequences. Never one to delay the inevitable, I followed her down the corridor. She stopped at the staff break room. I waited as she checked it. Then I followed her inside, unsurprised when she locked the door behind us.

"Dr. Pat?"

"Jax, you look like you haven't slept in days. Are you all right?"

I nodded. Then I shrugged. "I'm tired. I'm sleeping, but not well. I can't seem to shut down my brain when I got to bed. There's too much to do, too much to learn. Too many unanswered questions."

"I was worried that might be the case." She reached out and ran a hand gently across my brow. Almost instantly, the band of tension I'd forgotten was there eased. "I'm calling in something for you to help you rest." When I opened my mouth to argue, she simply shook her head. "I'm only giving you enough for a couple of nights. But you need to get some rest. We need you at your best now more than ever before."

"All right. Thanks." I smiled and gave her a quick hug. "What can I do to help Miss Serena?"

"You're already doing it. You've taken much of the stress off of her. I can't say you've taken all of it because she is always going to worry about those she loves and about our town. For now, do your best to keep her calm and remind her that she can help no one if she suffers another heart attack."

"I will." When she glanced at her watch and winced, I touched her arm, waiting until she looked at me. "Go on. I know that look. You've got patients waiting."

She grinned and nodded, relieved I understood.

"I do. That was my office reminding me."

She gave my hand a squeeze. A moment later, she unlocked the door and was gone, leaving me looking after her, wondering how much sleep she'd been getting lately.

"Jackie." Miss Serena smiled as I entered her room and held a hand out to me.

I smiled, relieved to find her awake. She still looked too small and ill for my peace of mind, but her eyes shone brightly and I had to admit she looked better than she had the day before. Not wanting her to know how worried I'd been, I hurried to her bed. As I took her hand in mine, I bent and kissed her cheek.

"You're looking better." I gently brushed a lock of white hair from her brow.

"I've been telling everyone I'm fine." She cast a look at Judith and Amy that spoke volumes.

"And we've been telling her she scared us and she is going to have to do exactly what Dr. Pat and the others say." Amy looked so much like her grandmother in that moment I grinned.

"She's right, Miss Serena. You scared all of us." I gently sat on the edge of the mattress. "I can't stay long, but I wanted to make sure you're okay and see if you needed anything."

She frowned at Amy before looking at me. "I need for everyone to stop hovering and let me go home."

"You'll be there soon enough, Grandma." Amy moved to the other side of the bed and reached for her grandmother's free hand.

"She's right, Miss Serena. In the meantime, Jimmy and the crew are making sure everything's getting done. I'm keeping an eye on the stock and Amy and Brian have moved in and are keeping an eye on the house."

Miss Serena smiled almost apologetically at her granddaughter. "I'm sorry."

Amy's brow knitted. "Why?"

"You two just bought a house."

"Grandma." Amy shook her head in exasperation. "I told you. Brian and I want to do this. We love your house and there's more than enough room for the three of us. Besides, the realtor said she already has a buyer if we want to sell our place."

"Miss Serena, you don't worry about them or anything else besides getting better."

"Jax is right, Serena," Judith said from her place at the foot of the bed. "You made sure everything was in place in case something like this happened. Now you need to trust us to do as you've taught us."

"Jax."

"Shh. She's right. We've got this." I squeezed her hand. "That's not to say we don't need you because we do. But we need you healthy and we need you to understand you don't have to do everything by yourself."

"Good girl." She smiled as her eyelids began to droop.

"Rest now. I'll come back soon." I brushed my lips against her cheek. As sleep settled on her, I stood and motioned for Amy and Judith to follow me into the corridor. "Has she said anything more about what happened?"

They shook their heads.

"She's been sleeping mostly," Judith said and Amy nodded.

"All right." I thought for a moment. "I'm going to see if Bitsy and maybe Miss Olivia can sit with her tonight. We need to talk."

"All of us?" Amy asked in concern.

Now it was my turn to nod. "I'll explain then."

"All right. Where?"

I thought for a moment. Before I could answer, Judith did for me. "My place."

"Thanks." I smiled in appreciation. "About eight?" Hopefully, that would give me enough time to get everything done.

"Perfect. I'll contact everyone for you."

I gripped her hand, hoping she knew how much I appreciated it. Then I smiled in understanding when Amy looked back at her grandmother's room. "Go on. I'll see you tonight."

She nodded and disappeared inside the room. Once she did, Judith and I moved further down the corridor. When we stopped, Judith studied me, a frown tugging at the corners of her mouth.

"You're up to something, Jax. What?"

"Just chasing down a few things. I can't help feeling things are about to come to a head. If we're not ready for them, we're screwed."

"What do you want me to do?"

"Stick close to Miss Serena and call the others about tonight. I'll touch base with you throughout the day, keep you in the loop."

"You'd better."

"I will." I leaned in and gave her a quick hug. "Now I need to run. I want to stop by the courthouse. Miss Olivia said she has at least some of the information we talked about earlier. Knowing all the players and potential players will help."

Judith nodded. "It's as complete as Olivia, Mary Kate and I could come up with."

With the three of them working on it, I didn't doubt that for a moment. "Let me know if she needs anything." I didn't need to explain who I meant.

"I will. Be careful."

"Always."

With that, I made my way back downtown and to the DA's Office. I smiled as I stepped inside. Annie might not have been in office for long, but that didn't matter. Miss Olivia had taken the staff well in hand. The receptionist greeted me as soon as I entered. Before I could say anything, she assured me Miss Olivia was expecting me. If I wouldn't mind waiting, she'd let her know I was here.

"Well, what do you think?" Miss Olivia asked as she escorted me into the private part of the office a few minutes later.

I looked around and smiled, proud for Annie and for Miss Olivia. This was what Annie was meant for, at least at this part of her life. Meg could keep the law firm going until Annie was ready to return. In the meantime, there was no one I thought better suited to be the county's top prosecutor.

"I think Mossy Creek and Harkin County will be well served by Annie and you."

Miss Olivia actually blushed. Then she led me to her desk outside Annie's private office. I glanced at it and then arched one eyebrow. Miss Olivia understood. "She is following in her grandfather's footsteps." Approval shone in her eyes. "She makes the rounds of each of the courts every morning."

"Tell her I stopped by." I leaned in so we couldn't be overheard. "If you can, be at Judith's tonight at eight. It's important."

"I'll be there. Do you want Beth there as well?"

I didn't hesitate. Not only would she keep an eye on Meg, but she would do everything possible to help us. She always had.

"Please."

"We'll be there." She reached into her lap drawer and pulled out a flash drive. "This might help."

I palmed it and thanked her. We chatted a bit longer and then I left. There was a lot to do today and time was passing much too quickly. If I wasn't careful, I wouldn't get everything done before end of day.

21

"Jax, are you sure this is what you want to do?"

Meg sat behind her desk and looked at me in concern. I knew she didn't approve. No, that wasn't quite right. She didn't understand. Not that I blamed her. She'd grown up with a mother who loved her more than life itself. Despite the fact Meg was the product of rape, her mother did her best to make sure her daughter not only had a good life but knew she was loved. Never did she let on to Meg the truth surrounding her conception. Because of that, Meg had a difficult time imagining how a family could be as dysfunctional as mine happened to be.

I nodded. Much as I wished I never had to see either of my parents again, I needed to do this. Somehow, they fit into everything that had been happening and it was past time I found out how.

"I don't understand and, as your attorney, I can't recommend you do this. Have you talked to Bitsy about it?"

I nodded again and then grimaced. My aunt had not been pleased when I told her what I planned. Not because I decided it was time to finally have it out with my parents but because I told her she wasn't to attend. For as long as I can remember, she's stood with me against my parents. It wasn't a lie when I said she had been more of a parent to me than either my mother or my father had. But this could blow up in my face and I didn't want her caught in the fallout.

Besides, if things went as I expected, I didn't want her targeted by whoever was behind what had been going on. I'd come too close to losing Miss Serena. I wasn't going to risk Bitsy.

"You don't have to be here, Meg. In fact, it would probably be better if you aren't."

Oh, she did not like that. She leaned back and looked at me as if I'd suddenly grown a second head. Then her eyes narrowed and her expression hardened. I waited, wondering if she'd fling lightning at me or, worse, send for Annie and Quinn. Instead, she surprised me. She relaxed and motioned for me to explain.

"I don't think anything's going to happen, but you have the baby to think about." I nodded to her slightly swollen belly.

"And they are both normals. If you think I can't handle myself." She left the rest of the sentence hanging.

I blew out a breath. Why did everything have to be so difficult?

"Meg, they might be normals but they aren't harmless. They also love filing lawsuits, as you know. It doesn't matter if the suit has merit or not. They will go after you and they will try to get you disbarred. You may be willing to risk it but I'm not."

"And I'm not willing to let you face them—and their attorney—without representation." When staring me down didn't work, she surprised me by grinning and relaxing. "Look at it this way, Jax. They think they are going to be dealing with the teenager they could bully and threaten. They don't know Dr. Jax nor do they know Jax the Guardian."

I chuckled softly. She was right. But that still didn't change things. I knew them. If they felt they couldn't get to me, they would go for her. I couldn't and wouldn't let that happen.

"And they don't know me," she added.

I nodded, willing to admit she was right. Maybe she was also right about being in the meeting with me.

"You've got a point." I grinned when she looked at me as if she didn't quite believe she'd heard correctly. "So this is what I have in mind."

I quickly outlined my plan. She listened, her expression thoughtful. When I finished, she said nothing for a few moments. Then she glanced at the notes she'd made. With a nod, she looked up and her expression was enough to make even the largest predator think twice before attacking.

"I like it, but I have a couple of suggestions I'd like you to consider."

"Such as?"

"They're expecting you to play by the rules." She waved off my objections. "Jax, they always do and you usually comply. Not this time. But you also aren't going in as the Rogue. You are going to play the game better than they do, starting with what you wear."

Now it was my turn to narrow my eyes. "Go on."

I listened, my smile growing as she laid it out. No wonder Annie trusted her to be the managing partner in the law firm while she acted as the county's DA. Meg knew the law and she knew how to get what she wanted.

Better yet, she wasn't afraid of playing hardball when necessary.

And it was very necessary right now.

"I like it."

"Then let's set the stage." Meg grinned and climbed to her feet.

As she did, I left the office through the back door. I had half an hour to do my part. That meant I needed to hurry.

Half an hour later, I sat in Meg's office, watching the video feed from the conference room. When I returned a few minutes earlier, she let me know of one additional change to the plans. I chuckled and nodded, liking the way her mind worked.

"Where is she?"

Daniel "Dante" Powell sat on the far side of the conference table. To his left sat their attorney, some poor sap from Dallas he and my mother somehow managed to con into representing them. To his right sat his wife and the woman I used to think of as my mother.

None of them looked happy to be here. Little did they know they would be even less happy in a very short time.

"Calm down, Dante," the attorney said. "She's not late—yet."

"She won't show up," Emma said. "This is just another of her childish attempts to embarrass us."

If that wasn't the perfect cue, I didn't know what was.

A few moments later, I opened the conference room door and stepped inside. I nodded to Meg and ignored my parents, something I'd become an expert at doing over the years. Without a word, I moved to take my seat next to Meg. As I did, my two Rottweilers settled on either side of my chair.

"Get those monsters out of here," Dante snapped.

"Meg, I don't think you've had the pleasure of officially meeting my parents, and I use that term loosely. Daniel—sorry, *Dante*—Powell and his wife, Emma." I smiled and rested my right hand on Odin's head. Then I glanced at their attorney, arching a brow as he continued to sit in silence.

"You always were an ungrateful child." Disdain fairly dripped from Emma's voice. "At least you dressed properly for this."

I glanced at Meg and fought the urge to laugh. She'd called that one right. Appearances were everything to the two of them, second only to money. Growing up, I never dressed and behaved the way they wanted. Because of their constant put-downs and obvious disapproval, my first instinct today had been to appear at this meeting in jeans and a tank top, letting my sleeve of tattoos show. Instead, following Meg's suggestion, I wore black slacks, vest and jacket. The one concession she made was agreeing the leather slacks would have more impact than a pair of dress slacks. Everything else was appropriate for the board room—in their eyes at least.

"Let's get down to business. I don't have time to waste on the two of you." I placed the folder I brought with me onto the table in front of me. Then I turned my attention to their attorney. "And you are?" I pointedly ignored my parents. I also made no attempt to hide my feelings about the fact he had yet to introduce himself.

"Spencer Chalmont, their attorney." He didn't—quite—stammer it out.

"Then, Mr. Chalmont, I hope you got payment for your services up front and that you've already cashed the check. Otherwise, you are going to be sorely disappointed when it comes time for payment."

"Show some respect, Jacqueline," Dante snapped.

"I will when someone earns it." I opened the file. "In case they haven't been forthcoming with you, Mr. Chalmont, Dante and Emma Powell are up to their ears in debt. Their previous attorney is currently facing multiple criminal charges and has been disbarred. I also happen to know civil charges will be filed against him within the next month or so."

To prove it, I slid several pages across the table in Chalmont's direction.

"But Sawyer is not the reason I asked you and your clients to join me here. For the record, I am here in my personal capacity and not as a member of the Board f Directors for Powell Properties."

"So noted." Chalmont opened his tablet and made a quick note.

"In this file, you will find copies of various legal documents, ranging from my grandfather's will, to the pertinent corporate records to more recent legal motions and judicial orders concerning your clients. There is also a list of every legal action filed against them in the last decade and as well as the pertinent dispositions. As of last night, more than a dozen judgments have been entered against them, amounting to close to a quarter million dollars before interest and penalties are added in."

Dante slammed his hands down on the tabletop and surged to his feet. "That has nothing to do with you!"

"Unfortunately, that simply isn't true." I leaned back, waiting until he returned to his chair. "Each of those spurious suits and the judgments entered as a result impact my reputation in this community simply because we're related by blood. They also impact me as a shareholder and member of the board for Powell Properties. If I were here in my official capacity, I'd also point out that your actions have negatively impacted the company and would inform your attorney the board of directors is considering filing suit against the two of you because of it. But, as I said, I'm not here in my official capacity."

My father paled but my mother, bitch that she is, glared at me. If I'd ever wondered how she felt really about me, I now had my answer. Hatred filled her expression. The little girl in me who had tried so hard to win her love died a little in that moment. But the Rogue? The Rogue prepared to destroy her, figuratively if not literally.

"However, I am here to offer you a way to get out from under those debts. Please don't be foolish enough to believe I'm doing this out of the goodness of my heart or out of some sense of duty, at least not to you. I have conditions and you must meet each and every one of them or I will instruct Mrs. Grissom to file every lawsuit she can come up with against you. Then I will request the authorities begin investigating your actions. I have no doubt it will be easy to prove you've engaged in at least one ongoing criminal activity."

My mother started to say something, only to stop when my father placed a hand on her arm. Then he looked at me, his gaze hard as flint. I waited as he considered his options.

"What's this big plan of yours?"

God, he was such an ass.

"You will give a statement here and now about everything concerning your relationship with Sawyer, how you came to use him as your attorney in the attempt to force Aunt Bitsy and me to return the stock you sold in violation of Grandfather's will. You will tell us everything you know or have heard about the attack on Annie Caldwell that happened around the time you retained Sawyer. You will also tell us everything you know or have heard about Winston Reed and his co-defendants. Finally, you will sign legally binding documents acknowledging that you waive all past, present and future claims you might think you have on my holdings in return for me making those debts go away. Think of it as me giving you your inheritance early."

"There is one more thing," Meg put in. "You will agree that any" family relationship between you and my client is over and you will not claim any such relationship—ever."

They didn't like it. Not the part of basically being divorced from me. They had no problems with that. What they didn't like was having to give up any claims on my inheritance and any future income or holdings I might come into. Well too fucking bad. They put themselves in this position.

"There is no way I can allow my clients to even consider something so out of the ordinary without studying the proposal and you so-called supporting documentation." Chalmont reached for the file and climbed to his feet. "We will be in touch after I've had a chance to do so and after we've discussed it."

When Meg started to stand, I reached over and laid a hand on her arm, stopping her. Then I stood.

"If you walk out of here, all offers are off the table. We'll give you ten minutes to talk with your attorney. One second longer and I leave and Mrs. Grissom moves to legally destroy you." I let my eyes bleed to amber and smiled as the three across the table from me paled. "And don't whine. You've spent most of my life doing your best to break me and destroy the best this town has to offer. No more. It stops here and now. How it does is up to you."

With that, Meg and I left the conference room, the Rottweilers on my heels. As we entered her office, Beth appeared with coffee for me and herbal tea for Meg. Then she slipped out, closing the door behind her after promising to let us know if we were needed.

"You were right, Meg. Thanks." I cradled the mug between my hands and sipped, enjoying the rich brew I recognized as having come from the café.

"Now to see what they do." She crossed to her desk and checked the stack of messages Beth had left for her. "My biggest concern right now is making sure Chalmont doesn't screw it up by being totally incompetent."

"Do you think that's possible?"

"Maybe." When I looked at her, she shrugged. "The fact he wanted to see the documentation reassures me, but we have to remember we're dealing with your parents. That means we have to keep in mind they very well may file to dismiss anything they agree to based on incompetency of counsel."

I frowned, knowing she was right. "So how do we play it?"

"We stick to the plan and we make sure they sign off on everything they agree to." She paused and thought for a moment. "If they agree to our terms, we'll get it on video. That way, I can go over everything, point by point and get their agreement on the record. If they refuse, then we call this a wash and proceed with Plan B."

"I'll leave that part to you. What do you want me to do?"

"Sit there and look serious and businesslike. Don't say anything else unless I signal that it's all right. Unless I miss my bet, they're going to try to get you to do or say something foolish that they can use against you later. Let's not give them the chance."

"Understood." And agreed.

Before I could say anything else, a knock sounded at the door. A moment later, it opened and Beth stepped inside. With a glance over her shoulder, she eased the door shut. Then she grinned like a kid on Christmas morning. Meg cocked her head to one side, inviting her to explain.

"Chalmont came out a few moments ago to ask that the two of you rejoin them." Her lips twitched as she tried to control her smile. "Before that, there was a lot of raised voices, a lot of finger-pointing and the like."

"And?" Meg prompted.

"I think Chalmont's starting to figure out he's never going to get paid."

Interesting. That happened quicker than I expected. Hopefully, it worked to our benefit.

Meg glanced at her watch and arched one brow. "They barely made it. Nine minutes thirty seven seconds."

"Let's go see what they have to say."

Meg nodded and then glanced at the Rotties where they lay under the far window. "Why don't you leave them here? They might be counter-productive right now."

I knew what she meant. It would be just like Dante and Emma to claim we used the dogs to intimidate them into doing what we wanted. I nodded and then moved to the dogs, petting them and telling them I'd be back soon.

"I understand you're ready to proceed," Meg said as we returned to the conference room.

Chalmont nodded and waited until we took our places at the table. Then he opened the file folder holding the various documents Meg presented earlier as well as his tablet.

"I've had a chance to review your documentation and go over it with my clients." The look he cast in their direction spoke volumes. He was not happy but he was smart enough to know he needed to at least appear to be trying to protect their interests.

"Well?" Meg folded her hands on the tabletop and waited.

"We have a counter-offer."

"Oh dear." Meg sighed like a disappointed parent and pushed back her chair. "I guess I didn't make our position clear. There will be no negotiation. This is a onetime, take it or leave it offer." She stood and, following her cue, I did the same.

"We told you they weren't interested in anything except making a mockery out of the justice system," Dante all but spat. "Well, Jacqueline, you can take your offer and shove it. We'll see all of you in court."

"Sit down, Mr. Powell." Meg spoke softly, not that it fooled me. Any moment now and she would circle for the kill. At least for the metaphorical kill. "Mr. Chalmont, assuming you did review the documents as you said you did, then you know my client's offer is more than generous. You also know your clients have no legal leg to stand on with regard to the lawsuits they have filed against her and others. Assuming you realize that, you also realize I would be negligent in my duties as Dr. Powell's attorney if I didn't alert the Bar to the filing of so many frivolous lawsuits."

His expression hardened. He most definitely did not like that. Too bad.

"Assuming these documents are true copies."

Meg's eyes narrowed and I leaned back. I did not want to be in the line of fire when she lost her temper. Instead, she smiled slightly and reached for her cellphone. "Beth, bring in the original certified copies of the paperwork you pulled together for this meeting."

She placed the phone down on the tabletop and leaned forward, her expression betraying none of the anger I felt coming off of her. "Mr. Chalmont, I will assume you made such an ill-informed and ill-advised statement because you foolishly believed your clients. However, my good will is very finite where they are concerned. Once you see certified copies of everything in that folder, I not only expect an apology, but I expect a good faith response to our proposal."

She paused as Beth entered and handed her another file. She glanced inside and then thanked Beth. A moment later, she slid the file across the table in Chalmont's direction.

"Because you had the temerity to suggest I might stoop to presenting falsified documents, the rest of this meeting will be on the record. Don't like it? You can leave and all offers are off the table. I need your answer now."

Thank goodness I'm a good poker player because it was all I could do to keep my expression from changing. Part of me wanted to laugh long and hard at the look on Chalmont's face as he glared at his clients. Another part of me wanted to drag the three of them up by the scruff of their necks and teach them a lesson they wouldn't forget about how foolish it was to insult people I cared for. Instead, I sat there, doing my best to look bored as I pulled my phone from my pocket and checked for messages. While I did that, Meg activated the room's video cameras and waited for Chalmont's answer.

Meg might kill me when this was over, but I'd had enough of waiting.

"This is getting us nowhere." I pushed back my chair and stood. "If you were smart enough to graduate law school and pass the Bar, Mr. Chalmont, you should realize how badly your clients have misrepresented the situation to you. You should also realize that if they refuse the offer, we will carry through with our promise to file against them. I will see them ruined. I will see them in prison for their crimes."

"I believe Dr. Powell has made her position very clear," Meg said as she, too, stood. "Your answer now or this meeting is over."

"Wait." Chalmont blew out a breath. "Give me another few minutes with my clients."

Meg nodded. This time, when we left the conference room, we didn't go any further than the work area outside. Before Meg could rip me a new one, I stopped her. This wasn't the time. She could lecture me all she wanted when this was over.

"He didn't know. He took their word for everything and now he's finding out they lied," I said softly.

It didn't take long. Less than five minutes later, Chalmont asked us to return. The moment we stepped inside, I knew we'd won.

"All right, Dr. Powell," Chalmont said as Meg and I returned to our seats. "Exactly what do you want from your parents?"

I leaned back and shook my head. How many different times and different ways did I have to say it?

"I want to know everything they can tell me about Sawyer, about what happened to Annie Caldwell, what relationship they had with Mia Caldwell, and anything else they happen to know or suspect about what has happened to Annie, to Quinn O'Donnell, to Meg Grissom and anyone else here in town. I also expect them to execute the legal documents you have in front of you. In return for that, I will make sure their current debts are cleared."

"We don't know anything you might be interested in. We hired Sawyer to represent us because he didn't ask any questions and was willing to work for a contingency fee." Daniel—sorry, Dante—sat back and smirked.

"Then we have nothing else to discuss." I couldn't even get angry. I knew going in the chances of success were slim to none. But that didn't mean I wouldn't get at least a little satisfaction. "Meg, turn over everything we've uncovered about these two to the DA's Office and contact all applicable federal agencies. It's past time they learn they can't continue to bilk people out of their labors and their money. Mr.

Chalmont, if you're smart, you'll fire them as clients before you get caught up in all this."

"You can't!"

I shook my head as Emma pushed to her feet, visibly vibrating with outrage.

"I can and I will. You and your husband have abused the good will of the people of this town for too long. You have defrauded local businesses. You have defaulted on loans and ignored court judgments. You have lied and swindled and who knows what else to get what you want and you've done so without a thought for those you hurt along the way. No more.

"My grandfather loved this town. That was why he opened the business here and why he kept it here. He taught me to love the town and everyone who lived here as well. He also taught me how important it is to protect the town and all it stands for. That includes protecting it from the likes of you."

"I swear, they must have switched babies at the hospital. There is no way you're my daughter," my mother spat.

"Trust me, it's been no walk in the park being your daughter. As far as I'm concerned, we no longer have any relationship, blood or otherwise. Just to make sure you can't cause others the heartache you've caused Aunt Bitsy and me, I've executed the appropriate legal documents making sure you have no legal claim on any of my past, present or future holdings or interests." Thank God, I didn't have to deal with them any longer. "Mr. Chalmont, you have my sincerest pity for having to deal with the two of them." I stepped away from the table. If I didn't get out of the room soon, I wouldn't be responsible for what happened next.

"Sawyer was right. They should have dealt with you first," my mother—No, I could finally quit thinking about her that way—Emma spat.

I stopped. The hand that reached for the back of my chair shook slightly. At the same time, my animal side pushed for release. Holding that part of me in check, I turned slowly to face Emma. As I did, one part of my brain registered Chalmont looking at her in disbelief. Meg stood at my side. Anger flushed Dante's face. He might agree with her, but he did not like the fact she'd spilled the beans.

Without thinking about what I was doing, I eased off my jacket. As I draped it over the chair to my left, Emma and Dante gasped softly. Fear lit their expressions as they stared at my tattoo sleeve. Good. They recognized the danger. Gone was the respectable Dr. Powell. In her place stood the Rogue, the woman who could and would make the tell her everything if it helped protect the town and find the person responsible for what had been going on these last few years.

"Easy," Meg said softly.

When she gently touched my left arm, I glanced down. My tattoo sleeve was more alive than I'd seen it in a long time. It wouldn't take much to shift. That was something my parents obviously suspected as they slid their chairs back from the table and prepared to stand.

"Sit!"

The order echoed off the walls of the conference room. Then I nodded at Meg, letting her know I was all right. She didn't say anything as she returned to her chair. Without a word, she produced her cell phone and sent someone a text. It didn't take a genius to guess she'd contacted either Drew or Quinn. Either worked because I was about to destroy my parents and there was nothing they could do about it.

Now to let them know it.

"Meg, contact the Sheriff's Department and ask them to send deputies here." I didn't look away from the two who should have been willing to risk their lives to keep me safe but who would rather I drop dead because I was *inconvenient* to them.

"Dr. Powell?" Chalmont looked at me in a mixture of fear and concern.

"Mr. Chalmont, my parents—and I use that term loosely—apparently kept you more in the dark than I suspected. First, I am an Other. I am an Earth Elemental and a Walker. That makes me very rare and very powerful, something they obviously forgot."

Or, more likely, refused to admit.

"I take my responsibilities as such very seriously. So when I realized my best friends were being targeted by someone, I came home to see what I could do to help protect them. I've stayed for a number of reasons, not the least of which centered around your clients. It goes beyond their trying to coerce my aunt and me into not only returning the stocks your client sold in violation of my grandfather's will and the paperwork he signed when the will was read after Granddad's death, paperwork where he acknowledged he not only knew but understood the provisions of the will and would abide by them. For years, pretty much as long as I can remember, your clients have actively worked against the best interests of this town and the people who live here. It is long past time for them to face the consequences of their actions."

Chalmont opened his mouth to say something and snapped it shut when I leveled my gaze on him.

"She." I pointed at Emma who shrank against the back of her chair, fear lighting her expression. "She just admitted knowing Sawyer was involved in what happened to Annie and probably the others. Her own words show she, and probably Dante, discussed the situation with Sawyer. Yet they have kept this information to themselves even though the sheriff, not to mention the former and the current District Attorney, have repeatedly asked for help from the public. That makes these two, at the very least, accessories after the fact. So yes, I am going to turn everything over to the Sheriff's Department."

Before I could say anything else, Meg spoke up.

"Mr. Chalmont, you have just become a witness to Mrs. Powell's admission. You have a decision to make, one that will impact your professional career going forward."

He blew out a shaky breath before dropping his head into his hands. When he looked up, I wondered if he might not be considering resigning from the Bar and running as far from Mossy Creek as he could. Then he nodded once before climbing to his feet.

"Mr. and Mrs. Powell, you have put me in an untenable position. Not only have you lied to me about the facts surrounding the reasons you hired me, but you, Mrs. Powell, have just admitted to having knowledge of a criminal act. I am not a criminal attorney. I also will not represent clients who tie my hands the way you have. Consider our professional relationship concluded."

He turned to Meg and me. "Mrs. Grissom, Dr. Powell, my apologies. I will do whatever I can to assist you moving forward within the restrictions placed upon me by attorney-client privilege."

"We understand, Mr. Chalmont, and thank you." Meg shook his hand and walked him to the door.

"You won't get away with this," Dante said as he and Emma stood.

Did they really think I'd let them leave before Lucas got a deputy here?

"I believe the only ones no longer getting away with anything are the two of you."

I glanced over my shoulder as the door shut behind Meg. Interesting. I didn't think she'd leave me alone with my parents, not when she knew how angry I was. Then I realized why. She wanted to make sure a deputy was on his way. Otherwise, she'd send for Quinn. Either way, these two—Never again would I think of them as my parents. For the first time, I truly understood why Meg spoke of the Luíseachs as her mother's egg donor or sperm donor. They were no more family to her than these two were to me—were going nowhere.

"Now sit the hell down and, for once in your lives, be smart. Tell me what you know about everything that's happened. If you do, I will make sure the DA knows you cooperated. Hell, much as I hate it, I will even ask for leniency—with the provision you not only leave town but that you also never bother Bitsy or me again."

One moment they looked at me, as if considering what I said. The next saw the world erupting into madness. Dante lunged across the table in my direction. As I stumbled back, his fingers brushing against my tank top, Emma dug inside the small purse she carried. My hands grabbed Dante, dragging him across the table. Before he could react, I slammed his face against the tabletop. His cry of pain was lost in a sudden explosion of sound. Something slammed into my left shoulder, staggering me. Across the room, Emma stood, a small gun in hand. A second explosion of sound came from behind me as the door was blown off its hinges.

"You bitch!" Meg rasped as she rushed inside, Drew and Quinn on her heels.

I sank onto a chair, my brain trying to catch up with my eyes. Not that I wanted it to. Blood seeped between my fingers where they grasped my shoulder. Then, as that thrice damned Dante moaned and tried to push to his feet, I swiveled in the chair and—oops!—my knee connected solidly with his jaw and he dropped like a rock.

"Drop the fucking gun or I will drop you," Drew ordered, his voice colder, more deadly than I'd ever heard.

"If he doesn't, I will," Quinn said as she moved to stand protectively at my side.

For a moment, it looked as if Emma considered refusing. Then she let the gun drop to the carpeted floor. Fortunately, it didn't go off. A moment later, Drew had her cuffed and was reading her her rights. As he did, another deputy entered the room. He pulled Dante up and cuffed him. Then he led the two of them outside, reading Dante his rights as he did.

"What the hell happened?" Quinn asked as she turned my chair so she could examine my wound.

"Mrs. Powell admitted Sawyer said *they* should have dealt with Jax first. She didn't say if he identified who he meant. That was enough for their attorney to quit. I was showing him out when I heard the gunshot." Meg dropped onto the chair next to mine. As she did, her right hand moved protectively over her baby bump and she breathed deeply, struggling for calm.

"I'm taking you to the ER." Quinn put away her gun. "Then you are going to give Drew a full statement about what happened. Once you do, I'm going to have a little chat with Sawyer." Anger roughened her voice and I doubted she realized flames danced around her hands.

"No, you aren't," Drew corrected. He didn't blanch when she shot him a look that would have most men pissing themselves. "Lucas and I will have a talk with him—after we discuss what happened with

Alvarez. In the meantime, those two will be booked on charges of attempted murder and anything else I can come up with."

Then he turned his attention to me. "And you will go to the ER. You will let them treat you and if they want you to stay there, you won't argue. I'm calling Rafe to make sure of it."

I did the only thing any mature woman would do in the situation. I flipped him off.

22

"**D**amn it, I'm fine."

Okay, maybe I wasn't fine. Maybe my friends had reason to worry. After all, this was the second time I'd been shot in the last few months. The first time, I'd been in one of my shifted forms. That time had been worse. A larger caliber gun had been used and there'd been more damage done. This time, Emma's small caliber gun—hell, it was so small it barely qualified as a gun—was nothing in comparison. Better yet, the wound was a through-and-through and nothing vital had been hit and no bones had been damaged.

But everyone was acting like I needed to take to my bed for a month and that was not going to happen.

Only Amy seemed to be taking everything in stride. Of course, I didn't doubt for a minute she'd give me a lecture once we were alone. But at least she wasn't demanding I stay in the hospital.

"Someone better tell me what's been happening." I paused and checked my watch. "The last three hours. Otherwise, I'm marching straight to the jail to have a little chat with Dante and Emma and then with Sawyer on my own and there's not a hell of a lot any of you can do to stop me."

We stood outside the entrance to the emergency department.

Although he stood at my side, ready to help if I needed it, I knew Rafe agreed with the others. He wanted me to go home and rest. I didn't doubt for a moment that he planned to head to the SD in my place. That was not going to happen. This was my fight and, by damn, I would finish it.

"All right. Annie and Lucas are on the warpath." Quinn actually grimaced. "Annie because she can't deal with Sawyer himself. So she's called in Alvarez and he's already meeting with Drew about what charges to file against that bastard as well as the Powells."

"And Lucas?"

"He's having to deal with Dante's threats, Emma's caterwauling, and doesn't have the reward of smacking them or Sawyer around. He is also waiting for search warrants for the Powell's residence, cars, electronics, etc."

I smiled a slow, deadly smile. I knew my parents. Confident no one would ever look closely at their actions, they kept records of everything they did. I didn't doubt the warrants would result in more than enough evidence to charge them with much more than shooting me. Better yet, we might get lucky and learn more about what had been going on. I only hoped it wasn't too late.

"I want to talk to Sawyer."

"You can't, Jax. You know that," Quinn said.

Instead of arguing, I pulled my phone. Before they could argue, I called Jason Alvarez. He listened closely as I laid out my plan. I few minutes later, I slid the phone back into my pocket and grinned. He had his own conditions, but he agreed. I'd get to talk to Sawyer. The SOB could demand to be returned to his cell once he realized I was his "visitor", but we'd cross that bridge when we came to it.

"Quinn, you can quit looking at me like that. I'm not going to do anything foolish." At least not too foolish. "But he knows something and I plan to find out what. Trust Alvarez to make sure it is done in a way Sawyer, Dante and Emma and everyone else involved never sees another day of freedom. Now go reassure Annie I'm all right and will be by the office later so she can see for herself."

"Jax." She ground the word out.

"I mean it." I paused and counted to ten. Emotions were high for all of us. The last thing we needed was to be at one another's throats. "Quinn, short of searching Dante and Emma before they entered the conference room, we couldn't have prevented what happened. This," I gently touched my injured shoulder, "is a small enough price to get to the bottom of what's been going on."

I turned to Meg who still looked like she blamed herself for what happened. "And you can quit feeling guilty. This is not on you. Hell, it's not even on me. This rests solely at the feet of the two who will never again be referred to as my parents. I will use what happened today as the lever we've been looking for to make sure they cause no more problems for the company or for Bitsy. I'd like you to go back to the office and start drawing up the paperwork for any civil suits you feel we need to initiate. Also, touch base with our corporate counsel and brief him on what happened."

"You don't do anything else foolish." She pinned me with a look that promised dire consequences if anything else happened to me.

"Yes, Mom." I grinned as she muttered under her breath before walking off, Quinn at her side. "Amy, not a word to your grandmother."

She actually chuckled. "Do you really think she doesn't already know what happened? If the usual grapevine hasn't told her, she'll have heard the nursing staff talking about it. How do you think I found out?"

Now I groaned. I hadn't thought about that. Shit!

"Don't worry. I'll make sure she knows you're all right. But you might want to come see her sooner, rather than later."

I so did not look forward to that but I nodded. She was right. But that brought up something else I needed to do. I needed to let Aunt Bitsy know what happened. Wouldn't that be a fun conversation?

As if that was the signal, my phone buzzed in my pocket. I didn't need to look to know who was calling. I blew out a breath, metaphorically pulled up my big girl panties and answered.

"I'm fine." I rolled my eyes as Bitsy demanded to know what happened and what she needed to do to pound her brother into paste. "Aunt Bitsy, really, I'm all right. They aren't keeping me in the hospital."

"Let me talk to Rafe."

Oh, hell, she was not going to take my word for it. I didn't have any choice. I handed Rafe my phone and started down the drive to where he'd parked when they told him I could leave. By the time he joined me, I sat in the front passenger seat.

"I don't know whether to take you over my knee for scaring the hell out of me or laugh because your aunt is truly pissed and threatening dire consequences over what happened." He slid the key into the ignition. The truck's engine roared to life and Rafe carefully pulled away from the curb. "I told her what I could and promised we'd stop by to see her before dinner. Sorry, Doc, but this is a battle you aren't going to be able to postpone."

I nodded. Maybe by then I'd have something to distract Bitsy.

I leaned back and closed my eyes. A moment later, Rafe's hand closed around mine. I smiled and linked fingers with him. He might be angry, but he didn't blame me for what happened. At least not too much.

Thank goodness.

"I know you aren't going to rest right now, Doc, but you need to take it easy. Lucas texted while I was getting the truck. He said Alvarez will meet you at the courthouse. Once you're done, stop by Annie's office. Reassure her you're okay. Then call me and I'll come get you. Then, whether you like it or not, you're going to rest. Then you can come back to see Miss Serena before we go to Bitsy's and then Judith's."

I didn't like it, but that was a battle I wasn't ready to fight.

"What are you going to do?" I turned my head and watched him as he guided the truck toward downtown.

"Let's just say Sam and I have a couple of things we want to look into."

I knew better than to ask more. At least not right now. But later was a different matter.

It didn't surprise me to find Quinn waiting with my dogs as I climbed out of the truck in front of the courthouse. She leaned in through the passenger window and promised Rafe she'd keep an eye on me. Then, as he drove away, she gave me a look she must have learned from her mother, one that had me squirming like I'd been caught doing something I shouldn't be doing.

"At least tell me you got one shot in."

I grinned and nodded. "Not a shot but I did manage to bloody Dante. Probably broke his nose." That had to count for something, right?

"And the bitch who shot you?"

"Meg interrupted before I could do anything."

"So, where was your gun?"

She gave me a look that spoke volumes. She knew I'd been unarmed. Crap.

"I had the dogs with me. I didn't think I'd need my gun." I shook my head before she could interrupt. "Quinn, not once have I ever seen either Dante or Emma with a gun of any sort. Remember when we were growing up. They refused to let me go to the shooting range with you guys. They didn't believe in guns."

Which made what Emma did more difficult to understand.

"And what do you plan to do about it all?"

"Charges are being filed. Civil suits as well. I gave them their one chance to make things right. They refused. So they will face the consequences of their actions, all of them."

For a moment, Quinn didn't say anything. Then she nodded, apparently satisfied by my response. She handed me a lead and, with the other lead in her left hand, escorted me inside. The message was clear. Alvarez was waiting for me.

It didn't take long to set up. Sawyer's court-appointed attorney— who looked all of thirteen—was already there, doing his best to get Alvarez to explain why he'd asked for the meeting. When Quinn and I entered the conference room Alvarez was using as an office, I ordered the dogs to lie down in the far corner. Quinn made sure I was all right and then stepped outside. She couldn't be part of this and she didn't like it one bit. She'd made that very clear on our ride up in the elevator.

I didn't say anything to Sawyer's attorney, leaving it to Alvarez to explain. My job, for the moment at least, was to look and listen.

"And what will my client get out of talking with Dr. Powell?"

"If he cooperates and answers her questions, I'll take life without parole off the table."

The defense attorney shook his head. "Not good enough. Probation with the State not fighting when he applies to be reinstated to the Bar."

Alvarez shook his head, his expression betraying nothing. "That's not going to happen and you know it."

He glanced down, as if studying the file on front of him. When he looked back up, his expression turned hard and I wondered if Sawyer or his attorney understood how formidable an opponent he happened to be. Sawyer should. After all, he worked for Alvarez for five years or more before being fired. Then again, no one ever said Sawyer learned from his mistakes. It remained to be seen if his attorney was any smarter.

"Mr. Garland, I suggest you review your client's history. Even if I were inclined to do as you propose, there is no way the Bar will ever consider reinstating him. For one, this isn't the first time he's gotten into trouble with them. When he worked as an assistant prosecutor, he routinely violated the rules of evidence and violated defendants' rights. Several of those resulted in the Bar sanctioning him. He did the same thing in the case against Julianna Grissom Caldwell's mother is what got him fired from the DA's Office and finally convinced the Bar that it's only option was to suspend his license. He has been reprimanded on at least three occasions that I know of since being reinstated. Each time was for filing frivolous lawsuits. He has been implicated—strongly implicated—in the attacks on both Mrs. Caldwell and on Mrs. Grissom."

"Implication doesn't mean you have solid evidence." Garland leaned back, a satisfied expression on his face.

"I'm going to assume you aren't as naïve as you're acting,

Garland." Alvarez didn't react to the younger man's quick flash of anger. "But, if you are, talk to your client. He may be an expert at manipulating people when it comes to implications and no solid evidence, but I'm a far better attorney because I don't have to play dirty. I can and do build cases that not only convince juries to convict but that will stand up on appeal. If you don't believe me, I suggest you check my record. Then check the record of cases tried by your client and then reversed on appeal while he worked for the DA's Office."

Garland and Sawyer leaned close together, whispering softly enough overhearing became difficult. Not that I needed to hear to know what was being said. Garland wanted Sawyer to leave the negotiations to him. Sawyer wanted nothing to do with any of us. When he glanced in my direction, fear and hatred filled his eyes. Good. I could play with both.

"Mr. Sawyer has no intention of discussing anything with you as long as Dr. Powell is present. Her vendetta against my client is well known."

Garland carefully folded his hands on the tabletop and did his best to look both intimidating and experienced. Unfortunately for him, he simply looked like a young man well out of his depth who didn't realize it. I knew he couldn't be more than five or six years younger than me but everything about him screamed youth and inexperience. I did give it to him for trying to do his best by his client. It was just too bad that client happened to be Sawyer.

I carefully changed positions and took a moment to study Sawyer. Less than twenty-four hours earlier, he'd been taken into custody for violating the terms of his release. This time, his mother not only refused to help him, she had refused to take his calls. Now he sat at the table in his orange county jail jumpsuit and white shower shoes. It was difficult to take him serious at the best of times. But seeing the little weasel of a man like this? Well, let's just say it did my heart good.

"Dr. Powell?"

Alvarez glanced at me and nodded. Interesting. I hadn't expected him to let me say anything this soon.

"Mr. Garland, we don't know one another but let me give you a word of advice. When dealing with Sawyer, you'd be wise to take everything he says with a grain of salt. Then you'd best verify it before acting on it. But don't take my word on it. When we're done here, take a few minutes to stop by Miss Peggy's café. Talk to the people there. Wander around downtown and stop in the shops and businesses. See what they have to tell you about your client. While you're at it, ask them about any vendettas there might be and who might be behind them. I'm confident when you do, you'll see the instigator is and always has been Sawyer.

"Do I like your client? No. He has waged war against people I care a great deal about. He has filed frivolous lawsuits against me, my aunt and Powell Properties, the business my grandfather spent his life building. He has threatened to negatively impact my veterinary practice as well as Caldwell Construction where my husband works. He has conspired with Dante and Emma Powell not only to extort an ownership interest in the business from my aunt and myself but to alter the terms of my grandfather's will, terms his clients not only understood but agreed to abide by."

I held up a hand to stop either of them from interrupting. It was time to lay my cards on the table, at least some of them.

"While investigating Dante and Emma Powell in preparation for the various lawsuits currently filed in connection with their actions, information has come to my attention that more than implicates your client in certain criminal activities. Activities that can land him in prison for the rest of his life without a hope in hell for release on parole should he be convicted."

"She's lying." Sawyer sneered, making him look even more like a weasel.

"I may do a lot of things, but I don't lie." At least not too often.

"Lay it out or this meeting is over." As if to make his point, Garland shut the cover on his tablet and slid his chair away from the table.

Now Alvarez smiled, looking very bit the predator after scenting his prey.

"Before I do, let me ask you this, Sawyer. What do you think my investigators found when they executed search warrants at your house and at the storage facility you failed to reveal to the court or to your probation officer when you were released on bail?"

A small smile lifted the corners of my mouth as the color drained out of Sawyer's face.

"What do you want?" Sawyer waved off Garland's objection. "Let's hear it."

In the end, it didn't take long. Alvarez was still drawing information out of Sawyer about everything that had happened, but I had what I needed. When we took a break for Garland to consult with his client, I stepped into the corridor with Alvarez. As we emerged, Quinn hurried in our direction. Her expression said it all. She was worried about me, curious about what we had found and more than ready to go hunting anyone we needed to "talk with" next.

"Do you need anything else from me?" I asked.

"No, and thanks. You were right. Seeing you put both Sawyer and Garland off-balance. Once I finish here, I'll be meeting with the investigators who executed the search warrants. Sawyer's reaction when I mentioned them tells me there's something there."

"Is there anything I can do?" Quinn asked.

He shook his head. "Not yet. I'll let you know what my the next step is after I've talked with the investigators." He shook my hand. "Go get some rest, Dr. Powell. You've earned it."

"Thank you." I watched as he walked down the hallway in the direction of the break room. Then I turned to Quinn. "Let's go. I'll fill you in once we've checked in with Annie."

Maybe then she could help me figure out what our next move should be.

23

Annie sat behind her desk, the end of her pen tapping out a rhythm that betrayed her anger. So did the way her eyes flashed, their color closer to amber than their normal blue. At least she managed to maintain control over her abilities. Still, I had a feeling it wouldn't take much to push her over the edge and I did not want to be anywhere near when that happened.

Especially since most of her anger was currently aimed directly at me.

"Well?" She arched one brow, a patented mother look.

"I'm sure Meg's already filled you in."

Her expression darkened and her eyes narrowed. Oops. Maybe that wasn't the best way to respond.

"My law partner said you'd tell me what happened."

I swallowed hard and made a mental note to have a long talk with Meg who would, I had no doubt, say she couldn't say anything because of attorney-client privilege.

"Your law partner is a coward," I muttered and then glared at Quinn when she chuckled softly. "As for what happened, you probably know pretty much everything already." I nodded at the to-go cup from the café.

When Annie continued to look at me, I relented. "Meg and I miscalculated when it came to Emma and Dante, Emma in particular. But it worked in our favor. Not only do we now have confirmation at least some of what's been happening is connected but it gave us the leverage needed to force Sawyer to cooperate."

"What do you mean?" Her anger dissipated as she waited for me to explain.

"Annie, I'm not going to give you specifics."

"Jax."

"I can't. You know that." Not that I blamed her for wanting to know. "But you've already had to recuse yourself from the cases involving Sawyer and the others. You and Alvarez have done a great job making sure the office itself can still be involved. Let's not risk that. Please."

I watched her struggle with what I said. The prosecutor in her knew I was right. But the friend, the mother and the daughter in her wanted to know everything that might impact her family and those she cared for. I understood but those details were for Alvarez to review and decide what she could know without jeopardizing the various cases.

"I don't like it." She spoke softly.

"I don't either," I admitted.

"Are you all right." Her eyes went to my injured shoulder and the sling my arm rested in.

"I am. I promise."

"She really is," Quinn said, surprising me. "I checked with Amy and Dr. Pat while she was with Alvarez. She needs to take it easy and be careful, but they didn't even try to keep her in the hospital."

"All right." She leaned back and shook her head as if by doing so she could clear away the mental cobwebs and confusion. "You're sure at least some of this is connected?"

I nodded. "Emma let something slip and Sawyer confirmed it. Alvarez was still with that SOB and his attorney. You know he will do everything he can to get further confirmation for us."

"What now?"

"I'm going to take Jax to check on Miss Serena," Quinn said before I could respond. "Rafe's going to meet us there. He'll take her home and make sure she rests some. We're all still meeting at my place tonight." Now she grinned as she glanced at me. "But before that, she gets to have a chat with Bitsy."

Annie looked at us, amusement dancing in her eyes, her lips working as she tried not to laugh. Then she gave up. She threw her head back and laughed long and hard. Then she pointed at me, still chuckling, and shook her head.

"You are so screwed." She snorted—SNORTED—as she started laughing again.

"Some friend you are." I grinned, knowing she was right. Bitsy was going to have more than a few things to say about what happened. "And to show I know how to return the favor, I'll just say this before Quinn and I leave. If things have progressed to where Emma would risk getting her hands dirty by taking direct action, then all of us are in danger. That includes our families. So you need to consider having your mother—and her babies—move in with you."

Annie's eyes widened and she went pale at the thought of her mother and those thrice-damned poodles moving in. Then she swallowed hard.

"Do you think it's that bad?" Gone was the teasing friend. In her place was the worried daughter.

"Honestly?"

She nodded.

"I don't know but I'd rather overreact than risk our loved ones."

She drew a bracing breath and nodded. "I'll talk with Sam and Gran. We'll figure out the best way to approach Mama." Then she grinned broadly.

Quinn barked out a short laugh. "I know what you're thinking and Meg will kill you."

I looked between the two of them and then it dawned on me. There was an alternative to Catherine and her "babies" moving in with Annie. She could move in with Drew and Meg. They had more than enough room and it had the added benefit—from Annie's point of view at least—of letting Catherine be close to her pregnant daughter-in-law and out of Annie's hair.

"And the two of you think I'm the evil one." I grinned, fully appreciating what Annie had in mind. "But that is one piece of news I'll let you discuss with your twin and his wife, Annie. Friendship only goes so far."

"Maybe Gran will suggest it."

I knew better. Mary Kate would smile, probably pat Annie's cheek, and leave it to her to suggest. In other words, Mary Kate was smart enough not to get involved. Since this promised to be entertaining, I wondered if there was some way to sell tickets and watch—from a distance, of course.

"We need to get on our way." Quinn stood and glanced around the office. Then she frowned. "Where's Brigid?"

"I could ask you the same thing. Where are your dogs?" Annie pinned us both with a firm look.

"In my office," Quinn said simply and then waited for Annie to answer her question.

Without a word, Annie stood and moved to the door behind and to the right of her desk. I'd assumed it was a closet of some sort. When Annie neared, I realized the door had been ajar. It opened onto a private restroom. Inside, curled up on a dog bed was Brigid, her German shepherd.

"Satisfied?"

Quinn nodded. "I'll be back as soon as I drop Jax at the hospital. We need to discuss the Bell trial that's set for week after next."

Annie cocked her head to one side. "Problems?"

"Possibly."

"All right. I'll take a look at the file before you return." She bent and made a note. "As for you." She pinned me with a look I knew I'd see from others before the day was done. "You don't take any more chances. Call me when you get ready to leave the hospital."

"Yes, Mother," I drawled.

She laughed and moved around the desk to give me a careful hug.

Then she walked with us to the door. As she did, Miss Olivia let her
know her next appointment as there. Annie thanked her and said
she'd see us soon.

"Well?" Quinn asked as she slid in behind the wheel of
her SUV.

"Well what?"

She carefully backed out of her parking space and headed toward
the parking lot exit. Before turning onto Main Street, she glanced at
me and grinned. "Any bets on where Catherine winds up staying?"
Amusement danced in her eyes.

"With Annie."

Quinn glanced at me, surprised by my answer.

"Drew will play the pregnant wife card. I can hear him reminding
Annie that Meg doesn't need any additional stress in her life, that she
has enough getting used to running the law firm. Then there's the
danger we all agree is coming. The last thing she needs is their mama
and her babies."

Quinn kept her eyes on the road, but that didn't keep me from
seeing her grin. "Maybe I should make sure they have a very hungry
looking dog, one that would give Catherine's babies a heart attack if
they saw it."

I glanced over my shoulder to where the Rotties lay on the backseat, carefully secured so they wouldn't be hurt if Quinn had to slam
on the brakes. If I thought I could get away with it, I'd loan one of
them to Meg just to make sure she didn't have to deal with her
mother-in-law more than necessary. Catherine meant well but I knew
she'd drive Meg crazy within a day or two. But I wouldn't be able to
get away with it. Besides, I was starting to bond with them.

"I have a feeling they'd both thank you if you did."

Drew certainly would. He might be a grown man but he'd been
known to turn his truck around and drive in the opposite direction at
the sight of his mother and "the terrible trio" jogging down the street.
Not that I blamed him.

Of course, Catherine would never forgive her.

"What's our next step?"

"Other than making sure Annie and Drew don't go to war over who has to deal with their mother?"

Quinn nodded.

"We need to finish making sure everyone is protected. How long before the rest of the dogs are ready?"

"It's going to take time before we get all of them." She wasn't happy. "I'll have dogs for Amy, Bitsy and Mom this weekend. The rest will be arriving over the next few weeks. The trainers are having to reach out to other trainers to get what we need and it isn't cheap."

"Don't worry about the cost. I'll take care of it." I might as well put my trust fund to use for something worthwhile.

"You don't need to. Bitsy has arranged for it to be covered. Amy's insisting on paying for her own dog as is my mother. So I'm going to let the three of them fight it out over who pays for what."

"Smart woman." I grinned at her. "And I do appreciate you making sure Bitsy's covered."

"Jax, she's your mother in every way that matters. Of course, I'm going to make sure she's protected." She reached over and lightly grasped my hand. "Now, what's next?"

"We need to find out where Benjamin Luíseach is and how he connects to the rest of the players beyond the connection to Meg."

"Lucas is already on it and I have no doubt Annie will put me on it as well. Once Ciara's home, she can help."

"I'm going to put Rafe and Sam on it. They won't be constrained the way the rest of you will be."

Quinn didn't like it. I could tell. But then she had always been the one to follow the rules. At least she didn't argue.

"What else?"

I thought for a moment. There was still one of our group who hadn't returned to Mossy Creek. I doubted he ever would, at least not permanently. His gifts were similar to an empath's and that made it difficult for him to be around too many people. It was hard to block out their thoughts and emotions. Normally, I'd never consider asking him to come home. But with everything that had been happening, I'd begun wondering if I didn't need to.

"Have you talked with Ciaran recently?"

She turned into the parking lot in front of the hospital and began searching for a parking space.

"We talked day before yesterday." She pulled into the first spot she found. "Why?"

"Has he mentioned anything happening up there that seems out of the ordinary?"

She turned in her seat and looked at me in concern. Then she cursed softly. "You think whoever is targeting the rest of us might go for him?"

"I don't know." That much was true. "Technically, they haven't tried for Ciara. Since Ciaran's still in Alaska, they might not even know about him." Although I doubted it.

She leaned her head back and closed her eyes. I waited, knowing she was considering the different possibilities. One of her talents was being able to see patterns. Right now, she would be looking for anything that might tie back to her older brother. When she looked at me, her expression betrayed nothing and that worried me.

"Quinn?"

"I'm going to call him when we finish up here. It's past time he and I have a serious discussion about everything that's been going on."

Meaning she'd left much of the previous discussions to Ciara, his twin. I didn't blame her. I would have done the same.

"Let me know what he says?"

She nodded, her expression thoughtful. "He almost came home after you brought Maddy back from Ireland."

That surprised me. "Why?"

"Why do you think?" She smiled, amusement easing some of the tension in her expression. "He wasn't happy about Ciara getting involved with someone who wasn't willing to be with her, even if it meant being here in Mossy Creek."

I didn't know whether to laugh or give Ciara a head's up. Assuming she didn't already know how her twin felt—which she probably did. Then again, I wondered if Ciaran's concern went beyond that of a brother worried his sister might get her heart broken.

I was still considering the possibility when my phone rang. Seeing Amy's name displayed, I turned it so Quinn could see. She grinned and told me to answer it. No doubt Miss Serena was asking where I was because she wanted to see for herself that I was all right.

"Hey, Amy. I'm about to head inside." To put actions to my words, I opened the door and released my seatbelt.

"Maddy, you shouldn't be here."

I swallowed hard and looked around, as if I could see where they were inside the hospital. God, what if they weren't at the hospital?

Damn it, what was going on?

"Where is she?" That was Maddy but something about her tone didn't sound right.

"Where's who?" Amy asked.

I bailed out of the SUV and jerked open the back door. By the time I had the Rotties unloaded, Quinn was there, Zeus and Sasha at her side. Once again, her expression was closed. She might not know what was going on, but she knew it wasn't good.

I put my phone on speaker and pulled my injured arm from the sling. Quinn narrowed her eyes at me but didn't otherwise react when I tossed the sling inside the SUV and slammed the door.

"Serena." Maddy bit out the word.

I didn't dare risk doing or saying anything that might warn Maddy we were there. So I silently mouthed for Quinn to alert Lucas. As I did, I sent a text o Rafe. Hopefully, he was already there.

"She's having some tests run, Maddy. Your mother and the other doctors don't want to release her from here to a regular room until they're sure she's all right."

From here.

That meant they had to be in the step-down unit or close to it. Maybe one of the waiting rooms. Without waiting to see if Quinn followed, I took off at a run. Odin and Loki ran next to me, one on each side. I hit the lobby doors, cursing as we had to slow down for them to open. Someone called out to me as we ran inside. I ignored them. They could either follow or live with the fact I'd brought two dogs inside. Behind me, Quinn ordered someone to contact Security. Then she raced after me, the sound of her boots on the tile floor matching mine.

"Stairs," I rasped over my shoulder as I ignored the elevators and ran around the corridor.

Heart pounding, lungs straining, I took the stairs two at a time. Pain lanced through me from my injured shoulder. A warm dampness seeped into the bandages. Dr. Pat was going to kill me, but that was a small enough price to pay if I managed to keep anything else from happening.

"I need to see her, Amy. Now."

I slid to a stop at the third floor landing and held up a hand. Quinn slowed and then stopped next to me. I tried to see down the corridor through the narrow window in the door but couldn't. Doing my best to ignore my injured shoulder, I considered our next move.

"Lucas is five minutes out," Quinn said softly as she checked her phone.

"We can't wait." I closed my eyes and sought my center. "Stay here with the dogs. Let me go first."

"The hell I will." Her eyes flashed and I knew she wouldn't change her mind, at least not without a very good reason.

"Quinn, we don't know what's going on. We could be overreacting and both of us barging in with four dogs ready to attack would undo all the inroads we've made with Maddy since Ireland."

"I don't give a damn, Jax. I'm not going to risk you, Amy or Miss Serena."

I understood, but that wasn't enough to change my mind. There had to be another way. Hearing the door a flight up open and close, I had the answer.

I hoped.

"Let's do it this way. You and your dogs go up a flight. Then come down the back stairs. It will put you on the other side of the unit. If that's where they are, we'll have them boxed in between the two of us."

She didn't say anything for a moment. Then she bent and lifted the right leg of her jeans. When she straightened, she held her backup piece in one hand. She extended it, her intention clear. I was to take it or we'd still be standing here arguing when Lucas and the others arrived.

I took it and slid it under my belt at the small of my back. Then I watched as she started up the stairs, Zeus and Sasha on her heels. I blew out a breath and took my phone off speaker.

Now to figure out how to walk down the corridor with the Rotties and not draw attention to us.

24

I pushed open the door and stepped into the corridor. As I did, one of the nurses appeared from a patient's room across the corridor. She started to say something, definitely not pleased to see the dogs, then she clamped her mouth shut. Whether she saw something in my expression or something else, I didn't know and I didn't care. I placed a finger to my lips and then motioned for her to duck back inside the room. I didn't care if she called Security. Hell, I hoped she did. I had a sinking feeling in the pit of my stomach things were about to go south. I blew out a breath and made sure I had a good hold on the dogs' leads. Praying none of my suspicions and concerns showed, I walked down the corridor in the direction of Miss Serena's room. As I did, I tried to convince myself the fact I'd heard nothing from Amy for the last few minutes didn't mean anything, that I'd get to the room and everything would be all right.

I stopped a door down from the room and signaled for the dogs to stay. My phone vibrated once and then again.

On other side, ready to move in, Quinn texted. **Status?**

About to go in.

I slid my phone into my pocket and took a moment to just

breathe. I couldn't put it off any longer. I shifted the leads to my hand. As I did, I felt the stitches pull. Doing my best to ignore the pain, I signaled the dogs to come.

I pushed open the door and stepped inside. "Hey, Amy, how's it going?"

"Dogs in a hospital, Jax. I'm disappointed." Maddy looked at the Rotties and shook her head. Then she glanced at Amy who stood pressed against the wall, as far from her as she could be. "Amy, be a good girl and put the dogs in the hallway and then make sure Jax isn't carrying any unpleasant surprises."

Sweat pricked out on Amy's face and she shook her head. That was all I needed. Anger cooled and the world focused on Maddy. I dropped the dogs' leads, trusting them to stay where they were until given a command. I needed both hands free because I wasn't going to let this go on any longer.

"Amy, you okay?" I didn't take my eyes off Maddy as I asked.

"Fighting it," she rasped.

"Maddy, care to tell me what the hell's going on?"

"Just taking care of a few things, Jax." She took a step in my direction, stopping when Loki growled in warning. "Now, Jax. Why don't you put them in the hallway so the two of us can talk?"

I glanced at Amy, worried about how long she'd be able to hold out against whatever compulsion Maddy tried to place on her.

"Tell you what, I'll agree if you send Amy out with them and she doesn't come back in, doesn't leave the hallway until you and I finish our *chat*."

"N-no," Amy stammered.

Maddy took a moment to consider my suggestion. As she did, I looked for anything in the room I might be able to use as a weapon. Unfortunately, she stood between me and most of the possibilities.

"All right." She grinned like a kid about to get exactly what she wanted for Christmas. "Amy, take the dogs out in the hallway and stay with them. We'll be leaving soon. I promise."

Amy looked at me, something close to panic in her eyes.

"It's okay, Amy. The dogs will stay with you. Nothing else is going to happen."

As she neared, I told the dogs to go with her. Then I stepped to the side, giving them room to leave. I waited until the door started closing behind them before moving back to my previous place. With Amy gone, I could focus on Maddy.

Except I wasn't sure it really was Maddy. At least not the Maddy I'd grown up with. This was the Maddy we found in Ireland, but more so. It was as if someone managed to reestablish at least one of the bindings and were manipulating her like a puppeteer and his marionette.

"Tell me who it is, Maddy. Who got to you this time?"

She blinked once, as if my question surprised her. Then she laughed softly, the sound so menacing a chill ran down my spine. At the same time, however, her eyes betrayed a different emotion, one totally at odds with the laughter. Fear, bone-chilling fear, looked out at me. Somewhere beneath the compulsion, Maddy still existed. I needed to connect with her, with Maddy, and bring her forward.

But how the hell was I going to do that?

"Well?" I cocked an eyebrow and did my best not to look like I might attack—or make a run for it—at any moment.

"How about you answer me a question instead. How come you're here?"

"C'mon, Maddy. You know the answer to that. I've been stopping by several times a day to check on Miss Serena since her heart attack." Which was the truth without actually answering her question.

"That's right. You come here instead of coming to see me."

Pain filled her voice but it didn't ring true. Instead, I felt the push from her as she tried to influence me. It slid over and around me, searching my shielding for a weakness. Her eyes narrowed slightly. She surprised me by waving her hand in front of her, as if brushing away a spider's web before she walked into it. Almost instantly, the probing withdrew.

"Maddy, listen to me. You aren't getting out of here. Not without answering for what you did to Amy, not without telling me what you want with Miss Serena."

I shifted positions slightly, balancing my weight on my toes, hands held at the ready. Then I let my eyes bleed to amber. The Maddy I know would recognize the warning that presented. If not, the way my tattoo sleeve came to life should have warned I wasn't fooling around.

"You know what I want, Jax. I want things to be like they were. I want to be part of what's going on. I want my friends back."

"Get over it, Maddy. I'm tired of the same old litany from you. We've all tried to prove to you that we still love you. If anyone's pulled away, it's been you. You are the one who decided your job was more important than coming home for major events and celebrations. You're the one who let yourself fall under Roben's influence when you could have asked for help. You're the one who has dragged her feet on working with us to make sure you were protected from ever becoming someone's victim again. You're the one who came here, somehow managed to at least partially roll Amy. I'm guessing there are others as well." Disappointment and a touch of anger showed in my voice.

Her eyes flashed and her right hand fisted at her side.

"Don't." I let my gaze drop momentarily to that hand, letting her know I'd seen. "Remember who you're dealing with, Maddy."

A touch of hysteria filled her laugh. "I remember. I remember the woman I had on her knees not long ago."

I clinched my jaw. My right foot slid back some, letting me blade my body in relation to hers. My Walker side pressed against my control. I held it in check as I *reached* through the floor, down through the building into the earth below. I gathered energy around me, weaving it into my personal wards, following it through the ground, along the energy paths to the ley line that ran through Miss Serena's property to mine. I carefully tapped it, holding the power in reserve.

"You won't hurt me, Jax."

She spoke confidently. But there, for just a moment, I saw the Maddy I knew reflected in her eyes. Then it was gone. Whatever happened, Maddy was still there but she was being pushed down, buried under someone's compulsion. Or was it possible she was being possessed? Until this moment, I didn't believe in possession but it would explain what had been going on. Not necessarily the movie version of possession where some evil spirit takes over an innocent's body. But Maddy had been bound by at least three people. We had no idea what the long-term impact of that would be on her. Was it possible a back door of a sorts had remained, making her easier to take over so that the binding made her man extension of whoever controlled her?

And, if so, how the hell did we break the binding and protect her going forward?

"That's where you're wrong."

I lifted my right hand, palm up. The fingers of my left hand drew a quick sigil in the air. Almost instantly a six-inch column of fire rose from the palm of my right hand. The flames danced and then twisted, spinning until it took on the shape of a tornado. Flames turned to air and water, turning into a water spout. Then it turned dark, muddy, but kept spinning, building.

I kept my attention on Maddy as she watched the display, something I'd never done in front of her before. She hissed out a breath and took a step back. Her expression went from hostile to surprised to scared to showing a trace of hope. It was like watching a war play out, one Maddy was losing.

Fire replaced mud. I pushed a little more energy into it. The temperature on the room rose. Maddy's breath came faster. She lifted her left hand. She looked at it. Confusion drew her brows together and had her biting her lower lip. I'd seen her do that before, when we were in school. She was trying to remember what to do in a situation like this and how to do it.

Either that or the Maddy of old had enough control in that moment to try to act—but in what way?

"Trying to intimidate me, Jax?"

I smiled, wiggling the fingers of my right hand so the fire once again transformed to water and air.

"Not at all. If I were trying to intimidate you, I'd be a bit more direct."

So saying, I eased my control and pictured my cougar-self. My eyes turned a deeper gold, the pupil turning slit-like. My features blurred as feline and human blended before settling back to human. It hurt like hell to allow the shift to barely manifest and then stop it. But it was something else Maddy had never seen me do, something I prayed put whoever controlled the binding off-balance.

"Abomination!" she rasped.

Except it wasn't her voice. Not really. But I had a pretty damned good idea whose it was.

For one long moment, she gaped at me. The hand she'd used to begin drawing her sigils stilled. One finger, shaking like a leaf, pointed at me. But it was the eyes again that told me what I needed to know. I'd shaken the binder, weakened his hold on Maddy. This was my chance.

But I had to be careful. Maddy might still be in there, somehow trapped in her mind, but she wasn't in control. She'd already managed to at least partially roll Amy. God help us if she managed to start a binding. I couldn't let her touch me or get past my personal wards.

And I held the weapon I needed in my hand.

Air and Water. Fire and Earth. I pulled on all of them. My hand tightened into a fist. Energy flowed from the ley line, through the Earth and up into me. I was nothing but the conduit, gathering and then directing. It filled me, intoxicating and tempting. I controlled the desire to keep drawing on it. Instead, I focused it in my fist.

"I'm sorry."

I flung my hand out in front of me, fingers opening, releasing the energy. The elements combined, exploding in a flash of light and sound. A wave of heat and wind followed a split-second later, like the immediate aftermath of a bomb going off. It hit Maddy, sending her tumbling across the room and into the far wall. She hit with a sickening thud. Then she lay there, unmoving.

I released the rest of the energy, sending it back into the ground.

Then I sank to my knees, barely registering the sounds of someone racing into the room.

"Jax!" Quinn pulled me to my feet and held me at arm's length, checking me for injury.

"Secure her. Glove up first." I scrubbed my hands over my face. "Amy?"

"Mom's with her."

I nodded. Judith knew what to do.

"Miss Serena?"

"She's in the ICU." She shook her head before I could respond. "She's all right. It's just easier to protect her there right now."

"She needs to be secured but we need to check her for another binding, break it if we can." I nodded as Lucas entered, Drew on his heels. "Can we take her to your house and keep her secured there until we can get to it?" There was something else I needed to do first.

"Yeah. You know the house won't let her out of whatever room we put her in."

"Do it. Go with them and make sure she's secured." I didn't mention any injuries Maddy might have incurred just then. It was hard to feel anything but anger right now. "We need to find Dr. Pat as well, make sure she's all right."

"Marcus too," Drew said.

"Quinn and I will see to it."

Lucas bagged Amy's hands much as Drew had before. Then he cuffed her arms behind her back. She was beginning to regain consciousness as he pulled her into a sitting position. As he and Quinn led her out of the room, I turned and found myself pulled against Rafe's chest.

"I'm okay." I thought. "I need to check on Amy."

His lips brushed against mine. Then he nodded. With his arm around my waist, he led me into the hallway, Drew on our heels.

"Judith's taking care of her. She said to tell you she didn't see any binding attempt. Her guess is Maddy somehow got hold of more of the lotion or ointment or whatever and used it on her. She's getting her cleaned up and will let you know if she needs you."

"Drew, go to her. Stay there until Judith is sure Amy's all right and we don't need to do anything else."

"What are you going to do?"

"I need to find Dr. Pat."

"That I can help you with," Mary Kate said as she approached from the direction of the nursing station. Dressed in slacks and striped blouse, sneakers on her feet, I had a feeling she'd been fixing a meal for everyone when the SOS went out. "She's in surgery right now. She has been for the last three hours."

I relaxed. That meant she didn't know what happened.

"Good." So very good. I hoped. "Will you stay with Miss Serena please?"

"Of course. Bitsy and Peggy are on their way."

That helped. The three of them would let nothing happen to their friend.

"What about you, Jax? What are you going to do?" Drew asked.

"Find the person responsible for today."

And I had a damned good idea who it was. Unfortunately, it still didn't make any sense.

"Who?" Rafe asked.

"Where?" Drew rested his hand on his gun, as if in case the SOB was near.

"I need to check one thing first." And I needed to do something about my shoulder. "Go check on Amy. Tell Judith what we're doing regarding Maddy and then we'll get together and figure out our next step."

He gave me a look that warned of grave consequences if I did anything he considered foolish. Then he nodded and hurried off.

Once alone, Rafe turned me to face him. His expression worried, he looked deep into my eyes, as if trying to touch my soul. I slid my right arm around him and stepped closer, resting my cheek against his chest.

"What happened and what are you planning?" he asked.

"I'll tell you in the car." I looked around for the dogs, relieved to see them stretched out next to the wall.

"Then let's go. I want Judith to have a look at you before anything else happens."

Since I wanted the same thing, I reached for his hand. As I did, I told the Rotties to come with us. Then I stopped. There was one thing I needed to do before leaving the hospital.

I needed to see Miss Serena.

25

"Sit still!" Judith snapped, her temper as frayed as mine.

Since I'd rarely seen her like this, I complied. I knew she was worried. Hell, that was putting it mildly. We'd gotten lucky today. If Amy hadn't been able to hold out against the compulsion Maddy put on her... If she hadn't been able to call me without Maddy realizing it... If we hadn't been able to keep Maddy away from Miss Serena....

God, so much could have gone wrong and didn't.

"How's Amy?"

"Resting now." From the way Judith said it, I had a feeling it hadn't been easy. "About as upset with herself as you were when it happened to you."

I nodded, understanding. "And Maddy?"

"She's awake and not happy but, honestly, I don't care."

I looked at Judith in surprise. She saw it and shrugged.

"This is twice now she's tried to use a compulsion on one of you. We know she's used it on others, her mother included. We have to admit to ourselves if no one else that she presents a danger to all of us right now and will until we deal with the person or persons responsible and until she finally admits she needs help and asks for it."

"I overstepped when I told Lucas to bring her here. I'm sorry."

She shook her head. "No, this is the only place we can keep her right now. But I'll be honest, Jax, I want her out of my house as quickly as possible."

"She will be." I winced as she probed my shoulder.

"Tell me what you plan. I know you have something in mind."

"I do, but I need to verify something first." I glanced at the clock across the room and considered another factor as well. "Ciara should be here in a couple of hours. She may have more information for us, but I don't think we can wait."

"You know something."

"Maybe." I closed my eyes and hissed out a breath as she finished re-bandaging my shoulder. "There was one point when it felt like I was no longer talking to Maddy. Whoever it was pointed a finger at me and called me an abomination."

Shaken, Judith sat down heavily next to me on the bed. "You're sure?"

I nodded.

"The Luíseachs"

I shook my head. "Not all of them. We know enough to know that. Sawyer named Benjamin Luíseach. That's who I have my money on."

"But he always agreed with his parents when it came to the Others."

"I know that's what it seemed like from everything you and the others have said. Still, he left town and we don't know what he's been up to since then."

She nodded a little reluctantly. "What are you going to do?"

"We need to find him. For him to have gotten to Maddy so easily, he has to be close by."

"How do you plan on finding him?"

As she helped me into a clean shirt, I explained. She didn't like it. Hell, I didn't like it. But I didn't see any way around it, not if we wanted to stop this particular threat before anything else happened.

Half an hour later, I looked around and blew out a breath. Behind the protective stone fence of the house, away from prying eyes, we gathered. Judith, Mary Kate and Bitsy stood together, discussing the plan and casting concerned looks in my direction. Lexie stood with Amy, her worry about what happened to Amy clear. Quinn, Annie and Meg stood with their husbands, waiting.

"Jax, are you sure about this?" Annie asked. "Wouldn't it be better to make sure Maddy hasn't been bound before going after Luíseach?"

I shook my head. I'd been round and round that question myself and the answer was always the same. As much as I wanted to make sure Maddy was safe—for herself and for the rest of us—doing so would warn Luíseach or whoever he was working with that we were onto him. It was bad enough he probably knew by now that we had Maddy secure where he couldn't get to her. I found myself hoping he hadn't left the area yet and gone to ground

"I would like nothing more, Annie, but we can't."

"She's right."

Quinn sounded as if she liked the situation even less than I did. Which might be the truth. She would always be a cop deep in her heart. What I was proposing went well beyond the general bounds of law and order.

I smiled slightly and held a hand out to her. She moved to my side and took it. As our palms touched, the Guardian bond kicked in. When Judith took her other hand, it felt almost complete. Unfortunately, Dr. Pat was still at the hospital and we didn't dare wait on her.

"Lucas, Drew, you can't be part of this. So I'm asking the two of you to go back to the hospital. Protect Miss Serena. We can't risk her now when we're so close to answering at least some of our questions."

"Jax," Lucas growled.

"Please." I freed my hand from Quinn's and moved forward. When I stood in front of Lucas, I stopped. "Lucas, you know I'm right. The only way we can protect our town is to stop this latest attack and see if we can't learn something from Luíseach."

"I'm going with you." Meg spoke firmly even as she placed a protective hand over her unborn child.

"No, but you will take part once we have him secured." I stopped her when she started to object. "Meg, if I'm right about this, he will strike out at you, no matter how poor the odds are in his favor. I am not risking you or your baby."

I didn't need to look at Drew to know he agreed.

"You're not leaving me out of this," Annie warned.

"No, you are our ace in the hole." Something else I'd done a lot of thinking about. "If I'm right about this, his family will know what he's been up to. When we get confirmation, you're going to get together with Alvarado and draw up additional charges against them as well as any and all charges you can think of against Benjamin Luíseach. Then you will talk to the Feds about what's happened. Convince them to also prosecute because they have better facilities to hold people with talents like Maddy's and I have no doubt Luíseach or someone he's working with have just such an ability."

"Jax," she drawled.

"Annie, please." I scrubbed my face with my right hand. What I wouldn't give for a week in bed with no emergencies, no need to get up unless I wanted to. "I'm asking you to do this and to keep the kids safe."

Okay, it was playing dirty, but if it keep her safe, I'd do it.

"We will discuss this later."

Her blue eyes flashed and I nodded. I had no doubt we would.

"You aren't going without me." Rafe crossed his arms over his chest, his expression determined.

"Not a chance in the world," I assured him. "Lucas, will you confirm where the Luíseachs are right now?"

Since their release on bail, they had been forced to wear ankle monitors. Those monitors would tell the police and the Luíseachs probation officers where they were at any time. I needed that information now.

Lucas looked at me for a moment, holding my gaze. Then he dipped his chin.

"They are at the old man's house."

"Then let's get going. I want this done as quickly as possible."

I also wanted it done before they could think of any other objections. But, before leaving, I wanted to talk to Judith one more time. It didn't surprise me when Mary Kate and Bitsy followed us into the kitchen, Quinn on my heels.

"I want you to lock this place up as tightly as you can when we leave. Tie into the ley line and use it to give the wards a boost." One of the four ley lines that ran through Mossy Creek ran beneath the back of the property. "No one in or out unless you are convinced they are safe, that includes Dr. Pat."

"Jax."

"Judith, you know I'm right. God, this is killing me but we have to admit there's the possibility Maddy has put a compulsion on her. When we finish with Luíseach, we'll find out and we will do whatever it takes to help both of them—Marcus too if he's been rolled. But we need to focus on the deepest threat right now and my gut tells me it is Benjamin Luíseach."

"All right."

"What can we do?" Aunt Bitsy asked.

"Stay here, keep the lines of communication open. Contact Miss Peggy and Miss Olivia. They need to know what's about to happen. They'll keep their eyes and ears open for additional trouble."

"You be careful." Bitsy pulled me into a tight hug.

"I'll be back. I promise." I turned to Quinn who stood in Judith's motherly embrace. "Let's go."

She nodded and whistled for her dogs. Rafe, along with our three dogs, met us at the door. With five dogs who most definitely were not the size of Catherine's "babies" in tow, the question of what vehicle or vehicles to take became important. Quinn quickly settled it for us. She would take her SUV. Rafe would follow in his truck. We'd meet up a block away from the Luíseach home and go from there on foot. Since I had an idea about how to do it I hadn't yet shared with the others, I agreed.

"You're with me," Quinn said as we walked toward the cars.

Rafe shrugged and continued on to his truck, Fenris on his heels.

"What?" I secured the Rotties and climbed into the front passenger seat.

"I understand why you have to do this but there are rules, Jax."

She closed her door and slid the key into the ignition. Instead of starting the engine, she turned in her seat to look at me. "You will go in after me. You will not put yourself in danger. If I tell you to get out, you will do so, no arguments. We can fight about it later."

"Quinn."

"No. You are the head of the Guardians now. We are already weakened by our concern for Miss Serena and by the fact we can't pull Dr. Pat in right now. If anything happened to you, it would put more than just you, Rafe and me in danger. It would put everyone in town, the very town itself, in danger. That is not going to happen."

She was right, but I didn't like it. We'd be having a serious discussion once this was over. There had to be a happy medium somewhere.

Right?

"Agreed."

She eyed me suspiciously for a moment and then started the engine. At least we avoided one battle. The one looming ahead wasn't going to be as easy.

26

I stood in the shadows of the trees across the street from the small house Mathias and Eileen Luíseach rented on the far side of town. Mossy Creek might be small by some standards but we still had two very different "sides" of town. People on this "side" were almost to the person normals who felt Others were anathemas until God. Oh, not that they were all religious. But their hatred for anyone who might be different from them bound them together. After their arrests and indictments for trying to steal Meg's inheritance and then trying to kill her, much of the support the Luíseachs enjoyed disappeared. Even the most fervent of those who stood against Others drew the line at cold-blooded murder. Add in how they had abused their own daughter, Meg's mother, and encouraged the assault and rape of Faith later and few of their friends wanted anything to do with them now. As a result, they lost their home and had moved into what was little more than a cottage with their son, Mathew, and his wife, Caroline.

"Ready?" I asked Quinn as she rejoined me.

"Ready."

I nodded once and took another moment to study the area. It was almost dark. That helped, especially if we stuck to the shadows.

With Rafe watching our backs, we raced across the street in the direction of the small house. I stopped the moment my feet hit the front yard. With Quinn moving ahead to cover me, I dropped to my knees. Odin stood to my right and Loki to my left, their heads swinging back and forth, as if looking for trouble. Trusting them—and Quinn and her dogs—to keep me safe from the front and Rafe and Fenris from the rear, I placed my right palm on the grass. My fingers dug through the blades and into the dirt below. My awareness narrowed to my hand and the energies running through the earth beneath me.

I broke contact and lifted my hand, four fingers raised.

Four people inside. I'd really hoped we'd find Benjamin there.

I stood and brushed my hands on my jeans. Then I moved forward. As I did, I studied the front of the house. A light shone from the window to the left of the front door. Another light shone from a window on the east side of the house. A three or four year old sedan was parked in the drive. From the dust covering it, thick enough to be seen in the faint light, it hadn't been driven for some time. On the surface, at least, it looked like the Luíseach had been complying with the terms of their bond.

Not that I believed it for a minute.

"*Steh*," I instructed the Rotties, using the German word for *stay*.

I carefully climbed to the small front porch. With Meg at my shoulder, her dogs behind us, I placed my hand, palm down, against the door. A moment later, I nodded, a grim smile on my lips. Quinn grinned and motioned me back. As I complied she stepped forward. Her fist pounded on the door three times as she announced our presence.

If you could actually classify both of us as Harkin County deputies.

Before anyone inside had a chance to open the door, she took care of it. She stepped back and lifted her right foot. Her boot stuck the door just under the doorknob. It swung open with a satisfying thud. As it did, the sounds of chairs scraping along the tile, silverware dropping to the floor or onto plates filled the air. She entered, gun in hand, the dogs on either side of her. I followed more slowly.

"Get out!" Mathias Luíseach yelled.

The months since his arrest had not been kind to any of them, but especially not to Mathias and Eileen. They had aged. If possible, they looked even more bitter than before. The four of them stood around a small table in the kitchen, staring at Quinn in disbelief. Then Mathew's fingers closed around a steak knife.

"Don't!" I snapped and the Earth rolled beneath our feet, a warning of what I could do.

The knife clattered onto the table.

"I'll have you arrested!" Eileen screeched.

"That will be hard to do from prison," Quinn said. "Sit down and keep your hands on the tabletop."

"I'm contacting our attorney," Mathias threatened.

"Do that. When you do, explain to him how you've been consorting with someone the Sheriff is currently looking for in connection with an attempted murder and more."

The looks on their faces were priceless. They also spoke volumes. Caroline, who still tried her best to look like a younger version of her mother-in-law, gaped at Quinn. Either she was a much better actress than anyone gave her credit for or she had no idea what Quinn meant. But the others knew exactly who and what she referred to.

Their expressions also told me they had no intention of telling us anything.

Time for a little *encouragement*.

"Contact the court and tell them we have proof they've been in violation of the terms of their bail on multiple occasions," I said, handing Quinn my phone. "I'm sure Alvarez will have no problem arranging for them to be kept in separate jails to keep them from further conspiring together."

"Now, Jax, you know our instructions. We're to see if they will cooperate first." She looked at me as if she didn't approve of my hard-nosed attitude. Then she turned her attention back to the four.

"We're not going to tell you anything." Eileen glared at us before turning that exact same gaze on her family.

"Really?" I mused as I stepped forward. "Tell me something. When did you realize your son is an Other?"

I almost laughed at their expressions. Caroline sat there, her mouth opening and closing like a landed fish trying to breathe. Eileen refused to meet my eyes. Mathias looked like he swallowed something distasteful. Mathew, however, would never make a good poker player. His eyes flashed and his features tightened. He knew what I was talking about and I'd bet good money on his mother knowing as well.

"These two." I indicted mother and son.

Quinn nodded and reached for Eileen.

"What do you mean?" Mathias demanded.

Quinn stopped reaching for the man's wife and turned her attention to him. "Your son is an Other and has been using his talents to harm others in town."

"You fool!" he laughed. "Mathew has been here with us, as you'd know if you checked with those monitoring us."

"We're not talking about Mathew," I said, moving to stand behind him and resting my hands on his shoulders. He jerked slightly as I did but otherwise didn't react. "We're talking about Benjamin."

"They lie, just as all their kind do," Eileen spat. "Our Benjamin is a good man, one who loves his family."

"Really?" Quinn cocked her head and looked at the older woman like she would some strange insect. "If he's such a good man and loves you so much, why did he leave town?"

"You leave him out of your vendetta against us," Caroline said.

"Call for backup. We'll take them all in and sort it out at the station," I told Quinn. "You can file the paperwork to revoke their bail at the same time."

"No!" Mathias roared. "You claim my son is an abomination like the two of you. Prove it."

I gave him a slow smile. Good. He had his doubts about his son before now.

"He has been identified by several of his victims." Not the truth but I had no doubts we'd find victims once we started looking for them. "Several of his co-conspirators have also handed over evidence connecting him to a number of crimes."

"Talk. That's all it is. Just talk."

And he knew better and I said so.

"Then let me put it to you this way." I patted Mathew's shoulder and smiled slightly as he flinched. You'd think he worried I might shift and take a bite out of him. "Tell us what we want to know and we will make sure the court knows you cooperated."

"All charges dismissed," Mathew said.

"Not a chance in hell." Quinn gave a quick laugh. "But it will mean your parents here may actually live long enough to get out of prison."

It wasn't likely, especially since we weren't going to argue too hard in their favor. But there was always the possibility they would live to be close to one hundred.

"And us?" Caroline's voice shook. She might be a fool about a number of things, her choice of husband being first and foremost, but she wasn't a complete idiot.

"The same. We'll let the court know you cooperated. The judge will take that into account when handing down your sentence."

"That assumes you can get a conviction and you won't." Venom dripped from Eileen's voice.

"You really are out of touch with reality." I shook my head, disdain in my voice. "Your husband and son, not to mention Winston Reed, attacked Meg Grissom in front of witnesses, witnesses who will testify truthfully if called to do so. There is a pile of evidence showing you egged them on and you helped plan some of the actions taken against Mrs. Grissom. Then there will be Reed's testimony that it was Benjamin who told you about Meg and her return to Mossy Creek. Now why would he do so unless he knew what you had in mind and wanted to be part of it?"

"Reed lies," Eileen said.

"Does he, Mathew?" I dug my fingers into the muscles of his shoulders, my face a mask as he sucked in a breath between his teeth.

"Go to hell."

"Tsk, tsk. Is that any way for a—how did your mother put it when she confronted Annie Caldwell?—is that any way for a God-fearing person to behave?"

I might not have been in town when Meg squared off against her maternal grandparents and the bastard who raped her mother, but I'd heard all about it.

"Last chance. Tell us where we can find Benjamin or we'll treat you to a one-way trip to jail." Quinn dangled her cuffs from one finger, making sure everyone saw.

Eileen glanced at the clock on the wall and smiled. "You'll never get there in time."

My stomach plummeted through the floor. Then anger rose, cold and deadly.

"Get where?"

"You'll find out soon enough." She laughed, her expression a bit mad.

"Where?"

I released my hold on Mathew and pulled the old woman to her feet. Her fingers clawed at the hand fisted at her collar. I ignored the pain as her nails raked my skin. Instead, I pulled her close. As I did, gold and then black flooded my eyes.

"Tell me!" I lifted her higher, not quite off the floor but high enough to be uncomfortable.

"Stay where you are!" Quinn snapped before the others could react.

"The café. But you'll never get there in time."

I shoved her back onto her chair. Then I turned and was out of the room, Quinn cursing behind me. I heard her calling for backup and then yelling for Rafe to stop me.

"Doc?"

He caught me around the waist as I ran outside. We both staggered several steps before righting. I tried to push past him but he held firm. He wasn't going to let me go until he knew what was going on.

"The café," I rasped. "She said we won't get there in time."

"Get in the truck."

He pulled out his phone and started running to where we'd parked. I considered and decided not to follow. There was one way I might get there in time. A way I hadn't tried in years because it frankly scared the shit out of me. But if we were going to have any chance of saving our friends, this was it.

I ducked into the deeper shadows at the side of the house. Even before I pulled my tee shirt over my head, pain wracked my body, dropping me to my knees. I toed off my shoes and wriggled out of my jeans. Gritting my teeth against the pain, I rolled shirt and jeans together, using my belt to hold them tight. Rafe's voice calling to me filled the air as I ran the fingers of my right hand over the soaring eagle near the top of my tattoo sleeve. Bone broke, muscles tore. The world spun and went dark before it once again came to life.

"Jax!" Rafe yelled as I took flight.

Wings beat upward. I circled the house once before angling back toward downtown.

27

I knelt on the rooftop of the gallery across the square from the café. My heart still pounded and sweat covered me. Never again. I didn't care what the reason, never again would I shift into anything that didn't keep all feet or paws on the ground. Flying was for the birds and, Walker or not, I was not a bird. Didn't want to be, wasn't going to be. Never again.

Stomach still churning from the last shift in air currents that almost sent me plummeting to the ground, I forced my lungs to work. Oxygen was good. The ground would be better. But before I did that, I needed to put some clothes on. Thank goodness, I hadn't dropped the bundle of jeans, tee shirt and shoes I'd tied together using my belt. Underwear would have been nice but I'd settle for this.

Dressed and feeling closer to normal, I once again crept to the edge of the building and looked down. Cars lined both sides of the street. Some were there for the local movie theater. Others had carried people downtown to do some window shopping. But a good number of them belonged to diners at the café.

Moving quickly and carefully, I made my way to the rear of the building and searched for the fire escape. Praying I didn't fall, I slung my leg over the side of the building and dropped onto the ladder.

Doing my best not to make too much noise, I climbed down, dropping the last six feet to the pavement of the alley behind the building.

"What the hell's going on?"

I yelped and spun, my hands up defensively. Seeing Drew, I blew out a breath. Then I punched him in the stomach. He stumbled back a step with an *oomph!* before righting himself. Glaring, he grabbed my arm and pulled me further down the alley.

"What's going on and how the hell did you get up there?"

"He's at or near the café and I flew."

"You... flew?"

I nodded, pulled my arm free and took off. As I did, I pulled on my Walker abilities, needing the speed and strength it gave me. I reached for my Earth abilities, drawing more power from the ground beneath my feet. Drew cursed and raced after me.

As I rounded the corner, I slowed. I ran a hand over my face, wiping away the sweat and who knows what else I might have picked up in-flight—and to make sure I no longer had feathers and a beak. I inhaled once, twice, and nodded to myself.

Show time.

Keeping a watchful eye out, I crossed the square and moved in the direction of the café. Behind me, Drew kept back and moved at an angle away from me but still in the direction of the café. Now to see if the threat was real or a ruse to keep us away from Benjamin's real target.

The bell over the door jangled as I pushed it open and stepped inside. Like most evenings, every table was filled. So were the stools at the counter. To the casual eye, everything looked normal. But I wasn't looking at the scene with a casual eye.

And things were far from normal.

Miss Peggy stood at the far end of the counter, face pale, anger and fear reflected in her eyes. A man stood in front of her, a slight smile on his lips. At first glance, he seemed so normal. Medium height and build, dark slacks, grey shirt with the sleeves rolled up above his wrists. His once dark hair was thinning and now sported more silver than dark. But it was his aura that had me fighting the instinct to attack first and ask questions later. I recognized its look and its *taste*. I'd encountered it before, several times in fact. Each time we'd had a situation with Maddy.

"Hey, Benjamin, let me welcome you to town."

I dropped to one knee and thrust my right hand against the tile floor. I tore through them, down, down, deeper until I felt the Earth energies. I grabbed them, pulling them to me. The Earth groaned and rolled. Silverware clanked against plates. Drinks splashed out of their glasses. A few hit the ground, shattering.

Benjamin Luíseach staggered back. His arms flailed before his right hand found a nearby table. He grabbed at it, struggling to stay on his feet. As he did, the family that had been sitting there, rolled away, taking cover behind an upturned table several feet away. Mossy Creek might be peaceful the vast majority of the time, but folks here knew what to do when the Rogue came out.

Before Luíseach could regain his composure, I sent another series of what scientists would call aftershock-like events through town. At the same time, I cast a quick look at Miss Peggy. Janny appeared from the kitchen and dragged her mother through the swinging doors. Before the Earth quit pitching, Janny was back, cleaver in hand. She positioned herself in front of the door, her message clear. If Benjamin Luíseach wanted her mother, he'd have to go through her.

"You must be the one she calls the Rogue." Luíseach rolled his shoulders and twisted his head this way and that, his neck cracking. "This is going to be fun."

"I assume you mean Maddy." My voice remained calm even as fury coursed through me.

"Such a dear girl." His voice sent chills down my spine, chills that were quickly replaced by a need for vengeance. "She's been so much fun to play with."

"How?" I ground it out.

"She's so needy and so wants to prove her worth. You and your friends really should have kept a better watch on her."

He took a cautious step forward, stopping when I once again placed my palm on the floor. Satisfied he wasn't going to try anything

—yet—I stood, keeping my arcane hold on the energies flowing through the Earth under my feet.

"How did you get to her this time?" I shifted slightly, keeping between him and the diners nearest the door.

"It wasn't difficult. A delivery made while her parents were gone. She accepted it, opened the box and the connection was made." He glanced at his hands almost as if admiring his manicure. "And how did you know I'd be here, Rogue?"

"Your family proved to be as self-serving where you're concerned as you all were with regard to your sister."

His eyes flashed and, for a moment, uncertainty lit his expression.

"Faith was like you, an abomination."

"Funny you should say that considering you're an Other as well."

He hissed in a breath and I shook my head. He hadn't expected us to figure that out. Hell, I had a feeling he still tried convincing himself he really wasn't an Other, that his abilities were something else. Something with another explanation he could live with.

"Perhaps, but I am dedicated to seeing the end of you and your kind."

He reached toward Mrs. Haverstock. The woman, old enough to be my grandmother, gave him a look that would have withered him where he stood if he'd been looking at her. Then she stabbed his hand with her fork. He cursed and grabbed his hand back, shaking it before looking to see if she'd broken the skin. Before he could retaliate, Mrs. Haverstock slid out of her chair and slipped into the kitchen, where more and more of the diners were taking refuge.

"Why?" I asked, motioning for those nearest the door to leave.

As they slipped out, I breathed a little easier. Luíseach might want to hurt the town, but he wasn't foolish enough to try to take on a large group by himself. Besides, with the others out of the line of fire, I could, hopefully, find out more about what he was after and who he might be working with.

"Why target your friend, why come back here or why something else?" He glanced around, whether for a weapon or something else, I didn't know and didn't plan to find out.

"I wouldn't if I were you." I pulled another strand of energy and the ground rolled again, just enough to rattle the dishes on the tables around us. I really didn't want to do anything to damage the café, but I would if necessary to stop him and protect the town.

"What are you going to do? Bring the café down around us?" He started to step forward.

"There's a reason they call me the Rogue, Luíseach." I dipped my chin slightly as Drew caught my attention through the window behind Benjamin. Then I thrust my right hand out in front of me. A gust of wind whipped through the café, knocking Luíseach back three steps. "Now answer my question. Why?"

"Because your kind stole from me and mine. The money left to my bitch of a sister should have been ours. We deserved it. My parents worked hard for it and that senile old woman left it to Faith instead."

"And that justified your parents abusing her when she was growing up? Justified you and the others tracking her down, beating and raping her? Justified trying to kill her daughter on more than one occasion?"

"I do what is necessary to protect my own."

"If that was true, you would have protected Faith from your parents and the others." I glanced past him, barely more than a flick of my eyes. The last thing I wanted was to have him realize Drew was there. "So you've been manipulating Maddy. Who else? Who else did you bring in to abuse her?"

"I wasn't the first." He gave a slight shrug. "Which is really too bad. I would have loved to be the one to break her. But that happened long ago and the one responsible is no longer alive." Now he smiled, as if he knew something I didn't.

"So, Rogue, we seem to have a stand-off here. Back away from the door and we'll call it a draw."

"I don't think so." I gave him a confident grin. "The way I see it, you aren't a challenge. The only reason I haven't opened the Earth to swallow you up is I don't want to damage the café. But don't think that means I won't do whatever it takes to defeat you here and now."

"He said you were stubborn to a fault." He shook his head, as if disappointed to learn the truth.

"Who?"

"Not yet. You haven't earned it yet."

I yawned. "This is getting boring. Either say something to keep my interest or we're ending it now."

He frowned. This wasn't going the way he expected. Too fucking bad. He'd hurt people I cared for. He did it without a second thought. While I wanted to know why, I wasn't going to let him get away with it.

For a moment, he stood there, motionless. I waited. This was the tipping point. He either gave up or he forced my hand. It was a toss up what he'd do. I waited, pulling the energies I'd tapped into close to me, weaving them into my personal wards. The fingers of my left hand moved at my side, drawing protective sigils in the air. As they did, I focused on Luíseach, looking for any indication that might give away what he planned to do.

His muscles tensed. His aura darkened. Without any other warning, he lunged forward, hands outstretched. My lips peeled back. My body bladed. Twisting at the waist, I reached back. Then I flung my arms forward. Energy burst from me. A wall of wind, as solid as concrete, met him before he managed to get within reach. From behind me, another blast of air joined it, lifting Luíseach from his feet. He looked like someone jerked a cord tied around his middle as he flew back.

He hit the window. For a moment, he hung there. Time slowed and the glass began to splinter. Spider webs crept away from his body as fracture lines appeared. Then time snapped back and the world once again spun on its axis with an explosion of sound as the glass shattered and he flew through the window, landing in a heap on the sidewalk at Drew's feet.

"Don't let him touch you!" I yelled as Luíseach weakly groped along the concrete, as if searching for Drew's foot.

Somehow, I went from standing inside the diner to standing on the sidewalk a short distance from Luíseach. I swallowed hard. There was blood everywhere. It seeped onto the concrete from cuts, so many cuts on Luíseach. When he turned his head in my direction, my stomach heaved. His face looked like raw meat on one side where he rolled across the concrete. His breath rasped. Blood bubbled around his mouth. Still, he smiled as he looked at me, as if he were the victor.

"Tell me who else." I dropped to one knee, just out of reach of his seeking hand. "Who are your working with? Who attacked Miss Serena?"

His lips curved up. Then he coughed, blood flying in droplets from his mouth. I looked closer and cursed. Sticking out of the far side of his neck was a shard of glass. A very large shard of glass. Blood oozed from the wound, coating the ground beneath him. From its position, I knew if we removed the piece, he would bleed out in seconds. As it was, we couldn't do anything until we secured his hands.

"Here."

Quinn shoved a thick plastic bag at me. I looked from it to her, not understanding. Then, seeing how she slid it over one of Luíseach's hands and then secured it with a zip tie followed by round after round of tape, I followed suit. Once I had, I fell back on my ass, too tired to do anything else. Someone grabbed me under the arms and started to pull me away. I shook my head and climbed to my knees, moving closer to the bastard who had caused so much trouble.

"You're dying, Luíseach. Tell me who you've been working with. Tell me and I'll ask the judge to go easy on your parents." I didn't care that I was lying to a dying man. If it got us the information we needed, I'd do it again and again.

"You'll find out soon enough." He struggled for breath. Then he turned his head so he could see me.

"Give me his name."

He smiled, the light going out of his eyes.

"Who?"

"Carson would be proud of him."

The words were barely more than a whisper but they made my blood run cold. When I looked at Quinn, her expression mirrored what I assumed mine must look like. Stunned, angry, worried and more. Then came the determination. I wasn't going to let anyone else get hurt.

"He's gone," Drew said softly as he checked for a pulse.

"Tell the ME to take precautions. Just because he's dead, it doesn't mean he isn't still dangerous." Quinn sat back on her heels and shook her head as she looked at Luíseach. "What now?"

"Now I'm taking my wife home and we're having a discussion about her not taking unnecessary risks," Rafe said as he hauled me to my feet.

"Wait a minute!" Quinn clamored up and stared at us. "Did you say wife?" She narrowed her eyes and grabbed for my left hand. Not finding a ring there, she simply glared at us both.

"Yes, wife, and you can just deal with it." Rafe was pissed. "We'll tell you about it tomorrow. Everyone's to meet at our place for breakfast. But right now? Right now I'm taking my wife home. I'm going to make sure she eats and gets some rest and then we are going to have a long overdue discussion."

I swallowed hard. Then I gave Quinn a shrug before following Rafe to his truck. Once there, I reached for his hand. He stopped and looked down the street long enough that I worried I'd gone too far this time. Then he pulled me close and wrapped his arms around me.

"Don't ever scare me like that again, Doc. Please."

"I'm sorry." I reached up and framed his face with my hands. Then I brushed my lips against his. "I'll be honest, that's only the third, maybe fourth, time I've shifted into an eagle. It will be the last time. I hate flying."

Absolutely hate it.

His lips twitched and he hugged me once again. Then he held me at arm's length. "Are you all right?"

"Been better. My shoulder hurts like hell. I'm exhausted. I'm even hungry. But most of all I'm pissed and scared."

"We'll figure the rest of it out, Doc. I promise." He reached beyond me to open my door. "All you need to do is figure out how to explain to the girls why you didn't tell them about us getting married."

"I have to figure it out?" I arched a brow at him. "You're the one who let the cat out of the bag. But let's worry about that later." I glanced back at the café. "Can you make sure someone comes right out to repair the window?"

"Already done." He lifted me inside the truck. "Let's go home. Everything else can wait until morning."

28

———————

"Are you all right?"

Amy slid her arm around my waist and gave me a quick hug. Then she looked at me in concern. For more than an hour, we'd sat on the back deck, our friends and family surrounding us, discussing the events of the last few weeks. It still felt like I'd been on a rollercoaster from Hell.

"Yeah."

At least I thought so. Glancing back at the deck, I smiled slightly. Most of the others had gone inside to help finish preparing breakfast, set the table, make sure the kids were all right. All the normal things normal people did before going to work. Except we were not normal and never had been.

This was Mossy Creek after all.

"Jax." She didn't believe me.

"I'm as all right as I can be." I stopped and watched the dogs playing in the dog run. "I'm tired and sore. I'm terrified we aren't going to be ready for whatever happens next."

Then there was the fact I had to talk with the Texas Rangers later about what happened at the café. Thank God, Miss Peggy had agreed to having a security camera installed. It showed I'd acted in self-defense and that Quinn had reacted to protect me. But I still had to jump through the legal hoops when I'd rather be making sure everyone was all right.

"We will be." Amy smiled at me in reassurance. "You need to trust yourself and the rest of us."

"I do."

"Then what's bothering you?"

I blew out a breath. She waited, giving me the time I needed to figure out what to say. The problem was that there was no easy way to say it. All I could do was say it and help she understood what needed to happen next.

"Dr. Pat came by before everyone got here."

Hell, she'd come early enough I wasn't out of bed yet.

"Maddy?" Amy looked at me in concern.

I nodded. "She's going to be all right, but it is going to take time. Luíseach's death severed the new binding and ended the compulsion. Judith confirmed it. But Maddy's damaged right now, more than any of us suspected. Pat's worried about her and rightly so. She's also feeling guilty for not realizing how bad it was for Maddy. Nothing I said got through to her."

Amy frowned as she considered what I said. "I was afraid of that. What happened then?"

"She and Marcus are taking leaves of absence and they're going to take Maddy away from here. She knows several healers she thinks can help Maddy both mundanely and arcanely. She said she would stay if I wanted her to but I couldn't do that to her, Amy. She needs to be with Maddy for both of their sakes. If I asked her to stay, she would be a liability because her heart and her head wouldn't be here."

"And her role as a Guardian?"

"It can't go unfilled." I looked at her, knowing what I was about to ask might not be welcomed. "I had a chance to look through the book after she left and before everyone else started arriving."

I didn't need to explain what book I meant. She knew the book better than anyone except her grandmother. But, just now, she didn't have any idea what I might have found in it.

"And?"

"There has always been a member of your grandmother's family as a Guardian. I can't help but believe there's a reason for it." I stepped away, praying I found the right words. "Amy, I want you to take Pat's place. I've already discussed it with Judith and Quinn. They agree with me. We need you to join us."

She closed her eyes. A myriad of emotions crossed her expression, everything from worry to fear to excitement and more. When she looked at me, I knew she'd made up her mind. The only thing I didn't know is what she'd decided.

"All right."

I blew out a breath I didn't realize I'd been holding. Then I smiled and held out a hand. The moment she took it, I pulled her into a hug. If her grandmother couldn't be a Guardian any longer, Amy was the next best thing. Besides, she knew what she was getting into, something I certainly hadn't.

"We'd best go join the others." She nodded to where the men were arranging tables and chairs while Quinn, Meg, and Annie carried out platters of food.

"You go ahead. I'll be there in a minute."

She studied me for a moment and then smiled in understanding. Without a word, she left me to my thoughts. Not that they were comforting. We might have dealt with one danger but the real threat was still out there.

"Jax, it seems you've been holding out on us," Quinn said, grinning, as I joined everyone on the deck.

Much as I wished Rafe hadn't slipped and let the news out, I was also relieved. We'd had much longer than the initial forty-eight hours Judge Caldwell gave us. Even the kids had managed to keep the secret. Now it was out and I planned on making the most out of it.

"I have." I smiled as Rafe came to stand with me. "Today, we'll deal with the aftermath of last night and the last few weeks. Tonight, you're all invited back here. We'll grill some steaks and Rafe and I will do our best to make it up to you for not telling you." Then, seeing Sam looking very interested in everything but what was going on around him, I grinned.

"Of course, if you really want to ask anyone about why you weren't told, you might start with Sam."

His head jerked up and he looked at me in disbelief. Then, feeling his wife's gaze, he swallowed hard and held his hands up in surrender.

"They kidnapped me. Then they blackmailed me into keep silent. Jax threatened to have the Earth swallow me."

"Samuel Caldwell." Annie narrowed her eyes and crooked on finger at him, motioning him closer.

He shook his head and backed away.

"That's my story and I'm sticking to it." He nodded emphatically.

"It seems your husband has been keeping secrets, Annie," Quinn teased.

If that wasn't the perfect opening. . . .

"Well," I drawled. "He's not the only one."

Quinn looked at me and then at Lucas, who quickly assured her he hadn't known anything about us getting married. "Mom?" She turned to Judith who shook her head.

"You really can be slow sometimes, Moira Quinn," I teased. "Your daughter and your son." I pinned Annie with an affectionate look.

"W-what?"

"Remember the night everyone was at our place and Ali came in needing help with her homework?"

The two mothers nodded slowly.

"Ali saw right away something had changed. I told her and Robbie."

"I'll be damned," Lucas chuckled.

"All right. You two get to grovel tonight. What can we do in the meantime?"

"Exactly what you will be. We need to get any legal hurdles that might come up because of last night dealt with as quickly as possible."

"And then?" Ciara asked.

She'd arrived back from Ireland about the time everything went to Hell in the proverbial handbasket last night. Liam Murphy was with her. He'd agreed to Pat and Marcus taking Maddy away for a while to recover. But they were to check in with him daily. That way, Maddy wouldn't be in violation of her probation.

I suspected he and Ciara had news I needed to hear as well. But it had to wait until I dealt with the Rangers. Meg would be with me. Then we'd meet with Ciara to go over what was said. Hopefully by dinner, I'd be able to put the previous day behind me.

"There is one thing I want to say. Each of you here had a hand in helping protect Miss Serena, our loved ones and this town. We've managed to survive yet another attack and that's what this was. But Luíseach was a minor player, a pawn in the greater chess game. Now we need to find the real manipulator. We have a clue, but I don't know if we can trust it. Because of that, we have to keep looking into the Luíseachs, especially Benjamin."

"What's the lead?" Ciara asked.

"Just before he died, Luíseach said Carson would be proud of him. 'Of him' not 'of me'. So there's another player out there. It might be a relative of Carson Alexander or just someone he knew. Luíseach could have meant Carson would be proud of whoever it was because of what they were doing, not because of any relationship. But we need somewhere to start. So lets see how Luíseach intersects with Carson and go from there."

I looked at my fellow Guardians, at the friends and family who supported us without question. Seeing them, hope filled me. Hope that we could win this war. Hope that no one else would be hurt. Hope that this soon came to an end and we could get back to our lives.

I lifted my mug. It might not be champagne, but it would do.

"I give you Mossy Creek, our friends and family, each of you and my fellow Guardians. We will not be defeated."

Everyone rose and echoed my toast. They even sounded like they believed it. Maybe they were right. After last night, I could feel hope, something I hadn't felt since realizing just how much trouble Mossy Creek faced.

I moved to the edge of the deck and looked out across the lawn.

Whoever you are, I won't let you win. You underestimated us and you underestimated our town. That will be your downfall.

———

To FIND out what's in store next for Mossy Creek and those living there, sign up for my newsletter.

REQUEST FROM THE AUTHOR

It has long been said that the best form of advertising is word of mouth. That is especially true when it comes to books. Friends and family members trust reviews and suggestions for books that come from people they know.

That word of mouth goes even further in this digital age. If you enjoyed this book, do me a favor. Spread the word. Tell people on your various social media accounts. Leave a review. If you're a blogger, write a post about it. All that does help. Besides, it is the one way we, as authors, know you really enjoyed our work.

Thanks!

ABOUT THE AUTHOR

I'm older than twenty and younger than death and that's all you'll get from me about my age. After all, it's not polite to ask a woman how old she is. I'm a mother, a daughter and was a wife. I've spent most of my life in the South and love to travel. The only problem with that is my dog always thinks I've abandoned him when I do and it takes weeks to reassure the poor thing and my cat resents the fact I came back before he could figure out a way to kill the dog and hide the body. My house is haunted - it is, really. I swear it. What else explains the table that plays music and the light that comes on by itself? - but it's mine and I love it. Okay, I'm a little strange. But that makes life interesting.

———

To keep up-to-date on new releases, specials, and more, please sign up for my newsletter.

ALSO BY THE AUTHOR

Writing as Sam Schall

Honor & Duty Series

Taking Flight

Battle Bound

Battle Wounds

Battle Flight

Vengeance from Ashes

Duty from Ashes

Honor from Ashes

Fire from Ashes

Betrayal from Ashes

Risen from the Ashes

Victory from Ashes

Writing as Amanda S. Green

Nocturnal Lives Series:

Nocturnal Origins

Nocturnal Serenade

Nocturnal Interlude

Nocturnal Haunts

Nocturnal Challenge

Nocturnal Rebellion

Nocturnal Revelations

Cat's Paw

www.ingramcontent.com/pod-product-compliance
Lightning Source LLC
Chambersburg PA
CBHW020327180626
46812CB00001B/84